P9-EMC-959

The Restless Heart

The Restless Heart

HELEN WINGO

AVALON BOOKS
THOMAS BOUREGY AND COMPANY, INC.
401 LAFAYETTE STREET
NEW YORK, NEW YORK 10003

Library of Congress Catalog Card Number: 91-92097
ISBN 0-8034-8885-8

PRINTED IN THE UNITED STATES OF AMERICA
ON ACID-FREE PAPER
BY HADDON CRAFTSMEN, SCRANTON, PENNSYLVANIA

To my mother,
a charter member of my cheering section

Chapter One

Of course, she didn't have to work at Wayside.

Allison Parmer pushed the Stop button on the recorder, ending the night nurse's report. There were over three hundred hospitals in southern California. Chances were, Case no longer worked here. She grinned wryly. So why did her heart jump every time she saw a tall, tanned man with sun-laced, pecan-brown hair striding down the corridor?

The door of the report room opened, and a youthful night nurse swept in. "What a night!" Mona Clark, at twenty-four, was a year younger than Alli, but with her mid-thigh split skirt and flyaway hair, she looked more like a teenager. "With everything else going on, Mrs. Tober in 301 has been awake since five. She's redone her makeup three times that I know of."

Sighing, she widened her eyes. "Not that I blame her. If that handsome hunk who's director of physical therapy had promised to help me walk today, I might break a leg." She grinned mischievously, picked up a cup, filled it with coffee, and sauntered to the window. ''Isn't the view spectacular? I just love living here, don't you?''

Alli glanced toward the distant mountains. ''Magnificent.'' She glanced at her notes. ''But I grew up here. I don't plan to stay here any longer than necessary.''

Mona took a sip of coffee and scowled at the cup. ''Witches' brew . . . tastes like someone used saline solution and has been boiling it since midnight.'' She set the cup on the windowsill. ''I hung Mr. Soames's IV for you. He's the elderly gallbladder surgery transferred from ICU yesterday . . . 304. He's a little confused. Wanted to know what I was giving him. When I told him five percent dextrose in water, he said his roses needed watering more than he did. Said if I'd let him go home and water them, he'd come right back. I left him calling his wife to check on his garden.''

''Thanks.'' Alli stood, stretching her five-foot, four-inch frame, and tucked the notepad into a pocket of her tunic. ''Since I'm in the float pool, I had to wait for an assignment, so I'm late getting report.''

Mona made a face. ''Moving from station to station is not for me.''

''I suffer from restless feet,'' Alli said. ''I travel a lot in my regular work.'' She clipped a ballpoint pen beside the notepad. ''I'm off to make rounds, or it'll be noon before I get meds out.'' She thought of asking if Mona knew Case Sherman and hesitated. Even if he had finished college, why would he work at Wayside with larger hospitals just over the horizon? "I'll check on Mr. Soames first," she said instead.

Leaving the report room, she walked briskly to the nursing station to gather an assortment of alcohol swabs, gauze squares, and tape rolls. Nodding at the other nurses, she walked down the wide hall toward Room 304.

She quickened her step at the continuous beep of a monitor in distress. *Darn! If it's 304, let it be a pinched tubing. I don't have time to restart an IV.* She swung around a corner in time to see a patch of hospital gown and a thin, shaky leg slip through the door to the stairwell across from 304. Without running, she lengthened her stride to follow the vanishing leg.

By the time she opened the door, an elderly patient stood on the second step of the stairs, struggling to pull the IV pole towering over him down the first step.

"Can I help you, Mr. Soames?" Alli asked calmly. She reached forward, released the kinked intravenous tubing from his fingers, and reset the monitor. The beeping stopped. "I don't know where you're going, but it might be easier to use the elevator." She uprighted the slanting pole.

"I'm going home to water my roses. My wife doesn't know they have to be watered oftener in the summertime."

"Summer is three weeks away. You'll be home by then."

"It looks like summer," he said defiantly.

"It does. But it could be cool tomorrow." She added a lilt to her voice, experienced eyes checking the flow of fluid in the drip chamber. "Are you ready to come back up the stairs?" She stepped down to his level. In the background she heard a door open on the level below and hoped she could get her patient up the stairs before some physician asked her why she hadn't been watching the patient in the first place. Balancing her feet firmly on the step, she grasped the frail waist before her. "One step at a time," she said with more confidence than she felt.

Mr. Soames lifted one foot, wobbled precariously, and toppled backward. Alli swayed like an elm in a Santa Ana windstorm.

"Could you use a little help?" a deep male voice sounded in Alli's ear, and the patient jammed an elbow in her rib cage.

Alli gasped.

"I'll take that as an affirmative." The husky voice vibrated with humor. Muscular arms circled Alli to grasp the unbalanced patient. For a second Alli felt her body crush against the body attached to the strong arms. Then Mr. Soames was pushed upright, and the arms loosened their grip on Alli without releasing the patient.

"Slip under my arms and take care of the IV." The well-remembered tone caressed her ear.

"Sure you can hold on to him?"

"If we both go down the stairs and end up in ER,

just ask someone to admit me to your unit.'' He grinned at her.

Alli restrained a groan. Even in a ludicrous situation Case still made lukewarm jokes. ''Just don't let him fall,'' she said. She ducked under Case's arms and caught the IV pole before the shaky patient could grasp it. ''Easy, Mr. Soames. You're in good hands.'' She bent to lift one feeble, bare foot and place it on the upper step, then straightened to take his arms. ''Bring the other foot up. Case won't let you fall.'' With a smile she gazed calmly into the distraught eyes of the unsteady patient, but her thoughts were on the brown-haired giant supporting the man.

''It isn't far.'' Alli shifted her gaze to find Case looking at her. ''Mr. Soames is in 304. It's right across the hall.'' She looked away, feeling her heart start a continuous beep like an IV monitor in need of attention. Without warning, Mr. Soames sagged against her arm.

''Catch the IV pole.'' Case reacted swiftly, scooping the frail body into his arms.

Alli followed, watching the athletic man carry the patient with seemingly little effort. She refused to let a rising memory of the feel of those arms mature. That was long ago, and she'd left once. Just as she meant to do again.

Moments later, Mr. Soames was clutching the telephone and talking to his wife. Alli moved away from the bed.

''Thanks for the help,'' she told Case, keeping a

professional note in her voice, wishing she could reset her heartbeat as she could an IV monitor. She looked at the friendly face. He was as good-looking as she'd remembered. Even better looking, to be honest. Age seemed to emphasize the creases beneath his high cheekbones and increase the warmth in his humorous brown eyes, if that was possible.

He seemed bigger, but maybe it was because he had added a few pounds to his once lean body. Her gaze flicked across the broad chest and tanned forearms exposed by the short sleeves of his beige tunic. The added weight certainly wasn't flabby. The body looked as if its owner spent every spare moment weight lifting.

"I'm glad you happened by," she added finally, pretending to check the clipboard fastened at the end of the bed for a note of the patient's vital signs.

"A hospital gremlin must have directed me up the back stairs." He grinned, white teeth contrasting with his tan. "It's good to see you, Alli." His look lingered on her momentarily. "It's been seven years. Don't tell me you've stopped traveling to work in Wayside?"

"Only for a few months." Alli clutched the clipboard as if it were a life raft. Why did he keep looking at her so intently? "I'm staying with Gran."

"I thought she lived in New York." The lightness left his voice.

"She moved to Wayside." Alli stared blindly at the notations on the clipboard. She didn't blame him for the edge in his tone. Still, she'd told him when she left that Gran wasn't responsible for her leaving. She would have left Wayside, anyway.

"That's long enough to change clothes twice."

"What?" She lowered the clipboard.

"I believe your words on leaving last time were to the effect that if you ever came to Wayside again, you'd only stay long enough to change clothes."

Putting down the clipboard, Alli thrust her hand into her pocket and withdrew the notepad. "Have you been working here since I left?"

"Off and on." His voice was affable again.

Alli stepped closer to peer at the name tag on his tunic. "Oh." She drew back, warmth rising at the base of her throat. "Director of Physical Therapy. I heard you mentioned in report. Seems a patient is anxious to see you today." She tried to sound casual and knew she failed miserably. But a little breathlessness was expected after the experience with Mr. Soames, she told herself.

"Mrs. Tober. I talked to her last night," Case remembered. He seemed unaware of Alli's breathing difficulty. "The therapist assigned to teach her crutch walking has the flu. I told her I'd help her."

"The director of PT is teaching crutch walking?" Alli shifted her feet. Maybe if she put the patient between them, she could breathe properly.

"In a small hospital a department head fills in when his staff is shorthanded."

"I thought you were going in for anesthesiology."

She walked around the bed and bent over Mr. Soames, peering closely at the intravenous site, checking to see that the needle hadn't become displaced. The patient blinked at her blindly, absorbed in his conversation on the telephone, and pushed a cotton blanket off the bed. Alli caught it deftly. When she turned, Case hadn't moved.

Alli folded the light blanket and carried it to the closet. "Anesthesia?" she repeated.

"I switched to physical therapy. People laugh at my jokes better when they're awake."

"Laugh? If I remember, people laughed more before you told a joke than after." She couldn't suppress a grin. "I suppose you write the punch line on your palm now."

"I'm getting better."

In more ways than one, Alli thought. Her gaze swept over the broad shoulders, narrow waist, and long legs. She turned and placed the blanket on a shelf. No way was she going to let thoughts like that beat in her heart again. Case had made it clear long ago that he was a settler. With equal determination she'd told him she was a traveler. And from the looks of things, neither of them had changed. She turned and Case flashed his devastating smile.

"Maybe I'll catch you in the coffee room later." He strode toward the doorway.

"Maybe," she said. *And maybe not,* she added to herself, wary eyes following his departing figure.

Case left the room and slowed his step to a stroll, his thoughts centered on Alli. Talk about second chances! *He* had almost fallen down the stairs when he'd discovered that the nurse in his arms was the girl of his dreams. The girl he couldn't forget. But the girl had become a woman. Soft and curvy in the right places. She even smelled feminine. The sable-dark, silky hair brushing his chin gave off an aroma of fragrant shampoo, and the brief encounter with her smooth cheek left a delicate scent of cosmetics. Even her breath smelled fresh and minty.

Her eyes hadn't changed from the startling blue-green they'd been when she was seventeen. Or was she eighteen before he looked beyond the effervescent personality to notice her bright, intelligent eyes? Everything about her seemed imprinted on his senses. And all of her was here in Wayside again.

He'd blown it once. She hadn't returned to Wayside for the holidays, as they'd planned, and he hadn't had enough money for a ticket to New York. Then he'd become interested in physical therapy, and the hospital administrator had offered to pay his college tuition. Their correspondence waned. By the time he could afford to visit New York, Alli was practically engaged to a doctor—so her sister said when he'd called to ask how he could reach Alli. He hadn't tried to call her again.

But no rings circled a finger on her left hand, he mused. He reached the bank of elevators before he realized he'd gone far past the room where Mrs. Tober waited for him.

Assured that the intravenous line was patent, Alli left Mr. Soames's room and met Mona coming from the nursing station. "Not off duty yet?" Alli asked, giving her a sympathetic smile.

"I clocked out and remembered my jacket. Probably Freudian. It gives me a chance to pop in and say good morning to Mrs. Tober"—Mona tilted her head, letting a teasing look settle on her pretty face—"and anyone else who might be in the room."

"He should be there by now." Alli grinned.

"Ah, you've seen him. Didn't I tell you he's a hunk? And you do have the advantage."

"Advantage?" Alli quirked an eyebrow.

"You work days."

"Not for long."

"I remember . . . restless feet," Mona said, smiling. "Your loss will be the nursing staff's gain."

"The nursing staff, or whoever, has my best wishes," Alli said firmly. She strode past Mona, ignoring the small voice that questioned the veracity of her words.

It was one o'clock by the time Alli settled a new post-op patient and left for lunch. A few hospital personnel and several visitors occupied the dining room. One nurse sat alone on the outdoor patio. No one stood before the food bar. Swinging past a row of empty tables, Alli entered the food line.

She gazed at a pan of beef Stroganoff without one twinge of hunger. She bypassed the lasagna and a chicken dish covered with some kind of white sauce and decided she was too tired to swallow one mouthful. Getting a late start was bad enough. Being new to the unit made it worse. She sighed and selected a tuna salad and a carton of milk. Next week would be easier. There were only so many nursing units in a small hospital. Working an occasional weekend at the hospital near her apartment wasn't enough to keep up her skills for the specialty units.

After paying for her food, she made her way through the dining room to the shaded patio. The decorative, open brickwork of the walls allowed an occasional breeze to pass over the diners, bringing with it the scent of jasmine.

Alli joined the middle-aged woman dressed in a colorful tunic. "Pediatrics, huh?" She gestured at the flower-bedecked top. "I worked there yesterday." She introduced herself.

"Laura," the older woman said. "Did you like it?" Her warm gray eyes sparkled with interest. "I wouldn't want to work anyplace else," she added before Alli could say it was her favorite unit. "I was helping PT work with a toddler who's just out of a lengthy coma. Time gets away from you when you're absorbed." She indicated her lunch tray.

"Would that be Lenny?"

Laura nodded. "My, it takes patience! But with Case

Sherman, patience is spelled with a capital P. The little ones love him." She opened a milk carton. "Have you met Case yet?"

Alli stabbed at her salad. Is that all anyone had to talk about today? She made an indistinct sound that could be interpreted either way.

"We go back a few years," Laura said. "I knew him when he was a student working part-time as a lab assistant."

So did I, Alli said silently. *And I know all about his quiet, mile-wide smile.* When she was a seventeen-year-old Volunteen, that smile could have willed her to follow him anywhere. But Case didn't want to go any farther away from Wayside than the Colorado River. And she wanted to get as far away from the small town as she could travel.

Laura touched her lips with a paper napkin. "Case just returned from vacation. Good thing. He's short two staff people, and everyone is yelling. But he'll have things smoothed out in a few days, even if he does double shifts. Administration couldn't have chosen a better replacement when Laytes retired."

Alli nodded, taking a sip of milk to stall a response. Case would be a good department head. And he'd probably be happy to stay right at ole Wayside until *he* retired. "The census was down in pediatrics when I worked there," Alli said, hoping to change the subject of the conversation.

"It's still down, but we admitted a couple of tykes

who need extra care, so we're busy.'' Laura lifted one hand and waved in the direction of the food line.

Alli looked up and quickly returned her gaze to her plate. But not before Case smiled broadly in her direction. A few minutes later he slid his loaded tray on the table and sat down opposite her.

Laura groaned enviously at the sight of his selection. ''I'd trade my day off for one slice of chocolate cake.''

''Be my guest.'' Case picked up the dessert and placed it in front of her. ''My eyes forget about my waistline.''

Laura shook her head. ''Mine don't.'' She grinned. ''Have you met Alli?''

He nodded and gave Alli a friendly smile. ''In the type of meeting that has my best recommendation.''

''Oh?'' Laura inquired with a roll of her eyes.

Case grinned and lifted a cube of beef to his mouth.

Laura turned toward Alli. ''If Case isn't going to tell me, you have to,'' she teased.

''I sort of fell into his arms on the stairs.'' Alli felt her cheeks warm, and she glared at Case. ''One of my patients decided to go AWOL, and I tried to keep him from falling down the stairs.'' Her explanation tumbled out in a rush. ''Case helped me get him back to bed.''

Laura awarded Case a gold medal with her smile. ''You can come to Peds and help me anytime,'' she chortled. She glanced at her watch and stood. ''Nice to meet you, Alli.'' She waggled her fingers at Case and carried her tray toward the conveyer belt.

Case looked at Alli, but before he could speak, a young man bounced across the room. "Ya' seen Dr. Ronson?"

Case shook his head.

The anxious man paused. "Hey, Case . . . missed you at basketball. It's not a game without you."

"Next Tuesday. Promise."

The man grinned and trotted back out the dining-room entrance.

Case turned back to Alli. "What are you doing working at Wayside?" He directed a fork full of beef and noodles toward his mouth.

"I need a job."

"I thought you had a job in Chicago." His expression was bland.

"I took an emergency leave." She wondered how he'd known she was based in Chicago.

Concern flooded his eyes. "Emergency leave . . . your family?"

"Mother and Gran were in an accident."

"I didn't know."

"It was in San Bernardino, and I doubt if it made the front page of the papers."

"Are they all right?"

"Mother's fine. One arm is still in a cast. Gran will take just a little longer to heal."

"I'm glad to hear it. I guess that means you won't have to unpack your suitcase."

Alli produced a mock scowl. "I'm staying until Gran

doesn't need me. She doesn't want to stay with my folks, and Mother couldn't care for her, anyway. The least I can do is care for her when she needs me."

"Of course," he said quietly.

Alli sipped at the near-empty milk carton carefully.

"I gather you're not ready to make the stay permanent." He looked at her steadily.

"Are you ready to leave . . . permanently?" She looked away, staring at the profusion of jasmine draping a corner of the patio. She knew his answer.

"Afraid I'm here for a while. A couple of years at least. Administration paid my tuition through college."

"And you're giving service in return," she said dryly.

The corner of his mouth tilted. "I like it here."

Alli looked away. *And I don't.* Gran's offer of tuition and a room with a view of the city had been a convenient way for her to escape Wayside.

"I hear you travel a bit with your job," Case said.

"You hear?" Alli tore open a package of crackers beside her plate.

"I run into your dad now and then."

Alli punctured the tuna salad. "I travel five days a week. The company I work for sets up health programs for universities and colleges and companies."

"What kind of health programs?"

"You know the kind of medical-history page you fill in when you apply for a job or visit a doctor? Well, our company includes questions on life-style and other things. Actually, it's a wellness program. Preventive medicine is popular these days.'' Her voice was animated. ''By running the data from the questionnaires through a computer, we can set up health-care programs appropriate for the people involved. And the traveling comes in when I set up new programs or troubleshoot old ones.''

''Sounds like you like your work.''

''I do. It's educational, challenging—exciting.'' She toyed with a cracker. ''And you—I hear you've been on vacation.''

''More work than vacation,'' Case said wryly. ''I drove to northern California to talk to a therapist about an outpatient physical-therapy clinic. Had to return before I managed the vacation bit.''

Alli nodded in empathy. ''Laura told me your department is short of staff.'' She looked up to see a slender black woman with short, curly hair lowering her tray at the end of the table.

''Can I join you?'' The woman's look flicked past Alli to rest on Case.

''Please do.'' Alli doubted if the woman heard her.

Case lifted his head, smiled in recognition, and introduced the new arrival. Alli caught the word ''respiratory'' and gathered the young woman worked in RT. With a quick smile at Alli, the therapist slid into a chair. She turned to Case. ''About the employees' picnic. . . .''

Alli nibbled at a whole-wheat cracker. Case spread

his charm over everyone—men, women, and children loved him. No doubt he had a dog waiting at home with a wagging tail and a cat that seldom roamed. And from the way he'd been acting, he wasn't averse to adding her to his list.

Alli stood up, nodded to Case and his coworker, and picked up her tray.

"Leaving so soon?" Case looked at her, disappointment in his eyes.

"I hear call bells ringing," Alli said lightly. She pulled her gaze away from the brown eyes that continued to ruffle her heartbeat.

She carried her tray resolutely to the conveyer belt. One way to avoid a contagious disease was to wear isolation apparel. Or not to get near the carrier. She made a wry face. A paper gown and mask were faint protection against Case's charm! A more preventive measure was to avoid him, even if it meant brown-bagging a peanut-butter sandwich to eat in the nurses' lounge and checking the halls before she made rounds.

Chapter Two

Alli pulled her time card from the clock, grimacing at the inked numbers. Fourteen minutes over. She twisted her lips wryly. Why did she always find one last task to do for a patient, knowing the undeniable stamp meant explaining to a supervisor her inability to get off duty on time? She strode down the hall, veering around a corner toward a heavy glass exit door. Outside, a young woman, juggling a baby in one arm, struggled to open the door and guide a child inside. Alli quickened her step to hold the door open.

"Emergency room," the woman said in a high, strident voice. "Please, show me the way to the emergency room."

Alli's look darted to the baby in her arms. She didn't see any blood. The infant's cheeks glowed pearl-pink, and a muted rose colored her lips. No indication of respiratory distress appeared in the soft rise of the tiny chest. Alli glanced back at the distraught woman.

"My son." The woman shoved her keys into the pocket of her green shorts.

Alli shifted her scrutiny to the boy.

"I broke my arm." The boy's left hand supported a limp arm. "I slid into home plate."

"The emergency room," the woman repeated in a strained voice.

"Down this hall." Alli lifted her hand and paused. One look at the distraught mother's face convinced her the woman might easily turn toward the cafeteria instead of the emergency room. She suppressed a thought of Gran. How long could it delay her to take the trio to their destination?

Alli smiled at the boy in his Little League outfit as he shuffled beside her, and she controlled an urge to bend to hug him and assure him he'd be fine. "It does look a little out of whack, doesn't it? But you know, you may be the only guy in class with a cast—everyone will be lining up to initial it."

"Jason had a cast last year." The ball player looked at his mother for confirmation.

"Yes, he did, Kenny." The mother smiled wanly.

"He didn't go to school for weeks. But Mom says I may get to go to school tomorrow."

"Let's see what the doctor says." Alli touched his shoulder, hoping his bravado held up a little longer.

Stopping her charges at the admitting office, she indicated a chair in front of the desk. "The clerk needs you to sign some papers and give her a little information—your insurance company—that sort of thing. Kenny can sit right beside you."

The mother made no effort to move. "Insurance?"

Glazed eyes stared at Alli. ''I must have left my purse in the car.''

Alli's eyes softened. ''I'll stay with Kenny while you get it.''

''I'd be terribly grateful.'' The woman hesitated. ''If you'd hold the baby, I could go faster.'' She looked at her son, taking in his look of trepidation. ''Three minutes, tops.''

Alli held her arms out for the infant. ''Kenny can help me watch the baby. Right, Kenny?''

Kenny blinked, his gaze following his mother, and Alli looked at the admitting clerk.

''Let me check with the nurse,'' the clerk said, leaving the desk. She returned a minute later to escort Kenny to the trauma room. ''The nurse will be in as soon as she can,'' she explained to Alli.

''I'll stay here until your mother returns.'' Juggling the baby, Alli touched Kenny's shoulder as a young physician approached. ''This is Kenny,'' she said cheerfully, hoping her voice reassured the boy. ''His mother will be back in a minute.''

The doctor glanced at the infant in Alli's arms. ''Haven't seen you working in ER before, have I?'' He reached for Kenny's injured arm and examined it skillfully.

''I don't—'' Alli cut off the denial when Kenny groaned.

The physician paused, asking Kenny about his ball game. Then his fingers moved gently over the arm again. He spoke to Alli without looking up. "I want some X rays as soon as possible. May need lab work and a signed surgical consent, but I'll wait for the X rays. Call me as soon as they're done."

He strode away before Alli could tell him she didn't work in ER. She pulled aside the curtain to look for a nurse and saw Kenny's mother instead. With a sigh of relief, she gave the baby to the breathless woman. "The doctor was here. He'll be back to talk to you." Alli turned to Kenny. "Wish I could stay and autograph your cast, but I have to go." She winked. "Have a good day at school tomorrow."

Alli was almost out the door before she remembered the physician's orders. She stopped at the desk. "Did the doctor write orders?" she asked the clerk hopefully.

The clerk shook her head. "He left before I had a chart made up. He's with a stab wound." She made a sympathetic face. "Everyone is tied up right now. Can you wait a minute?"

By the time Alli relayed the physician's orders and hurried from the hospital, car keys in hand, the minute had stretched to fifteen.

Another twenty minutes passed while she tried to start her car. Finally she pulled the key from the ignition and looked at her watch. Gran would be anxious by now. She might even get out of bed by herself. She hurried back inside. Slowing when she reached a corner, she glanced down to rummage in her purse for change. On the edge of her vision, a wheelchair moved toward her, and she stepped aside. She looked up when the wheels stopped and Case peered at her with a pleasant, questioning look.

"Do you have a problem, Alli?"

Of all times to run into him!

"It's almost five, and I believe the day shift goes off duty at three-thirty. It looks to me as if you're coming in, not going out," he said.

His husky voice did nothing to alleviate Alli's already agitated pulse. She jostled the contents of her purse, running her fingers through the inside corners of the leather. "Do you want the whole list?" She added a long-suffering sigh.

"One at a time will be fine," Case told her.

The calm tone didn't soothe Alli. "Change," she said shortly. "Any other time, I have so much change, one shoulder is lower than the other from carrying my purse."

"Your first problem can be solved without calling in a banker," Case said, with a note of humor. "What's the second?"

Alli didn't answer. Her fingers felt a cache of coins. Grasping the loose change, she withdrew three pennies and a dime.

"Well?"

Alli's sigh of resignation reverberated between the walls. Case always had been persistent. "Mom stays with Gran until two, when she goes back to bed for a nap. And I'm usually home by four. But I got delayed.'' She plunged her hand back into the purse. ''Now,'' she said with exaggerated patience, ''Gran's car won't start. I can't find a telephone to call a towing service, and I can't find any change even if I could find a telephone. Ah.'' She took a deep breath and held up a quarter triumphantly. ''The rest can't be too difficult.''

''I'll make it even easier.'' He extended a set of keys. ''Take my truck.''

She shook her head. ''I'll call a towing service,'' she said firmly. ''Gran has insurance.'' She hoped it wasn't a lie. But letting Case play hero to her damsel-in-distress role wasn't the way to stay clear of the handsome guy.

''Don't argue. Your grandmother's alone.'' He took her right hand and opened it, pressing the keys into her open palm. Then he closed her fingers gently over the keys. ''I have to see a patient; then I can look at the car. It may be a little while. Let me have your keys and telephone number. I'll call you when I get off.''

The warmth from his fingers weaved treacherously through Alli's veins, wilting her determination. Case was right. Gran might be alone, and it could take an hour for a tow truck to arrive. She withdrew her hand from his more slowly than she'd intended and reached to find Gran's keys. ''It's the brown Ford, about four years old, in the last row of the back parking lot.'' She relinquished the keys without touching Case.

''Mine's parked on the next row over. The eleven-year-old, sandblasted green pickup with the *I'd rather be skiing* tag on the license-plate holder."

"Figures," she said briskly.

"That's not what I'd rather be doing now."

Alli closed her purse with a firm zip. Of course, he could mean getting off duty. But the warm gleam in his eyes suggested his thoughts weren't on work or recreation. She watched his fingers slide over Gran's keys, and the remembered touch of his fingers returned.

"You're right. I should go home and see about Gran," she said breathlessly, her professional tone forgotten. She scrawled Gran's number on a slip of paper. "Call me." Her voice sounded off-key. "And thanks, Case."

"What are friends for?"

She almost ran for the nearest exit. Friends indeed! Case had more than friendship in his look, not to mention touch. Some success she'd had in avoiding him! She couldn't get through one day without running into him as routinely as giving meds. And it wasn't over yet. She had to return his truck.

Alli drove out of the parking lot and, fifteen minutes later, parked in the curved brick drive beside a Spanish-style stucco house. Trimmed grass followed the pale-pink brick to the entrance. A pair of coconut palms stood at one side of the doorway.

Grasping the doorknob of the broad mahogany door, Alli hoped Gran and her next-door friend had their heads together, sharing neighborhood news. But the locked door indicated the neighbor hadn't used her key to visit, as she often did until Alli arrived. Alli inserted her key into the keyhole and opened the door.

"Gran, sorry I'm late," she called. "You okay? I'll be right in to see you."

"I'm fine, honey."

With relief, Alli dropped her purse on the entry table. She looked at Case's keys for a moment before she placed them beside the purse. When Case called, she would suggest he take the car home—providing he got it started. She could meet him at work to exchange vehicles. She nodded in satisfaction, as if she'd solved a nagging problem, and walked down the hall toward a large bedroom facing the street. Leaving Case's keys with his secretary would eliminate seeing him at all, she thought as if inspired. That was what she wanted, wasn't it?

She stopped in the doorway of Gran's bedroom. "You look fine," she said cheerfully. "How's the leg?"

Gran Parmer sat upright in the rented hospital bed, her white hair neatly blow-dried and her makeup carefully applied. Small aquamarine earrings matched the bed jacket she wore over a spaghetti-strapped gown. Alli noticed she'd added a touch of lavender above her intelligent blue eyes.

"It's not losing any weight. Still, I'd rather have a fat cast than be tied to those rope and pulley things." A look of concern touched her eyes. "What's with the truck? Is something wrong with the car?"

"Nothing to worry about, Gran." Alli sank into a chair facing the bed. "Your car wouldn't start. A therapist at the hospital offered me the use of his truck to come home." She slipped off one white shoe. "He'll try to start your car when he gets off duty."

"Sounds like a nice man." Gran lowered knitting needles and an unfinished coral-and-blue afghan. "Time you made friends here."

"I knew Case before I left Wayside. He worked part-time at the hospital when I was a Volunteen."

"The name sounds familiar. Didn't he write you in New York?"

"Uh-huh." Alli nodded, unbuttoning her tunic. At first Case had written long letters, telling her he missed her and hoped she'd be home for Christmas. She had written an equally longing response. But then Grandfather Parmer died, and she didn't make it home for the holidays. And during summer break from college she'd accepted a position as a ward secretary at a nearby hospital. The next December she and Case had exchanged Christmas cards, and by that summer she was dating a medical student.

"And he's still at the hospital." Gran's voice cut into her thoughts. "Sounds like a good, stable man."

"Gran." Alli chuckled. "No matchmaking with Case Sherman. He is definitely not the man for me."

"He's engaged?"

"I didn't ask." Alli pushed off the other shoe and wiggled her toes.

"He has halitosis?"

"You're as persistent as Case, Gran." She padded across the carpet and kissed her grandmother on the cheek. "Shall I help you into the wheelchair before I start dinner?"

"No, I'll watch the six o'clock news first." She feigned a pout, but a smile sparkled in her eyes. "I thought it would be nice if you found a young man in Wayside so I could see you without having to break a leg."

"You could visit me," Alli said cheerfully. She picked up the remote control from beneath the colorful yarn and handed it to her grandmother. "I'll change and check the fridge."

"Alli."

Alli stopped in the doorway and turned. From the lilting tone of Gran's voice, she knew the subject of Case wasn't over.

"You could set an extra place for the young man who's fixing the car."

"He may have other plans, Gran. Most likely, a date. It's Friday."

"Just thought I'd mention it, dear."

Inhaling with elaborate control, Alli made no comment as she left.

In her bedroom, Alli changed into brown walking shorts, a persimmon T-shirt, and tennis shoes. Tossing her uniform into the hamper in the adjoining bathroom, she went to the kitchen to take fish and vegetables from the freezer. Gran wanted a man settled in Wayside, did she? Alli grimaced. She'd have to keep Case and Gran apart. Just avoiding him at the hospital took more effort than she'd expected. She didn't need Gran's romantic interventions to add to her problems.

She yanked a head of lettuce from the vegetable keeper. She had two younger sisters. Why couldn't Gran concentrate on their love lives? Of course, Candi was married and expecting her first child. But Gwen's recent recovery from a mildly bruised heart had possibilities, even if her availability for grandmothering was limited to college holidays and an occasional weekend.

Thumping the head of lettuce against the drainboard as if it had disagreed with her, Alli removed the core. Maybe Gran *would* come to Chicago and live with her, she mused. She quartered a tomato with less hostility. She missed Gran. She hadn't realized how much until now. She added chunks of broccoli and carrots to the salad, covered the bowl, and placed it in the refrigerator. Dawdling, she walked to the door of the bedroom.

"Baked halibut, rice, and green beans sound good, Gran?" she called over the sound of the newscaster's voice. "And a green salad."

"Alli!" Her grandmother's mock groan floated toward the door. "You're not feeding a farmer."

Alli wrinkled her face. "Can't have that leg reducing too much."

"Sounds great," Gran said faintly.

Alli grinned. "You say that every night." She knew that, given her choice, Gran would rather eat fried tacos and pizza with mozzarella and black olives.

She returned to the kitchen, wondering if Case might return the car without calling, and felt a rise of anticipation at the thought. He'd hand her the keys and close her fingers over them gently. She shook her head in annoyance. She couldn't let such fantasies linger. Proximity to Case endangered her present life-style. As if the thoughts might follow her, she closed the back door firmly and went through the patio to Gran's herb garden.

Standing before a slender plant of dill weed, she stared at the lemon-colored clusters topping the slender stalks. Why couldn't she conjure up a vision of the last place she'd traveled? Restlessly, she bent to savor the licorice scent of a dill bouquet.

Alli looked toward the distant mountains and felt a stab of nostalgia. She and Case had spent an afternoon by the mountain lake before she'd gone away. She'd just turned eighteen, and he'd kissed her in a special way for the first time. She bent to snap a slender twig of rosemary, crushing it in her fingers, concentrating on the sharp scent to force her mind away from the mountains. She had to remember Chicago and work she enjoyed, and an apartment for which she had to keep up her share of the rent.

The memory wavered. Perhaps her last assignment

was more enticing, the time spent setting up new programs in Hawaii. The dreariness of the tiny apartment had brightened with the fragrance of frangipani drifting through the window and the sound of rain on the broad banana leaves. She smiled at the memory of the sudden flurries of rain sending unwary tourists skittering for shelter. She loved it—the frangipani and ginger and miniature orchids, the brief sprays of rain, and the brilliant azure sky above an even bluer ocean. Funny, she'd had to *force* herself to think about it today.

The ring of a telephone pulled her thoughts back to California. She felt her heartbeat quicken even faster than the steps she took to reach the kitchen. The ringing ceased as she opened the door. With only a second's hesitation, she walked to Gran's bedroom. She paused in the doorway, chagrined at her reaction. She'd acted like a teenager expecting a call from a boyfriend. She breathed heavily, alarmed that the rapid beat of her pulse could be more from the anticipation of hearing Case's voice than from jogging across the yard.

Gran replaced the receiver calmly and looked up. "That was your young man."

Alli took another deep breath and put up her hands, palms out. "Gran, he's not *my* young man. For all I know, he's engaged to be married next week." A trace of good-humored exasperation tinged her voice.

Gran ignored her outburst. "He said the battery was dead. He had someone jump-start it, and he's bringing it here to pick up his truck."

Alli suppressed a grimace. So much for the plan to exchange vehicles at the hospital. But she wasn't sure she was upset. "I'm glad it was nothing worse." She turned to leave.

"Oh, yes." Gran's voice halted her.

Alli turned, with a look at her grandmother that said, *I'm waiting for the other shoe to drop.*

"I asked if he had an engagement this evening."

Alli lifted her eyes toward the ceiling.

"What trouble could it be to add a little rice to the water and a leaf or so of lettuce to the salad? I don't eat much."

"Sometimes I don't think you'd eat at all if I didn't coax you." It was all Alli could think to say. Her thoughts were spinning like clothes in the dryer.

"Stop nagging like you're on duty. Don't you bully people enough eight hours a day at the hospital?" The smile on Gran's face denied any hostility.

"Gran, I don't mean to nag," Alli said contritely. "Maybe I get overenthusiastic about my work and bring it home with me."

"I thought you nursed kids."

"That was yesterday." She grinned. "I mean the health programs I put in place. Part of the program is to help people stay well—to have them take responsibility for their own health when possible."

"Okay." Gran lifted her hands in resignation. "I'll eat that raw, green vitamin-stuffed concoction." She burst into laughter. "You'll be sorry. I'll look so great, you won't dare bring a date home for coffee or tea."

''Ha! You look so gorgeous now, I'm not letting Case Sherman in the front door.''

''This evening you have to.''

''Not if we swap keys at the door,'' Alli quipped.

Gran smiled with elaborate serenity. ''You have it all figured out?''

''Right.''

Gran reached for her knitting. ''Seems Case has nothing planned this evening, so I invited him to dinner. The least we could do.'' Her eyes rounded with the innocence of a toddler.

Chapter Three

Expecting the buzz of the doorbell didn't prevent Alli's nerves from erupting like Mt. Kilauea in Hawaii. With effort, she spread the last of the dill mixture over the defrosted halibut fillets, waiting for the lava flow of tension spreading through her to subside. Why did Gran do this to her? Adjusting to a new workplace was stressful, even without the threatening presence of an old love she wished to avoid.

She glared at the hapless halibut. Home, albeit a borrowed home, should be a haven where you could toss your daily armor into the clothes hamper and not expect to don a fresh suit until the next shift.

She lifted the oven-ready dish and moved to the stove. She couldn't cope with the feelings that arose when she thought about Case, let alone the emotional havoc created when he moved within touching distance. Telling herself to step back was no help. Closing the oven door with a thud, she walked to the front door.

Case stood on the broad porch, dangling the car keys from one bronzed hand. He'd changed from hospital attire to faded jeans that encased his long legs with the snugness of stretch fabric. Alli pulled her gaze away from his narrow waist to his broad chest. The yellow-and-brown cotton shirt covering his torso did little to conceal the muscles beneath the fabric. She told herself she should breathe at regular intervals and decided it might be easier to accomplish that task if she looked at his face.

"Hi." Her voice sounded husky in her ears. "Gran said you'd found the problem." She took the keys, remembering to avoid the touch of his fingers, and stepped aside. "Come in. Gran is anxious to meet you. She's in the bedroom. I'll get her up for dinner." Her words tumbled out like a television picture on a vertical roll. "You are staying for dinner, aren't you?" She finally managed to get her voice under control.

"Thank you, I'd like that," he said cheerfully. His eyes sparkled with sunlight. He brushed past her and paused in the entry.

"Your keys are right here." Alli reached for the keys beside her purse and accidentally brushed them off the table. Flushing, she bent to retrieve them. Apparently she hadn't controlled her nerves as well as she thought. She straightened and extended the keys. "Come and meet Gran. Her room is down the hall." Her feet fairly flew over the carpet before Case could get near her.

"Are you always this energetic after a long day?" he called from behind her.

Alli ignored his teasing voice. "Gran," she called, her voice preceding her through the bedroom door as if she were eager to establish her grandmother's presence. She stepped inside and waited until Case followed her into the room. "I want you to meet Case Sherman. Case, my grandmother, Alene Parmer."

"Mrs. Parmer." Case stepped forward to take Gran's hand. "I've been looking forward to meeting you."

"Call me Gran." Blue eyes sparkled in greeting. "I'm sure we're going to be friends."

"Any grandmother of Alli's. . . ." Case's deep voice boomed pleasantly.

"And any friend of Alli's. . . ."

Alli looked from Gran to Case and back again like an amazed tennis watcher. Gran thanked Case for starting the car and inquired about the weather, as if the drapes hadn't been drawn since dawn. Case responded politely to the gratitude and said summer had sneaked in a few weeks early. Gran sat up straighter and kept her eyes fastened on Case's face as if he'd just told her an undisclosed scientific secret. He leaned nearer and asked what she was watching on television.

Alli coughed twice before their conversation paused. "I'd better see about dinner," she commented dryly.

Case turned his head toward her. "Can I give you a hand?"

''Of course you can,'' Gran said, preventing Alli's open mouth from uttering one word. Her look was angelic.

''Of course,'' Alli echoed with resignation. She gave Case a wan smile and steamed past him like a toy locomotive.

She didn't slow down until she reached the kitchen and opened the oven door to peek at the fish. The aromatic odor wafting from the oven smelled wonderful but did nothing to improve her mood.

Closing the door with a bang, she bent to rummage in a cupboard, clattering pots and pans to cover the thud of her heart. She knew Case was watching her. Measuring water into two copper-bottom pans, she placed them on back burners, pretending his scrutiny wasn't playing havoc with her heartbeat.

''Are you going to let me do something?'' Case lounged in the doorway.

''You could set the table. Get the salad out of the refrigerator.'' Alli measured precooked rice into a cup, keeping her eyes on the rice as if she had to count the grains. ''Plates are in the cupboard on my right,'' she said in a monotone, setting the cup down. She turned and almost bumped against him. She wondered when the kitchen had shrunk.

''Whose right?'' he asked, the direction of his eyes focused toward her face.

She motioned with her right hand. ''I'll get the place mats.'' Her tone indicated she might need to launch a long search. She ducked around him and sprinted toward the dining room.

Before she had the second buffet drawer open, Case stood at the end of the mahogany cabinet, his eyes bright with humor.

"I meant what can I do in the kitchen. I don't have five thumbs around a stove."

"There isn't much left to do. I have to pour a little rice into one pan and plop a plastic bag of beans into another." She slid through the narrow passage between his body and the buffet. "In fact, I must see about the water." She slung place mats and napkins on the table rapidly.

The water wasn't boiling, but her nerves were approaching that point. If Case would just stay out of the kitchen, she might get the rest of dinner on. As it was, she might cook the salad and pour dressing on the frozen beans.

She removed the wrapping on a package of frozen beans as Case returned, and she placed the pouch near the pan, as if to assure herself she couldn't make a mistake. Mentally she made a checklist to put the rolls in the warmer, set out the margarine, and find the salad dressing. Case was underfoot everywhere she went, searching, he said, for glasses. The kitchen got smaller and smaller.

She patted her forehead with the back of her hand. "I should have turned on the air-conditioning when I came in." She looked at Case to see if he was buying her story.

"Seems comfortable to me." He opened the refrigerator, looking as cool as the salad he removed. "Dressing?"

"I'll have to look for it." She turned off the burners under the pans. "Everything is almost ready. I'll get Gran up in her wheelchair."

"It'll be easier if I help."

There was no sense telling him that his presence turned her hands to inept clumps of dough. He was already on his way to the bedroom. Without a smile, Alli followed. Case had the wheelchair beside the bed, positioning it in line with Gran's body. Gran grasped the swinging bar over the bed with a minute grimace, despite Case's cheerful monologue.

Alli moved beside the chair. "Case is going to show us how it's really supposed to be done, Gran."

"Flattery will get you anything." Case grinned at Alli wickedly. "If you lift the casted leg, Alli, I'll do the easy part." He shifted his feet, his thigh brushing against Alli, and leaned to place his hands beneath Gran. "Ready?" He looked at Alli.

"Ready," she said. It wasn't easy to focus on lifting the encased leg with Case looking at her as if Gran wasn't even in the room.

"Now."

Alli swung her gaze to his arms and raised the casted leg as he lifted Gran. Together they lowered her to the chair.

"That was nice." Gran sighed gently. "You two make a great team. You do well together."

"I think so," Case said, winking at Gran. "Maybe we can work something out to do it more often." He bent to reposition the casted leg, and Alli felt his breath warm her neck.

He did it so smoothly, she thought wryly. He moved in on her space with the ease of an expert. She stepped back, watching Case gently shift the casted leg and tuck the corner of the pillow under one side. Alli knew she was being silly. Case was simply doing the same things he would do for any patient. And if she'd been helping any other therapist, or male nurse or physician, she wouldn't notice the close working quarters. Thinking Case deliberately moved near her was imagination. She had to keep her thoughts in perspective. His words and deeds were a mixture of friendliness and kindness.

Case moved behind the wheelchair, talking to Gran as Alli placed a light cover over Gran's uninjured bare leg. Then he wheeled her to the dining room. Gran eyed the table skeptically, her look traveling to her extended leg.

"We've been eating on trays in the family room," Alli said to Case, noting Gran's look.

"It's a lot easier," Gran said wistfully.

"I can make it just as easy and comfortable right here," Case promised. "Or we can move to the family room."

"That's too much trouble," Gran said. "This is fine."

"You're sure, Gran?" Alli felt a twinge of guilt.

Why hadn't she asked her how she felt about eating in the dining room? She'd been so concerned about her own feelings about Case, she'd forgotten that Gran might find it uncomfortable to change from her familiar routine.

She watched Case push the chair to the corner of the table, letting the casted leg rest beyond the overhang. He moved the place mat in front of her and made small talk. Alli stared. He was so . . . so *big* to be so gentle. She turned away quickly and went to the kitchen to get the food.

Alli served Gran, standing over her in silent protest until Gran added a few spoonfuls of each dish. "I'm getting even for all the times you made me eat breakfast before I left for class," she teased lightly.

"Ha!" Gran scowled at the salad. "You ate like an anorexic bird."

"You can't say that now." Alli placed the salad on the table and sat across from Case.

"For which I'm glad," Gran said emphatically, prodding a bean with her fork. "You look a lot better with a touch of padding here and there."

Alli passed Case the rice and caught the sparkle of laughter in his eyes. His gaze lowered, not from embarrassment, she was sure.

"Green beans?" Alli asked. She lifted the dish, aware of the slow swirl of heat rising inside her, and shoved the beans toward him without meeting his eyes. What was wrong with her? She'd gotten over Case long ago. Teenage love, she'd told herself when she thought about him. Yet, there'd never been anyone else she'd thought about seriously. No one quite measured up. No one had ever made her feel like she felt now. Warm and wanted—and confused.

She turned toward her grandmother, refusing to yield to the hypnotic pull of his look. "Salad dressing, Gran?" She reached for a bottle and placed it near her.

"I'd prefer blue cheese," Gran said with a lilt in her voice.

Alli added a cruet beside the first bottle and picked up her fork.

"Vinegar and oil would be fine too." Gran's voice sounded amused.

Alli wrinkled her forehead in puzzlement and looked at Gran, who grinned. Alli lowered her fork. Why Gran found a bottle of salad dressing funny was a mystery to her, but she reached for the first bottle she'd given Gran. "Do you want me to mix your dressing, Gran?" She stood, reaching for Gran's salad bowl, and looked at the bottle in her hand. Flushing, she replaced the bottle on the table. Catsup. No wonder Gran's grin was as broad as a saucer.

"I'll see if there is any blue cheese, Gran." She glanced at Case, but he carefully spooned beans onto his plate without a hint of a smile on his handsome face.

Alli sprinted noisily to the refrigerator for salad dressing and swished a cruet of oil from the cupboard as she went by.

Case glanced at her as she placed the dressing beside Gran's salad and continued talking. "Range-of-motion exercises are necessary to keep your muscles in good working condition." He reached for the oil at Alli's unspoken query. "Do you have a therapist come to the house, or does Alli help you with the exercises?"

"Is that those bending and twisting tortures Alli insists I do?" Gran smiled.

Alli handed the vinegar to Case. "You'll thank me when you're ready to walk, Gran," she said from habit. "And we don't exercise as much as we should." She added blue-cheese dressing to her grandmother's salad bowl.

"What do you mean, 'we'?" Gran retorted. She glanced at the salad dressing on the greenery in her bowl. "Don't be sparing with the dressing if you expect me to eat that mess," she added with alacrity.

Alli rolled her eyes, feigning a look of shock. "I don't exercise when I'm lifting your leg!" She looked to Case for support, her planned reserve momentarily forgotten. "Gran's physician suggested a therapist should come out to the house, but Gran says we . . . notice that *we*"—she paused to laugh softly in Gran's direction—"*we* can do fine."

"Alli." Gran put her fork aside and straightened. "What did you do to the fish tonight? It's tasty. I would like another helping."

Alli almost dropped her fork. Gran hated fish.

By the time Alli had placed another portion of halibut

on her grandmother's plate, Gran had smothered any discussion about the dreaded exercises with a new topic.

"It's a lovely place to live. Only a few hours' drive to the mountains or the ocean or the desert," Gran was saying to Case. "Have you lived here long?"

"Years. I even commuted when I went to college." He took a bite of the halibut and nodded appreciatively at Alli. "I made it somewhat permanent a few months ago. Bought one of those ranch-style houses built on a couple of acres of land. A few fruit trees grow on the property, and I intend to plant more. Maybe get a couple of horses. There's a stable area."

"Planting roots?" Gran picked at her beans, but Alli could almost see gears spinning beneath the carefully coifed white hair. "Alli's dad likes to plant roots too."

"I can't say the same for my dad." A mixture of affection and resignation blended in Case's voice. "He is an unrepentant nomad. And Mother is a 'whither thou goest' wife. I was lucky to stay in one place long enough to finish a school year." His grimace held no hostility. "We lived in Wayside when I graduated from high school, and I decided to remain in one place for a while. My folks went on to Arizona."

"Where is your family now?" Gran asked.

"Alaska, when I heard from them two months ago. My sister Emily married a serviceman. She and her family are in Texas. Mother did mention something about going to see Emily before Emily's husband was transferred again, so they may be en route, so to speak.'' He chuckled softly. ''Sometimes I feel like one of those post-office boxes where people have their mail sent. When Mom and Emily haven't heard from each other in a while, they send their letters to me—to be forwarded. Even when I moved to the new house, I met my former postman in our new mall, and he asked about my mother. There's something to be said for small cities.''

Gran beamed at Alli with a look that was almost audible. *Responsible. Now, here's a young man who's responsible.* ''Didn't I tell you, Alli?'' she said, ''that you should stay in Wayside? I'll bet you don't even see your postman in Hawaii.''

Alli blinked. What did knowing who delivered the mail have to do with living in Wayside? But Gran had gone on to another subject.

''Alli tells me you're the director of the physical therapy department at the hospital,'' she said with interest. ''Sounds impressive.''

''It does, doesn't it?'' A twinkle lit Case's eyes. ''Luckily, few people notice I changed positions a few years ago.''

Alli chewed on a green bean. She could just see Gran lapping up the charm of this man who didn't take himself too seriously. The trouble was, Case probably believed what he said. She stabbed another bean.

''You have a choice of desserts,'' Alli informed Gran and Case with a bleak smile. She had to stop these two. ''Vanilla ice cream or vanilla ice cream.''

"Ice cream?" Gran arched an eyebrow. "Three times this week? And no comment on my cholesterol count?"

"I would've had an angel-food cake *baked*, but the bakery doesn't deliver." Alli wrinkled her face at her grandmother.

"Pay no attention to Alli," Gran told Case. "She's a great cook. I'll bet she doesn't even own a can opener."

"Modern career women pop a package into the microwave, Gran." Alli stood. A little late to resume talk about Case's career, she thought, but dessert might detour Gran's present course. "I think I saw a package of frozen strawberries for topping." If she didn't erect a barricade right now, Gran could have Case proposing and Alli pondering an unacceptable future before the month was over.

Five minutes later, having served a dish that looked as enticing as a centerfold in a dessert calendar, Alli restrained a moan as a back tooth came in contact with a cold, rigid berry. With trepidation, she glanced at her dinner companions. Case lifted a strawberry-and-cream peak to his mouth and chewed cautiously, making appreciative sounds. Alli glanced at Gran, who was lowering a berry to her plate.

"Sorry. I forgot to pop that package into the microwave to defrost." Alli made a face.

"Delicious." Case made appreciative sounds. "Wish my waist could stand seconds."

"There's plenty." Alli slid her spoon beside her dish and started to rise.

"A second helping would mean I have to walk a few extra miles this evening."

"Walk?" Alli sat down. "I walk enough at work."

"You know it's not the same thing." He pushed his dish forward an inch. "Doesn't keep the old pulse rate up long enough. Tell you what. I'll pick you up every evening if you want to walk with me."

Alli smiled at him with mild exasperation. "I'll pass." She stood up and glanced aside as she stacked dishes. "Do you want to watch television in the den while I put the dishes in the dishwasher, Gran?"

"Not really."

Alli turned her head toward her grandmother. She'd expected a routine yes.

"I'd rather put the dishes in the dishwasher," Gran said, her face in a resigned scowl. "But it looks like you get that pleasure."

"Gran, let me take you to the den," Case offered, rising, "then I can help Alli with the dishes." He leaned down and released the brake on the wheelchair. "Though it's a difficult decision to make."

"Difficult decision?" Alli couldn't help voicing her puzzlement aloud.

"Which one of you lovely women to leave alone."

Me, Alli wanted to scream, but Gran was already assuring Case that Alli could get out of the kitchen faster with a little help.

Pushing the chair, Case glanced back at Alli. "Don't go away. I'll be right back."

She smiled graciously, but she didn't feel gracious. What did he think he was doing? She wanted him to be nice to Gran, but he didn't have to go overboard. Gran didn't need any buttering up to decide he was the man she was looking for—for Alli.

She stacked plates haphazardly, jammed the cutlery together, and strode to the kitchen. Opening the door to the dishwasher, she yanked out the lower tray and dumped her load amid the wire slots. The cutlery wobbled precariously atop the wire cage instead of in it, and Alli took a deep, calming breath. With controlled effort she rearranged the silverware and realigned the plates. When she looked up, Case approached with an assortment of glassware in each hand.

"Got a place for these?" He walked to the dishwasher, extending two glasses, and stood next to her, enclosing her in the nook between the L-shaped cabinet and the open door of the dishwasher. Alli withheld a sigh and leaned past him to pull out the upper dish rack. When she raised up, she was aware of the warmth building in her veins. Did he have to stand so close?

Case placed the glasses on holders; then he straightened, turning his head to grin at her like a small boy who awaited praise for a job well done. Alli gave him a faint smile and waited with mounting impatience for him to move. But he didn't move one inch. He didn't even seem to notice she was trapped inside the small enclosure. She stiffened her spine and kept the smile on her face. She was not going to let him see he affected her one bit. She leaned over and tried to shove the rack back into the washer. It stuck halfway.

"If you're finished with whatever you're doing, could you move?" she asked calmly.

"Move?" He didn't budge.

"Step aside. Move one foot and let the other one follow," she said with rising frustration. He turned as she straightened up, and she stared at his chin.

"Satisfied?" he asked blandly. His body didn't touch hers, but it was so close, she could smell the scent of his after-shave.

"Not this way." Alli raised her hands to press them against his chest. She looked up and found his eyes filled with amusement and something else that disturbed her already wobbling emotional equilibrium. It wasn't enough that he had her in a corner without an inch to retreat. Now he'd invaded her airspace. Her breath caught in her chest while the warmth in her veins mushroomed up and floated down to engulf her body.

"Maybe you could show me." The amusement in his eyes spread to tilt the corner of his lips.

"You don't need me to show you how to move!" she sputtered.

"Show me where to put this bowl," he said calmly and stepped back.

Alli looked down to see that he held an ice-cream bowl in one hand.

She moved to yank the rack out again and point to a slot on the rack. This time she'd moved into his space. And he didn't seem to mind one particle. Gran's kitchen had never seemed this small before.

She knew she should laugh and say something witty.

"What else can I do?" he asked innocently.

She shoved the rack in. Didn't he know he was more distraction than help?

"Detergent." Her mind seized on a word. "It's in the cupboard under the sink."

When he moved to get to the cupboard, she fled to the dining room. She lingered over gathering the place mats and replacing Gran's silver centerpiece of fruit on the table. When she returned to the kitchen, Case was bent over the closed dishwasher, studying the dials. She moved toward it, planning to turn the water on, and remembered the water she'd left running in the garden.

"I just remembered—I left the water running on the roses. Maybe you could start the dishwasher while I dash out back and turn it off." Without waiting for an answer, she darted toward the back door. She needed time away from the nearness of the man. She couldn't think properly.

She turned off the water and bent among the roses to retrieve the hose. She took time to coil it neatly. Not that it helped much, she thought. She couldn't stay here all night. And Case wouldn't leave until she ushered him out the door. All she had to do was show him to the door, tell him good night, and get back on track—that is, stay away from him. She'd wined him and dined him and thanked him properly for helping a damsel in distress. Hadn't she?

With a firm step she turned toward the house and found Case watching her from the patio doorway.

"Everything okay?" he asked.

"Fine." She paused, waiting for him to step aside.

"Lovely evening," he said huskily, reaching to touch her cheek.

Alli's nerves reacted like a monitor alarming. Just as she thought it was safe to go back into the house, she thought wryly.

"You don't need this." He held up a leaf before he dropped it. He reached to brush his fingertips across her cheek lightly, and Alli looked at him. His fingers paused, then moved to her jawline, tracing it gently, his look meeting hers. "I let you leave too easily the first time."

The look of intensity in his eyes made her speechless. Then he took a step back, waiting for her to enter the kitchen. For a moment she simply stood there. Then she brushed past him and hurried to the den.

Dimly she was aware that Case followed her to say good night to Gran and that she walked him to the door. She watched his old truck pull into the street, her heart still sounding an alarm she hadn't been able to reset.

Chapter Four

Alli reached for the telephone and continued grating cheese, expecting to hear her mother's voice travel into the sunlit, bacon-scented kitchen.

"Good morning, Alli." The rich tone of Case's voice rumbled through the line.

Alli held the receiver aside momentarily. She didn't need this call. She'd overslept because of a restless night. Keeping her balance, verbal or otherwise, with Case was a challenge anytime. Still battling the doldrums of sleepiness, it would be like hiking up the mountain in a snowstorm. "Hello," she finally said.

"I called to thank you for the great dinner last evening."

Alli winced at his bright, cheerful tone. "Glad you enjoyed it," she said, working at rousing her vocal cords.

"Car start all right?"

"Fine," she said, amazed at what a little effort did for her voice. "I had to run to the market for eggs before I could start an omelette for Gran. One turn of the key, and the car was wider awake than I was.''

She finished grating the last sliver of cheese and set the bowl aside mechanically. Not a good start, she warned herself. She'd vowed to avoid him, and yet here they were again. And the sound of his voice was threatening to ruin her carefully made plans. . . .

''Speaking of food—'' He paused. ''I'd like to take you to dinner tonight. I could come early and bring you back to see my place before we go to dinner.''

Alli stared at the bowl before her as if remembering the microwave recipe could forestall a response. Methodically she lifted a bowl of egg yolks and slid them into a snowy cloud of beaten egg whites. ''Sounds nice,'' she said into the receiver, reminding herself she'd spent half the night chairing a meeting in her mind concerning the pros and cons of Case Sherman. With effort she recalled the final vote. ''But no can do, Case.'' She hoped her voice sounded firm. She'd drained her determination cup.

''I know. Gran. I'm ready to solve that problem. I have a friend who loves to sit with grandmothers.''

Alli poured the mixture into a glass dish, slid the dish into the microwave, and punched in the time code. The oven purred softly. ''A sitter is not what I need. In fact, three sitters are due to arrive in a couple of hours and stay through dinner.'' She chuckled, wide awake now. ''And Gran hasn't had breakfast yet.''

''Three sitters?''

"Relatives," Alli explained. "And I was exaggerating when I said 'sit.' Mom and Gwen will help in the kitchen."

"Sounds like today's out. How about tomorrow?"

"I'm working tomorrow. If I make it to evening church services, I'm going to bed ten minutes after I get home." Her determination was on a roll.

An exaggerated sigh echoed over the telephone. "Ah, the trials a man goes through to get you alone! I'll give you a rain check this time."

"Did I ask for one?"

"You didn't have to. Working with patients who rebel at moving a muscle, let alone relearning to walk or crawl, has taught me something. I have the patience of a sphinx. I'm aggressive and optimistic. Stubborn." Humor rippled through his voice. "Which trait do you think might be most successful in the pursuit of, uh, a date?"

Aggravating, annoying, obtruding—and shamefully sexy, Alli added silently. Even over the telephone his voice raised unwanted feelings.

"None of the aforementioned," Alli said with mock severity. "Case, I don't have time for fun and games. As soon as Gran is able to walk, I'm returning to Chicago."

"So?" he drawled. "What harm could it do for us to enjoy each other's company while you're here?"

A warning bell sounded in her head. Case fever. That's what the harm could be. Just because she'd caught it once didn't mean she was immune to it now. She realized Case was saying something. "I didn't catch that, Case," she mumbled. "I'm sorry."

"I'm the one to apologize. You did say you were making breakfast for your grandmother, and I heard the microwave alarm."

"Oh, yes." She rallied her thoughts enough to push a square on the control panel of the oven. "What were you saying?"

"Let me call you back when it's more convenient for you," he said and then laughed. "Though from the sound of your schedule, that's sometime between midnight and two in the morning."

"That's about right." Alli breathed easier. At last he was seeing the light. She had no time for a romantic interlude in California.

"I'll set my alarm. Which is better—midnight or one o'clock?"

"Persistent." She groaned. "You didn't add persistence to your résumé of questionable qualities."

"I'll remember that," he drawled. "By the way, I give personal attention to any rain checks I give. I don't just mail out postcards. 'Bye," he added before she could retort.

Alli replaced the receiver and took the pan from the oven. Mustard-colored glue covered the congealed creation in the pan. She lifted her eyes in frustration. Even long distance, Case was hazardous to her health. Case fever, she thought grimly. One date would be like eating one potato chip. She'd want another and another. She could end up staying in Wayside, like her mother, and making those she loved miserable.

Alli had the dishes in the dishwasher, Gran bathed and in her wheelchair, and a roast in the oven by the time the family arrived. Her mother, hands full with a basket of food, gave her a peck on the cheek. Her sister Gwen smothered her in hugs, and her father touched her shoulder briefly before he turned his attention to his mother.

"Gwen, great to see you home from college for the weekend," Alli said affectionately. "I wish Candice and her husband could have come too."

"We would have had a party, huh?" Gwen squealed. "Hi, Gran," she said over Alli's shoulder. A minute later she hurled herself toward the wheelchair and flung her arms around her grandmother.

Alli grinned. Age hadn't slowed Gwen's bubbling spirit. Caught in the merrymaking, she was reluctant to return to help her mother, but the clatter from the kitchen was an undeniable demand for help.

"Mom, your salad looks beautiful. Almost Christmasy with all that red-and-green stuff."

Gail Parmer continued changing the colorful Greek salad from the plastic container to a clear glass bowl. "Thank goodness for supermarket delis." She dropped the empty container into the trash bin. "I see you found the roast. I'd hoped Candi and Ted would be here, but Ted's working this weekend." She covered the bowl with plastic wrap. ''Candi called this morning. Said she's feeling well. Pregnancy agrees with her. She's scarcely had any morning sickness, you know. Unlike me.'' She grimaced. ''My morning sickness lasted all day for nine months.''

Alli made an inarticulate sound, bent to remove potatoes from a bin, and smiled with patient indulgence at her mother. Gail Parmer was still slender and attractive with her dark hair and blue-green eyes. Her hair was shorter now than in the publicity stills she kept from the time when she sang with a band, before she'd married and settled for solos with the church choir.

''She seems to be happy,'' Gail said, almost in amazement. ''Though I told her, just as I've told you a thousand times, think about it long and hard before you settle down. There's so much to see and do.'' She crossed the room to put one arm around Alli's shoulder. ''I'm so glad you took my advice. You've got a good career ahead of you. You're independent and footloose.'' She sighed. ''It must be wonderful to be able to travel and see the exotic places I just dream about.''

''It is, Mom.'' Alli dropped a peeled potato into a bowl of water. ''But you could travel now. I tried to get you to visit me in Hawaii.''

''I know,'' Gail said wistfully. ''But I didn't want to leave Mother Parmer when you asked. Now I can't go anywhere until she recovers.''

Alli picked up another potato and tried to remember what her mother's excuse had been last year.

* * *

After setting the roast before her father to carve, Alli made her way to the empty chair beside her grandmother and sat down. Her gaze roved around the table, lingering on the face of each loved one, as voices erupted into a confusion of merriment. An unfamiliar ache arose in Alli. Even more unfamiliar was the thought that followed. How wonderful to be in Wayside! She blinked furiously, her look darting from Gran to her mother as if she might have spoken the words aloud. But Gran was talking to Gwen, and her mother was telling her dad how to carve the roast. She breathed a sigh of relief. *But I wouldn't want to live here,* she amended vigorously.

Gran turned toward her son. "Did Alli tell you about the young man who helped her when the car wouldn't start the other day?"

"Why didn't you call me?" Alli's father looked at her as if she should have.

"No problem," Gran said calmly. "This nice man who works at the hospital got it started. Case Sherman—isn't that his name, Alli?"

Alli nodded, managing not to glare at her.

"I know Case." Alli's father concentrated on slicing his beef. "He's been in the nursery a couple of times lately." He looked at his wife. "Remember, you mentioned he'd dated Alli years ago."

Without comment Gail Parmer passed the salad to her mother-in-law.

"If I remember, Alli used to talk about him like he was the only man alive," Gwen bubbled. "Is he still a tall, dark, handsome hunk?"

Alli ignored her sister's teasing look and gazed intently at the contents of the table. She must have forgotten something. Maybe if she looked in the refrigerator, she could remember the missing item. She rose and strode purposefully toward the kitchen. When she returned with another set of salt and pepper shakers, the conversation had switched to Candice's pregnancy.

On Sunday, Case drove into the hospital parking lot as Alli hurried in front of him to catch up with Laura. Nuts! He probably wouldn't see her all day. How any two people could work in a small hospital and not trip over each other at least once a day was a puzzle. It was almost as if Alli scouted the territory and scooted away if she saw him in the distance. He'd even checked the dining room at different hours, but he never managed to catch her at coffee or lunch breaks. He parked the car and strode toward the time-clock entrance. Maybe he could catch her there.

But only Laura stood near the time cards, talking to another nurse. Case nodded, hurrying past. He paused at the sound of his name.

"Case, what are you doing here so early?" Laura hurried to fall into step with him.

"Paperwork. I never seem to catch up." Case looked down at the plump nurse. "How's pediatrics?"

"Not as crowded as usual. We're between respiratory season and vacation accidents."

"I thought I saw you with Alli Parmer a few minutes ago. Is she working on pediatrics today?"

"Medical floor, I think." Laura stopped at the turn in the corridor. "Good nurse. Nice girl too. You should get better acquainted."

"Maybe I should," Case said, as if he'd never thought about it.

He waved at Laura and turned in the opposite direction and went to his office. Spreading a sheath of papers across his desk, he stared at them.

Get better acquainted with Alli! He was in love with her again. That is, if he'd ever been out of love with her. She'd grown up and still kept all the qualities he'd loved when she was an enthusiastic Volunteen. Age had enhanced her beauty, and despite her effort to appear cool and professional, her career had increased her warm and caring nature. He'd tried to avoid thinking about her, but she was in his thoughts before he went to sleep and dancing in and out of his dreams until he awoke.

Common sense told him she avoided him at the hospital, but not seeing her didn't get her out of his system. In fact, it only heightened her appeal. Maybe it was time to change tactics, to haunt her literally as she haunted his thoughts. Proximity might overcome the obsession she had with leaving Wayside. He had to convince her Wayside was as good as any place to live when you were in love. At least, until he could go with her. He loved her.

With persistence maybe she would admit she loved him. He wasn't bad looking; he was reasonably personable. Lots of people liked him. Gran liked him. Laura liked him. He grinned. Maybe he should think about that. From the conspiratorial wink Laura had given him, she wouldn't be averse to sprinkling a little sugar on a romance. He rearranged the papers with fresh intent.

For a change Alli clocked out on time. It had been almost a routine day on the medical floor. One of her patients had a violent reaction to his medication. By the time she arrived at the room in response to a nursing assistant's summons, the man breathed with difficulty. She reached for the telephone to call a Code Blue and dialed the emergency room instead. Waiting to ask for the physician on call, she sent the assistant for the crash cart and bent to place a blood-pressure cuff on the patient. Seconds later she wondered if a code call would have brought a faster response. She watched the door anxiously, as if she could hurry the arrival of the physician and the crash cart, and monitored the patient's breathing. Had she done the right thing?

When the physician strode through the door, he barely glanced at Alli and the approaching crash cart and ordered the patient transferred to ICU.

Alli and the nursing assistant wheeled the bed to the

intensive care unit, and Alli parted with her patient reluctantly. But she couldn't stand around waiting to see that he recovered. She knew she had a patient waiting to be admitted. When she returned to her unit, the unit secretary handed her a page of orders for an elderly dehydrated woman being transported down the hall on a gurney. Alli hastened to see that a fresh bed had been rolled into the vacant space left by the "reaction" patient.

She started an IV on the new patient, sent a request for medicines to the pharmacy, and spent ten minutes trying to reassure the patient's stricken husband. In between she cared for her other patients—dressings, medicines, transfusions, and rounds with the doctors. All in all, it was a peaceful day. No one mentioned Case.

On Monday notices on the bulletin board about the upcoming employees' picnic made that the topic for the day. During coffee break, over charting, and passing coworkers in the hall, someone invariably mentioned the picnic.

"You're going, aren't you, Alli?" Laura asked when Alli sat down to chart.

"I don't think so. I volunteered to work so someone who's worked here longer could go."

"Oh, I forgot to tell you," Laura said. "The staffing secretary called to say she has enough nurses and no one wants to take off. They'll go to the picnic before or after their shift. So—'' She paused dramatically. ''We need volunteers for the children's booths at the picnic.''

Alli made a face. ''If I don't work at the hospital, my grandmother needs me at home,'' she said with ambivalent feelings. She liked children.

''You told me about her. But I'll bet your parents would stay with her for the day. You said they usually come by, anyway. And it would do you good to meet your fellow employees away from the hospital. It's two weeks away. That'll give you time to make arrangements. At least go to the committee meeting with me,'' she coaxed. ''Free lunch.''

Alli agreed reluctantly.

At noon there was no way for her to back out of attending the committee meeting. Laura waited for her to give a twelve o'clock medicine. ''I'll show you the way to the meeting room.'' She hovered like a big sister until Alli notified the charge nurse she was taking a lunch break.

Laura led the way across the dining room and through a door to a smaller room. Long tables were covered with bright-blue paper cloths and orange napkins. At one end a buffet table held trays of sliced meats, cheeses, breads, and fruit. Laura joined the line near the plates, beckoning for Alli to precede her.

Carrying a plate, Alli speared two paper-thin slices of beef and a slice of Swiss cheese. She added a small pickle and a few cubes of cantaloupe to her plate and dawdled until Laura selected a place to sit.

"Nice spread," Alli said, sliding into a chair next to Laura. "Does the dietitian do this often?"

"For committee meetings, usually." Laura opened a fat roll and placed two slices of beef inside. She looked across the table and smiled.

Alli followed Laura's gaze and smiled a welcome to the newcomer also. Mona, the night nurse Alli had met earlier, slid her sparsely filled plate on the blue cloth and sat down across the table.

"Hi, Mona," Alli said. "Isn't this a bit early for you?"

"Could say it's a bit late. I haven't been to bed yet. But I don't mind losing a few hours' sleep to volunteer for this committee."

"This is the committee for the children's games, you know," Laura reminded her.

"I know," Mona said, grinning broadly.

"I thought you didn't like pediatrics."

"Sick kids and well kids are different. Besides, there'll be lots of adults around the children's booths." She cut a millimeter of meat from a thin slice and eyed it warily.

"It wouldn't be the chairman of the committee who induced you to give up a day's sleep, would it?" Laura said in a teasing tone.

"Now how would the night shift know who's in charge of the committees?" Mona widened her eyes innocently. She tasted the meat, and her gaze roved the room. "Speaking of chairmen, I think I see ours now." Her eyes brightened.

Alli looked toward the door and saw a ward secretary she'd worked with on the surgical unit. The woman was about twenty-four, with a bright, witty disposition that took nothing away from her efficiency. If her work on the unit was any gauge, she'd keep the committee laughing while they worked, Alli thought. Suddenly she noticed someone sliding a plate on the table beside Mona. Her eyes rested on a beige tunic.

''Room for one more here?'' Case folded his tall body onto a chair beside Mona and looked into Alli's eyes.

''About time the chairman showed up,'' Laura quipped. ''You know I panic when I pick up a microphone, Case. The thought of having to start the meeting had me so upset, I could hardly eat.'' She held up the sandwich with a hefty bite removed from one side.

Case chuckled. ''So I see.'' He looked at Mona. ''Hello. Glad to see the night shift represented.'' He shifted his gaze to Alli. ''And the float pool. Glad you're here, Alli. We need new people with fresh ideas.''

''I have a fresh idea.'' Laura put her sandwich on her plate. ''How about making animals with those long balloons like you used to do for the kiddies in pediatrics?''

Case topped rye bread with ham and cheese. ''That was a long time ago.''

''Yeah.'' Laura wrinkled her face in a grin. ''When you worked a little.''

"You don't call all that office paperwork work? Besides, I'll probably be so busy seeing that things run smoothly, I won't find time for anything extra."

"Come on, Case. The kids love those giraffes and puppies and kitty-cats." She looked at Alli and Mona for support.

"Sounds good to me," Mona said, looking at Case with adoring eyes. "I'd be glad to help."

"Enough. I know when to agree." He looked at Alli. "Do you have any suggestions?"

Alli pushed the cantaloupe around on her plate. "Arts and crafts. Maybe I could have a crafts table. There may be some children who can't participate in the games."

"Good idea," Case said, as if she'd proposed a way to get to the moon. He pulled his look back to the group at the table. "Do all of you know the picnic will be held at a private park at Big Bear Lake? The theme is the Renaissance Faire. The diet kitchen has a menu planned. Barbecued chicken, beef, or spareribs, I believe, corn on the cob, assorted salads, and fresh vegetables. They asked us to come up with something for the kids."

"Hot dogs on a stick and soft ice cream and lots of soft drinks," a young woman on the other side of Case said.

"Fine. Save those ideas." He glanced around the table. "Looks like everyone is about finished eating. So I'll get started." He looked at Laura. "Did you bring something to take notes on?"

Laura reached in her pocket and brought out a small notebook and a pen. ‘‘I’m ready when you are.’’

Case stood for a moment. ‘‘I think everyone could hear me if you moved to this table; then I wouldn’t need to use the microphone.’’ He waited until the few scattered employees had moved to the long table. Then he repeated the location of the event, the theme, and menu. ‘‘I haven’t thought of any games to tie in with the theme, but I hope some of you can. Is pin-the-tail-on-the-donkey a twentieth-century game?’’

Alli watched Case and only vaguely heard suggestions about dunk tanks and water-balloon fights and fishing booths.

‘‘I believe you had a suggestion, Alli,’’ he said.

‘‘Arts and crafts,’’ she said tentatively.

Laura nodded in support and made a note on her pad. Case smiled warmly before turning to someone else.

‘‘I’m not all that thrilled about the Renaissance Faire theme,’’ one of the nurses said. ‘‘I have four girls. How could I possibly find time to make four costumes—not to mention one for me—even if I wasn’t working overtime next week?’’

‘‘Maybe we should bring that up to the other committees.’’ Case asked if there were more comments or suggestions, then closed the meeting.

Mona stood and caught his jacket sleeve and leaned to speak to him. As Alli gathered her dishes, she caught Case watching her.

"Thanks for volunteering, Alli." His smile was radiant. "See you at seven," he added.

She smiled briefly, wondering if his department was short of help. He usually came on duty at eight in the morning.

Walking back to the pediatrics unit with Laura, she asked her coworker about the balloon figures someone had mentioned.

Laura glanced at her watch. "Case calls them balloon sculptures. He blows up a long, skinny balloon and twists and turns it into the shape of a puppy or airplane or giraffe. It delights the kids. Of course, he pops one occasionally, and the kids laugh even more. And he warns them that their new toy may burst, so they won't be frightened—or disappointed. He uses rubber gloves once in a while. He's so good with the kids, but then he's just as patient with a reluctant, elderly patient."

Or a stubborn nurse, Alli thought.

Chapter Five

Surrounded by newspapers and a stack of mailbox ads, Gran kept her gaze glued to a *Magnum P.I.* rerun when Alli trudged in to see her.

"Have a good day?" Gran asked without missing a minute of the televised action.

Alli dropped into the lounge chair and glanced at the screen. Magnum, as usual, shorts-clad and sockless, vanquished a seedy villain with his bare hands. For a fleeting second Alli imagined Case dressed in shorts. She shook the thought away. "Had lunch on Mars," she said, glancing at Gran mischievously. "Returned only a few minutes late to make rounds and check IVs."

"That's nice." Gran looked away from the television as the commercial interrupted Magnum's plunge into a pool. "Did you see that young man—uh, the therapist—today?"

Alli leaned back, letting her head rest on the high back of the chair, and closed her eyes. She should have seen this coming. She'd even predicted it, hadn't she?

"As a matter of fact, Gran, I did." She opened her eyes and met Gran's bright, interested look. "I volunteered to help on the committee he chairs for the employees' picnic."

"What committee?" Gran ignored Magnum's unscathed emergence from the swimming pool.

"Games and booths and, uh"—she hesitated, remembering her suggestion with a feeling of trepidation—"crafts."

"Crafts?"

"You know, forming carnations out of pink tissues. Or wind chimes from cardboard toilet-paper rolls."

"Just what I would have expected." Gran's eyes were shining. "Your mother said you were crazy about kids, even when you were little. You insisted on helping her when it was her turn to work in the church nursery."

Insisted, Alli scoffed silently. From what she remembered, her mother signed up for nursery duty and dragged her along to do it.

"And this young man, Case, is the chairman?" Gran shuffled the mailbox ads languidly before replacing them on the bed.

"Umm." Alli turned toward the television, hoping a subtle reminder of the program would make Gran forget Case. Gazing at the screen, she found herself overlaying Case's face on Magnum's body as the latter stuffed his muscular physique behind the wheel of the Ferrari. She shook herself mentally. Daydreaming was worse than talking to Gran about Case when her goal was to forget him. She pulled her gaze from the screen, staring unconsciously at the stack of ads near Gran's hand. A colorful oversized pizza advertisement filled her view.

Gran looked back at Alli at the next commercial break. "If you're gonna do any laundry this afternoon, would you toss my bed jacket into the washer?"

"I might as well." She looked toward the window at the green lawn drying in the sun. "I'd better start the sprinklers too." She pushed herself upright.

Gran removed her bed jacket, leaning to hand it to Alli, and the colorful ad slipped to the floor. Alli bent to retrieve it.

"Gran, let's have pizza delivered for dinner."

"I don't know, dear. All that fattening stuff." Gran looked back at her program.

Alli stared at her in surprise. Pizza was practically her favorite food. Alli squinted at the ad, ignoring the thought of the calories crammed into the tantalizing slice almost leaping off the colorful page.

"But you have so much to do," Gran added, seemingly absorbed in Magnum's word battle with Higgins, "you shouldn't worry about cooking dinner." She tilted her head to get a better view of Magnum. "Order two while you're at it."

"Two?" Alli pointed to the huge replica in the ad.

"I like leftover pizza." Gran abandoned Magnum momentarily and took the paper from Alli's hands. She folded it neatly so that the telephone number appeared prominently, then returned it to Alli.

"Right." Alli looked at Gran warily, but only a bland smile curved her grandmother's lips as she reached for her knitting. Alli looked at the ad again. She was almost out the door when she added as an afterthought, "You're missing your program, Gran."

In the garage, Alli sorted clothes and dumped them into the washer before switching on the sprinkler system manually. Satisfied at the spray of water starting up outside, she went back into the house and changed to shorts and a T-shirt and called the pizza-delivery service.

None of which forestalled her thoughts returning to Case. Why had she volunteered to do crafts for the employees' picnic? For that matter, why had she let Laura drag her to the committee meeting in the first place? She'd meant to avoid involvement with anyone at the hospital, except on a professional basis. *Especially* Case.

Restlessly she wandered to the living room, staring absently at the chocolate-and-cream-colored sofa and cantaloupe-colored armchairs. Fruitwood tables, spotlighted by shafts of the lowering sun, showed a near microscopic film of dust. With forced momentum, Alli walked to the utility closet and returned with a dust cloth. Almost half an hour later she remembered the sprinklers.

In the garage she adjusted the dial to a new station and turned the manual switch with a mild sense of frustration. She could skillfully insert a needle into a vein, start an intravenous injection, and regulate the flow of fluid by drops in minutes—even without the latest state-of-the-art technology. But she couldn't read a pamphlet and reset the automatic sprinkler system! She'd worked on it for a week without success.

Pondering her inability to pass on a few simple instructions from her eyes to her hands, she strolled toward the living room, stopping to look for a can of spray wax. When she pulled her head from beneath the cupboard under the sink, the sound of the water from the sprinklers sounded unusually loud. Striding to the back door, she glanced toward the sliding-glass door leading to the patio. Water pounded against a glass panel, moved on to the open door and, unimpeded by the screen door, flooded the patio with unfailing regularity.

Alli shrieked silently. One rainbird sprinkler had gone berserk. Instead of arcing across the lawn, it spun in a circle, sending a torrent of water crashing against the glass panel and onto the patio.

Dashing across the room, Alli ducked the spray to slide the glass door shut. She stopped to catch her breath and watched the wild sprinkler slam a wave of water against the glass. Then she slid the door open again and bent to catch the spinning sprinkler. A torrent of water struck her across the chest. Firmly she turned the spray away from her body and found the wire guides beneath the plastic cap. With the water directed toward the yard again, she went inside the garage, shifted the controls to Off, and returned to the yard.

Assured the sprinkler was tame, she lowered herself to her knees. She prodded the sprinkler lid up and peered under it to readjust the spray pattern. Then she went to turn on the system again. This time the spray directed itself at her face as she walked through the patio. Irritably she shut the sprinklers off again, and the doorbell rang.

After scrubbing at her wet face, she scuffed her wet shoes on the doormat. Then she grabbed some money for the pizza and yanked the front door open.

Case stood on the porch with a cheerful grin on his face. He tipped his wrist over, tapping his watch. "Five minutes after seven. I'm late."

Alli scowled. "Late for what?"

"Your grandmother's exercises."

Alli's scowl deepened.

"Your grandmother's range-of-motion exercises," Case said patiently. "I called to ask how she was feeling and mentioned her exercises. The way she hemmed and hawed, I knew she hadn't been trying too hard."

Alli winced. She'd meant to see that Gran exercised every day, but with work at the hospital and cooking, cleaning, and caring for Gran, the exercises slid by some days.

"Your grandmother agreed she could use some assistance," Case explained. "I checked with her doctor this morning." He peered at Alli's sodden clothes without comment.

Alli felt her cheeks redden, knowing her clothes clung to her like a second skin. Brushing damp hair from her face, she opened the door wider. ''I'm having a little trouble with a rebellious sprinkler.'' She tugged her T-shirt loose from her skin. ''I'm sorry I didn't realize you meant you'd be here at seven tonight.'' She walked down the hall with Case to Gran's room.

''Hi, Case,'' Gran greeted. She glanced at Alli. ''I thought you were doing the laundry,'' she said. ''Did you forget to get out of your clothes before you put them in the washer?''

''The sprinklers attacked me,'' Alli said wryly.

''Um.'' Gran turned to Case. ''Not that I don't enjoy your company,'' she said with a trace of humor, ''but I'd hoped you'd forgotten about the exercises.''

''Didn't even have to circle it on my calendar to remember,'' he said.

Alli shuffled self-consciously in her sodden clothes. ''If you don't need me, I'll get back to the sprinklers.''

''Alli, I'm sure Case could use your help. We'll wait for you to change, won't we, Case?''

Alli restrained a scowl. Gran could be so transparent at times.

When Alli returned, Case was holding Gran's right hand, rotating the forefinger.

Alli moved to the bed, avoiding Case's eyes. ''I'll do Gran's other arm.''

''No need.'' Case cupped Gran's elbow in one hand. ''I have time. Why don't you sit and talk to us? I know you've had a busy day.''

''No busier than yours, I'm sure.'' She perched on an arm of the lounge chair. ''The count in pediatrics is down. Laura says we're between colds and calamities.''

''That's one way of putting it.'' Case laughed.

Gran looked at Case. ''Alli tells me she's working with you on some committee.''

''The annual employees' picnic.'' Case rotated her forearm. ''It's being held at Big Bear Lake this year. The committee hasn't chosen a place this far from the hospital before. They've rented a space in a trailer park by the lake and worked out transportation problems. We'll transport food and equipment and have a van available for employees who need transportation.'' Case lowered Gran's arm. ''We're all pleased Alli is joining the group. We have a good time. And''—he sent a warm look toward Alli—''your granddaughter seems to have some ideas for keeping the kids busy.''

''Sounds like fun.'' Gran's eyes glowed with interest.

''I could come by and get you and Alli if you'd like to go. Employees may invite a relative.''

''Not this year,'' Gran said. ''But it's nice of you to ask.''

''Does that mean you might consider it next year?''

''Probably. But it depends on whether Alli is still working at Wayside, doesn't it?''

''It's a great place to work,'' he said.

''Convince Alli.'' Gran winked at him. ''I'm on your side.''

Alli looked from Case to her grandmother with a sinking feeling. She'd anticipated a problem if they got together. But how could she know Case would find an excuse to make house calls? She was grateful to hear the doorbell ring before her spirits fell any lower.

This time it was the pizza deliveryman. And Case stayed for dinner. "I'll have leftovers for lunch if you don't stay," Gran said, trying to pull a look of misery across her cheerful face.

For a fleeting second Alli wondered if Gran had planned to invite Case to dinner all along. She shook her head. It had been her idea to order pizza. And she hadn't even thought about it until she saw the ad on Gran's bed.

Alli found it more difficult to avoid Case the next few days. She worked on Pediatrics, and Case found an excuse to walk into the unit at least twice a day to see Laura. Something to do with the committee, Laura said. On Tuesday evening he arrived at Alli's house with Chinese food and stayed for dinner after Gran's exercises. Wednesday was committee-meeting day, and Case sat across from Alli at the luncheon, his warm eyes meeting hers every time she looked up. As if that weren't enough to rattle her, he bent over her shoulder to peer at Laura's notes when the meeting ended. It was unnerving.

After the meeting Alli returned to the pediatrics unit with Laura and hurried to check on the IV of the toddler in bed four. She found the plastic container almost empty. Hanging a new bag of solution, she returned to the nursing station to pour one o'clock medications. She concentrated on administering the medications without one thought of Case. But when the last med was charted and she went to bottle-feed an infant, thoughts of Case arose.

She wondered if she could gracefully resign from the children's committee. Not resign from helping with the picnic—just the committee chaired by Case, she amended. Just because he'd jotted her name down beside arts and crafts didn't mean the commitment was chiseled in stone. Anyone could help children make a few pinwheels or paper carnations.

She settled the sleepy infant in one arm, tilted the bottle to fit comfortably in the baby's mouth, and leaned back in the maple rocking chair. To be honest, it was ludicrous to change committees. She could cope with Case for one day. She was an adult and a professional at that. She could react competently in an emergency and in less than a minute, with steady fingers, slide a needle into a vein to start intravenous solution without so much as a change in her pulse. But let Case sit across from her in a room filled with people and lock his warm, teasing gaze on her eyes. . . .

When he bent his head over hers, it was worse. The faint scent of his after-shave lingered long after he'd moved away. She lifted her eyes toward the ceiling in mild protest at herself. With everything she had to do, how did she find so much time to think about Case? If she'd keep her mind on her job at the hospital, the hundred-and-one tasks to be done when she stepped through the door to Gran's house, and the job she was anxious to return to, there shouldn't be a minute for Case to invade her thoughts.

Thinking of him didn't help, anyway. There was no solution to their dilemma. Case couldn't leave Wayside until he had paid his debt to the hospital. Frankly, she doubted if he'd leave even then. She tilted the bottle to keep up with the infant's suckling. And she wouldn't stay in Wayside. It wasn't only that she liked her job with the health program. Her mother had told her often enough the misery caused by making the wrong choice. Gail wanted more for Alli, she said time and again. She wanted her to see the world she longed for. To visit every exotic place with strange-sounding names she'd fantasized about.

Actually, Alli didn't know whom she was more annoyed with, Case or herself. She wasn't sure if she scanned the halls to see that he wasn't there, or spent an extra minute to linger outside a patient's room on the chance the tall, muscular figure would stride into view. Occasionally when leaving the nursing station to give a medicine or check an IV or answer a call light, she felt a jolt of anticipation at the sight of a distant male figure, and somehow a feeling of disappointment when the man approached and he didn't have sun-streaked brown hair and his smile was simply ordinary.

"Alli?" Laura stood a foot away, carrying the toddler from bed three.

Alli looked up dreamily, trying to corral her wayward thoughts and focus her attention on Laura's words. "What?"

"That baby has been asleep for five minutes, and Joey is getting crankier and crankier."

"Oh, thanks for picking him up." Hastily Alli placed the infant in the slatted crib and raised the rail, listening for the locks to catch. She pulled down on the top bar to double-check the lock before she turned to take Joey from Laura.

Alli settled Joey and for the next hour didn't think of Case until Laura asked her to go on a break.

"Want to go to the cafeteria for iced tea?" Laura asked.

Alli nodded. The pediatrics unit was no safer from Case's presence than the cafeteria. How he found time away from his department so often was a puzzle. But, to be honest, Case spent less than two minutes on break each time. It was the aftermath of seeing him that lingered for hours.

"Let me check on Joey." She moved to the crib, then made sure another nurse would check her patients during her break.

The tables in the dining room were occupied by visitors as well as employees, and Alli tried to find a group with two places left at their table. Finding none, she pushed open the door to the outside patio, pausing to see that Laura would follow her.

Alli sank onto a chair at an unoccupied table, glancing at the outside parking lots. Waves of heat rose from the asphalt. She looked away. For a moment she pictured the greenness outside the apartment in Hawaii. With surprise she realized she hadn't thought of Hawaii for days. She glanced toward the corner of the patio, searching for the honeysuckle vine clinging to the corner wall. She breathed deeply, straining to draw the scent of the flower to her. The fragrance was barely discernible in the stilled afternoon heat.

Laura slid a glass on the table, interrupting Alli's thoughts. "I noticed we're working the weekend together," she said, plopping on a chair across from Alli.

"You too?" Alli tore open a packet of sweetener and sprinkled it over her iced tea.

"I don't really mind, now that the children are grown. My husband and I arrange our days off to coincide when we can."

"Sounds great." Alli tasted the tea. She'd spoken automatically, but for a brief minute she thought the idea of spending your days off with someone special *did* sound great.

"Listen," Laura said. Her eyes met Alli's with candid calm. "Since we're off the same days, too, how about coming to the river with us? My daughter and her friend are going with us. They're only a few years younger than you."

"That's nice of you to ask, Laura. But, you know, I take care of Gran on my days off."

"You've told me. But all work and no play. . . ." She raised her eyebrows dramatically. "You know, you do look a little tired."

Alli raised her glass to her lips and let the cool liquid linger in her mouth for a moment. She shouldn't be tired. Her schedule here was mild in comparison to some of her travel schedules. Maybe it was the heat. Or maybe she wasn't getting enough sleep. Avoiding Case in her dreams was as difficult as avoiding him in the daytime.

"Alli, you should take some time off," Laura urged. "Maybe one of the other nurses would like to go. Someone your age. Is there someone you'd like to ask?"

Alli shook her head. "Really, Laura, it's nice of you—"

"Partly self-serving." Laura chuckled. "We need good pediatric nurses at the hospital. This is my contribution to keep you happy, healthy, and content in Wayside."

Alli smothered a groan. "You know this is only temporary."

"Is it?" Laura picked a chocolate chip from a cookie. "I thought you had family here."

"I do. I also have a job I love and an apartment in Chicago."

"You mentioned you travel a lot. Last time to Hawaii, wasn't it?" she said wistfully.

Alli nodded.

"Mac and I talk about taking a vacation on the islands, but we always end up going to the river." She took a gulp of tea. "A few days on the water does wonders for my disposition, not to mention what all that smogless air and sunshine does for my skin and lungs." She finished the cookie. "Think about going with us, Alli. Nurses should think about their health too."

By the time she went off duty, Alli had agreed to call her mother and arrange for her to stay with Gran. Between changing diapers and charting, she decided the opportunity to get completely away from the threat of seeing Case could vastly improve her mood. Just clearing her mind of the masculine menace might secure some inner peace. Case would be working at the hospital Thursday and Friday while she soaked in the sun at the river, and she'd be working Saturday and Sunday while he was off duty.

Four whole days to strengthen her resistance.

Chapter Six

"Anyone for Scrabble?" Laura asked after introducing Alli to her husband, her daughter Jan, and her daughter's friend. She bounced up the step to the lengthy motor home. Turning, she looked at her daughter. "You did bring the Scrabble game, didn't you?"

Jan laughed. "Would I dare forget it?" She motioned Alli to go into the vehicle. "Sometimes I think Mom goes on these trips so she'll have someone to play games with her."

"Would you have me go along to look for boys?" Laura mocked affectionately.

Alli stood gazing at the interior of the motor home. Across from the doorway stood a dinette, the benches upholstered in gray with patterned leaves of mauve. To her left, mauve and gray velvet covered a couch and matching lounge chairs. Beyond the compact kitchen she could see a large bed with a mauve spread.

"It's beautiful," Alli told Laura.

"Our one extravagance," Laura said, working at

concealing her pleasure at Alli's words. "Sit next to the window so you can look at the scenery."

"Mother will be looking at the Scrabble board," Jan said, laughing. She opened an overhead cupboard and removed a slender box. "See, I didn't forget." She slung her bare legs beneath the table as Mac entered.

He slid into the spacious, velvet-covered chair behind the steering wheel, switched on the motor, scanned the panel in front of him, and turned to grin confidently at his passengers. "Ready for takeoff?" he quipped.

"Fasten your seat belts," Laura said, opening the Scrabble board. Industriously she began to distribute tiles to each player.

Jan pulled her tiles toward her without turning them over. "Mom says you travel all over the country, Alli. Your job sounds exciting."

Alli grinned at Jan's enthusiasm. "It is." She placed a tile upright, noticing the letter C printed on the wooden block.

"Mom wants me to enter the nursing program, but I don't think I could cope with people suffering and dying. Especially little kids."

"A lot of people get well too," Alli said. "In a way, that's what my job is about."

Jan leaned forward with interest. "What do you do?"

"I work for a company that sets up health programs

for colleges and businesses. We use questionnaires to evaluate student and employee life-styles and health problems.''

''Is that all?'' Jan looked disappointed. ''Where does the traveling come in?''

''We have client companies in a lot of states, and once the program is set up, I make regular calls on my clients to assist with problems and reinforce the program. I travel across the continental United States and Hawaii and Canada. It's really interesting.'' She felt her voice gathering momentum. ''I learn so much about people and their life-styles in different areas.''

''Do you get lonely, always being in a new town?''

''Not really. I'm meeting old acquaintances when I visit my client businesses. And I'm usually home on weekends. Not always. For example, the company sent me to Hawaii for four weeks. That was the longest I was away from my home base, however.'' Alli paused for breath, wondering if her eyes were as bright as Jan's. She liked her job, and it probably showed when she talked about it.

Laura tapped a tile at her daughter. ''Didn't I tell you the options were numerous? Not all nurses work in hospitals.''

''To hear you talk about the children at the hospital, I thought that was the only field a nurse would consider,'' Jan teased. She uprighted her tiles. ''I'm ready if you are.''

Half an hour later Alli looked at her tiles to see she

had formed the word CASE on the wooden stand. Reluctantly she removed the C to use in a word on the board. Thoughts of Case were still interrupting her concentration on the game when the motor home stopped.

Alli looked out the window, realizing she'd watched very little of the passing scenery during the drive. And they'd arrived at the campsite. Or had they? It didn't look like a campground. But Jan and her friend were already opening the door to the outside.

Without questioning, Alli followed them into the bright California sunshine. Adjoining the parking lot were a large restaurant and a number of shops. Farther along the street, Alli could see a supermarket sign, a gas station, and a number of other buildings.

Seconds later Laura joined them. "We usually stop before we go on to the campground to have lunch." She stretched her shoulders. "You might want to go with the girls and look around. I need to pick up a few supplies I've thought of on the way. No matter how well I plan my shopping, I always forget something." She pulled her T-shirt loose. "It's hot already. Think what it'll be by the end of June. There's a general store on the campgrounds, but sometimes they're out of whatever I've discovered I can't do without, so I'd better shop while I can. We'll meet you at the restaurant. Jan knows the place."

Joining Jan and Beth, Alli strolled into a nearby shop. She bought postcards and looked at a glass case displaying Indian jewelry. Purchasing a pair of earrings, she looked up to see the girls had moved on and hurried after them. In the next shop she bought soft leather moccasins for her grandmother.

And all the time Case kept cropping up in her thoughts. Once, she thought she saw his long-legged figure stride through a doorway. *Ridiculous,* she scolded herself. *Case is working at the hospital.*

After lunch they returned to the motor home, and Mac drove to the campground. Again, Jan and Beth were the first ones out the door. Alli followed, marveling at their campsite. Cabanas, tables, benches, and barbecues appeared to furnish each site—and all within walking distance of the river. And few of the campsites were vacant.

On the beach, children frolicked under the watchful eyes of nearby mothers. Bronzed bikini-clad beauties, covered, Alli hoped, with a layer of sunscreen against the rays of the brilliant sun, lounged on low chairs or mats. On the river, a variety of boats skimmed the sun-splashed water. Alli turned her head as the roar of a powerful motor split the air. A skier behind a boat dropped his ski rope and skimmed gracefully onto the shore, stepping off his banana ski without stepping into the water.

She turned away from the scene, aware Laura carried chairs and supplies from the camper. Accepting two beach chairs, she placed them beneath the covered patio and returned for another load. As she lugged a loaded cool chest, she thought she saw a sandblasted green pickup, and her heart picked up an extra beat. Case? She shrugged mentally. Any number of green trucks could be in the campground. And the sandblasted exterior wasn't unusual on vehicles daring the desert sandstorms to reach the river.

She had to get over this obsession. Coming on the trip was supposed to give her time to reinforce her plans, not confuse them. Instead, Case might as well be here. He crowded her thoughts all the time. She rested the heavy cooler on the edge of the table and looked up at the sound of a vehicle braking a few yards away. She blinked and read the *I'd rather be skiing* sign on the license-plate holder.

Case leaned his head out the open window. "This must be the place."

Alli shoved the cooler onto the table, leaning against it as her heart rose like a balloon in her chest. Her heart drooped like a deflated balloon the next moment. Realization set in. Case was here, and he should be in Wayside seeing that his department employees were helping their patients. What was he doing on the Colorado River? More specific, what was he doing at this campsite on a Thursday afternoon?

Alli smiled weakly at Case, and Laura bounced down the step of the motor home. "You found us," she said with exuberance.

"Don't I always?" Case pulled the truck forward, clearing the boat trailer behind the motor home. "I see I arrived in time to help get the boat in the water."

Mac walked forward to greet Case warmly. ‘‘Don’t you always?’’ he added.

Case stepped from his truck. ‘‘Hi, Alli, Laura. Where’s Jan?’’

‘‘Scouting the beach for bodies, if I know her and Beth.’’ Laura looked at Alli and grinned at the puzzled expression on her face. ‘‘Boys,’’ she explained, lifting her eyes upward. ‘‘Men.’’ She rolled her eyes toward her husband. ‘‘That other part of the population that we women chase until they catch us.’’

‘‘Laura, my lollipop,’’ Mac guffawed. ‘‘You’re finally admitting I didn’t have a chance of losing you.’’ He slid an arm around her shoulders.

‘‘Not while I was breathing,’’ she said affectionately, leaning against him briefly. ‘‘Enough of this dawdling.’’ She moved to close the motor-home door. ‘‘It’ll be easier for us to unload the rest of the stuff after you get the boat off and park the trailer.’’

‘‘I know,’’ Mac teased. ‘‘You want the canopy set up so you can sit in the shade and supervise.’’ He winked at Alli and Case. ‘‘She says this is her time to relax. I not only have to catch the fish, I have to cook them.’’

Laura stood on tiptoe to kiss Mac on the cheek. ‘‘If you don’t get started, we won’t have any dinner, because you won’t have time to catch any fish.’’

‘‘Pay no mind to them,’’ Case told Alli. ‘‘It’s something about the river. They start acting like a couple of love-struck teenagers by the time they’re here thirty minutes.’’

Alli grinned, despite her trepidation at Case's appearance. Mac and Laura seemed so different from her parents. She couldn't remember her parents teasing and having fun as if they really liked each other.

"We're trying to set a good example for you two." Laura laughed. "Don't give me that innocent look," she said to Alli. "The hospital grapevine may not know it yet, but I've seen the way you both light up when you meet."

"Lollipop, will you stop matchmaking long enough for us to get the boat in the water?"

Laura raised both hands, palms out. "Go. We'll be here."

Case's gaze touched Alli with a promise that he might be a few yards away but his thoughts wouldn't.

"Wait a minute," Laura shouted, hurrying toward the motor home. She went inside and reappeared carrying a green jug. "Okay," she signaled to Mac. Placing the gallon thermos beside the ice chest, she turned to Alli. "I made lemonade, though I don't know if anyone will drink it except me."

"I drink lemonade," Alli told her. She couldn't get any enthusiasm in her voice.

"I thought all you young people drank diet colas."

"Vitamin C," Alli said. "But I'm not a fanatic about it." Her gaze followed Case's tanned body as he climbed into the motor home. The cotton walking shorts he wore exposed long muscular legs, and a faded T-shirt seemed to have shrunk after he stretched it over his broad shoulders. "I didn't know Case was joining us." She tried to sound casual, despite the alarming sound inside her rib cage.

Laura opened the cool chest and peered inside. "Didn't I mention it on the way here?"

"No, you didn't." Alli laughed to cover the edge invading her voice. Laura didn't have to tell her whom she'd invited on the river trip. Maybe she should have asked who might join them, Alli thought. But how could she even guess Case would be here? He was a department head. Department heads took days off during the week to attend workshops and conferences and meetings. She wouldn't have been surprised to see him in San Francisco dressed in a three-piece suit. But wearing walking shorts on the Colorado River on a weekday!

Had he lost his mind? Or his job?

"Does Case usually come with you?"

"On weekends." Laura rummaged among the cartons on the table. "No cups, and I'm as thirsty as if I'd just finished a marathon. I think this sun drags liquid out of my body as fast as I put it in." She withdrew a straw hat from a box and plopped it on her head. "Let me see if Case packed any."

She trudged across to the bed of the pickup. A moment later she returned with a package of paper cups. Holding a cup beneath the thermos spout, she filled it and handed it to Alli. "We may as well relax while Mac and Case launch the boat."

She filled a second cup and carried it to a slatted lounge chair. She sat back and drank half the contents of the cup. ''Case came by as I was asking a couple of the nurses if they wanted to join us. They couldn't, but he could. Said he could take two days off. He was short of help for the weekend, so he'd planned to fill in.''

''I don't suppose you mentioned I was going with you.''

''Probably. You don't think Case came for my company, do you?'' She grinned wickedly. ''I thought you liked Case.''

''Case is all right.''

''He's more than all right. And believe me, from the way he looks at you, no one else in sight has a chance of landing the man.''

''You're exaggerating.''

''I don't think so. In fact, I wonder who Case coaxed to take the weekend off so he'd have an excuse to take a weekday off.''

Alli sipped at the bittersweet liquid. She'd been thinking the same thing. ''I don't want to 'land' Case Sherman,'' she said emphatically. ''I'm leaving California as soon as my grandmother is walking.''

''Ah, too bad. But more than one female employee will be delighted to help you pack and drive you to the airport.'' Laura chuckled and sipped her drink and looked toward the beach where the men pushed the boat into the water.

Alli blinked. Laura's words were familiar somehow. But then, if so many women were interested in Case, why wasn't he married? Shading her eyes, she let her gaze follow the direction of Laura's. At the water, Mac had backed the boat trailer to the river's edge, and he and Case were unhooking the boat.

Case raised his arms, and even at a distance Alli could see the muscles in his back strain beneath the taut T-shirt as he gave the boat a firm push. The boat skimmed over the rollers on the trailer and slid into the water. Deftly Case caught the rope attached to the bow ring and pulled the boat forward until it touched the sand. After securing it on the beach, he looked up and waved at Alli.

Alli raised one hand limply, but her heart made up for the lack of enthusiasm, bouncing toward her throat in anticipation. She lowered the hand feebly. If she had any sense, she'd catch the first bus leaving for the city. Any city. But she only sat statue-still, watching Case stride toward the cab of the coach, thinking how magnificent he looked with the sun gilding his hair and bouncing off his bronzed legs.

She stood up as the motor home came to a stop, meaning to help Laura unload whatever she wanted from inside. Instead, she waited for Case to emerge. When he did, his eyes roved over her appreciatively.

"Great to see you here, Alli," he said warmly.

She smiled, but the smile didn't reach her eyes. As if he didn't know she'd be at the river! Smooth, Case, smooth. ''Laura made lemonade. Can I get you a glass?''

She'd meant her move away from him to be calm and cool, but she almost bumped the corner of the table in her haste to move. She managed to fill the glass without overfilling it and hand it to him without spilling one drop.

''Refill, Laura?'' She reached for Laura's cup before Laura could answer. She filled a third glass as Mac approached. Case was still looking at her when she turned away from Mac.

Alli raised her glass to her lips, draining it as if she had sieves in her heels. The midday sun had suddenly increased its heat output, she thought.

''Want to help me unload my stuff?'' Case placed his empty glass on the table.

''Of course.'' Alli followed him slowly. What else could she say? *I don't want to help you do anything. I want to catch the first wheels leaving the campground.*

Case lifted a sleeping bag, and she stepped forward. He slid the lightweight bundle into her arms and caught her hands. ''It's wonderful to see you here.''

His touch sent slivers of burning embers up her arms. ''I hear you have to work the weekend.''

''Worth working four weekends in a row.'' His gaze lingered on her face.

She pulled her hands from his grasp and carried the bundle to one of the benches beside the table. This wasn't in her plans. Four days of staying away from

Case had become four days of staying near Case. Or at least two days. How could she avoid him without snubbing him when he was sharing their campsite? She couldn't do that without antagonizing her hosts. After all, he was their guest too.

Case placed another cooler on the table. "You can put my sleeping bag under the canopy when Mac sets it up." He motioned toward the motor home where Mac and Laura were unrolling a canopy attached to the side of the vehicle.

Put Case's sleeping bag under the canopy? Laura had said the girls and Alli could sleep there. Alli scowled at Case's back as he bent over the bed of the truck. Did he think she could sleep one wink with him lying a few feet away?

Case returned with a carton of groceries and glanced at the bag in Alli's arms. "Just leave it on the bench. I see Jan is returning, so I'll get the ski while you change into your suit. I can't wait to see you"—he paused with a mischievous grin—"on a ski."

Alli emerged from the motor home last, dawdling as Jan introduced her friend Beth to Case. She tugged at the high-cut French legs of her suit and looked toward Case self-consciously.

He looked good in his swimming trunks—too good. Alli simply stared for a few minutes, telling herself this was no way to avoid Case fever. Maybe she could say she preferred sunbathing while he took Jan and

Beth waterskiing. But she knew it would only cause a debate and she'd end up getting in the boat.

"Sit up with me," Case said, sliding behind the steering wheel of the small craft. "Jan can be the observer while Beth skis."

Alli moved to the front seat. Squinting against the brilliant glare reflected off the water, she rummaged in a straw carryall for her dark glasses.

Moving the boat away from the shore, Case idled the motor and glanced back at Jan, who indicated they weren't ready yet. He looked at Alli. She was gazing at Beth's attempt to straighten her ski rope. If she knew what her nearness did to his thoughts, she'd not only sit in the back of the boat, she'd stay on the beach.

It wasn't easy to control his thoughts when he saw her in her nurse's uniform; in a bathing suit that was more provocative than protective, it was impossible. He hadn't thought about that when he planned this strategy. He'd envisioned hours on the sunlit water and evenings watching the moonlight gild the river. One more stroke toward tying her to Wayside.

He gripped the steering wheel of the boat as if he had to keep his hands from touching her. It wasn't easy, this self-imposed discipline. He blinked when he realized Alli was speaking to him.

"I think Beth's ready." She motioned to the skier who held the rope in one hand and secured her foot on the single ski. Case nodded, waiting for Jan to signal, and shifted one hand to the speed control. The boat picked up speed, and Beth stood up on the ski, gliding gracefully over the water.

"Seems like you see fewer skiers these days," Case said, leaning close to Alli to make himself heard above the motor. "There's more interest in jet-skis." He pointed to a pair of jet-skis skimming the water some distance away. His bare shoulder touched her arm.

Alli leaned forward, breaking contact with his sun-warm skin and peered at the one-person, motorized watercraft. Concentrating on the skier and staying six inches from Case didn't help. The warmth of his shoulder still burned.

"I'd like to buy one." He leaned forward again so she could hear him. "But something at the ranch always seems more important." He glanced back at Jan. She smiled, giving him an okay sign. "Speaking of the ranch, when are you going to let me show it to you?" he continued.

Would right now be too soon? Alli said silently. At least on the ranch Case wouldn't need to lean so close to make himself heard. She was saved from answering by Jan's yell.

"Beth's finally gonna let me take a turn."

After Jan skied, Case offered Alli the ski next, but she declined. "Let me work up to it. I haven't been skiing for a few years. We have tomorrow."

"What do you do on all the beautiful water in Hawaii?" Case lowered himself over the side of the boat.

"Surf," Alli yelled at his head. "Or watch the surf-

ers.'' She scanned the water for nearby boats, indicating a skier was in the water as she'd seen Jan do.
''That's for me,'' Jan yelled above the idling motor. ''Watching those gorgeous surfers.''

Alli grinned at her exuberance, never taking her eyes from Case as he retrieved the ski rope and ski. There were nice physiques on the Hawaiian sands, but none of them compared with Case's, she thought. Embarrassed at her thoughts, she wanted to look away, and yet she was glad she had to keep her eyes on him. Skillfully he pulled himself up on the ski and with languid grace skimmed the water, crossing the wake to ski to the side of the boat. My, he was . . . beautiful! Alli could think of no other word at the moment.

The spray touched her face and dried in minutes and, mesmerized, she never took her eyes from the figure flying on the water.

They ate at sunset, and after dinner Jan and her friend invited Case and Alli to join them at a party farther down the beach.

''Go,'' Laura encouraged. ''Unless you want to stay here and play pinochle with the old folks.''

They walked to the beach party, staying to dance on the sand to the sound of taped music. Flashlights doubled for strobe lights, and Alli joined in the festivities, ignoring the voice that warned her against dancing with Case. She had a grip on her emotions, she told herself. But she wasn't so sure when he took her in his arms.

By the second dance she suggested they leave, deciding pinochle with Mac and Laura would be advantageous to her heart.

But Case strolled in the opposite direction. "We wouldn't want to interrupt Mac and Laura's game, would we?" He took her hand in his.

Without warning, Alli became aware that the campfires and campers and people were far behind them, and that they were alone, watching moonlight cast a silvery line across the water. Case turned her to face him and looked into her eyes. And then he bent his head to place his lips on hers. Alli felt she was on the mountaintop at the lake again, being kissed in that special way for the first time.

When he released her, he stepped back, but he caught her hand. "We could go for a moonlight swim."

She shook her head. A moonlight swim wouldn't *lower* her temperature.

With the memory of Case's lips covering hers, Alli glared into the darkness and turned in her sleeping bag for the tenth time. If ever she needed an antibiotic against Case fever, it was now. It had just been one kiss. But it was enough to contact Case fever. She could tell. Her emotions had a raging temperature.

Chapter Seven

For someone on the verge of succumbing to a debilitating malady, Alli awoke with amazing alacrity, sliding out of the sleeping bag in one silent movement. Standing, she stretched her arms and inhaled deeply. The smell of a campfire blended with a scent of sage in the cool air. In an hour the sun would reverse the temperature. Alli took another deep breath, grinning broadly. She felt brighter than the early-bird sun peeking over the low range of mountains on the Arizona side of the river.

As if an alarm clock sounded in her mind, she squashed the smile and pulled her gaze from the distant view to peer guiltily at Jan and Beth. They appeared to be sleeping peacefully, cocooned in envelopes of down. Alli drew another breath, this time with relief. Feeling like a spy, she looked toward the cabana where she knew Case had placed his air mattress and sleeping bag. There was no sign of either the sleeping bag or Case.

Slowly she rolled her sleeping bag and stashed it in

a corner of the shelter attached to the motor home. Then she stepped inside a closet-sized enclosure to replace her oversized shirt with a T-shirt and cotton shorts. After combing her hair with her fingers, she picked up her toilet kit, pulled a towel from her overnight bag, and left the cabana.

To her surprise, the spot where Case had parked was vacant. She turned slowly, scanning the other campsites to see if he had moved to another location. Nowhere did she spot a paint-peeled pickup.

She should be glad, she told herself. Case had returned to the hospital, and she could spend the whole day splashing in the sun-warm water or skiing with Jan and Beth. But somehow the sunshine in her heart had slipped back behind the mountains.

After finishing in the rest room, she crept past the sleeping women to store her bag in the canvas closet. She walked along the shoreline, enjoying the morning quiet over the river despite her sunken heart. She waved at one lone camper setting a battered aluminum coffeepot on a camp stove. He waved back without speaking, as if neither of them wanted to break the peaceful silence. Farther ahead, the sound of a motor ruffled the silence, and far across the lake a boat putted to a stop. Fishermen, Alli thought, wondering why she hadn't checked to see if Mac's boat was tied to the shore. Maybe Case and Mac had gone fishing.

She left the shoreline, circling a lengthy motor home, and turned back toward the campsite. Then she saw

Case's old truck. Her heart rate accelerated like a motor being revved up for a speedy takeoff. He hadn't left without telling her. Even before the truck slowed and Case waved, she was walking toward the road.

The truck came to a stop, and Case grinned broadly. "Need a lift?" he asked.

"Not really," Alli lied. Her heart thudded against her rib cage. "It's a beautiful morning for a walk."

"Hop in," he coaxed. "Let's see if we can find a coffee shop. It may be an hour before our group wakes up."

Without hesitation Alli climbed up the short incline to the road and around to the passenger side of the truck. "What are you doing up?" she said cheerfully, amazed at how suddenly the sun could rise again.

"I was awake early, and an old guy down the way was having trouble pushing his boat trailer down to the water. I drove over. Thought we might hook it to my trailer hitch, but we managed to push it to the water."

"The fisherman?" Alli motioned toward the boat on the water.

"Yeah."

Case parked in front of the western storefront of the general store and slid from his seat. "Come with me. I'll buy you a doughnut to tide you over until we breakfast. If I know Laura, she'll cook pancakes and sausage and a raft of other goodies." He extended a hand.

Pretending not to see the offered help, Alli swung

her feet on the step and leaned forward to step onto the ground. Instead, one foot slipped slightly, and she found herself overbalanced. Two large, capable hands caught her waist and lowered her easily to the soft sand. Alli took a startled breath and lifted her eyelids. Case's eyes met hers. His hands remained motionless, spanning her waist, and the look, the unusual look, in his eyes darkened with warmth. It was possessiveness, Alli realized with a start. Case's look had subtly changed from stalking to staking a claim. He released her waist, sliding one hand casually down to clasp her hand.

"You may find the coffee a little strong." He released her hand to open the door. "Jake perks it in an old pot for the early fishers." His hand circled her waist casually when they entered the store, directing her toward a glass-enclosed tray of doughnuts and breakfast rolls. "But it's not bad for dunking doughnuts."

He was doing it again, Alli thought. Telling everyone in sight she was already spoken for. For a moment she let his hand rest easily. Then he released her and lifted the glass door, and a pinpoint of conscience stabbed her declining willpower.

Case fever might be spreading, she told herself, but she still had some control. It was just a matter of lasting out the day. No more moonlight maladies. No more star-bright fantasies. She'd be back in Wayside tonight. Back to checking the halls and eating a sandwich in the nurses' lounge.

"Glazed, sugared, or chocolate?"

Alli pointed to the chocolate.

He paid for the coffees and doughnuts, and they walked back to the truck. Setting his coffee on the hood, he helped Alli onto the high seat. Then he handed her his cup. "There's a holder on the dash," he said. "I drink coffee on the way to work."

He drove to an open site overlooking the river. "By the weekend every space will be filled," he told her.

For a while they sat quietly, watching a young man start a jet-ski boat and skim across the calm morning water. Slowly the dove-gray water silvered with the increased light. High overhead, a plane streaked across the smogless sky. Somewhere nearby a bird called. Alli sipped her coffee and felt an unfamiliar sense of contentment.

Case drained his cup and placed it in the holder. "I imagine everyone at the camp is up. Maybe we should get back, or Laura might start rumors we've eloped." He grinned wickedly at her. "Not that that's all bad."

"Case, you're impossible," she said with pretended hostility. "We can't elope. We're not even engaged."

"We could be."

"Drive," Alli commanded with mock severity, knowing her wariness was wavering. She dunked her doughnut into the coffee and lifted it to her mouth. She felt too good to rebuild her fortress right now.

Laura was flipping a pancake on a grill set over the camp stove as they walked toward the campsite. "Coffee's hot.'' She turned another cake on the grill. ''Easier to serve 'em hot when I cook at the table.''

''Smells good,'' Case said, filling two paper cups. His eyes sparkled as he handed one to Alli.

''I gather you two have been watching the sunrise.'' She didn't wait for an answer. ''Want to turn these while I wake up the girls?'' She handed the spatula to Alli. ''This one is ready to come off.'' She lowered the volume on the radio beside the stove. ''How those kids can sleep through all this racket is beyond me!''

She watched Alli scoop a pancake atop others on the plate beside the stove. ''Mac says their hearing is impaired from all that loud music they play, but he wasn't home with them when they were small. Youth has a built-in ability to tune out undesirable information.'' She laughed. ''Like, 'It's time to get dressed for school.' Or, 'Did you bring home your report card?' '' She walked to the sleeping bags and prodded Jan with one hand. She turned her head toward the camper. ''Mac, bring the butter and syrup when you come out.''

Alli turned her attention to the grill, aware Case worked on the other side of the table. She pushed the spatula beneath a pale cake, endeavoring to flip it over as Laura had done, and met with resistance. The cake pulled apart, leaving a trail of batter across the grill. She groaned and Case looked up.

''That's something we have in common. I undercook 'em or overcook 'em.'' He placed a stack of paper plates at the end of the table.

''Practice,'' Laura said, returning. ''Like marriage, it takes years of practice.'' She reached for the spatula. ''Want me to take over?''

''Where do you keep the cutlery, Laura?'' Case asked, rummaging in the box where he'd found the plates.

''Keep digging. Mac put them away last night.'' She took the pancake turner from Alli and said good morning to her daughter. Dressed in a brilliant two-piece suit, Jan blinked sleepy eyes at Case. ''Are you ready to take the boat out?''

''Do you think we could eat first?'' Laura asked her with a look of tolerant indulgence.

Jan lifted her eyes in mild exasperation and plopped on the bench by the table. She slid over to make room for Beth. ''You might as well sit down. Knowing my mother, she's probably hidden the key to the boat until we have what she calls a 'good breakfast.' ''

Making no comment, Laura reached for a plate, scooped two plump pancakes onto it, and handed it to Case. She smiled at her husband as he set the syrup bottle on the table. ''The fish can wait to eat until after you do,'' she said cheerfully. She filled another plate with pancakes.

Alli refilled the coffee cups, passing one to each of the men and raising a questioning eyebrow at Beth and Jan. They both declined, and Jan stood up to search through the cold box for soft drinks. Replenishing Laura's cup, Alli filled her own and stood watching

Laura cook. What a lovely family! They seemed so compatible. Or maybe, like Laura said, it took practice. Perhaps if her mother had tried. . . . Maybe if she'd gone on a fishing trip with Alli's dad and taken the family. . . . But Gail hated the smell of fish—she'd said so often enough. The only way she'd let them in the kitchen was if her husband cleaned and cooked them.

Mac interrupted her reverie. "Honey—" He stood up, looking at Laura. "I gotta go. Bert's waiting for me."

Laura waved the pancake turner at him and then scooped pancakes onto a plate to hand to Alli, who wondered if she could slip the cakes onto Case's plate without Laura noticing and decided against it. Laura was already refilling his plate.

Laura sat down as Jan stood up. "Now can we have the key, Mom?" she said in a mock plea. She lifted her partially filled plate and walked to the trash bag beside the motor home. Pushing her plate in, she turned with a satisfied grin. "My dishes are done." She eyed Case's plate. "Case, the river may dry up before we get a chance to ski if you keep eating."

"Last bite." He laughed and stood up, dangling the last piece of a pancake on his fork. "You don't want me to hurt your mother's feelings." He looked at Alli. "Finish your breakfast. We'll push the boat into the water." He motioned for the girls, but they were already headed for the boat, carrying the ski, a cool chest, and carryall.

"I'll stay and help you clean up," Alli suggested, finishing the last of her coffee.

"No cleaning up to do." Laura motioned at the trash bag.

"You're sure?" Alli asked with mixed feelings. Spending another day with Case leaning over her shoulder, brushing against her skin and looking at her with that sort of proprietary look was not conducive to a speedy recovery. On the other hand, as long as she recovered, did a few hours matter?

"I'm settling down with a cup of coffee and the adventures of a heroine in a romance novel by my favorite author." She grinned. "Jan thinks my passion away from home is games, but it's really reading."

"I won't disillusion her." Alli gathered the remaining plates and cups.

"I can't really read at home," Laura said with a trace of apology. "There's always something that needs my attention." She poured syrup on a pancake with measured casualness and looked up brightly. "If you can drag Jan off the river, I think checkout time is around two."

Alli lifted the plates. "I get it. I'm going." She dumped the plates into the plastic bag. She wasn't sure if Laura liked to read as much as she said or if she was pushing her to join the skiers. And Case.

She changed into her bathing suit, picked up her carryall, and headed to the boat with a feeling of excitement.

With little encouragement Jan and Beth eagerly took turns at skiing on the sun-glazed water. Finally, knowing she couldn't delay longer, Alli went into the water. With surprise she rose smoothly on the banana-shaped board on the second try. She reveled in the feel of sailing on the silvery surface, even knowing Case watched her with that look of possession lingering in his eyes.

Caught in reverie, she watched a boat approaching, aware of the wide wake left in its path. She pulled her gaze back to her path, but she was already wobbling in the choppy water. Releasing the ski rope, she tumbled into the river. Sputtering, she lifted her head above the water and looked for the boat. In the distance she saw Case lifting an orange flag as the boat made a wide sweep to turn around. Embarrassed, she swam toward the nearby ski and waited for the boat to reach her.

"You okay?" he asked, lifting her smoothly into the boat before she could comment. He reached for a towel.

She grinned sheepishly. "I haven't skied in a few years."

"Do you want to try again?" He pulled the towel around her shoulders.

She shook her head.

"It happens to all of us," Jan called. She moved to the back of the boat, pulling in the ski rope as Case reached for the ski.

"Who's next?" Case held the ski in the water.

"What say we go up the river for a while?" Jan suggested. "Beth wants to learn to steer the boat."

Case lifted the ski into the boat. "Fine with me." He looked at Alli, and she nodded. She'd survived the dump in the river. Anything the occupants of the boat wanted to do had her approval.

Jan returned to the front of the boat, changing places with Beth. Jan indicated the throttle, bending to explain something to Beth, and the boat shot forward. Jan moved the throttle again, and the boat slowed somewhat. Beth shot an embarrassed grimace at Case and Alli.

Case returned a wide smile. "We're fine," he shouted.

Alli lifted a hand to her damp hair, ruffling it through her fingers gently. The towel dropped from her shoulders when she raised her other hand to fluff her hair dry. Lifting her face toward the sky, she closed her eyelids, letting the sun dry her skin.

"Feel good?" Case asked.

His husky voice sent rays of sunlight coursing through her veins. "Wonderful."

"I think Jan and Beth have some admirers." His breath warmed her ear as he bent close.

She lifted her eyelids slowly, reluctant to break the spell, and turned her head toward a boat veering toward them. Two muscular, tanned young men waved, smiled, and shouted words scarcely audible. Beth and Jan returned their waves with enthusiasm.

"They look like the guys they met at the beach party last night," Alli said.

The boat with the boys aboard slowed, and Jan tapped Beth on the arm and pointed to the throttle. Glancing at the throttle, Beth took her hands off the wheel momentarily before she remembered she must steer also. She jerked the wheel around, and the boat slowed and came to a jolting stop.

Beth yelled and Jan moaned. Alli lurched forward and felt Case's arms catch her. "What happened?" she gasped, reluctant to push away from his chest.

"We must have hit a sandbar, or Beth steered into shallow water." He released Alli and moved to look over the side of the boat.

Alli glanced at Beth sympathetically. She was near tears, and Jan attempted to calm her. The young men in the other boat pulled near and idled their outboard motor. As Case slid over the side of the boat and into the water, the darker-haired man in the other boat did the same. "Hit a sandbar, huh?" he said.

Case made a comment inaudible to Alli. In a few minutes he signaled Beth and Alli to enter the water; then he and the young man pushed the hull of the boat free of the sandbar. Watching Case examine the motor, Alli, Beth, and Jan waited as anxiously as relatives of an ailing patient for Case to deliver a diagnosis. When it came, Alli and Beth breathed easier at Jan's sigh of relief, though neither of them knew what a sheared pin meant.

"It's no big deal," Jan said. "Dad sheared a pin when I was with him once. He fixed it himself." She looked at Case. "Right, Case?"

"It's no problem—if you have a pin," he agreed.

"Dad carries a tool chest in the motor home," Jan said.

"We'll give you a ride across the river," the young man in the water offered.

"Is that okay with you?" Jan turned to Case and Alli. "If we can't find a pin in the toolbox, we'll go along the river and find Dad. It may take a little longer if we do that. I don't know where he's fishing."

"Let's push the boat to the beach before you go." Case looked at the young man for help.

"You don't mind?" Jan asked anxiously. "There are soft drinks and snacks in the cooler."

"We'll be fine," Alli assured her. But looking at Case's broad shoulders straining to release the hull of the boat from the sand, she wasn't too sure. Holding her feelings for him at bay with a crowd was difficult. Alone with him, even in midmorning under a brilliant sun, was another matter.

Wading from the cool water onto the warm sand, Alli turned to wave at Beth and Jan. The young man who had helped Case swam toward the boat and, minutes later, leaving a trail across the water, the boat moved away. Ignoring the faint tremor of anxiety as the boat became smaller, Alli turned at the sound of her name and walked to the beached boat.

Case handed her the towels and her carryall. ''Hope you brought some sunscreen. Between the sun and the glare off the water, your skin starts feeling like a grilled hamburger in a few hours.''

She tossed the towels onto the sand and lowered the carryall. ''It doesn't take an hour to cross the river,'' she scoffed, looking up at him.

He lifted a cooler over the side of the boat. ''Maybe not. But we might as well eat, drink, and prepare to tarry. I wouldn't be surprised if Jan and Beth's admirers encourage a cruise along the river to look for Mac first.'' He grinned. ''That's probably what I'd do in their case.''

Alli laughed. ''You don't think they planned this meeting, do you?''

''I don't think they planned to run the boat onto a sandbar.'' He balanced the chest on the rim of the boat. ''Can you steady the cooler while I get down?''

''Sure.'' She grasped the container. ''Maybe I wouldn't blame Jan if she went along with looking for Mac. That guy was good-looking.''

''You are a romantic, after all,'' Case accused. He lowered the chest to her.

''Absolutely. I cry when I watch sad movies and prefer books with happy endings.'' Turning, she lowered the chest and shoved it near the boat, seeking a sparse column of shade. Then she retrieved the straw bag and carried it farther from the water.

After spreading the towels on the sand, she lowered

herself to a sitting position and looked around. She'd been too busy to notice the isolation of the area before. For all the traffic on the water and the motor homes and campers on the other side of the river, the shoreline where they'd landed was sparsely occupied. Far down the sand, two fishermen supported their poles languidly while lounging in plastic webbed chairs. Beyond the fishers, a sun-faded truck and camper stood motionless in the heat.

Case sank on the towel spread beside her. "Did you find the sunscreen?"

She reached for the bag, withdrawing a tube of sunscreen and a plastic bottle of lotion. She tossed the lotion on Case's towel and took the lid off the sunscreen. "I'll trade you bottles after I smear this on my face."

"I meant it for you." He eyed her light skin speculatively, a look of appreciation glinting in his eyes. "I'm used to the river."

Alli finger-brushed the cream over her cheeks with broad strokes, letting her gaze rove over Case's bronzed shoulders. "I can tell."

"I may have to forego the river trips for a while. I'm thinking of taking on a second job."

She groaned with exaggeration. "You're beginning to sound more and more like my dad. A workaholic."

"I'm not too fond of the idea."

"Neither was Dad—so Mom says. But he stayed in Wayside, anyway."

"I know." Case looked toward the fishermen. "And she hates it."

"It wasn't Dad's fault exactly," she said defensively. "Grandpa developed multiple sclerosis, and Dad moved back to Wayside to help with the nursery. Finally, Grandpa just turned the business over to Dad, and he and Gran moved to New York so Gran could be near her mother, who was ill. Of course, Dad is a workaholic. Even now he thinks the business will go bankrupt if he isn't here to keep an eye on things."

"I guess owning your own business, or being an executive running a company, can take more attention than an eight-hour-a-day job. And some marriages go bankrupt when the business succeeds." He looked at Alli intently, compelling her to look into his eyes. "But I think it depends on the couple."

He wasn't talking about her father and mother, Alli thought. He was explaining his long hours at the hospital and the possibility of a second job, and he was leading up to the "couple" bit. She pulled her gaze free and looked across the water, following the flight of a skier jumping the wake of a boat.

"Turn around," he said.

At the sound of his words, she jerked her gaze back to him. But he studiously watched a thin stream of lotion pool in his palm.

"Let me put this on your back."

The scent of coconut oil, warmed by the sun and spread by Case's soothing fingers over her shoulders, permeated Alli's senses for an unaccountable time. She knew she should shrug his hands free of her skin, but she felt mesmerized by the sweetness of the fragrance and the warmth of the sun and feel of the fingers sending a different kind of warmth beneath the skin. It took effort to pull away from the pleasant sensation Case's fingers invited.

She felt a sense of relief when he refused her offer to oil his shoulders. He stood up and went to rifle through the cooler, returning with soft drinks and varied snacks. He asked about her work on pediatrics, and she breathed another silent sigh. Talking about the hospital would deter him from talking about other things.

They talked about pediatrics and the physical therapy progress made by a patient with Guillain-Barré syndrome. The sun tilted minimally toward the west, and Case gathered drink cans and food wrappers and placed them in the boat. "I think I'll have a look at the motor." He scanned the river. "Jan's probably lost track of time, and Laura will be worrying because we're not back by checkout time."

Alli followed him, watching as he rummaged in the boat. "You mean you might fix it?"

"I could try. If I can find something to use as a pin."

"What?"

"A nail or something like that. You wouldn't have a bobby pin, would you?"

"Bobby pins went out with bustles, I think," she said dryly. She frowned in concentration. "Now, if you wanted to do a tracheotomy, I have a ballpoint pen. I saw a medic use one in a movie."

"Let me see it." He waited for her to go through the contents of her carryall, then scrutinized the proffered pen thoughtfully. Removing the cartridge from it, he slipped over the side of the boat.

Alli watched intently, not sure what he was doing, until he motioned her to get the towels. Then he helped her aboard and pushed the boat into the water.

He started the motor. "Wish us luck. Just because we have power doesn't mean we're going anywhere."

Alli looked at him questioningly.

"The shear pin protects the motor from serious damage." He pushed on the throttle. "It's such a small thing—costs less than a dollar, and it can save a hundred-dollar or so repair bill on the motor, but when you don't have one, it's like for lack of a horseshoe, et cetera, et cetera." He grinned broadly as the boat moved.

"You could have fixed it hours ago," Alli said suspiciously.

"Now, how come you said Jan's new friend was romantic when you thought he was negotiating a way to spend time with her and you give me that suspicious look?" he said, glancing at her with a smile.

Alli lifted her hands in pretended frustration.

With Alli and Laura's help, Case had the boat on

the trailer and was hitching it to the motor home when Mac and the girls returned.

Laura left to scold them for returning after checkout time, and Case touched Alli's arm.

"Ride back with me, Alli," he said, his eyes compelling her to look at him.

She felt a familiar rush of warmth. She wanted to reach and touch his sun-streaked hair; she wanted to tell him she'd had a wonderful day. She was shocked to find she wished he would repeat the kiss of last night—despite the unromantic sun blazing overhead and a throng of people nearby.

She pulled her hand free, her mother's words flashing across her mind. *"Don't make the same mistake I did, Alli. Once the glow of romance dies, you're left with the monotony of diapers and dishes. Adding cheese to the macaroni casserole becomes an exciting event in your day."*

She turned away. "I don't think that would be a good idea, Case."

Chapter Eight

Gran lowered the volume on the television set and welcomed her granddaughter with enthusiasm. "Alli, you look wonderful!" She peered at her lovingly. "I was afraid you'd be pink as a petunia after two days in that desert sun. But you look radiant. Did you have a good time? Tell me all about it."

"Gran, I haven't been away a month. Not even two whole days." Alli rested her overnight bag precariously on the edge of the coffee table in the family room. "Where are Mom and Dad? Did they leave you alone?"

"No, little Miss Worrywart. They didn't leave me alone."

"I don't see anyone else with you."

"You just missed him."

"Missed him. Missed who? Dad?"

"The young man you were with at the river."

"Gran, I was at the river with the MacCabes."

"Picky, picky," Gran mocked with widened eyes.

Alli exhaled in mock frustration. ''If you mean Case Sherman, he just happened to come down later,'' she said emphatically, letting the bag land like a soft exclamation mark on the carpet. ''And what do you mean, I just missed him?'' she added, wondering why Case would have stopped to see her grandmother and how he could have arrived before she did. He had still been securing his gear in the bed of the truck when Mac stopped the motor home at the dump station. And they hadn't stopped on the way home. Laura had fixed lunch while Mac was driving.

Alli voiced her thoughts suspiciously. ''What was Case doing here?''

''He was concerned about me,'' Gran said placidly, smoothing the lacy afghan covering her legs. ''He was checking to see that one of the therapists came to help with my exercises.'' She smiled benignly. ''He's such a thoughtful young man—so sincere and stable.''

Alli didn't even let out a sigh this time. She lifted the bag from the floor.

''As to the rest of your question''—Gran's voice rose as if she were losing her audience—''your dad's in the garage, and Gail went to get Chinese takeout. So you can stop frowning,'' she said complacently.

Chinese takeout. Alli lifted her shoulders feebly. Gran probably hadn't had one nutritionally balanced meal since she left. Artery-clogging pizza, hamburgers, crisp-fried tacos, and goodness knows what else! She walked down the hall, making a wry face, and dropped the overnight bag, the straw carryall, and her body on the bed. Refusing to think about Case, she removed her sneakers.

Alli lifted a bite of chow mein toward her mouth, daring the gob of vegetables to drop from the inexpertly held sticks in her right hand. "Dad, the weather was wonderful. You should go fishing at the river."

"Case said the same thing." John Parmer balanced a fried shrimp between his chopsticks. "Invited me to go with him sometime."

Alli fumbled for another bite of food. So Case had included her father in his campaign to encourage her to change her mind about leaving Wayside!

"I may even take him up on the offer. Of course, I got the impression he wouldn't mind if you came along too." His grin was teasing.

"I'm surprised he didn't ask Mom and Gran to join us too." Alli abandoned the chopsticks and fled to the kitchen. "I forgot," she said when she returned, waving a fork in her hand, and continued her speech as if she hadn't left the room. "He's already invited Gran to the employees' picnic. That just leaves you, Mom."

"Sounds like he wants to be a part of the family," Gail said wryly.

"Is that bad?" Gran asked. "As far as I know, we have as many murderers on the family tree as millionaires." She pointed a chopstick at her son.

"Huh!" Gail said in a voice to reach Alli's ears

only. ''Your father is just like his father when it comes to business sense—he gives away more plants than he sells.''

Alli glanced at her father with a warm look of sympathy, but he merely smiled complacently at his wife and turned his attention to his daughter. ''How about it, Al? Isn't it about time you settled down? Stop all that running for planes and trains and things?''

Gail scowled at her husband. ''Don't nag Alli. She likes her job.''

''Some job!'' Gran sniffed. ''Never in the same city a month at a time.''

''I was in Hawaii four weeks,'' Alli said.

''If I recall, that was unusual. You were setting up new programs for a number of clients on the islands.''

''I'm home every weekend.''

''Home? An apartment with an airline stewardess who's gone as much as you are. What kind of life is that? I bet you don't even find time to meet a young man, let alone be around long enough to accept a date.''

''Mother, she's been dating an airline pilot for months,'' Gail said to Gran. ''Don't you remember I told you when Alli wrote me about him?''

''Another traveler.'' Gran dismissed the suitor with a sniff.

Alli stuffed a pea pod into her mouth, silencing any discussion on her part. To tell the truth, the airline pilot was her roommate's brother, and she dated him about as often as she saw her roommate. Of course, she dated the manager in the home office, and a physician finishing his residency in orthopedics at the hospital occasionally. Her social life wasn't all dull.

''Did I tell you Candice called while you were napping?'' Gail said to Gran, turning the conversation to the subject of her younger daughter.

Alli smiled at her mother gratefully.

The activity in the surgical ward of the pediatrics unit the next morning left little time for Alli to reminisce about moonlight on the Colorado River. Toweling her three-year-old burn patient dry, she glanced toward the entry door of the spacious room as the swinging double doors opened. A plastic-covered cart preceded a central-supply technician through the doors. Alli breathed easily, her glance lingering on the cart as it crossed the room.

She wasn't looking for Case, she told herself. But if he came into the unit and strode toward her with that charismatic grin, a little notice would give her time to summon forth a casual greeting without getting tongue-tied.

She patted Sean's scarred left leg gently and encouraged him to recite the alphabet. Reaching for clean pajamas to slip over the scarred skin left by the damaging flames of a house fire earlier in the year, she concentrated on her patient.

Carefully she drew the short pants over the dressings on the right leg, keeping Sean's attention on the alphabet. The three-year-old had returned to the hospital for a skin graft on the leg, but Alli had noted the physician's orders to continue therapy on his hands. She'd half expected Case to appear to do the therapy. Declining his invitation to accompany him on the ride from the river to Wayside hadn't deterred his appearance at Gran's house. And inviting her dad to go fishing didn't sound as if he meant to abandon his efforts to keep her in Wayside.

The next time the door opened to the unit, her cautious gaze caught sight of Case. As if mesmerized, she kept her eyes on him as he strode across the room and stopped to speak to the head nurse. He nodded at the nurse and started toward Alli. She barely had time to lower her gaze to Sean.

''Morning, Alli.'' Case's voice was as bright as a desert sun. ''I see you're caring for one of my favorite patients.''

''We have good taste, huh?'' she said, echoing his cheerfulness—for the child's benefit, she told herself.

''Hi, Sean.'' Case's eyes made contact with the anxious boy. ''Are you ready to show Alli how well you use your fingers?''

The boy stared at Case warily. Taking his time, Case enclosed the small hand with gentle fingers. ''You remember me, don't you? I see you when your mother brings you into the Outpatient department for therapy. I don't help with the exercises you do, but you see me, don't you? I made a balloon giraffe when you walked for us.''

The child's eyes lit up. "Yeah." Then he made a face. "It went to sleep and wouldn't wake up. Mommy said it had to go back to the hospital for a refill."

"Is that the one that came back for a refill?" Case said, massaging the scarred fingers. "Maybe I can find it when we get through with the exercises."

The boy barely glanced at Case's manipulating fingers. Picking up the other hand, Case continued talking to Sean as he separated the fingers gently. Finally he lowered Sean's hand and looked at him. "Enough of my working," he said. "It's time for you to show me what you can do." He reached into his pocket, withdrew a plastic bag, and looked at Alli. "Let's put Sean at the play table."

Alli widened her eyes in question at Case, but he smiled and reached for Sean's slippers. He lifted the child and carried him to a low chair beside a small table.

"Join us, Alli. Sean hasn't tried this yet. You can pass it on to the nursing staff. It's really occupational therapy, but I want to see how well he uses his pincher grasp."

Case scattered half a dozen miniature rings on the table. They looked like Cheerios, Alli thought. "Let me see you pick them up," he said to Sean encouragingly. He concentrated on the child's misshapen fingers as they attempted to pick up the small o's.

Sean struggled to grasp a ring between a stiffened forefinger and an uncooperative thumb. Alli reached forward to help, then stopped in embarrassment. Picking the ring up for Sean wasn't the purpose of the play.

"Silly Putty is useful too." Case smiled at Alli as if he hadn't noticed her hand. "His mother has him working with it at home." He held the plastic bag open for Sean. "When they're all in the bag, I have a surprise for you."

Warmth built in Alli's chest as she watched Case work with the boy. He was so gentle with children. He'd make a wonderful father. He was probably the kind of man who'd be home for dinner every night. He'd be a Boy Scout leader and attend all the PTA meetings. She scowled at her thoughts. If she married Case, he'd be the one bathing and feeding the kids—and telling the children Mom wouldn't be home tonight.

Her gaze lingered on his face. Ruggedly handsome. But the face and the physique weren't the only things that drew her to Case. It was everything about him. His honesty, his loyalty, his compassion for others.

She looked away guiltily. There was no need trying to work out a solution. Case wasn't one for casual relationships any more than she was. And giving up her job wasn't in her plans. It wouldn't be easy to leave him this time. But she meant to try. Try? She meant to succeed.

She looked up as Laura approached.

"Hi, Case," Laura said. She turned to Alli. "Do you have a minute to help me with my little guy? I need someone to support his arm while I change the dressings.''

''You don't need me, do you?'' Alli asked Case.

''Do you expect me to answer that honestly?'' Sparkles of humor glinted in his eyes.

Alli gave him a disapproving look and looked in Sean's direction. ''I'll be back in a minute.''

''We'll be watching the clock,'' Case said with a chuckle.

He watched her move away, her soft-soled shoes quiet on the tiled flooring. She went around the high crib, lowering one side rail, and spoke to the blond child. She was good with children, Case thought. She'd make a marvelous mother. If only he could convince her she'd make a wonderful wife! But a wife and mother needed to be home. At least, part of the time.

He looked at Sean as he placed the last ring in the bag with nodding approval. He pulled a balloon from his pocket, filled it with air, and handed it to Sean. ''Hold this for me. I think I need three balloons for the hat I have in mind for you.''

He pulled two more balloons from his pocket, glancing back at Alli. She was no more into casual affairs than he was. If she made a commitment, she'd honor it, even if she was unhappy in the process. And she would be. She loved her job. And her job was traveling. She'd said some weekends she didn't even come home.

He blew up another balloon. She'd made it clear she didn't want to come home to Wayside. And his home was in Wayside. He reached for another balloon. If things worked out with his new therapist friend, his home would be in Wayside long after he paid off his obligation to the hospital.

Deftly he twisted the balloons together to form a hat with floppy ears. Holding it up for Sean's inspection, he first tried it on his head. Sean laughed in delight. "Now you try it on." Case extended the hat toward the boy.

Sean lifted it experimentally toward his head, looked at Case, and then grinned at Alli as she approached.

"Is my minute up?" she asked.

"Oh." A look of mock distress touched Case's face. "We were so busy, we forgot the time. But we're glad to see you back."

"See my hat?" Sean said gleefully. "Case made it for me."

"Magnificent hat." Alli touched one rubber ear.

"A reward for my favorite patient." Case stood and lifted Sean. "I could make one for my favorite nurse." He carried Sean to the bed, and Alli followed.

"I'm afraid to ask. What do I have to do?"

"I'll think of something."

Laura approached. "Case, do I really have to attend your body-mechanics class Tuesday? I practice what you preach every day," she moaned.

"Hospital regulations, Laura," he said. "If attendance wasn't mandatory annually"—he paused to grin at Alli—"and required for new employees, I wouldn't have one person in the class."

He placed Sean in the bed and raised the side rails.

Laura looked at Alli and rolled her eyes. ''I don't know about that,'' she said. ''If I were fifteen years younger, I'd go once a week just to watch Case demonstrate the technique of getting a patient into a wheelchair.'' She moved to the crib.

''Think of it as a time to get away from your little ones. And get paid for it.'' Case adjusted Sean's hat.

''It's not the class.'' Laura sighed. ''Wednesday is my day off. I usually clean, cook, and shop for the week. Since I went to the river last week, I really have to make up for it this week.''

''Maybe if I added a few jokes to my class and brought in one of those muscular bodybuilding types to demonstrate lifting a patient into bed, it might warrant a little enthusiasm for the employees to attend.''

''I knew I couldn't ditch class, but I thought I'd try.'' Laura sighed. ''I'll be there.''

''See you too, Alli.'' He waved at Sean.

''Right.'' Alli watched him walk away. He didn't need to bring in any bodybuilder to get her attention. That was her problem. Case was enough to get her full attention.

Tuesday was Alli's day off, and Case hadn't appeared for Gran's workout. By Wednesday she was embarrassed to find she watched the clock anxiously for the time to go to the body-mechanics class. No amount of self-scolding helped. It was as if she had to have a daily fix of seeing Case.

She sat with Laura in the second row of seats, noting that Mona sat in the first row. The open area in the front of the room was furnished with a hospital bed, a wheelchair, and a gurney. Case, dressed in white tunic and white trousers, stood before the small lectern. He riffled through a stack of cards, then looked up to smile in her direction. But then, she thought realistically, he could have been smiling at Mona, who sat in front of Alli and Laura.

"I need a volunteer patient," he said.

Alli smiled back blandly. Getting within touching distance of Case confused her sense of stability anytime, let alone before a crowd of people. Surely he wouldn't expect her to volunteer. Before she had a chance to reconsider, Mona stood up eagerly.

"Physical therapy is so fascinating," she said, turning slightly to speak to Alli and Laura. "I want to learn everything I can about a therapist's duties." She bounced toward the lectern.

"I wonder if she really means everything she can about a particular physical therapist," Laura whispered to Alli in a teasing tone.

Alli stared at Mona's trim, slender figure. Mona did seem to spend a lot of time with Case, she thought morosely. She'd seen her at the hospital in the afternoon twice and wondered what woke Mona early from her "night sleep" to return to the hospital. Now, she recalled, one of those times Mona had been going into the physical therapy department. Maybe she'd been coming to see Case each time.

She looked back toward the front of the room as Case's voice broke through her thoughts. Mona turned to face the audience, her gaze on Case, and lowered herself into a sitting position on the bed.

Case moved to the side of the bed, placing his hand on Mona's shoulder, and spoke to her. She swung her feet onto the bed and lowered her head to the pillow.

"You don't have to be that uncomfortable," Case told her, including the audience in his words. "You can raise the head of the bed to a semi-sitting position for now." He moved away to retrieve the wheelchair, explaining the procedure of locking the brakes on the wheelchair and raising the footrests before beginning to assist the patient from the bed.

"Consider the age and degree of debilitation of the patient and use whatever assistance is necessary to assist him or her to a sitting position. Let's pretend your patient is elderly and somewhat infirm." He looked at Mona and chuckled toward the audience. "In this case that might take some pretending, but try."

A young man across the aisle from Alli shuffled his feet and raised his hand. "If you need any help to lift this elderly lady, I'll be glad to volunteer."

"Thanks, Jess, but that's what this class is about. I know, lifting a patient may be faster for some of us, but this demonstration is on moving a patient with safety to both the patient and hospital personnel." He winked at the young man as if to say, *Nice try*, and turned back to the class. "Assist the patient to a sitting position.'' He levered one arm beneath Mona's legs, shifting her body, and swung her legs over the side of the bed.

Alli followed the ripple of muscles beneath the taut tunic stretching over Case's shoulders, thinking how he'd lifted Gran to the wheelchair with an ease that appeared effortless. Consider the patient, he'd said just now. In Gran's case he'd apparently thought his effort to move her to the chair was preferable to *her* effort. Mona stood, supported by Case, and he guided her onto the chair. He straightened and faced his audience again, and Alli realized the similarity of their career goals. He cared about people as much as she did. Only their life-styles were so dissimilar. He was a settler, and she was a traveler.

Case rested one hand on Mona's shoulder casually, and Mona lifted her eyes, listening to his words with rapt attention. Alli looked away. She had no right to feel an unexpected gust of dismay. Hadn't Laura told her half the single female population in the hospital would listen to Case with rapt attention? She shouldn't feel the least dismay if he turned his attention to someone who appreciated him.

A nursing assistant stopped Alli on her return to the unit to report a gallbladder patient needed a pain shot. Alli thanked her and went to check the patient's order sheet. After medicating the patient, she tightened his lower sheet, encouraging the middle-aged man to relax and sleep if possible. ''The pain medication will take effect soon,'' she assured him.

Straightening the top sheet, she paused to look out the window at the distant mountains. Wayside was beautiful this time of year. She was surprised at her thoughts. Even if she did settle down someday, would she even consider a small town dozing in the California desert?

Chapter Nine

Alli opened the drapes in her bedroom, glared with mixed feelings at the Saturday-morning sun, and crossed her fingers, wishing for an unseasonal rain. She was well aware that the odds were with the sun. To be honest, she told herself, hoping for rain and a cancellation of the picnic was as false as her dubious wish to avoid Case.

Hurriedly, she dressed in acid-washed jeans and a hand-painted T-shirt and cocked a straw western-style hat atop her dark hair. She was glad the sixteenth-century theme for the picnic had been recalled. Like the others who'd brought up the issue of costumes, she hadn't had time to make an elaborate dress.

After looking in on her sleeping grandmother, she went to make a pot of coffee. By the time her mother arrived, she stood on—or, rather, paced—the sidewalk, waiting for the MacCabes.

Half an hour later Alli sat cross-legged on the floor of the motor home. She'd had to store her hat on top of the microwave oven when she found a place to sit on the floor. Bracing her back against the oven door and the cabinet beneath, she rested her feet on one end of the dinette bench and gazed up at a forty-five-degree angle. Wall-to-ceiling hospital employees, clad in various forms of western attire, spread over the interior, laughing and joking as the motor home purred up the winding road high in the San Bernardino Mountains. She shifted her feet, allowing Laura to move by with a bulging box. Her thoughts floated back to Case. He'd probably left for the mountains before dawn.

He'd called a final committee meeting on Wednesday, friendly to everyone as usual. He hadn't lingered after the meeting, though he had smiled at Alli. He'd seemed preoccupied on Wednesday evening when he came to see Gran. He'd declined Alli's offer to stay for pot roast. On Thursday she'd caught a glimpse of him in the hall with Mona. On Friday he'd sent another therapist for Gran's range-of-motion therapy.

The sound of her name interrupted her thoughts. "Hey, Alli, I've pushed some of the supplies into the bathroom. There's room for you at the table now," Laura called.

"I'm okay." Alli pulled in one foot, leaving a few inches clear in the narrow passage.

"Not if someone wants to get by you," someone said.

"Why would anyone want to get by Alli?" another voice piped up. "The bathroom's stuffed with bags and boxes."

Laura returned to regain her position at the table. "Come on, Al, you're holding up the game. I've been looking forward to beating Tess at Scrabble all week."

Alli pulled herself to her feet and slid onto a mauve-colored cushion at the dinette table. If she concentrated on the game, she thought, arranging her lettered squares on the holder, she wouldn't think about Case. Or would she? The past few days, she could be listening to someone, and suddenly Case would be cavorting in her mind. While she helped Gran, the memory of his experienced hands massaging Gran's leg filled her mind. When she loaded the dishwasher, the memory of his nearness tugged at her senses. And the aroma of her breakfast coffee brought back the sight of him in the early morning at the river. She repositioned a birch-block C in front of an A dreamily.

"Your turn, Alli."

Alli corralled her wandering thoughts long enough to form a word and looked back at the scenery dreamily. She breathed deeply, savoring the mountain air scented with flowers and sage and pine. The motor home purred upward, and the air thinned. She glanced at the roadside, noting they'd reached the five-thousand-foot marker. The tree population increased, shading and sheltering the lower shrubs. Pinecones spilled everywhere, their burnished-brown hue reminding Alli of the color of Case's eyes.

She looked at the player across from her, aware the woman had spoken her name.

"Are you playing?" the woman repeated teasingly.

Alli grinned apologetically and turned her attention to the cubes in her hand. She kept her mind focused on the game until Mac turned off the road and parked the motor home.

Alli departed the vehicle in the midst of a group of hospital personnel, but when she stepped onto the ground, she could feel Case's eyes on her as if she were the only person in the park. She lowered her gaze and then raised it slowly. Above his scuffed boots, faded jeans clung to his narrow hips, rising to cinch in the waist of the checked, pearl-buttoned shirt covering his broad chest. On his head he wore a cream-colored Stetson sporting a brilliant blue feather. Alli wondered if there was a woman in the group who wasn't taking a second look.

"Hi," Case greeted everyone in his friendly, deep voice. His look paused on Alli briefly, and a familiar warmth rose in her veins. "I'm setting up the children's corner near those pines." He motioned toward a section of the park where half a dozen people mingled, laboring amidst laughter and squeals. He turned to Mac and Laura. "We appreciate your carrying part of our supplies in your motor home."

Laura accepted his thanks with a nod. "The bed is packed. I should have told everyone they couldn't leave the place empty-handed," she said, smiling.

"No problem. I'll find a few willing hands." He turned to Alli. "Let me show you the arts-and-crafts area. We used the picnic tables and benches already in the park. Put two together. Do you think that will be enough space?'' His warm look locked her eyes on his.

''Sounds fine.'' Alli wanted to look away and couldn't. Could it only be a day since she'd seen him? It seemed like a week. She wanted to reach out and touch him. ''The tissues and toilet-paper rolls and other stuff are in Laura's motor home. It's bulky, but not as heavy as some of the other supplies.'' She moved back to the motor home and found someone had already placed two boxes of her supplies outside the door.

Case reached for the larger box and carried it to the picnic tables set in the partial shade of a towering pine. He peered into the contents as Alli trudged to the table. ''How did you manage to find this many discarded rolls?''

''With a little talk and a lot of help.'' Alli plopped a carton filled with boxes of facial tissues, glue, and assorted supplies on the table. ''Almost everyone I come into contact with at the hospital has been saving discarded rolls for weeks.''

''Another thing about small hospitals—everyone gets into the spirit.''

Alli didn't comment. Maybe Case hadn't been making another point for Wayside.

''And the tissues?''

''Would you believe''—she paused for effect, tilting her head and rolling her eyes—''Dr. Calogen, though he may be the verbal scourge of the surgical unit, is not a Scrooge? The carton of tissues is only part of his contribution. I have a bag of gift certificates to a well-known 'chow for children' place. The kids don't even have to win, place, or show.'' She paused. ''Well, they do have to show up. But the word *gift* flies faster than a jet among the grammar-school set.''

''The paper?'' Case waved a sheath of oblong scarlet sheets in the air.

''Central Supply. They were going to toss them out.''

''Resourceful,'' he said, admiration glowing in his eyes.

''Early training. Scavenger. Anything I could find to keep my sisters busy when Mom was working. Besides, I was a Girl Scout for a few years.''

''Always prepared?''

''Not always.'' *Especially not now,* Alli thought. Her heart was beating merrily along like a lilting melody. And she couldn't find the willpower to tell herself to shape up and tend to the business of setting up her crafts table. Just being near Case made her forget all about wanting to avoid him. Right now it was even difficult to think about leaving California.

She took a plastic tablecloth from a box and fanned it over the peeling green paint on the tabletop. Case caught one end, pulling it toward him. She tossed two metal clips toward his end of the table.

''These look familiar.'' Case smoothed the cloth over the edge of the table and fastened it with the clips.

"They should. You saw them at the river," she said brightly. She wondered if she looked as euphoric as she felt. "Laura lent them to me. She did add a little request about returning the clips if possible. She said they don't cost much, but she forgets to replace lost ones and ends up anchoring the tablecloth with rocks most of the time."

"So we'd better see that she gets them back, or the MacCabes may not ask us to the river with them again." He opened a box of supplies and peered at the contents. "What are these?" He pulled Gran's pinking shears from the box.

"Another thing I'd better not misplace. When I told Gran we were making paper carnations, she insisted pinking shears were the thing to use on the petals. I think we just slashed the paper with scissors to give the petals that shaggy look when I made them years ago. But Gran wanted to be helpful, so I brought them along." She raised both hands in pretended horror. "Be just my luck to lose them—Gran said she's had them for forty years."

"I can see where it's going to be hard to keep an eye on them if you let everyone use 'em. Maybe you should just leave them in the box." He held them over the supply box, awaiting her answer.

"No. Gran will ask if the children used them, and I'm not very good at covering up. I'll just have to keep track of them."

Case handed her the shears and continued placing

tissues and cardboard rolls and various containers on the table. For all the wide-open space around them, Alli wondered why she felt as if they were limited to a few feet to move in. At times Case was so close, the aroma of his after-shave was stronger than the pine scent flowing from the nearby trees. A rustle of nerves, persistent as the shivers of pine needles overhead, laced through her euphoria. She was grateful when two members of the radiology department jogged up to ask for Case's assistance.

Separating the supplies, Alli saw her first group of prospective artists arrive, crowing over their prizes from the fish tank.

"You have to work a little harder for the prizes from this booth," she said with a mixture of enthusiasm and anxiety. "Find a place to sit." Two of the youngsters wandered on. Alli's tinge of disappointment was brief. She passed out dull-pointed scissors and pink tissues to the remaining three children.

Picking up a tissue, she fanfolded the paper slowly, explaining the process to her mildly interested audience. Bypassing Gran's pinking shears, she selected a pair of scissors from the box and held up the tissue, acutely aware of her lack of preparation for this performance. Why hadn't she practiced, or at least purchased a book on crafts before she volunteered for this project?

She continued with an approach as confident as if she knew what she was doing. "Now, cut the tissue in half.'' She snipped through the paper. ''Next, we fasten them together with flower wire. Then, pull each tissue apart.'' She was amazed when the creation began to resemble a pink paper ball.

Case passed by, grinning at her group. Feeling extraordinarily happy, Alli applied Gran's pinking shears to the paper, serrating the edges of the tissue to resemble a carnation. She dipped into a plastic jar and withdrew half a dozen green tulip-shaped objects and slid one on the wire holding the tissue. Passing one out to each child, she watched as they copied her action. She placed the pinking shears on the bench beside her when she found the dull scissors produced a ragged edge resembling a carnation petal.

The next time Case strolled by, half a dozen children clustered around Alli. The pinwheels, paper-roll wind chimes, and bouquets of flowers had caught on. ''Need a breather?'' he asked.

''Anytime.'' She gazed at two teenagers who'd joined the younger ones. They feathered yellow paper carnations, telling each other they'd done them before at summer camp. Alli grinned. Some things changed little, it seemed. She pushed a jar of glitter toward the girls. ''Try adding glue and glitter. It's lovely.''

Case picked up a spiral wind chime. ''Maybe I should do my balloon sculpture at your table. You seem to have the most customers.''

''Fine.'' She felt a surge of pleasure.

''Would you help?''

"Sure. But the kids are so enthusiastic and eager to learn, they'll be helping you in a few minutes. Even the preschoolers." She wrapped a length of green tape around the wire holding a paper carnation. "I didn't know playing with children could be so much work." Her grimace was more a grin than a frown. "Or so much fun."

"Maybe you should have been a kindergarten teacher instead of a nurse," Case teased, picking up one of the glitter-splashed paper spirals. "I've been watching. You're good at teaching."

"That's what my boss says . . . on rare occasions."

"Some boss, if he doesn't know a good employee when he has one."

"My problem is, I get carried away with the workshops for employees sometimes and keep them over, and the company has to pay for the time they spend with me. Clocks and I are not the best of friends; the hands pull me away from people or patients before I'm ready to leave."

"Did you ever think of being a mother? No time clocks in the nursery."

"Ha!" Alli laughed, keeping an eye on the striving fingers of a seven-year-old twisting a wire around a paper blossom. "Then you've never heard the alarm-clock yell of a two-year-old who wants dinner."

"I think I'd like to. Depending on who the mother is, of course."

Laura and Mona sauntered to the table, standing to

watch the children, and Alli was able to reserve comment on Case's remark.

"Case," Mona said, tilting her head to look up at him. "When are you going to do the balloon sculptures?"

"Any minute now."

"Need any help?"

"Alli volunteered." He cleared his throat. "But I can always use help."

An hour later Alli handed a balloon-fashioned dachshund to an excited six-year-old and stretched her shoulders, looking away from the mob scene around Case. She must have filled dozens of balloons with air. She felt like sagging from the effort. One of those helium-filled canister things would have saved a lot of wear and tear on her cheeks, she thought dryly. She picked up another balloon and glanced at Case and Mona. They looked like marathon runners who didn't even need to pause for liquid refreshment.

Mona watched Case closely, then attempted to imitate the figure he was forming. "If I help in the therapy department, I may need a way to entertain children," she said to him.

He twisted a balloon and held it while he prepared to blow up another one. "Probably." He took a deep breath. "And this isn't difficult, once you get the hang of it."

Alli glanced quickly at Case. He hadn't mentioned he needed a nurse in his department. But then, she hadn't seen much of him lately.

"Two more," Case said to an eager boy. "Then my lungs need to take a break."

Moans emitted from the crowd. "Maybe my new assistant will fill in for a while."

"I only know how to make one kind," Mona protested.

"I don't think they'll mind," he said, thanking her with a warm look. "But are you sure you don't?"

"I told you, I need the experience." She batted long lashes at him.

"Okay." Case handed her the limp balloon in his hand. "I'll send Laura over if I can find her. Alli and I are going to peruse the buffet table."

Chapter Ten

Case caught Alli's hand in a spontaneous gesture, pulling her away from the crafts table. "Come on. A pan of barbecued ribs on the buffet table needs my attention STAT or, at least, as soon as possible."

Alli couldn't restrain a giggle. "I worked with a ward secretary once who thought STAT and ASAP were the same thing. I tried to tell her that STAT means *now*—do it first—and ASAP means do it next. But she wasn't convinced. She said she processed every order as soon as possible."

Alli knew she was rattling, but just being with Case was so good. She stopped at the line leading to the table and was reluctant to release Case's hand to pick up a paper plate. She breathed in the air as if she could store it for future reference—the aroma of sauce and roast beef and pine and, above all, the faint scent of after-shave. *Careful,* she scolded herself mildly. *Case fervor could crop up again anytime.* She blinked at the mispronunciation, even though it was in her thoughts. *Case fever,* she amended and felt like giggling.

Watching Case pile his plate with barbecued ribs, Alli placed two sauce-covered bones on her plate. She added a sparse spoonful of potato salad, bypassed a crockpot of beans, and added an apple because it glowed like a ruby in a shaft of sunlight.

A vaguely familiar, middle-aged man, one of the costumed food servers, with a red bandanna circling his neck, placed a slice of rare beef atop the ribs on Case's plate. "Case, how's the business venture going?" he asked.

"Going, I hope," Case said optimistically.

"I hope that isn't going, going, gone," the man said with a kindly grin.

Case smiled cheerfully and moved on.

Alli shook her head when the cowboy-cook poised his knife over the mound of beef, wondering about the business venture he had mentioned to Case. She declined an ear of corn with a mild shake of her head. Her determination waned as a pioneer woman in a matching bonnet and full-skirted frock dipped the corn into a pan of butter and offered the dripping ear to the person behind her. She averted her eyes from the array of offerings and moved on. She had enough food on her plate and too much food for thought.

The band stopped playing as Case led the way to a costumed clan of western-clad diners and motioned to two vacant spaces on the bench. He waited for Alli to sit down first. Then he slid in beside her, his thigh brushing hers. She moved over an inch. She couldn't afford another bout with Case fever. Her resistance was at an all-time low now, and any renewed attack would be devastating.

She glanced around the table at the grinning faces greeting Case. Some teased him about the feather on his cream-colored Stetson. ''A peacock feather on a cowboy hat, Case!'' a young woman from the business office joked. ''Some westerner you are!''

''I knew even less about the Renaissance costumes, so I'm glad the committee changed *our* minds.''

''I liked the Renaissance theme,'' someone said adamantly. ''Next year I'm going to propose it again, so be prepared.''

''It was a good idea,'' the business-office worker agreed. ''We just need more time to make costumes. I'll go for it next year. How about you, Case?''

''I'm agreeable.'' He picked up a rib from his plate and grinned at Alli. ''I bet you'd look great in one of those low-necked, waist-hugging dresses.''

His voice was low, but Alli glanced up to see if anyone was looking at her. Luckily most of them were listening to a joke told by a man at the end of the table.

I'm not going to be here next year, Alli wanted to say. But there was no point. As long as she was here, Case meant to keep turning on the charm in hopes she'd stay. She shifted uneasily on the bench. Succumbing to his charm was okay for these people—they didn't have to make a lifelong commitment.

She turned as someone asked her about her grandmother, and, after a few minutes of polite answers to casual questions, she quietly nibbled at the spareribs. Conversation swirled around her like leaves in a windstorm. She listened vaguely, her mind busy with her own thoughts, even when Case's deep voice and laughter rippled above the other voices.

Why hadn't Case mentioned starting a business? Or maybe he had. She tried to recall some of their conversations. Maybe he had mentioned a business and she'd blocked the memory. If Case was contemplating starting some kind of business, he had no intention of leaving Wayside.

The couple across from Case left, and another couple took their place. A few minutes later Alli heard the band begin a lively melody again.

Case looked at her questioningly, then stood up. "If you'll excuse us. . . ." He took Alli's plate and waited for her to join him. But after dumping their used dishes, he didn't walk her back to her crafts table. "It's about time for the square-dance exhibition." He enclosed her hand in his again. "We don't want to miss that, do we?" Before she could object, he led her toward the music.

Four colorfully dressed couples stood on the concrete slab in an area cleared of pines, alternately looking from the band to the western-dressed caller at the microphone. Lace-trimmed, full-skirted dresses flounced around the knees of the ladies. The men looked only slightly more conservative in dark trousers, with red-checked shirts to match the colorful skirts of their partners. Sunlight flashed from the silver-clasped bolo ties of the men and the silver necklaces of the ladies.

Winding through the crowd already gathered around the platform, Case found an unoccupied space. He positioned Alli in front of him, inquiring solicitously if she could see the dancers. She nodded, feeling his chin brush her hair. Then his hands closed loosely around her waist. She felt a tremor of nerves. But it was difficult to think of a reason to step away from his touch.

The song started and the dancers moved onstage, following an intricate pattern of steps as the man at the microphone spoke. The women's soft-soled shoes seemed to barely touch the concrete as the scarlet skirts swirled and swished to the demands of the caller. Alli marveled at their agility, almost forgetting the feel of Case's hands on her waist.

When the music stopped and the dancers moved away, Case suggested they tour the other exhibits. They watched a puppet show and a demonstration of rope twirling and declined the offer of ice-cream bars from a fringe-jacketed vendor.

They strolled away from the crowd and walked along the shoreline of the lake, and Alli stopped to watch two waddling ducks test the water. Bobbing on the water, they moved away from the shore. She bent to remove a sneaker and sifted a spoonful of soil back onto the beach. Case put a hand out to steady her as she slipped the shoe back on her foot, and she looked up to thank him. She caught her breath at the look in his eyes.

"I love you," he said.

The words were so unexpected, Alli's heart didn't have time to change beats. She would have been prepared, she told herself, if he'd uttered the words in the moonlight on the Colorado River. But in the brilliant sunlight and carnival atmosphere, with the sound of western music blaring amid the laughter of the children behind them, she hadn't been on guard.

She watched a passing boat and felt his words touch her, lapping at her heart as tangibly as the wake-created waves lapping at the shore near her sneakers. She knew what little reserve she had was slipping away. She pressed her lips together in silence. Admitting her love for Case wouldn't change the way she felt about making a commitment to him.

"And I have something else to tell you," he said when she didn't answer. His voice held a note of controlled excitement.

"The business someone referred to." Alli pulled away from him and bent to pick up a pebble.

"You heard." He laughed. "I want to take you to see the building location."

She tossed the pebble into the water, watching it sink into a pool of circles. "Why haven't you mentioned it before?"

"It wasn't definite earlier."

"But you're planning to open a business, which

means you plan to stay in Wayside.'' Her voice was low.

He looked at her intently, enthusiasm fading from his face. ''I never said I'd leave.'' He placed his hands on her shoulders and turned her to face him. ''But I thought you might stay.''

''I'm afraid not.'' She tried to make her voice sound light and cheerful. And, without thinking, she added, ''In fact, if Gwen can come home for the summer and stay with Gran, I'll be returning to Chicago sooner than I expected.''

He caught her hand as if to hold her. ''Running away?'' His voice matched hers in tone, but his eyes were solemn.

''I am, Case. If I stay here much longer, I could stay forever and make you miserable. Or make us both miserable—like my mother did Dad.'' She looked at the water, bright and shining and lively with watercraft. Back at the picnic site, the band had started another spirited tune. Alli felt dark and depressed. Her voice dropped an octave. ''I love you too, Case. There, I've said it. But I don't want to see the sad resignation that I see in my father's eyes when he looks at Mother sometimes.'' She slipped her hand free and turned to stride along the shore.

Case caught up with her. ''Your parents seem as happy as the average couple.''

''If theirs is an average marriage, then I know I never want to get married,'' she said. ''Mother tells me often not to make the same mistake she did. When she married, she thought she and Dad would see the world together. Instead, they seldom travel as far as Los Angeles.''

''Do you think your mother is right—to blame your dad?''

She blinked. ''No. I told you, remember? Dad had to take over the nursery for Grandpa.''

''So you're doing what your mother wanted to do.''

''Maybe.'' She kicked a pinecone away from the water. ''If Mom and Dad had been like Mac and Laura,'' she said, ''it might have been different. I love the way the MacCabes tease. I know Mom and Dad love each other, but I don't know if they like each other.'' She stopped at a boulder near the water and sat down. ''My parents do so little together. Dad is always at the nursery, and Mom has worked as a hostess as long as I can remember.''

''At least they stayed together in Wayside.''

''Which Mom hates.'' Alli brushed sand from her shoes.

''Why?''

''Mom was a singer and traveled with a band.'' She shook her head slowly. ''She talks about the fun she had, the excitement of different cities and crowds, and she says there was no housework, because she didn't stay in one place long enough to clean a room.'' She shrugged. ''I guess she just liked it and Dad was willing to go along with her. Until his father became ill.''

"It's sad when people aren't happy with their lives," he commented.

"And my mother isn't. 'Don't do as I did, Alli,' she's repeated a hundred times. 'Have fun. See the world before you settle down.' "

"Your obsession with leaving Wayside is to make your mother happy?"

She felt a twinge of discomfort under his scrutinizing gaze. "No," she said slowly. "I didn't mean that at all. I like living in Chicago. I like crowds and people. I like traveling and seeing places other people only read about."

"You don't think you could do that in California?"

"You mean Wayside, don't you?"

"Yes." He locked his gaze on hers. "Does happiness depend on where you live?"

Alli was the first to pull her gaze free. She looked across the water, following the flight of a skier jumping the wake of boat. Why did he have to confuse her? "Case, your job is in Wayside, and mine is in Chicago. At least on weekends."

"Weekends?"

"I travel during the week." She looked at him.

"You told me." His voice was a growl.

"It's a great company to work for. The pay is better than hospital nursing. I fly all over the country and to Canada. I just went to Hawaii, and I'm going to Australia next year to explain our program to a company there." Her eyes sought his. She wished he could understand her enthusiasm for her work. ''I have a company car, a liberal expense account, a living allowance, plus a month's vacation, holidays, sick leave, and health insurance.''

''And no place to call home.''

''I've flown home almost every weekend. Except when I was in Hawaii. We were setting up new programs there, and I stayed longer. I'd planned to spend my vacation there too, but Gran needed me.'' Her voice lowered. ''Case, I can't see settling down in Wayside when there is a whole world out there to explore, and I can do it on an expense account.''

His eyes darkened. ''I guess working in a community hospital and living in a small city does sound dull compared to your life-style.''

Alli steeled herself to look away. If she kept looking into his eyes, she would weaken. She gazed at the mountains on the far side of the lake until they came into focus. The momentary rise of enthusiasm she'd managed while talking about her career sank like a stone in water. Her heartbeat thudded in her ears like a funeral dirge.

People spoke as Alli and Case returned to the picnic area, and with difficulty she returned their greetings. Looking at Case, she wondered if his smile was as forced as hers. When they reached the crafts table, it was slightly easier to meet Laura's eager welcome with a semblance of cheer.

"It's been fun," Laura said brightly. She handed a carnation to a preschool cowgirl and her scissors to Alli. "But I'm glad you're ready to take over." She gestured at the flowers, wind chimes, and balloons. "It looks like Mona and I have been making preparations for a wedding." She sighed wearily.

"Don't I wish?" Mona said euphorically.

"There's a saying that good things come to those who wait," Case teased Mona, waving to the group of youngsters waiting for his balloon creatures.

Mona tilted her head. "You should know by now, Case, patience was never one of my virtues."

"I'm getting the idea."

"All I want is a therapist of my own." She gave him a wicked smile.

"You keep telling me." He laughed.

Alli listened to their wordplay without interest. Her minimal display of cheerfulness was only skin-deep—and it was slipping. The laughter around her didn't penetrate her dismal thoughts. Even the joy of watching Case delight the children with his air-filled animal figures was missing.

She was relieved when he moved on to help at another booth. And more relieved when Mona returned to help her close her table and clean up. "Laura said they'd like to leave anytime." Mona boxed the leftover tissues. "Case says you have to work tomorrow," she added, "so I'll finish up if you want to go."

"I really appreciate it." A fleeting thought bolted

across Alli's mind, and she wondered if the volunteer cleanup duty was Mona's way of extending her time with Case. She shunted the thought aside with a sense of chagrin. Mona was so open and eager to help, Alli was ashamed of the thought. Besides, she'd just told Case her feelings for him weren't strong enough to keep her in Wayside. So why the touch of regret to think that Mona's feelings might be stronger?

Chapter Eleven

Alli trudged into the house, veering to stop in the family room when she heard music. Gail Parmer watched the television screen with rapt attention while her mother-in-law knitted industriously on the coral-and-blue afghan.

"Hi," Alli said. She included both her mother and her grandmother in the greeting, aiming a weak smile midway between them.

"Who died?" Gran said.

"What?" Alli blinked.

"I thought you went to a picnic, not a wake."

Alli forced voltage into the smile on her lips. "Gran, I had a wonderful time at the picnic."

"You could have fooled me," Gran said wryly.

"I'm just tired." Alli sank onto a lounge chair.

Gail picked up the remote control from the table beside her chair and pressed a button on the control panel. The television picture paused and began to run backward. "Of course you are, darling. I'm sure you're not used to baby-sitting on your day off." She gave her daughter an exaggerated look of sympathy. "And a picnic is so dull compared to your usual life-style." She sighed proudly. "I know you're counting the days until you can get back to the city. You probably would have gone to lunch in one of those fashionable restaurants at noon today and out to the theater tonight."

Alli looked at the ceiling morosely. Her mother wouldn't believe that she washed and ironed on Saturday so she could repack on Sunday. Startled at the tinge of irony in her thoughts, she lowered her gaze, looking at her mother to see if she'd noticed. Gail was still watching the television screen. Alli breathed easier. She was in no mood to discuss her career today. "Did you and Gran have a good day?"

A broad smile brightened Gail's face. "Enjoyed my favorite pastime. We watched old musicals on the VCR all afternoon." She got up to remove a cassette from the VCR unit. "I like happy endings." She sighed nostalgically. "I don't know why they make so few good musicals these days."

Her comment didn't seem to demand an answer, so Alli ignored it.

Gail replaced the cassette in a nearby rack and picked up her purse. "I have to run, dear. I told your dad I'd be home in time to go out to dinner."

"I hope I didn't make you late," Alli said. "You should have mentioned it this morning. I might have caught an earlier ride home." *Like about noon,* she thought. Her afternoon had been a disaster. But then, she had settled the nagging problem about Case, even if the decision was as unexpected to her as it must have been to him. Now she had to call Gwen and coax her to come home the minute her classes were over.

"There are cold sandwiches and deli potato salad in the fridge." Gail pulled a collection of keys from her purse and turned toward Gran. "Hope you enjoyed the movies as much as I did, Mother, though I know you prefer mysteries."

"They were fine, dear," Gran assured her. "And there's a little mystery in every movie, isn't there?"

Gail leaned over and kissed her mother-in-law's cheek. "I'll see you tomorrow." She waved at Alli and walked lightly toward the doorway, and Alli pushed herself up from the chair.

Gran lowered her knitting needles. "Alli, hand me the TV thing while you're up. The TV listing, too, if you see it," she added.

"I'm going to walk Mom to the car, Gran." She picked up the remote control and scanned the nearby tables for the program guide. Seeing it under Gran's chair, she bent to retrieve it.

She was on her hands and knees when the doorbell rang. She retrieved the booklet and handed it to Gran and then went to the entry hall. Gail turned in the open doorway, holding a pair of pinking shears.

"Someone called Mona said you left your pinking shears on the table at the picnic."

"Gran's shears." Alli gazed through the open doorway to Case's truck parked at the curb in front of Gran's house.

Mona slid into the front seat, leaning toward Case as he reached to close the door. Case pulled away from the curb, stopping suddenly as a cat streaked in front of him and Mona lurched against him. The sound of their laughter radiated across the front yard. A tiny poodle stopped on the curb, barking at the racing cat. It was over in a second, and Case eased the truck into the street without looking toward the house. Alli felt an unfamiliar pang of disappointment.

"Gran's pinking shears?" Gail repeated.

It took a moment for Alli to focus on the shears. "She lent them to me to use on the paper carnations."

"It was nice of the woman to bring them by. Or rather, nice of Case to bring her by with him."

"I thought you didn't remember Case Sherman."

"I didn't, when you were talking about him before. But your grandmother introduced me to him this morning."

"Gran introduced you this morning?" Alli asked in puzzlement.

"Gran said he did her therapy treatments."

"He came to do her physical-therapy treatments this morning?"

"No," Gail said with ill-controlled patience. "He came to see if you wanted to ride to the picnic with them this morning. But you'd already left with the MacCabes." She turned back toward the door. "I'd better go."

"Yeah. I doubt Dad would go to dinner without you, but don't keep him waiting." She looked toward the street, but Case's truck was out of sight. "Thanks for staying with Gran, Mom."

"Anytime, dear. I wish I could stay so you could get back to your job. But my arm isn't healed enough to care for Mother all the time."

"I know." Alli closed the door and carried the pinking shears to Gran. "I left them at the picnic, and Mona, one of the nurses on the night shift, brought them by."

"I wouldn't want to lose them, but she could have brought them to you at the hospital."

"She works nights, and I don't see her often." Alli opened Gran's sewing cabinet and replaced the shears in a box. "I'm sure it was Case who thought about it. I told him how long you'd had them. But it was nice of Mona to run them in." She closed the cabinet door with a thud.

"You don't sound like you think it was nice."

"What did I sound like?" She stared at the closed door.

"Like you thought this night nurse was moving in on your territory?"

Alli turned around. "Case isn't my territory."

"He could be. I've seen the way he looks at you."

"Gran, Case wants to stay in Wayside, and I don't."

"What's wrong with Wayside?"

"There's nothing wrong with Wayside if you want to live here."

"And you don't?"

Alli avoided her grandmother's eyes. "Look how unhappy Mom and Dad are. She wants to move anywhere else. Dad is perfectly content to stay home and work in his wood shop when he isn't at the nursery. They've never really been on a vacation out of California."

"Alli, I'm afraid Gail would be unhappy anywhere. Don't get me wrong. I love Gail, but her unhappiness needn't be yours. She wanted to be a singer or an actress. Either she didn't have enough talent or perseverance or maybe just the right break, so she blames her failure on staying in a small town. If she'd really wanted to act, there are little theaters nearby, and Hollywood is only a few hours away." Gran shifted uncomfortably in her chair. "I've heard her tell you not to make the same mistake she did. Well, don't make a mistake that could make you even unhappier." She switched the television set on, clicking the channel changer rapidly, as if she were annoyed.

Alli stared at the changing screen. For a second she wished she could be like her sister Candice—married and content to live in a place even smaller and more remote than Wayside. "I think I'll take a shower, Gran," she said, leaving the room quickly. With a slight frown she padded down the hall. Why did she have to be the one with her mother's restless feet?

The following week Alli seldom saw Case. She avoided him at the hospital as usual. But she couldn't help hoping to see him when he came to help Gran with her exercises. But on Monday she was shopping at the supermarket when he came. His car turned the corner to leave as she returned, and she told herself it was irrational to feel depressed, even for a moment. It would be easier to leave Wayside if she didn't see him at all. She turned into the driveway and remembered she hadn't tried to call Gwen.

On Wednesday, Case came to the house early, staying only a short time, and she met him in the hall as she came out of the shower. She thought her disappointment was minimally justified this time. She was leaving for Chicago to attend the monthly meeting held by her company on Friday. And maybe she should have asked him if Gran's therapy was progressing as expected. After all, *when* she called Gwen, it would be nice to tell her about Gran's progress.

She had to take Thursday as an extra day off in order to catch the plane to Chicago. She packed with less enthusiasm than usual, lagging until her father grumbled she'd miss the plane and he left the house to sit in the car with the motor running.

Turning off the San Bernardino Freeway, he stopped at the first traffic light to comment on the flow of cars. "I'll drop you off in front of the terminal," he said. "Parking in the main lot is near impossible these days."

Alli pulled her thoughts away from the hospital and the therapy department. "I remember. You were parked at least a mile away, and we had to take the commuter bus to the car when you picked me up a few weeks ago.''

''Doubt it's gotten any better,'' her father said laconically. He pressed the gas pedal when the light changed. ''But the problem is minor compared to the airport in Chicago. Not that I've been there or plan to go, but I can just imagine parking problems in a big city.'' He eased around a dawdling compact. ''Speaking of cities, haven't you had enough traveling? It's about time you came home and settled down with some nice young man. It would be nice to have one of my daughters nearby. I want to be a grandfather before I get too old to play ball with my grandchildren.''

Alli looked at him in surprise. ''I never knew you played ball.''

''I played ball when I was a kid. I was in Little League.''

''You never mentioned it.''

''I never thought about it.''

''Why now?''

John Parmer pulled into the airport lane of traffic. ''I've been watching Case Sherman's Little Leaguers play a few times.''

Alli stared at his profile. Before she could say anything, the car slowed to a stop, and her father slid out to open the trunk of the car. She moved slower. Her workaholic father took time to watch Case's baseball team!

He handed her luggage to an airport porter and turned to her. "Hurry back. I like the idea of having you around."

Alli gazed at him with amazement. "I'll be back Sunday afternoon."

In the plane, she settled back in her seat, expecting the usual rush of excitement at traveling to a different place.

She looked for mountain peaks and viewed rooftops and gray ribbons of freeways cluttered with cars vaguely resembling elongated marathon runners. Grimacing, she rummaged in her carryall for a paperback. Even that was disheartening. She glared at the cover depicting a lace-collared lady gazing rapturously at a jeans-clad man. In the background an oil well rose above a dilapidated shack.

Fingering the book absently, Alli turned it over, reading the blurb without interest. How could a romance novel be in her carryall? Then she remembered. Gran had helped her pack. But Gran knew she liked mystery novels. She grinned despite her irritation. Gran had probably arranged for her son to watch the ball games too. With a sigh, she opened the book.

When the stewardess approached with the refreshment cart, Alli reluctantly slid a forefinger between the pages of the book, lowered the tray attached to the seat in front of her, and requested a glass of tomato juice. As if she were on a time clock, she returned to the problems depleting the heroine's resistance. At a pause in the action, Alli lifted the glass to her lips and returned to her reading. Eyes watering, she paused briefly to blink at the glass of juice. Then she realized the contents of her glass might be the spicy liquid used for cocktails. It didn't deter her downing the remaining fluid. Surviving the problems of the paperback heroine needed refreshment.

By the time the seat-belt announcement sounded in the plane, prior to landing at O'Hare, the lace-collared lady and the jeans-clad man were discussing a lifelong commitment—despite their differences. Alli closed the book with a sigh of contentment. Too bad real-life problems couldn't be solved in the course of a few hours.

People that she usually found so interesting in airports blurred into a jostling crowd of uncaring strangers as she tried to locate her luggage, and hailing a taxi became an irritant instead of an adventure. She finally caught a commuter bus, anxious to leave the bustle around her. She needed to relax, that was all, she told herself. It had been a long day. Once she reached the familiar walls of the apartment she called home, everything would fall into place. Wouldn't it?

The apartment looked the same. Bright, clean, and sparsely furnished. She hadn't expected it to be any different. She and her roommate were seldom home on the same days. She kicked off her shoes and opened the drapes in the bedroom, planning to rest before she made a trip to her favorite deli for takeout and then call a friend to go to a movie. But at dinnertime she rummaged in the miniscule freezer instead, popping a dinner into the microwave. In the evening she changed television channels restlessly, trying to find a program to hold her attention.

Despite retiring late, she arose early Friday morning, eager to attend the meeting. Once she saw her familiar coworkers, she knew her enthusiasm would return like a boomerang. She listened to the reports for current programs and the plans for projected ones with interest. But even the report from the programs in Hawaii didn't keep her thoughts from flying back and forth to California.

After the meeting her supervisor told her he missed her, inquired about her grandmother's health, and asked how much more time off she needed. She told him she hoped her sister would be able to stay with Gran for the summer.

She went to lunch with two other nurses and thought about California only half a dozen times or so. She went shopping in the afternoon. She looked at the tall buildings and thought about Wayside's four or five two-story buildings. She passed the tall, sprawling hospital where she worked an occasional weekend when she was in Chicago to keep up her nursing skills, and thought about the one-level hospital in Wayside. She made a mental note to call the temporary nursing service and tell them she hoped to return soon. Viewing a park from the window of the restaurant where she'd stopped for tea, she thought of the magnificent mountains visible from the hospital in Wayside.

That evening she attended the theater with one of the men from the main office—and found herself comparing him to Case.

On Saturday she wandered around the apartment, undecided what to do for the day. By noon she realized the joy of traveling was marred by a longing she felt reluctant to identify. By two o'clock she knew her heart was in Wayside with Case. She dressed and went to the deli for pastrami and potato salad—and decided it would be less painful to dream about faraway places than to be far away and dream of Case. She went back to the apartment and tried to change her airline ticket to catch an earlier flight to California, with no success. She patched her nerves back in place for the umpteenth time by the time she caught her scheduled trip.

Awake before the sun squeezed a shaft of light through a crack in her bedroom drapes, Alli searched her closet for a clean uniform. She wondered if she could find an excuse to go by the physical therapy department before she clocked in. Some mornings Case came to work earlier than others.

"Alli," Gran called from the bedroom. "What are you doing up so early?"

"What time is it?" Alli asked innocently, as if she hadn't been checking the clock every fifteen minutes since long before dawn.

"Quarter to six."

"Just wanted to be sure I'm not late."

"Ha." Gran's exclamation drifted across the hall. "Don't tell me you missed the hospital!"

When she reached the parking lot, Alli scanned the area, but no sandblasted pickup occupied any space. She clocked in, lingering in the hall for a few minutes. She even walked by the dining room and looked in. Case might be having coffee before he went to work, she told herself.

She didn't find an excuse to go to the therapy department during the morning, and if Case walked in the halls, she didn't see him. She missed him at lunch, and at the afternoon break she was sitting on the patio with Laura and a group of medical personnel when Case and Mona came into the dining room. She lifted a hand to wave and lowered it in embarrassment. Case and Mona, intent on their conversation, apparently noticed no one else in the room, let alone the outside patio.

Alli gazed at the star-studded wall of scented jasmine, grateful Laura and the other employees at the table kept up a buzz of conversation that needed no input from her. She had only herself to blame. She'd told Case she wasn't the woman for him. So why shouldn't he look for a woman who was available—a woman who liked Wayside? She lifted her coffee cup and stared at the black liquid bleakly. He wouldn't turn to another woman for comfort so soon! Or would he?

Just the thought sent her heart lurching around her chest in near panic. Right now, returning to the travel and the work she loved seemed unbearable, for it meant losing Case. If she hadn't lost him already.

Chapter Twelve

Alli didn't see Case for the rest of the workday at the hospital. She lingered in the hall after clocking out and dawdled on her way to the parking lot. His truck wasn't parked in the usual place. Morosely she drove home.

Gran was still asleep, so she changed into shorts and a T-shirt and, unlike her, left her uniform in a discarded heap on the floor. Trudging to the kitchen, she poured a glass of tea from the sun-tea jar. When she heard the familiar sound of Gran's afternoon television program ringing through the hall, she poured another glass from the jar and carried it to the bedroom.

"Hi, Gran. Ready for tea?" Alli decided her voice sounded quite normal.

"Sounds good." Gran adjusted the bed to a sitting position and shifted her shoulders against the pillow.

"Let me fluff your pillow. It looks like half a dozen small boys used it for a football."

Gran leaned forward, allowing Alli to remove the pillow and shake it. "Why all the attention?" Gran said with mock suspicion. ''Did you dent a fender on the car?''

''How can you ask?'' Alli chided. ''Don't I fuss over you every day?''

''Yes, you do, dear.'' Catching Alli's hand, Gran squeezed it gently. ''And I'm going to miss you terribly when you go.''

Alli felt a lump rising in her throat. She'd realized weeks ago how much she'd missed Gran. Being with her again was wonderful. In fact, being with her family again was wonderful. She couldn't wait to tell them she planned to settle in Wayside. It would be a major announcement. She brushed away the thought of the look on her mother's face. Her decision trembled on the edge of her tongue. She busied her hands with straightening the cover on Gran's bed, reining in her runaway emotions until they calmed down. A wisp of wariness nagged at her. She had to tell Case first.

''I see you and Mom have been playing Yahtzee.'' She gestured toward the game on Gran's bedside table.

''In which I won.'' Gran smiled smugly, then grinned in candid resignation. ''No credit to me. Your mother would rather watch television, but she's a good sport.'' She swung her attention to her program, and Alli sank into the lounge chair, staring at the television screen absently. A commercial interrupted Magnum's argument with Higgins, and Gran turned back to Alli.

''Case called. Said he was sorry, but he'd have to leave the range-of-motion therapy to you this evening.''

"Oh." Alli was unable to restrain her disappointment. "I don't suppose he said why."

"No. He just said he was sure you could do fine without him."

Alli looked at the screen, grateful that Magnum once again was playing for Gran's attention. She couldn't do fine without Case. She knew that now. She stood up, mumbling something about dinner, and hurried from the room.

She didn't see Case for the next two days at work. He didn't come to the wrap-up committee for the picnic. Nor did Mona. She thought of asking Laura if she'd seen Case, but she couldn't. Her anxiety might creep into her question. She told herself to be patient a few more hours. He wouldn't miss Gran's therapy another day, even if he was upset with Alli.

She hurried home from work and left Gran watching television while she showered, put on a summer dress, and applied fresh makeup.

Gran widened her eyes at Alli's dress. "Do you have a date tonight?" she asked.

"No. I just thought it would be nice to put on a dress for a change." She rolled the wheelchair beside the bed. "I thought we might have steaks and baked potatoes tonight."

"You're going to give my cholesterol a break," Gran chortled.

Alli gave her an impish grin. "I took an extra steak out of the freezer. I'll ask Case to stay for dinner."

Gran frowned. "I forgot to tell you. Case sent another therapist to do my exercises this morning."

Alli bent to swing Gran's feet to the edge of the bed, keeping her head down longer than necessary. She didn't speak until she had Gran in the wheelchair. By that time she managed to pull her voice out of her shoes.

The next day she haunted the halls looking for Case. She offered to hand-carry physicians' orders to the therapy department and took morning, lunch, and afternoon breaks in the cafeteria. Misery clung to her like moss on a dank wall. Even seeing Case with Mona was better than not seeing him at all.

She'd clocked out at three-thirty and went to his office, only to find he wasn't in. His secretary said he was at a conference and she expected him to return on Friday.

Alli winced. Friday was her day off.

At home she moped all evening. Traveling was a distant memory. Not even a pleasant one. Friday morning she dragged herself from bed after a restless night. She took an hour to make breakfast, looking up a recipe for Belgian waffles. She microwaved bacon and peeled oranges, sliced bananas, and added half a can of leftover fruit cocktail for a fruit cup. She insisted they eat on the patio so Gran could breathe the fresh air. And she didn't eat three bites.

By ten o'clock she decided her present level of anxiety was unendurable. She had to know if Case was avoiding *her* now. Admitting the possibility shredded another layer from her already threadbare confidence. Had Case accepted her decision to return to Chicago and decided to look closer to home for a woman who would be happy to live in Wayside? Her anxiety level rose like a hot-air balloon. She had to tell him she'd changed her mind—to convince him she knew now she'd rather be bored in Wayside than miserable in Hawaii or Venice or any of the faraway places she dreamed about. Yet she was afraid he'd tell her he'd changed his mind too.

By noon she couldn't bear to stay home any longer. She showered, dressed, and told Gran she had to go to the store. Instead, trepidation pricking her nerves, she drove to the hospital. Her nerves received a momentary reprieve when the familiar outline of Case's old truck loomed in the back parking lot.

Her nerves kicked in again when she entered the physical therapy department's reception room. Case's secretary, her ear snuggled against the telephone receiver, glanced up and motioned Alli to wait. Alli went to sit down and then stopped. She hadn't been hesitant in rebuffing Case . . . and what she felt now was more important, so why was she standing in a waiting room? The door to his office was open, and he stood beside his desk, apparently alone.

Readjusting a downhill slide of insecurity to a radiant smile, she strode past the secretary and through the door of Case's office.

He was dressed in a dark suit, with his back to Alli, and she gazed at his broad shoulders admiringly. Unaware of her entry, he sank into a high-backed leather chair and picked up the receiver from the desk, swinging around to look up as he spoke into the telephone. A smile lit his face, and he motioned her to sit down.

If she'd thought he looked great in shorts at the river, he looked equally handsome in a three-piece suit. In fact, he'd look good to her in just about anything.

He replaced the receiver. "Good morning, Alli." His eyes lingered on her summer dress admiringly. "That doesn't look like any uniform I've seen around the hospital."

"Hi, Case." She felt like a fool. Her carefully prepared speech stopped somewhere behind the boulder in her throat and disintegrated at the look in Case's eyes.

His line buzzed discreetly again, and he looked at her with a resigned apology and picked up the telephone. This time the call was longer. She stood up to leave, and he motioned her to stay. She took the time to try to recall her speech. It was still lost on some brain disc when Case spoke to her.

"It must be your day off," he said cheerfully.

She nodded.

"You're just in the neighborhood?"

"Actually, Case, I came to see you."

"I'm delighted."

"I wanted to tell you. . . ." She hesitated. Where

were the words she'd thought so appropriate early this morning? She looked at a seascape behind his desk. He looked at her intently.

"I wanted to tell you that I want to take back everything I said in the mountains. I was wrong about my job being so important. I can't be happy traveling when my heart is in Wayside."

She wished he'd stop staring at her and say something. She knew what she wanted to say was coming out all wrong. "I plan to resign my position with the health-care company and accept a full-time position here in Wayside if one is available." She felt her heart sinking. His eyes didn't light up the way she'd expected.

"Alli, I've been thinking too. It was selfish of me to expect you to give up your job. No matter what you say now, I know how much you like your work. In time, just as you said, you would be unhappy here." He took a deep breath. "I don't think you should resign."

She felt numb. She'd told herself he might have changed his mind, but when it came down to it, she was shocked. He was still speaking, but she couldn't hear him. He didn't want her. That's all that was important. Apologies weren't necessary. He didn't have to try to soften the blow.

She saw his face change, and he looked over her shoulder and nodded. She pulled her thoughts back to the room, hearing his secretary's voice dimly behind her saying something about a Miss Clark waiting in the lobby.

Case stood up. "Alli, I'm sorry to have to leave, but I have a luncheon engagement."

"I understand, Case," she said in confusion. "I should have called."

"You never have to call for me to want to see you. But I do have an important appointment."

She stood up in a daze, vaguely hearing Case assure her he'd call. She nodded dully, then hurried out of the office and down the hall in the opposite direction of the lobby. She'd suddenly realized Mona's last name was Clark.

Depressed, she drove to the supermarket and sat in the car, staring at the people hurrying by. Her decision had been too late. Case had made his own decision. What was it Gran had said? Case might decide he didn't want a wife with her body in Wayside and her heart in faraway places? *"Maybe he's thinking of you more than himself—maybe he loves you enough to want you to be happy,"* Gran had said. Alli felt tears sting her eyes. How could she ever be happy again? Finally she started the car and drove home. But she didn't tell Gran how prophetic her words had been.

She fixed lunch and escaped to the backyard to weed Gran's herb garden. She moped through a television program while Gran slept. She dawdled about fixing dinner, finally ordering pizza, to Gran's delight.

When the doorbell rang, she expected the pizza man

and found a young man holding a basket with half a dozen balloon animals attached.

"Alli Parmer?" he inquired cheerfully.

She nodded, accepting the basket reluctantly as she peered at the English-Italian dictionary and sheath of travel folders resting inside. Who else but Case would send the familiar balloons? And travel folders? Was this a new way to send a Dear Jane letter? She blinked, barely able to mutter a polite thank-you to the man.

"Wait," he said with a grin. "There's more."

He bounced away, and Alli glanced at the floral-shop truck parked in front of the house. She gasped. He pulled a second basket from the panel truck, and even at a distance the red roses and a bouquet of red-and-white balloons was clearly discernible.

"Two more," he announced before Alli could open her mouth. He returned minutes later with the two baskets. Balloons bobbled in colorful profusion over a bottle of wine nestled in artificial greenery in one and an assortment of crackers and bread sticks and cheeses in the other.

Still clutching the basket of roses, Alli accepted the gifts one at a time and set them on the entry table. Her thoughts reeled.

"Wish I'd thought of this when I proposed," the young man said. Then he grinned sheepishly, his cheeks coloring, and darted back to the panel truck before Alli could move.

She didn't move for another minute. She looked at

the baskets and the contents, half afraid of the elation rising in her. Slowly she closed the door.

Wine, bread, cheese. . . . The words had a familiar ring, but she hadn't read poetry since high school—or was it junior high? Nostalgia surfaced briefly. She'd liked poetry, but time to read poetry dwindled when she had to read nursing journals and keep up on advances in nursing. She wondered when Case had time to read anything but therapy journals. Maybe he didn't. Maybe she was seeing sustenance for the soul when Case was merely sending food as an apology for not taking her to lunch.

The thought didn't keep her from savoring the scent of the roses as she sorted through the baskets. An English-Italian dictionary nestled amid a stack of travel folders for Venice, Italy, in the first one she looked at. She started and drew a deep breath, her heart swelling like a helium-filled balloon as she read the attached note. *I hear Venice is romantic, and I have vacation time. Do you?* It was signed, *Case*.

Alli placed the baskets back on the table and went to tell Gran the delivery wasn't from the pizza parlor.

"I can see that," Gran said. "I can also see Case arriving." She grinned. "I suggest you put some romantic music on the stereo. You might also close my door as you leave. That way the music won't disturb my television program."

Alli picked up the travel folders on her way to answer the door. Case grinned broadly, looking from the folders to her face.

"Do I see a yes in your eyes?"

Alli couldn't stop smiling. "To what?" she said mischievously.

"To a trip to Santa Catalina tomorrow?" he said. He pointed to the top folder.

She looked down and noticed the ad for the boat to Catalina atop the other folders.

"I'm working," she groaned.

"Sunday?"

"Working."

"How about a trip to Venice?"

"Venice, California?" she asked innocently.

"Venice, Italy. I hear it's a great place for a honeymoon."

"Oh, Case!" Alli placed the folders carefully on the table and stood on tiptoes to kiss him lightly on the lips. Before she could lower her heels, he pulled her into his arms.

"Not so fast. Does that mean yes, you'll marry me, and yes, we'll go to Venice?"

"Yes, yes, yes," she said, offering him her lips.

"Do you think we can learn to speak a little Italian by the end of summer?"

"Why the end of summer?" she said dreamily.

"That's when I put in for the rest of my vacation. I'd planned to spend the time getting the new business started. But business isn't as important as you are. So we'll travel."

Alli's heart soared. Anywhere with Case would be Venice.

"You didn't tell me what kind of business," she said languidly.

"You didn't ask."

"I'm asking now." She feathered kisses on his lips.

"I don't want to talk business now." His hands moved against her back as he returned her kisses.

She pulled back. "Gran told me to put a romantic melody on the stereo. What's she going to think if all she hears is silence?"

"She's going to think we're doing just what we're doing." He kissed her again.

The doorbell sounded, and Alli made a face and pulled herself from Case's arms. "I ordered pizza."

"I'll get the pizza," he said firmly, "while you find the romantic music."

Half an hour later, with Gran insisting she wanted to stay in her room to eat while she watched a television special, Alli placed the basket of roses and stack of travel folders on one side of the coffee table in the family room. "I'll find a corkscrew so you can open the wine while I slice the cheese." She started toward the kitchen.

Carrying the wine, Case followed. "I'm not letting you out of my sight tonight. You might change your mind."

"No chance." Alli beamed. "I'm afraid you're committed, Case." Her eyes clung to him lovingly.

He opened the wine and kissed the nape of her neck. She handed him glasses and kissed the hollow of his throat. When she reached for the cheese board, he wrapped his arms around her waist.

"Case, you'll waste away if you don't let me fix the food."

"I'm not hungry for food." With sighs of reluctance, he released her and sliced the pizza. "When I think of it, I should be hungry. I think I talked more than I ate at lunch."

Lunch. Alli's heart dipped fleetingly, recalling his appointment with Mona. She steadied her hand on the cheese board. "Did your luncheon appointment have something to do with your business venture?"

"It sure did." Elation rose in his voice.

"Well, are you going to tell me about it or keep teasing me?"

"I'm going into partnership in an outpatient physical-therapy clinic with Tom Carpenter. He's Mona Clark's fiancé." Case grinned with maddening casualness. "I guess you plan to eat in the family room, so I'll take the wine in and come back to help with the rest."

He returned minutes later, continuing as if he hadn't left the room. "We've been working on it for six months or so. I went to see Tom on my vacation. He came here today. I think it's about sewed up."

"How are you going to manage a business and work at the hospital?" Alli didn't really care about the answer. Her heart was too happy. He hadn't been interested in Mona at all, except as the fiancée of his new partner.

''It'll be almost a year before the building is ready. Then we figure it will take a little time to build the business so it will support us.''

''If I work at the hospital, could you afford to work at your business full-time?''

''You're forgetting, I still owe the hospital some time.''

Alli placed the cheese and bread on a tray. ''Will your therapy compete with the hospital?''

''No. In fact, the CEO was at the meeting. He'd rather have me opening an outpatient department than someone they don't know.'' He lifted the pizza pan. ''He's quite enthusiastic about our plans for a cardiac rehab exercise program and an aerobics class and an exercise program for weight reduction. He had a few suggestions. If people stay in Wayside for the programs, they're more likely to return to the hospital for necessary tests and hospitalization.''

Alli followed Case to the family room and slid her tray on the table. ''I'll send in my resignation to Chicago next week.'' She didn't even feel a twinge at saying the words as she sat on the couch beside Case. She still wasn't sure how long her elation would keep the boredom of Wayside at bay. But with Case nearby she'd work it out.

Case poured wine into the glasses and turned to face her. ''I want to talk to you about that.'' He fingered the ribbon of a balloon attached to the basket of roses. ''I've been selfish to think lead feet and love are synonymous.'' He pulled the balloon free. ''I don't want the love to leak out of our life because you're tethered to Wayside.'' He wrapped the ribbon loosely around her wrist. ''Your career is as important to you as mine is to me, so I have a suggestion.''

His fingers tap-danced gently on her arm. ''Nursing, as well as nursing hours, has changed at the hospital. Some nurses work four-hour shifts, and some work eight- and ten- and twelve-hour shifts. Some work weekends; some work three days or four. Maybe your CEO would accept a four-day week or, even better, a three-day workweek.'' He raised his fingers to move them slowly along her jawline. ''Didn't you say you spent your days off and holidays at home in Chicago?''

Alli nodded, watching his eyes sparkle.

''Why couldn't your home base be in Wayside? You could fly in for the monthly briefing as you did this time.''

Alli's heart soared. Having Case and her career too—it was more than she'd dreamed possible.

''If you need any help at negotiating, I'm experienced. I've been working on this outpatient clinic thing a long time.''

She leaned forward to snuggle against his chest, and her heart floated back into place. But it continued to beat with outrageous euphoria. Case fever, undeniably Case fever, she determined happily. She'd never recover . . . and she'd never want to, ever again.

	DATE DUE		

Little X

❋ Little X

Growing Up in the Nation of Islam

Sonsyrea Tate

HarperSanFrancisco
A Division of HarperCollins*Publishers*

 For information address HarperCollins Publishers, 10 East 53rd Street, New York, NY 10022.

HarperCollins Web Site: http://www.harpercollins.com

HarperCollins®, ®, and HarperSanFrancisco™ are trademarks of HarperCollins Publishers.

FIRST HARPERCOLLINS PAPERBACK EDITION PUBLISHED IN 1998

Library of Congress Cataloging-in-Publication Data

Tate, Sonsyrea.
Little X : growing up in the Nation of Islam / Sonsyrea Tate. — 1st ed.
ISBN 0–06–251134–3 (cloth)
ISBN 0–06–251135–1 (pbk.)
1. Tate, Sonsyrea. 2. Black Muslim—Biography. 3. Black Muslims—Controversial literature. 4. Afro-American women—Biography. 5. Young adults and religion/children. I. Title.
BP223.Z8L57769 1997
297'.87—dc20 96–25666

98 99 00 01 02 RRD(H) 10 9 8 7 6 5 4 3 2 1

To all the brothers who ain't here: Uncle Hussein,
Uncle Edward, Billy, Everrete, and Chris Reddick.

Also my homegirl, Robin, who fell in the struggle.

Contents

Acknowledgments

Thanks to Patrice Gaines for getting me started by insisting that "everybody has a story to tell." Thanks to my agent, Denise Stinson, for encouraging me to write my story down. And other editor-friends who helped me shape it for presentation—Tsi Tsi Wahkisi, Marc Tibbs, and Rosemary Armao.

Thanks to all the supporters at HarperSanFrancisco—Andrea Lewis, Kandace Hawkinson, and Caroline Pincus.

Thanks to my family and friends who completely and tirelessly supported me in thousands of ways, big and small. Especially Darren, GrandWillie, Uncle Avon, Uncle Wallace, Uncle Sharrief, Ma and Dad, and my other siblings for the memories. Thanks to Grandma and Grandaddy Thomas for love, room, and board. Also thanks to Aunt Brenda and Uncle Butch for believing in me.

A very special thanks to alla my ladies and my mens: Aunt Nell and Chee-Chee for hanging with me through countless hours of whining; to Chris Reddick and Uptown Mr. P. Brown for their broad shoulders to cry on; and D. R. Hunter for friendship.

Everyone offered so much encouragement. I would not have made it without them.

Introduction

It all started when a fair-skinned fellow named W. Fard Muhammad arrived in Detroit, Michigan, from the holy city Mecca. The year was 1930. Mr. Muhammad said he'd come to save the lost-found tribe of Shabazz. Came to save us—the so-called Negro. Here in this wilderness of North America. He said all we Negroes had to do was follow his program. We could rule the world, starting with this country. We were the Original Man. Maker. Owner. Cream of the planet Earth. Father of civilization. God of the universe.

Mr. Muhammad said he knew what our problem had been. We had been praying to the wrong God. There was no blond-haired, blue-eyed man named Jesus. No spook of a God looking down on us from someplace above the clouds. No such abstract entity held our fate in his hands. That's where we'd gone wrong, he said. Our ancestors' prayers had gone in vain because they had been praying to the wrong God. For four hundred years of slavery, the spook God had failed us, Mr. Muhammad said. And for a few generations after that, God's chariot still failed to swing low enough for our rescue.

When Mr. Muhammad arrived on the scene, all of America was depressed—economically speaking—and her Negroes were doubly devastated. So it was easy enough to believe in a man like Mr. Muhammad. Peddling silk scarves and self-esteem door-to-door, Mr. Muhammad built a sizable enough base in Detroit's ghettos. He established his first Temple of Islam. Then in 1934 he mysteriously disappeared, and his devout disciple, Elijah Poole, took over leadership of the organization and assumed the last name *Muhammad*.

The Nation of Islam encountered considerable opposition from the U.S. government early on. When the Nation opened its first school for the children, members were accused of going around to public schools begging the children to leave and go to the Muslim school. Elijah Muhammad was sentenced to six months' probation for refusing to take his children out of the Muslim school and put them in a public school. A year later, when another Muslim school was opened in Chicago, there were more charges of "contributing to the delinquency of minors," and another member was charged.

The Nation had other problems with the police and Federal Bureau of Investigation over the years, and in 1959 Detroit's State Department of Public Instruction, its fire department inspector, and two other government agencies poked through the Muslim school again and found enough holes in the walls to order the school closed down. But a few weeks later the school was back in operation.

In spite of considerable opposition, Elijah Muhammad expanded the Nation of Islam across the country and amassed power from the early 1930s to the mid-1970s. His Nation became the largest and most formidable all-black organization in America.

"Elijah Muhammad told the people what they needed to hear at the time," my grandmother told me. "They needed somebody to make them feel good about themselves. Somebody to tell them yes, they were good. Whereby the white man had treated us so bad and made us out to be the bad ones. Well, the Honorable Elijah Muhammad came along and did the reverse."

❋ ❋ ❋

My family was among tens of thousands who joined the Nation of Islam in search of a better way. In the Nation of Islam, we had our own identity and our own ethics. We had our own constitution, our own businesses, our own educational system—not just schools, but our own system and our own way of life.

When my grandparents joined the Nation of Islam, they replaced our family name with the letter X, a symbol that stood for hope deep-rooted and eternal. To a people weighted under racism, broken and embittered, disenchanted even with the black church, the Nation of Islam represented such hope. My family, like most black Americans, had been Christian for generations before my paternal grandparents joined the Nation of Islam in the early 1950s. My great-grandfather, in fact, had helped found a Holiness church. So for a long time I feared that the family chain linking me to my ancestors—and to my contemporary Christian relatives, for that matter—might forever be broken.

My grandparents liked the fact that in the Nation of Islam gender roles were clearly defined, rules were strictly enforced, and the individual god within each black person was acknowledged and respected. In the Nation little black boys and girls appeared well mannered because in school they were trained to believe that they were little gods and goddesses who would someday be leaders. In public school blacks were taught that our heritage began with us as slaves in America. In the Muslim schools children are taught that we were kings and queens in Asia while white men still were running around uncivilized and naked in caves.

Growing up with a sense of self-respect would mean growing up with a sense of responsibility. In the Nation children learned to love themselves and love people who were like us. This was the education my grandparents wanted for their children, the education my parents wanted for me. When I became a third-generation X, I, too, would learn self-reliance, discipline, and self-respect.

Most of the families in our Nation were poor, but we learned that killing and stealing from one another were not options. We were taught that if you had one green pea, you split that pea and shared it with your brother. If a mother had only five dollars, she should put hers with a sister's dollars to buy groceries together.

We were taught that cleanliness was next to godliness, and the sharp, clean, righteous men and women in the Nation provided examples of what I could become.

Looking at the carnage of black men through the eighties and early nineties, I considered it a sad excuse that we would kill one another for drugs. Or for anything. In the Nation I had learned that one of the white man's tricks would be to starve us and deprive us and turn us against one another.

When I watched the river of beautiful black men pour forth on the monument grounds as part of the Louis Farrakhan–led Million Man March in the summer of 1995, I thought about the many lessons that troubled young men and women could learn from the discipline exhibited by the Nation members involved.

While I was growing up, the Fruit of Islam, the security unit of the Nation of Islam, had made me, a small black child, feel safer than I felt at any other time in America. There were tense times and painful episodes. Indeed, my life as an African American Muslim girl was bittersweet.

❊ ❊ ❊

After leaving the Nation, my family journeyed through several interpretations of Orthodox Islam. But in the midst of praying five times a day, something went wrong and I watched my family fall apart. I wasn't sure whether we fell because of our Islam or despite it. I set out to examine my life to find some answers. I hoped that by writing it all down, spelling it all out, it would begin to make sense.

Opening Prayer

CHAPTER 1

I knew I wasn't supposed to, but I couldn't help myself. I had to peep so I could make sure everybody else's eyes were shut tight like they were supposed to be. I was always the one peeping, trying to see something. All nine of my classmates had their eyes closed while we recited our prayer to begin our day.

"Surely I have turned myself to Thee, O Allah. To Him who created the heavens and the Earth. I am not of the polytheists. I am of those who submit."

All our little-girl voices blended into one voice under our teacher, Sister Barbara, whose voice spread over ours like an umbrella. We followed her lead, pronouncing certain words in a high pitch and certain words low, just the way we were trained. For me, at age three, it was as easy as singing a nursery rhyme, though I didn't understand a word of it.

This was level one, the grade where we did kindergarten and first-grade work at Elijah Muhammad's University of Islam in Washington, D.C. All of us knew our ABCs. We could sing them and write them, but Sister Barbara pasted pictures of each letter across the top of the blackboard at the front of the class in case we forgot how to make a letter. She had Arabic letters up on the wall, too. And numbers going down the side of the board.

The dark green and black pictures stood out extra specially because the white walls were so bright. That's what I liked about our little classroom. Even though it was crowded with Sister Barbara's desk and a table full of papers under the window, and even though we had to squeeze past the other chairs to get out to the bathroom, the room was bright. We had three big windows with venetian blinds our teacher kept closed because she didn't want anybody off the street looking in on us.

At three, I was the smallest one standing around our long dark brown table. All of us had our heads bowed and our hands cupped in front of us. I moved my head from side to side and made tight fists with my hands to see if they would turn red. Anything to be different. Mostly, we were all the same. We all wore the same green uniforms, wide-legged pantaloons, long tops that reached almost to our knees like a short dress over our pants, and white headpieces.

"Surely my prayers and my sacrifice, my life and my death are all for Thee, O Allah. Lord of all the worlds. No associate has he and this I am commanded."

As my lips moved, I wondered what a "polytheist" was and what a "sacrifice" did. I knew what "my prayers" meant because my teacher had already explained that part. Saying prayer was like talking to God on an invisible phone, she had told us.

"I have been greatly unjust to myself and I confess my faults," our prayer continued. I'd have to ask Ma what a "confess" was later on when I got home. I knew a fault was when you sneaked to do something, thinking nobody saw you. Allah was always watching and always counting up your faults. Every time I sneaked a piece of candy out of my uncles' coat pockets, that was another fault. So I had to keep saying prayer, asking Allah not to be mad at me. The grown-ups had bigger faults, so they had to pray five times every day. I was little, so I only had to say prayers in school.

"Grant me protection against all my faults, for none grants protection against faults but Thou." I wondered if my classmates understood a little better since they all were a year or two older than me. When I peeped again, I caught one of the older girls doing the same thing. We both snapped our wandering eyes shut again.

"Oh Allah, bless Muhammad and the followers of Muhammad." That was us in the Nation of Islam, I knew. "As Thou did bless Abraham and the followers of Abraham. For surely Thou are praised and magnified. Amen."

With that we sat down and waited for Sister Barbara to give us our assignments. We said prayer at the end of the school day, too, and that prayer made me think of other questions. Every day when we prayed I thought about the questions and reminded myself to ask my mother when I got home. But every day I forgot because at home other questions popped up in my head.

❃ ❃ ❃

I rode the public bus home from school and wondered why I was the only one on there dressed in funny clothes. Nobody else wore a scarf tied under her chin, and nobody else wore balloon pants. Most of the women wore hip-hugging, flare-legged pants, with their hair picked out in a fluffy bush or Afro puffs. This was 1969, a time of self-celebration in the black community, and James Brown's "I'm Black and I'm Proud" was the number one song. A lot of people knew about the Nation of Islam, which had been around since 1930, so I didn't know why I looked so strange to some people I passed on the bus. Two ladies in particular pointed at me and whispered, but Uncle Sharrief, my teenage uncle who had brought me home on the bus, told me just to ignore the women, which I did. Still, I wanted to know why.

"GrandWillie, these ladies was pointing at me again," I told my grandmother as soon as I got in the house. GrandWillie always met me at the front door and helped me take off my coat. She wasn't that much taller than me, so she didn't have to bend too far to help me.

"I can do it," I said, preferring to unzip my own coat. I was a big girl now. I knew how to tie my own shoes and lotion my own legs getting ready for school in the mornings.

"Sonsyrea, your zipper is stuck. Hold still so I can help you," she said, tugging at my orange vinyl plastic coat. It was all I could do to keep balanced on my feet while she wrestled with my coat. GrandWillie had strong hands.

The house smelled like a forest again, which meant Ma was upstairs cleaning the bathroom with Pine-Sol. All the little kids Ma and GrandWillie baby-sat were down for their afternoon naps. So the house was quiet, all except for the TV playing Ma's favorite soap opera, *One Life to Live*, which she caught glimpses of through her chores. She wasn't supposed to be watching that junk. GrandWillie told her it wasn't good to watch that stuff because it would brainwash her. And GrandWillie knew what she was talking about because she listened to the Messenger every Sunday and read his newspapers and books through the week. Plus, she went to Muslim Girls' Training and General Civilization Class on Saturdays, so she knew what was best for Ma. But Ma still found a way to do what she wanted to do, so she let the TV run and did her chores during commercials.

"Saray, I laid your play clothes out on the bed," Ma said as she brushed past me and GrandWillie, still fiddling with my zipper. Ma called me Saray, Sonsyrea, or Ray-Ray, depending on what mood she was in. And GrandWillie would call me Ray-Ray, Sonsalay-lay, or my real name, Sonsyrea, which Ma got from a cowboy movie. Sonsyrea was the main female character, an Indian woman whose name meant "Morning Star."

Ma was short like GrandWillie, and they dressed the same—like me—in long clothes and scarves. Ma looked like Minnie Mouse on the cartoons she let us watch sometimes, and GrandWillie reminded me of Mama Bear in my *Goldilocks* book. We didn't have fairy tale books at my Muslim school because my teacher said we didn't need to read about any silly little white kids. But when Ma took us to the library, those were the only kinds of books they had in the children's section.

"Ma, did you match my clothes right?" I asked, because sometimes Ma put the wrong colors together and I had to get GrandWillie to tell her to let me wear something else. I knew Ma was smarter than me 'cause she was the mother, but since GrandWillie was the grandmother, she was the smartest. Still sometimes Ma got mad when I went behind her back to GrandWillie, so she made me wear the mismatched clothes anyway just because she was mad.

It was late in the afternoon, almost three o'clock, and the beautiful, bright sun washed over the street like lemon air. We lived in Washington, D.C., the best place in the world, a beautiful city with big green parks and downtown office buildings resembling oversized cereal boxes and animal cracker boxes. Some of the buildings were famous, for instance, the Washington Monument, the Lincoln Memorial, the Kennedy Center, and the U.S. Capitol building.

Our house was in the Kingman neighborhood in the northeast section of town. In our neighborhood, working-class black families lived in two-story brick row houses, each with a porch and small patch of yard, or in small apartment buildings. Girls jumped rope on the sidewalks, and boys played touch football in the street. An old man named Mr. Floyd owned the corner store, and in the evenings teenage boys met in front of the store and cracked jokes on one another.

"Man, your breath smell like the back of a Chinese restaurant," one would say, making the others burst out laughing. Sometimes Uncle Avon, who was about twenty, took me with him to the store, and I'd hear the guys going.

Whenever Uncle Avon walked up with me on his shoulders, the guys knew they had to watch their mouths because Uncle Avon had told them not to cuss around me. The men in our neighborhood treated us special—especially me, Ma, and GrandWillie—because they knew we were Muslims and you couldn't disrespect a Muslim woman. They didn't whistle at Ma the way they whistled at other women, and when the older teenage boys saw GrandWillie trying to flag a cab they helped her.

But the women treated us strange—and not just in our neighborhood. In the grocery store or on the buses, they would point, roll their eyes as they passed us, or say nothing at all. Ma and GrandWillie acted like they didn't notice, but I caught everything. GrandWillie said it was because I was too sensitive.

"GrandWillie, how come they was pointing? You not 'sposed to point, right?" I asked again one afternoon.

GrandWillie flung my coat over the banister and leaned over to explain it to me one more time.

"Sonsyrea, you're special," she said slowly and precisely, her deep voice falling over me. "Don't make no never mind if somebody else don't like the clothes you wear. You wear these 'cause you're a Muslim!" Anytime GrandWillie started pointing with one hand, the other one braced on her hip, I knew she was doubly serious.

"Don't make no never mind." Her words would stay in my head. I'm special, I thought. GrandWillie made it sound so good. Special. I didn't realize that *special* was also a word to describe kids born crippled. Children with one leg too short or one arm missing were special, and babies born with some kind of mental disease were special, too. Although GrandWillie didn't mean this kind of special, I later realized mine was a social handicap. Growing up Muslim was going to be special.

❊ ❊ ❊

Our house was on Corbin Place, a quiet street lined with old shady trees, flower beds, and street lights. The street would get noisy as the children started getting home from the public schools around us. They traveled in pairs and groups and laughed and pushed at one another like everything was so much fun. Some of them weren't even carrying books. What was so funny? Why did they think they had time to mosey down the street playing and stuff? Didn't they have chores and homework to do?

When I got home, I hurried to change out of my uniform and help Ma or GrandWillie with cleaning or cooking. Since my family was Muslim, I wasn't allowed to rip and run in the streets with the "uncivilized" non-Muslim children. Instead, I spent my time at GrandWillie's elbow, and I enjoyed having her full attention while we worked and talked from one end of the house to the other.

Aunt Gay had come in while I was upstairs, and I heard her Temptations eight-track playing from the basement. "Return your love to me. Forgive me for the wrong I've done. . . ."

I bopped to the beats and wished I didn't have my headpiece on so my plaits could swing free. The music played louder than the TV, which was still running, though no one watched. All three floors of our house stayed busy—and full. Someone was always passing through the front foyer, putting on a coat or taking one off. Going up the stairs or coming down.

Ma, Dad, my brother, and I had our own apartment in the same neighborhood, but we spent most of the day here at GrandWillie and Granddad's. Dad's piano, which he played some evenings when he was making up a new song, stood alone in one corner in the basement. The living and dining rooms were always full of the kids that GrandWillie and Ma baby-sat. Kids taking naps, eating snacks, or sitting on the floor coloring their daily lessons.

"Oh, oh, oh, P-lease give your love to me," the Temptations played on. I was grooving, but GrandWillie didn't seem to hear it as she stood at the sink snapping green beans for dinner. I pulled up my sleeves and slid my step stool next to her to help.

While GrandWillie and I snapped beans in the kitchen, Ma was busy tending to the children. Although the house was always busy, the busyness never bothered me and GrandWillie when we worked and talked. We chatted about the way things were when she was little, and I found her more entertaining than the TV or the music.

"When you was little, did y'all used to go to church as much as we go to the Temple?" I asked. I enjoyed listening to GrandWillie talk about her "good old days," the 1930s and '40s.

"See, when I was coming along, black people believed in the Church," she said. The Church, as far as we Muslims were concerned, included any that was non-Muslim.

"Back in my days, black people listened to their ministers," she said. "When you had a problem, if you needed help with your family, or if you was just feeling bad, you knew the minister could help you.

"There was always something to do at the church," GrandWillie told me. "You might be needed to cook or help clean and get it ready for service. Always something. And our church always knew they could count on the Haynie family to get things done," she said, remembering how her thirteen sisters and brothers always worked in the church. After all, their father had helped build the Bethlehem Church of God and Holiness.

Without looking at her, I could hear the smile in her voice. It was a kind of smile that confirmed her pride in our family's history, a pride she was trying to impart to me.

"Why did y'all stop going to church?" I asked, reaching into the bowl. My hands looked like small pecans, and GrandWillie's were dark and smooth like Brazil nuts.

"Oh, it's a long story," she said, offering nothing more.

I would piece together the story over the years.

❋ ❋ ❋

GrandWillie met her husband in the family church but left the church soon after they wed. One day in 1952, Granddaddy Tate had come home from his job at the railroad station, telling GrandWillie about a man named Elijah Muhammad. Mr. Muhammad preached that God was a black man who once walked the streets here in North America and that he, Mr. Muhammad, was God's messenger sent to teach black people about our true history and our true selves. A friend at the railroad where Granddaddy cleaned trains had told Granddaddy Tate all this, then had taken him to a meeting after work so Granddaddy could hear more.

Granddaddy had never even considered that God might be a black man. But such an idea certainly was worth looking into. When he and his friend from work sat in the little storefront building listening to the minister talk about a black God who came to America to save black people, it seemed to make sense. Maybe the white man was the devil and the black man was God, as the minister taught.

Only white devils would have brought Africans over here as desperate slaves and taught them to pray to a white man on a cross. "Christianity was a trick played on black people," the man named Brother Minister Isaiah said. "Free yourself. Come to Islam, come to freedom. Let us build our own Nation."

Granddaddy, who was cocoa colored and stout and usually wore dungarees or overalls, came home all excited after hearing the minister.

"Willie, you gotta see this man! I can't tell you 'bout him 'cause you gotta see him for yourself." Granddaddy talked more southern than GrandWillie because he was from North Carolina. He went to grab GrandWillie around her waist like he always did when he got home, but she stiffened up on him because she was mad.

It was late in the evening, dark outside, and the children had gotten hungry waiting for him to get home for dinner. GrandWillie, wrapped in her apron, short dress, and wedge-heel slippers, slopped pork and beans on my father's plate and proceeded around the yellow metal table in the dining room. My father, their eldest son, named Joseph after his daddy, was six years old. His toddler brothers, Avon and Edward, were perched on thick phone books in their chairs so they could reach the table, and their sister, Carolyn, who was the eldest, ate in the kitchen because there weren't enough chairs in the dining room.

"Willie, this brother went on and on about who the white man really is and how there gon' be a time when we take over." Granddaddy didn't pay no attention to GrandWillie being mad at him. He went in the kitchen and washed his hands, still talking. The boys knew better than to say anything when he was talking, so they kept their faces focused on their plates.

GrandWillie tipped back in the kitchen and reached for the pot of hot dogs with her potholder. She rolled her eyes at her husband because she had expected him home hours ago, right after work. GrandWillie never fussed or yelled, but she had little ways of showing when she was angry. She slammed the pots in the sink and cut her eyes some more.

"Willie, I'm gon' take the whole family to see him," Granddaddy told her.

The next Sunday morning, GrandWillie took out the avocado green skirt suit she used to wear when she had a job as a secretary. That was before she had kids and Granddaddy told her it would be better for her to stay home and take care of them. Since he was ten years older than she was, she figured he knew what was best.

"Willie, I can't find my socks," her eldest son demanded from the kitchen doorway as his mother stirred grits on the stove. Dad called her by her first name because that's the way Granddaddy got her attention. GrandWillie didn't care that her children didn't call her Mother or Mom. But Granddaddy insisted his children call him Daddy.

"They're in the basement with the other laundry, June," she told him. June was short for Junior. That's what they called Dad when he was little.

"Willie, where my good shoes?" Granddaddy shouted from upstairs.

GrandWillie was humming one of her old gospel favorites while she worked in the kitchen. "June, go upstairs and tell your father to look in the closet," GrandWillie said. She could have hollered upstairs, but GrandWillie was too modest to raise her voice.

Once they were all dressed they caught the bus, taking up only two seats because GrandWillie and Granddaddy kept the little ones on their laps. Everybody had gotten excited listening to Granddaddy talk about the new kind of church.

GrandWillie could tell when she first walked in that this group was different, and not just because all the women were wearing scarves on their heads and modest dresses cut below their knees. To her it looked like one big happy family.

"As-Salaam-Alaikum, my beautiful sister," the women at the Muslim church greeted GrandWillie and her little daughter before escorting them to the sister side of the audience.

The room was small with a rickety stage as the pulpit, but it was neat and sparkling clean compared to its surroundings in the poor neighborhood. There were no stained-glass windows like the ones at the church GrandWillie grew up in, and people sat in fold-up chairs instead of benches.

There was no singing of gospel hymns, no members of the congregation shouting, "Thank you, Jesus!" and the minister wasn't whooping and hollering at his audience. He spoke in a plain speaking voice instead of a loud singsong like black Southern Christian or Baptist preachers.

"Brothers and sisters, I'm here to tell you, stop praying to some man on the cross. How's he going to save you? Has that white man come down from his cross to save you from sickness and suffering and indignation? No." People closer to the front were nodding agreeably. GrandWillie kept her eye on the minister, thinking about his questions, not having enough time to answer them in her head before he asked another.

"Do you know anybody who's been to a heaven up in the sky and seen this invisible spook God they say this Jesus has become? No." He spoke in measured tones, at a deliberate pace.

Before she knew it, she was nodding in agreement. She would have time to ponder later. On the men's side, Granddaddy sat there smiling, his three boys seated next to him. It would be good to teach them about a black god. A couple of hours passed on the clock behind them, and the minister up front was coming to a close.

"At this time, we would like all those visiting us for the first time to please stand at your seat," the minister said. Ushers on both sides handed visitors an index card with blank lines for a name, address, and phone number, and tiny boxes at the bottom so they could write X if they believed what they heard during the service was true and if they wanted to join the group.

"Take a minute to think about what you've heard today," the minister continued. "And if you agree," he smiled. "And I'm sure you will because you're intelligent people. Complete the information on the card and give it to your brother or sister at the door. I leave you with the Arabic words of peace and paradise. As-Salaam-Alaikum."

GrandWillie put her card in her purse and sat back down. As they were leaving, Granddaddy was about to give his card to the brother, but GrandWillie reached for it and Granddaddy let her have it.

That night, he and GrandWillie talked about joining the Nation of Islam.

"Joe, I think we should think about it a little first," Grand-

Willie told him. "Won't hurt none to take a little time."

In those days the group was small, with fewer than fifty followers in Washington, D.C. When Elijah Muhammad first started organizing in Washington, he had to hide out because the government was always trying to find some reason to arrest him, GrandWillie had told me. For instance, he had been arrested and thrown in jail for dodging the draft in World War II and then got into more trouble because he advised his followers to "refuse to fight the white man's war."

"Joe, I'm going to turn in our cards today," GrandWillie said one Sunday morning as she took out her clothes for service.

She handed both their cards to the sister as they were leaving the service that Sunday, and Granddaddy winked at her.

By now, they'd learned that in order to become official Nation members, GrandWillie and Granddaddy had to write a letter to the Honorable Elijah Muhammad at his headquarters in Chicago. The next morning, GrandWillie read over the letter, which they had to copy from papers they got at the Temple. The letter read:

"Dear Savior Allah, our deliverer who came in the person of Master Fard Muhammad, to whom praises are forever due. I bear witness that there is no God but Thee and that Elijah Muhammad is Thy Servant and Apostle. I desire to reclaim my own. I desire a name from Thee. Please give me my original name. My slave name is as follows. . . ."

Initially, my grandparents and their children would be labeled X like babies born again into a new world. Over time they could earn a name that best described their character when the Nation officials deemed them worthy.

A few weeks passed, and my grandparents received a response from Chicago. Mr. and Mrs. Tate became Sister Willie X and Brother Joseph 10X. Granddaddy found a new brotherhood, and GrandWillie was embraced by the sisters.

Nation of Islam members paid special attention to new recruits. Two women from the Temple began visiting GrandWillie at home, helping her with her housework. Dressed in their Nation of Islam long dresses and headpieces, they looked like strange nuns or nurses when they arrived at my grandparents' house. They showed GrandWillie how to make bean soup and whole wheat bread. This was better than hot dogs, pork and beans, and biscuits, they told her. While they worked the sisters talked about the Nation's history and why they had so many rules to follow.

They told GrandWillie that her children shouldn't be running around with the uncivilized children in the neighborhood. They needed to be inside studying their schoolwork, and the girl, Aunt Carolyn, who was seven, should be in the kitchen with them.

The years passed, and GrandWillie got pregnant again and again. The sisters told her it was a wonderful blessing from Allah to be able to have children for the Nation. GrandWillie baked a cake for my dad's eleventh birthday since she always baked cakes for birthdays, but the sisters told her the only birthday they were supposed to celebrate was Elijah Muhammad's birthday, Savior's Day, in February. In subsequent years, she wouldn't celebrate her children's birthdays. Dad, more than the other children, missed the birthday cakes.

Dad's childhood was slipping away. Officials at the Temple told Granddaddy it was time to put my dad to work selling *Muhammad Speaks* newspapers for the Nation. Dad, who was skinny and bald headed, dressed in a dark coat, dark slacks, white shirts, and bow tie, began knocking on people's doors with the older brothers, hawking papers. Sometimes he got cold out there, GrandWillie told me, and a lot of people slammed the door in his face.

❃ ❃ ❃

Dad grew up and left the Nation. Now he had a bush, a thick beard, and a mustache. He wore colorful double-knit shirts with zippers because that was the style in the 1960s. In the Nation he had learned to be a responsible family man. So every evening he stopped by his parents' house to get me, Ma, and Darren after dinner and walk us home. Then he'd be gone again, seduced back to the embrace of his main squeeze, his music.

He played his saxophone at the Cocoa Club on H Street and at McPhael's Place on Benning Road, near our home. Sometimes he played up Georgia Avenue, and some weekends he stayed in New York because he was trying to make a record.

He had learned how to play the horn in eighth grade at Elliot Junior High, the neighborhood school he went to since they didn't have a Muslim school yet. It was a good thing Dad got to go to public school because the Muslim school wouldn't teach music, considering it frivolous.

My grandparents allowed Dad to play his horn as long as he took care of his other responsibilities at home and for the Nation. Granddaddy had a fight with the Captain when Dad was about seventeen, so Dad didn't have to sell papers and clean up at the Temple anymore. That gave him more time alone in the basement with his horn.

Dad fell in love. He could communicate with his horn. The more he practiced, the faster his fingers could go. Sometimes his brothers watched from the steps.

"Boy, you bad!" his little brothers marveled.

By the time Dad reached his senior year in high school, he had also learned to play piano and read music. He was so good he could listen to a Smokey Robinson song on the radio, then play it by ear.

Dad hung by himself. Just him and his horn. He met my mother, but his horn still came first. But after he had two kids, Granddaddy told him we had to come first. Dad had to come get us every evening to make sure we got home safely, because that's what real men did.

GrandWillie told Ma she needed to join the Nation so she could enroll me and Darren in the Muslim school, and Ma did. GrandWillie told her the Muslim school was better because they taught more and were more disciplined. But GrandWillie had learned her lesson about being too strict with children since her eldest sons and daughters were so unhappy and troublesome. Aunt Gay, Uncle Edward, and Avon were the worst. So she was going to help Ma be just strict enough with her grandkids.

Birthdays, for instance. GrandWillie baked birthday cakes again and made everybody stand around the dining room table and sing to us.

"Happy birthday to Ray-Ray. Happy birthday to you." I loved the family chorus. For my fourth birthday and my fifth they laughed and sang while I puffed my cheeks, trying to hold my breath to blow out the candles.

❋ ❋ ❋

By the time I was six, I was a perfect audience for Uncle Avon, who loved to tell tales.

"Uncle Avon, when you was little you used to beat up white people. Is that true?" I asked one evening.

Uncle Avon was the best. He was tall, slim, handsome, and so cool. He wouldn't just tell you a story. He showed you, making faces, using his arms, hands, legs, or whatever to emphasize his point. I loved to watch him in action.

"I remember one time, one time, okay. I was about this big," he said, leveling the palm of his hand about four feet from the floor, holding his sandwich in the other. "And your Uncle Edward was about this big." He raised his palm just a bit. "I guess we was about eleven and twelve, okay. And uh-rum, we had this little club called the White Hunters Club, right." He used all these *okays*, *uh-rums*, and *rights* trying to sound extra cool. He stroked his chin to draw the same effect.

"What we used to do, okay, was, we would go around." He paused for drama. "And beat up white people."

I burst out laughing. "Where'd ya'll find the white people?" I asked, knowing they didn't live in our neighborhood. GrandWillie came downstairs and sat in Granddaddy's recliner, stitching a hem in her skirt. She wasn't drawn into the story.

"We used to go up to the Union Station, right, and catch the white people coming and going. From the Capitol building. See, we'd be there, right, all of us in a group. Hiding in the bushes, okay. And we'd be like, 'There go one right there! Get her! Get her!' And whoever was initiating to get in the group, right, they'd have to go up and *kick* the white lady in the leg." He laughed. "And then we started running," he said, pumping his arms, head bobbing like he was running. "And running all the way to we got back on our turf."

By now I was hysterical. Uncle Avon finished his sandwich and moved into the living room for more space for his dramatics. I heard shouting and laughter from the boys' room upstairs where Darren, Uncle Hussein, and Uncle Wallace were playing foosball. Darren was seven, Wallace eleven, and Hussein twelve. They did everything together. Ma was in the basement with Aunt Gay playing Four Tops albums with my two-year-old brother, Furard, in his playpen. Aunt Gay came upstairs to get a bottle for her infant son, Beyete, and poked her head in the dining room to see what was going on.

"What ya'll doing?" she asked. Aunt Gay was dark with broad features like GrandWillie, broad nose and lips, wide hips. She wore her hair in a wild Afro with a band tied around it and hip-hugging jeans. GrandWillie and Granddaddy couldn't stand the sight, but they couldn't do anything about it.

"Uncle Avon's telling me about when ya'll was little," I told her.

"He's probably lying again," she said, smacking her lips and rolling her eyes as she turned away. She didn't remember anything funny about her childhood days in the Nation.

Being a Muslim had been harder for the girls. Aunt Gay got into fights when girls snatched her scarf off in elementary and junior high school. By the time she went to high school she found a way to go to a friend's house and change into short skirts before school, then change back before going home. She got pregnant right before graduation, and now that she was officially grown at nineteen her parents couldn't tell her anything.

Being a Muslim boy had made Uncle Avon special, too, but special in a different way. He learned enough about the white man at the Temple to impress his friends back home. They looked up to him. He told them that Elijah Muhammad hadn't taught him and his brother to hate and torture white people, he had just taught them how hateful and evil the white people were.

"See, black people already knew white folks was nasty," Uncle Avon said. "The Honorable Elijah Muhammad just explained in more detail what they already knew."

I thought Uncle Avon was so smart.

He said Elijah Muhammad was trying to teach them how to deal with their pain. Take the pain of poverty, for instance. Elijah Muhammad taught his followers that they didn't have to live in poverty just because the white man insisted on paying the black man lowly wages for his hard labor. He taught that by using God-given self-control, the black man could stop wasting his money on the white man's poisons—cigarettes, alcohol, and degrading entertainment—and save it or spend it on something more positive, like the Nation of Islam, which was designed to uplift the black race.

Elijah Muhammad taught us to stop complaining about what the white man wasn't doing—like giving blacks good jobs—and "Do for Self!"

Education: The Mind Is a Terrible Thing to Waste

CHAPTER 2

The morning sun was a pale blur as my schoolmates and I stood in line waiting for the doors to open for school. Our line snaked around the side and back of the tan arched building that was our Temple and school—dozens of girls in long skirts or pantaloons hanging beneath our coats.

The neighborhood around us was just awakening. Our place of prayer and learning was in the Shaw neighborhood, located less than two miles from the U.S. Capitol, where white men in dark suits designed laws that affected the world. By the time I was six in 1972, more than a dozen black men and women had been elected to help make the laws, but the Honorable Elijah Muhammad taught us that those black lawmakers were going to turn out to be just as bad as the white people they worked with because it was the whole system that was evil since white people had created it. That's why he said it was a good thing black people had a big college like Howard University, which was also located near our school, so they could become scholars and independent thinkers. At Howard they let strong black men like somebody named Stokely Carmichael talk about black power and stuff that we in the Nation of Islam could respect.

The one thing we didn't respect about black people not in our Nation, though, was the fact that they acted like they couldn't keep their own neighborhoods clean if the white man didn't help them. The streets around our school were dingy, but brothers from the Temple worked hard to keep the sidewalk on our street swept. Soon these dingy streets would be filled with parents going to work and children walking to the three public schools nearby.

School for us started at eight A.M., but we had to be there fifteen minutes early since we each had to be searched head to toe before entering the building. Our dean of girls, Sister Memphis, a tall, very thin, pinch-faced woman who looked like the wicked witch from *The Wizard of Oz*, and Sister Captain, Margaret Ann, who was stiff as a lady soldier, checked under our scarves, felt down our bodies, and searched our book bags and purses.

"As-Salaam-Alaikum, Sonsyrea," Sister Memphis greeted me as she slid her hands down my back and front.

Although these searches were necessary to ensure our safety since we in the Nation of Islam were God's chosen people and the devil was always trying to get inside to destroy God's people, I felt a little awkward. I had heard about how the white devils bombed a black church and killed four little children inside. That happened before I was born, but I heard about it from our minister when he was telling us why we should never be sitting ducks like the Christians. I was glad we had protection. I turned about-face and lifted each shoe so she could make sure no one had planted a tiny bomb in one of them.

"Wa-Laikum-Salaam," I said, returning her greeting. She fumbled through my book bag, then dismissed me with a smile. I walked off to class.

My class, level three, which was equivalent to third grade in public schools, was on the ground floor of this two-story building. Our classrooms were spaces cordoned off by rollaway blackboards and wooden dividers—except for level one, which was behind a vinyl curtain. The building was quiet except for the shuffling feet and hushed voices of the hundred or so girls.

"As-Salaam-Alaikum, Sister Doris," I greeted my teacher, who was standing at the entrance of our class.

Sister Doris 3X was short and wore round glasses. Like the other Muslim women, she was purposely plain. She wore no makeup and only nondescript jewelry.

Some of my classmates were already seated at the rows of desks and chairs. I went to my seat by the window, placed my notebook on my desk and my hands on my lap, and waited for class to begin. We stood and began with prayer.

There were about two hundred of us little Xs enrolled in the University of Islam in Washington, D.C., and in the "universities" in other cities there were thousands more. All with the last name X, all dressed alike, all being trained to think alike.

Girls went to school in the morning and boys in the afternoon because the Temple wasn't large enough to accommodate everybody at one time. Even if it had been large enough, we girls would have been separated from the boys so we wouldn't get distracted trying to impress each other.

To make up for going to school half a day, we went year-round, getting a two-week vacation in the spring and another two weeks in the winter, about the same time as the Easter and Christmas breaks of public school children. Those kids got the whole summer off, and I envied that. But GrandWillie told me I was going to be smarter since I studied all the time.

Our studies were different, too. While children in public schools learned that Christopher Columbus was a great man who discovered America, we learned that he was a wicked white man who stole land that already belonged to the Indians. While they learned that slain civil rights leader Dr.

Martin Luther King, Jr., had been a hero, we were taught he had been a coward. While they learned the history of America, we learned the history of our own nation, the Nation of Islam. They learned America was "land of the free, home of the brave"; we learned it was the most vile and wicked nation on Earth, one that would be destroyed.

Our reading, math, and science studies were more advanced than in public schools. We learned Arabic in level three, and kids in public schools learned a foreign language in seventh grade. Every day we were drilled on a few of our twenty-five Actual Facts, information about the dimensions of planet Earth and other celestial bodies. We were taught that our God, who came to North America in the form of Master W. Fard Muhammad, measured the Earth, all the other planets, and the distances between. This God wanted us to memorize the widths and weights of all the planets, our teachers said, because someday we black people, especially the few of us chosen for the Nation of Islam, would rule the world. We would need to understand everything about the universe in order to control it, so we had to learn the figures our Master-God had left for us.

By age six, I could rattle off facts and figures in cadence, more concepts I couldn't comprehend: "Earth is ninety-three million miles from the sun. It is seven thousand miles in diameter, and it takes three hundred sixty-five and one-fourth days to circle the sun."

I was convinced that our God was a powerfully smart God to have measured the sun and figured out how long it took to travel around it. I was proud that my little head could hold so much information. I practiced reciting to myself every chance I got. "Three hundred sixty-five and one-fourth days," I mumbled as I fell asleep at night. "Ninety-three million miles . . ."

We also had to memorize and recite Student Enrollment Rules of Islam, which were bits of history according to Elijah Muhammad. The histories of Christianity and Buddhism, according to his lessons, dated back 551 and 35,000 years, respectively, while the history of Islam was timeless. "It has no beginning and no ending," I recited.

Islam, we were taught, was the very first religion, from which all other religions evolved, and in the end everyone would return to Islam.

According to our lessons, dark-skinned people were the first people on Earth, and they developed a civilized society in Asia, while pale-skinned people were still running around like savages, living in caves in Europe. We had to memorize certain lessons at each level in order to get promoted to the next level. My memory proved sharp as I advanced through levels one, two, three, and four.

"Who is the original man?" my level four teacher commanded from her desk at the front of the room, while one selected pupil stood in front of her seat with the rest of us watching.

"The original man is the Asiatic black man, the Maker, the Owner, Cream of the Planet Earth, Father of Civilization, God of the Universe," came the answer.

"Sister Sonsyrea!" my teacher continued. "Who is the colored man?"

"The colored man is the Caucasian, white man, or Yacub's drafted devil, the *skunk* of the planet Earth!" I shouted back like a young soldier responding enthusiastically to a sergeant.

Like GrandWillie said, Elijah Muhammad flipped everything to the reverse. Out in the world, *colored* referred to African Americans, white represented everything good and pure, and black was bad. In our world, which the Nation of Islam had become, the exact opposite was true.

I was glad to be born a black person and extra glad that I was one of the special black people chosen to be in the Nation of Islam. When I got big, I was going to be an example to black people so they could see our true selves, how we could be smart and not be tricked by the white devil anymore.

We were taught that we, people of African descent, were not the ones in the minority. If we considered ourselves globally, we learned, we were in fact the majority.

The Honorable Elijah Muhammad said black people in America needed to show unity so they could become an example of solidarity for people around the world. The Nation would lead the way; that's why it was important for us to work in unison—to look alike, speak alike, act alike, even think alike. But even as a little girl, I could see people were different underneath.

I could look at Sister Memphis, Sister Captain, and my teacher, Sister Doris, all dressed in their long skirts and headpieces, and still tell they were different. Sister Memphis was very light skinned and mean. Plus, she had special powers. She could stop little girls in their tracks and somehow know they were hiding candy in their shoes. She always knew just when to go in the girls' bathroom and catch a couple of teenage girls meeting there when they were supposed to be in class.

"You have a problem," Sister Memphis said one morning, pointing her sharp nose down on a teenage girl named Nyeemah, whom she had pulled into the bathroom. I continued washing my hands and saw their reflection in the mirror in front of me.

"You insist upon doing evil. This is a bad habit you're getting into. Why do you do things you know you're not supposed to do?" Nyeemah stood there with her head bowed and shrugged her shoulders. She probably was too scared to speak. Sister Memphis was going to whack her a few times with her rulers in a few minutes, and I didn't want to be in there to see it. So I left without drying my hands.

Sister Captain, a statuesque, cocoa-colored woman, was strict but not as mean as Sister Memphis.

"Sister Donna," would be all she'd have to say to the teenage student about to sneak to the water fountain on her way back to class from the bathroom. She'd tilt her head in the direction of the stairs leading back to class and the young sister, Donna, with no comment or hesitation, would turn and go back to class.

Sister Doris didn't seem to care too much if somebody sneaked a piece of candy to class or took too long coming back from the bathroom. She'd just keep right on teaching unless one of us did something really bad; then she'd make us stand in the corner on one foot with our hands over our head. That's how most of the teachers disciplined us little girls. They sent the bigger girls to Sister Memphis, who took them in the bathroom and dispensed a prescribed number of lashes on the hands with a stack of eight wooden rulers bound at both ends by rubber bands.

❋ ❋ ❋

School, like everything else in the Nation, was serious business. We had no extracurricular activities: no art, music, sports, cheerleading, or any other unacademic things. Elijah Muhammad scorned what he considered "sport and play," saying black people had already wasted too much time playing and not taking life seriously.

We didn't waste much time in the classroom on petty squabbles among students or power struggles with the teachers, either. In our school you got in trouble for the least little things: for coming to school with your clothes dirty or your body stinking or "shoes excessively worn." Elijah Muhammad taught that cleanliness "is next to godliness," so being dirty was taken as an offense.

Discipline had to be strict, we were taught, because that was another problem with our downtrodden race. We lacked discipline and therefore had failed to command and direct our own godly wills. The white man couldn't keep us down once we commanded our will to stand up.

Anybody who got into trouble in school was supposed to get whipped at home, too. They'd have to have both parents sign a letter from the teacher, and one of the parents would have to schedule a conference with the teacher. I didn't get into any trouble. In fact, I tried to keep my school goddesses—my teachers, Sister Memphis and Sister Captain—appeased with gifts of potholders and woven baskets I made them at home.

We all tried our best to make honor roll so our parents would reward us with praise and our Nation would reward us with token prizes like free tickets to one of our banquets or bazaars. I got mostly As and Bs, and so did my brother, Darren.

We learned more than just academics. We learned how to handle our feelings, too. We were taught at an early age that we were not supposed to get emotional about anything. "Whenever you're faced with a situation, don't react on what's in here," Sister Memphis reminded us, pointing to her chest. "Use what's in here," she said, moving her finger to her right temple.

But for some of us, the feelings lay just below the surface, even though we weren't allowed to show them. Like the time one of my schoolmates' father went into a rage and busted her head open with a telephone, then killed her mother and hurt her three younger sisters and brothers. We had a special assembly so Sister Memphis could tell us the news and ask if anybody had any clothes or toys they wanted to give to her family. I didn't have any spare toys or clothes for my classmate, but I felt sorry for her losing somebody she loved. Soon, I would lose somebody I loved.

❋ ❋ ❋

Every evening I looked forward to jumping up on Granddaddy's lap, digging in his pockets for tiny toys he hid for me and Darren. I waited to hear him yell "As-Salaam-Alaikum" as he walked through the door, but this particular day a woman ran to the door instead.

"Mr. Tate's been hit!" she screamed. GrandWillie, Ma, and Aunt Gay went flying out the house. I stood at the front door waiting for somebody to come back, listening to the babies and other kids behind me making too much noise. Ma ran back in the house and headed for the phone.

Her voice was calm: "We need an ambulance immediately at the corner of 13th and C Streets, Northeast. A man has been hit by a car. Vital signs not good."

Ma rushed out the door again. Moments later, I heard the sirens of an ambulance.

When Ma came back I asked, "What happened to Granddaddy?"

"They had to take him to the hospital," she said.

I heard Ma telling somebody on the phone that Granddaddy couldn't move.

"Does that mean Granddaddy is dead?" I asked. Ma assured me he wasn't and told me to go to sleep. I fell asleep in GrandWillie's bed that night, very worried.

The house was quiet when I woke up the next morning. Ma was fixing breakfast.

"They didn't let Granddaddy come home from the hospital?" I asked. Somehow, I knew to whisper my question.

"No," Ma said in an equally hushed tone. "Your Granddaddy passed on last night."

"Passed on where?" I asked.

"Your Granddad passed on from here. He won't be coming home again." She couldn't tell me he went to heaven up in the sky because I had already learned in the Temple that no such place existed.

Granddaddy had to have his funeral at a funeral parlor because the minister at the Temple wouldn't let him have it there. GrandWillie didn't question him about why. She figured it had something to do with that argument Granddaddy had had with a captain at the Temple a few years back, but she didn't have time to worry about that right now.

One of GrandWillie's friends, Sister Marie 2X, a slender, fast-talking woman from the Temple, contacted a former minister who had left the Nation of Islam a few years earlier, and he agreed to conduct a Muslim funeral for Granddaddy at the parlor. Sister Captain Margaret from the Temple helped GrandWillie put together appropriate white outfits for the women in the immediate family to wear to the funeral. I didn't go to the funeral because Ma thought it was best to leave us little kids at home. GrandWillie's parents, sisters, and brothers all attended the funeral and stopped by our house afterward. Most of them were strangers to me.

GrandWillie started going back to the Temple after Granddaddy died because she needed some kind of family support while she was grieving, and she felt closer to her "sisters" at the Temple than she did to the ones she grew up with.

A few days later GrandWillie and Ma were back in the dining room teaching the toddlers, I was back in school, my uncles were back at work. Everybody acted as if nothing had changed. It was as if I was the only one missing Granddaddy.

I kept remembering his full laugh that shook his stomach, his cocked smile, his bouncing me on his knee.

"Sonsyrea, I don't want you thinking about nothing right now but your homework. Understand?" GrandWillie said.

I nodded my head yes, but I really didn't understand. I remembered Sister Memphis tapping her finger on the side of her head, teaching us to think our way out of difficult situations. I bit down on my pencil and swallowed hard to make the knot in my throat go away.

Nobody at school or home taught me it was all right to feel sad sometimes, all right to grieve, to cry. I was taught that I couldn't let life's disappointments and tragedies slow me down. Elijah Muhammad had taught us not to dwell on our emotions but to think our way through dilemmas.

When I was older, I would learn the hard way that emotions must be acknowledged. For now I wiped my tears and concentrated on the homework in front of me.

* * *

My school lessons became more complex as I reached levels four and five. Now I had to learn the Honorable Elijah Muhammad's Lost-Found Lessons, which further sought to explain our circumstances in America and how they came about.

We were taught that Asians and Africans, people of color, are all the same but that Caucasians gave us different names to try to divide us. I didn't question where all this information came from or whether it was accurate. As a little X, I was only supposed to learn it by heart, which I did.

The devil, I was taught, is a weak and wicked man. Only such a man would feel the need to brutally enslave people, oppress them, and exploit them. In short, the devil was all blond-haired, blue-eyed Caucasian men and women. I was learning to hate white people without even knowing them. The only white person I knew personally was Mr. Stevenson, who lived around the corner from my home. But he had dark brown hair and brown eyes, so I figured he wasn't like the white people I learned about in school.

Maybe the white people I saw going to work around the Capitol building, which I passed on my way to and from school, were evil, I thought. Maybe that's why my uncles used to beat them up. It would be years before I would meet any of them personally, after I grew up and worked there with them. Then I'd see that some of them really were evil but some of them were no different from me.

Darren was almost ten now, and I was eight and a half. The only other white people I saw were on TV, but we didn't have much time to watch TV anymore, since Darren went with our uncles to sell our Nation of Islam newspapers after school and I had to help GrandWillie more because Ma's stomach was so big with another baby.

Ma, Dad, Darren, I, and our little brother, Furard, had moved back into the family house after Granddaddy died so Dad could help take care of his three youngest brothers: Uncle Sharrief, who was sixteen, Uncle Hussein, twelve, and Uncle Wallace, eleven.

Some evenings Darren and I watched *The Brady Bunch* and *Partridge Family* because there were few shows on TV with black children. That's the reason the Honorable Elijah Muhammad told our parents not to let us watch TV, because he said we didn't need to be watching white kids, wondering why there were no black ones, and we didn't need to be patterning ourselves after them.

I knew that if I ever met Marcia Brady and we had to answer questions about history, science, or the size of the universe, I'd beat her. I was black and therefore naturally smarter, plus I was being trained very well.

On a typical day our teacher went to the chalkboard and wrote a vocabulary list that included words such as *atmosphere* and *hemisphere*. We looked up these words in the dictionary for homework and discussed them as part of a spelling lesson the next day. We didn't have textbooks, so the dictionary pretty much became our spelling book.

Sister Brenda 4X came to our classroom to teach us Spanish and Arabic. Elijah Muhammad said we had to learn Arabic because in the future we would need to be able to read the Holy Quran, the Muslim book of revelations, in its original Arabic. For now, the Honorable Elijah Muhammad did all our reading and interpreting for us. We read books he wrote: *Message to the Black Man*, *How to Eat to Live*, and others in which he told us what he thought we needed to know from the Quran and the Bible.

He required us to learn Spanish because he said one day there would be more Spanish-speaking people in America than white people and we would need to be able to communicate with them. I learned just enough to pass the class.

* * *

As much as our education was communal, our individual talents were not overlooked. Uncle Hussein, who showed a keen aptitude for math and science, was encouraged to become a doctor. Elijah Muhammad was planning to build a hospital for the Nation, and of course we would need doctors. Since I showed a talent for writing plays and short stories, my teachers, especially Sister Doris, encouraged me to read more and write more.

By now, at eight and a half, I had begun writing rhymes about studying hard and being good.

If you want to grow up strong,
make sure you're right
and never wrong.
If you want to grow up right,
you have to study
in the day and night.

I got the idea for rhyming from Dr. Suess books at home. Each time I finished writing a poem, I ran to show it to GrandWillie. She always said, "That's very good, Sonsyrea," and tucked it in her apron. She held onto those poems for years and years. Sometimes when my maternal grandmother, Grandma Thomas, came to our house for a Thanksgiving dinner or a baby shower, GrandWillie showed her some of my poems. "That's very good," she'd say. "You should keep it up."

By the time I reached levels five and six, I began writing short stories about a fictitious character named Tonya, a happy-go-lucky girl who played with her friends all day. Tonya said and did everything I wished I could. She played with the other children in the neighborhood and dressed like them.

I arranged my plays like the plays I found in books in our basement, among them a work by Ntozake Shange. We also had a collection of science books, encyclopedias, black history books, and poetry. I loved to write, and I thought perhaps I could write for the *Muhammad Speaks* when I grew up.

In class we read articles in the *Muhammad Speaks*, some of them written by women. We didn't read the white man's newspapers because the Honorable Elijah Muhammad said they were full of propaganda and negative news to try to make black people look bad or foolish. He told us—during Sunday services—that more black people should make their own newspapers and print news they liked.

When I got older and worked as a reporter myself, I heard the same complaints from people in the black community, but I believed it was my duty to do what I could to change the way whites viewed us. I would wind up working for large white-owned newspapers, and my family, which once refused to read them, would subscribe, proud that I was covering our community.

* * *

In order to recite our lessons perfectly in school, we had to rehearse them at home.

"All right, man, Lesson Number Ten: Why does Muhammad and any Muslim murder the devil? What is the duty of each Muslim in regards to the four devils? What rewards does a Muslim receive by presenting the four devils at one time?" Uncle Hussein drilled his younger brother, Uncle Wallace, on these lessons at night so they could correctly recite them in class the next day.

I could hear them in their bedroom going over this information while they put on their pajamas. I was already in my pajamas, lying in the twin-size, fold-up, roll-away bed I shared with GrandWillie. The thought of murder frightened me because I knew that black men couldn't go around killing white ones and get away with it.

"Because the devil is 100 percent wicked and will not keep and obey the laws of Islam," Uncle Wallace began answering. "His ways and actions are like a snake of the grafted type. So Muhammad learned that he could not reform the devil, so they had to be murdered."

He paused, then I heard paper rumple. He had to read the rest of the answer. "All Muslims will murder the devil because they know he is a snake and also if he is allowed to live, he will sting someone else. Each Muslim is required to bring four devils, and by bringing and presenting four devils at one time his reward is a button to wear on the lapel of his coat, also free transportation to the holy city, Mecca."

Even I knew that killing could guarantee a black man only a trip to jail. Uncle Avon and Uncle Edward both had been incarcerated for robbery, and I had missed them very much. The idea of losing two more people I loved to jail was too much to think about. I pulled the covers over my head, hoping the soft, warm flannel could somehow cover up my thoughts.

I didn't know that at eleven and twelve years old, my uncles already were beginning to understand that Elijah Muhammad wasn't talking about physically going out and killing four white people. Their teachers had explained to them that Elijah Muhammad was a prophet and that prophets don't always mean exactly what they say because prophets tend to speak in parables—symbolisms. He might have meant for his followers to go out and kill four people's devilish ways.

I was too young to realize that in our Nation of Islam and, in fact, in other religions, leaders used examples and symbols. Neither did I know that some grown people misunderstood the Honorable Elijah Muhammad's teachings the same way I did. Twenty years later, when new leaders, including Minister Louis Farrakhan and Khalid Muhammad, would teach these same old lessons, their words would again be misunderstood.

I would hear Mr. Khalid Muhammad talking about pushing old white people off a cliff, and I would be transported back to my childhood, back to listening to my uncles, as I wondered if he was really inciting violence or speaking in symbolism.

All Praises Due to Muhammad

CHAPTER 3

At eight years old, I didn't know that important things were happening around the country outside our Nation of Islam. I didn't know that living conditions had improved for us African Americans and that we were being elected to the U.S. Congress and local offices in greater numbers.

It was 1974, and the Civil Rights Movement had resulted in better jobs, housing, and educational opportunities for many blacks. And major colleges and corporations were recruiting minorities and women to fill new quotas. In my household, however, nobody reveled in this new sense of accomplishment because our Honorable Elijah Muhammad cautioned us against celebrating such gains.

Elijah Muhammad said that these gains were just another trick being played on the so-called Negro, that integration would bring about further decay of our race. Why should we want to live, learn, and work with the most wicked people on the face of this Earth? Our esteemed prophet wanted the United States government to give him a piece of America where his Nation—our all-black Nation—could live separately.

Our Nation had gotten bigger and bigger. GrandWillie had watched Temple Number 4 in Washington grow from fewer than one hundred members in the early 1950s to several hundred people by now. No one knew the exact figures because our officials kept it a secret. But on a national level, outside newspapers were reporting that we had grown from about 8,000 in the 1930s to more than 100,000 by the early 1970s. Around the Temple, GrandWillie now was considered a pioneer. You could tell she was proud by the way she carefully balanced her Nation-issued uniform hat on her head Sunday mornings when we dressed for service. Our head garments evolved from large square scarves tied under our chins when I was little to special veils rounded about our shoulders to hats.

GrandWillie stood tall, royally fixing her hat in the mirror. Her hat, a round box with a crescent, star, and the letters *M.G.T.* for Muslim Girls' Training on the front, was her crown. I stood next to her and balanced my little-girl hat, which looked like a spaceship with a ponytail on top.

Elijah Muhammad had inspired a minination worth 80 million dollars in businesses and assets and ten times that much in human potential. We owned our own temples, schools, restaurants, bakeries, fish stores, farms, banks, and service businesses. A majestic-looking Temple complex was built in Chicago, complete with classrooms for the kids. School buses were bought for our schools in Washington and several other cities, and now we were trying to build our own hospital. Although we didn't all live on a single compound, which would have made being a Nation more convenient, we were all of one mind-set.

We had a clothing factory in Chicago to make our special kind of clothes. Our newspaper, *Muhammad Speaks*, reported news the way we wanted to see it—always positive for blacks and negative for whites. And our eateries served food especially accommodating to our Muslim diet; pork, white bread, white rice, and white potatoes were forbidden. Elijah

Muhammad's Sunday morning radio broadcast aired on commercial radio stations all across the country and blasted through our house from the living room stereo so everyone at home could hear it.

It seemed like people were beginning to respect our Nation because black people were beginning to respect themselves. At fish fries African Americans wore dashikis and danced to the Temptations' "Ball of Confusion," which was popular. I didn't feel insecure about being special now because a lot more people in the black community were supporting our efforts through buying our newspapers and fish products and visiting our stores and restaurants. They respected our independence and industry even if they disagreed with some of the other, finer points of our program.

"Y'all Moozlems sure 'bout y'all's work," a passerby might comment, watching us file into the Temple so puffed up and proud. "I was going to become a Moozlem, but when they told me I couldn't eat no more pork, I said 'no way.'"

"I'd love to get me one of them men, but I can't see me wearing them long clothes through the summertime," came the comments from women.

I looked forward to going to the Temple on Sundays. I wanted to ride the public bus in my special uniform so everyone could see I was one of those sharp Nation of Islam children.

❊ ❊ ❊

It was snowing one important Sunday as we were getting dressed for service.

"Put your long johns on," GrandWillie said. "It's cold out there today. And get your boots."

"My boots're lost," I said. I knew where they were but didn't want to wear them because they were too big. My mother had gone shopping at a thrift store and couldn't find a pair in my right size.

"Girl, you better find those boots," GrandWillie said. "I've told you about putting your things where they belong."

GrandWillie slid her feet into her insulated boots that fit just right. I looked at my big yellow rubber boots in the closet and stooped to push them farther back, out of sight, hiding them behind empty shoe boxes and bags.

"GrandWillie, I don't see them," I said. I didn't mind walking through the wet, icy snow in my regular shoes. My feet might get cold and numb, but that was better than slipping and sliding in boots too big, I figured. Besides, I wanted to see my own footprints in the snow, not clumsy, awkward footprints made from misfitted boots.

"Chile, move out the way. I saw those boots somewhere just yesterday," GrandWillie said, pushing her way into the closet. She fished around just a few minutes before she found the yellow rubber boots.

"Girl, put these on your feet, and I don't want to hear another peep out of you," she said.

Darren and Uncles Hussein and Wallace had left about an hour earlier because it was their turn to set up the chairs in the Temple. I didn't know why Ma wasn't going with us, but I realized that she was staying home more and more these days. I was used to Dad not going.

The snow was just starting to accumulate when GrandWillie and I left. I slid my gloved hands along the porch rail trying to collect a snowball, but I couldn't because the snow was still too soft. GrandWillie opened her umbrella, and we proceeded down the street and around the corner to the bus stop. A few children were playing in the snow in the street, but we didn't have time to stop and speak. We arrived at the bus stop just in time for GrandWillie to pluck enough coins from her purse for our fare. While GrandWillie was dropping the coins into the box, I hopped into the passenger's seat right behind the driver. But GrandWillie motioned me to her favorite spot near the back of the bus. I slid into the seat next to the window, and GrandWillie sat beside me. There were only three other people on the bus this Sunday morning, and they were dressed for church. Looking out the window, I saw a woman pulling a laundry cart across the street toward the laundromat. The woman had big pink rollers in her hair and a dirty scarf tied around them.

"GrandWillie, she's lost, ain't she?" I said, remembering how Elijah Muhammad talked about women like her who went out in public looking any ole kind of way. He said people like that were lost and it was up to us members of the Nation of Islam to find them and bring them into our way of life so they could hear Elijah Muhammad and find their true selves.

We, black people, were the lost-found tribe of Shabazz, a people with self-respect and dignity. That was our true identity.

GrandWillie told me to stop pointing.

"But look at her, GrandWillie. She's outside looking like a fool," I said, using the term used at the Temple. "GrandWillie, did you used to come outside with rollers in your hair before you got in the Nation?"

"No," she said. "Even when I was in the church, they taught us not to go out in public looking like that."

"Hmpphh," I said. "Somebody needs to go and tell that lady, right?"

"Everything ain't for everybody," GrandWillie said.

Our transfer stop was coming up, so I sounded the bell to make the driver stop.

We got off the bus, and as we walked I paused to watch the large snowflakes fall to the ground, losing their oneness as they fell. They all became a single blanket of snow, and you couldn't tell one flake from the other. That's what Elijah Muhammad was trying to do with us in the Nation, make us all one unit that looked the same and sounded the same. Most of the people in the Nation had been vulnerable emotionally and spiritually, and in other ways downtrodden, when they joined the Nation. So it was easy enough to mold them. And those of us born into the Nation simply went along with the program. For the most part.

Some of my classmates rebelled, like babies refusing to eat a food that only they knew they were allergic to. Donna was a natural rebel and so was Linda, whose older brother must have been rebelling some kind of way because he wound up getting in trouble out in the world and going to jail. Linda and Donna were two and three years older than me, but they were my friends, and I looked forward to seeing them on Sundays. Linda didn't come that much because she would fake a stomachache so she could stay home. But Donna's father made her come all the time. My friend Saundra and I both learned to sugarcoat the isolation we felt and digest it like we were actually being fed a special privilege. Deep down, I hated going to school year-round and I resented the intense pressure to excel, but by the time I finished turning over my feelings in my head, I convinced myself that all the pain and strain was making me a better person, like the grown-ups said. I was better than the kids in my neighborhood who got to play all the time and run freely through the streets. God—not the little one inside me but the big God who ruled all us little gods—was going to like me better on Judgment Day because I followed all his orders. I wore all the right clothes, ate all the right foods, and said all the right things when called on in class, and I even tried to keep my thoughts in my head righteous.

One of my schoolmates, Kim, told me she hated Sister Captain, who was in charge of all the women and girls, because Sister Captain had told her mother not to come back to the Temple for four months because twice Kim's mother didn't show up for kitchen duty. I told Kim it wasn't right to hate, but when I saw her staring meanly across the room at Sister Captain some Sundays, I knew she had not taken my advice.

When GrandWillie and I arrived at the Temple, we had to stand in line to get searched upon entering. Low-ranking official sisters formed an assembly line behind the closed vinyl curtain in the space normally used for the first grade classroom, frisking incoming sisters from head to toe to make sure none of us was trying to sneak weapons or tape recorders into the Sunday meeting. I stepped in front of one of the sisters while GrandWillie stepped in front of the sister next to me. I lifted my arms like an airplane about to take off, and Sister Muriel smiled as she began patting my head to make sure nothing was concealed beneath my headpiece.

"As-Salaam-Alaikum," she greeted me. She was a short, thick, teenage sister who also went to the Muslim school. She was always nice to me, I think because she liked one of my teenage uncles.

"Wa-Laikum-Salaam." She slid her hands across my arms and down my sides, then I turned around and lifted each foot.

Sisters and brothers were hanging up their coats downstairs then moving quickly upstairs to get a good seat for service. GrandWillie and I hung up our coats, then she handed me a pair of my white gloves out of her purse and slid hers on. We always wore our white gloves to the Sunday meetings. Upstairs in the main meeting hall, the brothers sat on one side and sisters on the other. A few brothers in their F.O.I. (Fruit of Islam) uniforms stood post along the brothers' side. They looked sharp in their dark blue suits with a thick white stripe running down the pant legs, a high collar on the jacket, and the matching cap that bore a backward crescent and star, our Nation's emblems. The brothers on guard moved about with swift precision, walking straight lines stiffly, turning corners sharply with a click of their heels, just like well-trained soldiers.

The sisters on guard were equally dazzling in their special uniforms: a long white skirt, a knee-length cape, white gloves, and a white box-hat with flaps tied under the chin. Their hats had the letters M.G.T. and G.C.C., for Muslim Girls' Training and General Civilization Class, embroidered on the front. The sister officials who donned these hats had successfully completed Saturday classes for women at the Temple.

GrandWillie and I went to the Saturday morning classes, too, and I watched the teenage sisters and young women in drill rehearsals, anticipating the time I'd be old enough to drill. I couldn't wait to become a sister soldier, too.

Sunday service was considered a teaching session rather than an hour for praise. We didn't worship some invisible God up in the sky. There would be no heaven above the clouds after we died, we were taught. This life was it, and in order to experience heaven here on Earth we would have to exercise our individual willpower, our intellect, our individual god in a way that blacks were unaccustomed to. Heaven and hell were states of mind, we were taught. Martin Luther King and other civil rights leaders who got their heads beat while praying for integration were foolish, said the Messenger, Elijah Muhammad.

"I have the only solution to the problems of the so-called Negroes in this wilderness of North America," his voice boomed through the loudspeakers.

Collection baskets circulated several times during the service. A baby cried out during the lesson, and one of the uniformed brothers standing guard at the main hall entrances motioned to one of the sisters standing post on the women's side of the room to escort the baby and its mother out of the room. We had been at the Temple since eleven A.M., and now it was six o'clock in the evening.

Since this was a fourth Sunday of the month and Elijah Muhammad's lecture was being broadcast at all the Temples, we would be at the Temple until ten o'clock at night. I was getting tired of sitting, and I looked around, trying to make eye contact with one of my friends so we could go meet in the bathroom to talk. We had signals to arrange our meetings—one nod for "now," two nods for "in a few minutes." I couldn't catch Saundra's eyes or those of my best friend, Vernarda. So I went by myself.

"GrandWillie, I'm hungry," I said when I returned.

Without turning to look at me, GrandWillie reached in her purse and handed me a stash of raisins folded in foil. Since we weren't allowed to eat during the service, I had to hide them in my lap and eat them one at a time.

"It is the time for the ending of the American white people. This are the people mentioned in Daniel," Elijah Muhammad's voice boomed on. His speech was broken and his grammar was bad compared to the grammar we learned in his schools. But GrandWillie and the other grown-ups were spellbound. I didn't dare tell GrandWillie that he didn't sound so smart, so I convinced myself that he was so supersmart in his mind that his mouth just couldn't keep up.

"It has been prophesied . . . that beast must be taken and destroyed and his body given to the burning flames."

"Teach! Teach!" one of the brothers in the audience shouted.

"America is the most strongest government of the white race and the most vicious and cruelest when it comes to the so-called American Negroes," he continued.

"Teach, brother!" someone else shouted. GrandWillie silently nodded her head in agreement.

GrandWillie and the other grown-ups believed Elijah Muhammad was the smartest man in the world. Some of us kids were suspicious. Sometimes tears swelled up in Grand-Willie's eyes when she listened to the Messenger speak. She couldn't shout out like the brothers because we ladies weren't supposed to shout, but I could tell she wanted to. GrandWillie and the other grown-ups kept their focus straight ahead while listening to the Honorable Elijah Muhammad, even though there wasn't any motion to watch when the Messenger's voice was being broadcast. The only thing to look at in front was a row of uniformed brothers seated on the platform with our local minister, Dr. Lonnie Shabazz. They all sat stiffly upright with their hands folded on their laps. Behind them was a blackboard with an American flag on one side and the word *Christianity* above it. A cross and a painting of a black man hanging from a tree were underneath this flag.

The picture of the man hanging frightened me because he looked so helpless with his hands tied and his head bowed. In real life I saw strong black men who walked with their heads erect. If black men used to be helpless, I didn't want to know about it. In school we didn't talk about slavery and how vulnerable and helpless black people were when first brought to America, and I was glad. Instead we talked about how great and godly black people had been way back before America was even discovered. The blackboard up front must have been for the people visiting our Temple, the people who needed a picture to show them how evil the white man was. The words *Slavery*, *Suffering*, and *Death* painted in bold letters completed this side of the board.

On the other side of the board there was a painting of our Muslim flag: a crescent and a star on a fiery red background. Above our flag was the word *Islam*, and beneath it were the words *Freedom*, *Justice*, and *Equality*. In the center of the board the word *Allah* was painted in even larger letters at the top of the board with a question below: "Which one will survive the War of Armageddon?"

The speakers carrying the Messenger's voice made him sound larger than life.

"God has taken it for himself to deliver us by the hand of a Messenger. That Messenger has already been sent and is doing his work and progressing his work by the help of Almighty God, Allah, who came in the person of Master Fard Muhammad," his voice continued. "This work is not to bring about war and aggression upon America, but this work is to try to separate the so-called American Negro from his cruel masters as it were in the days of Moses."

Applause filled the room. "Teach!" "Teach!"

"GrandWillie, can I go to the bathroom now?" I asked.

"Go," she said. "And you come straight back. You hear?"

There was absolutely no room here for children misbehaving. We knew better than to breathe too hard during the service, especially when the Messenger of Allah was teaching. Downstairs in the ladies' restroom where mothers breast-fed their babies or changed their diapers, I heard two of the older girls whispering while we all washed our hands at the four sinks.

"I think Markus likes me. He winked at me," Donna told Nunita. Markus was our local minister's son.

"Oowh. For real?" Nunita got excited. They giggled. "He's so cute," she said.

"I know. I'm going to bump into him at the water fountain so he can ask me for a chance if he wants to."

Asking for "a chance" was our way of asking someone of the opposite gender to become a boyfriend or girlfriend even though in the Nation that kind of relationship was strictly forbidden, even for adults. Young adults were encouraged to get married right after graduation or even before if they wanted to start keeping company with somebody. But most of them didn't want to go that far. They just wanted to flirt and get to know each other like they saw normal kids on TV or in our neighborhoods doing. But the consequences of behaving like the uncivilized people outside our Nation could be frightening.

Uncle Wallace, for instance, would often call his favorite girl, Janice, when he was sure her father was at the Temple and wouldn't answer the phone. They had a code: let the phone ring twice, hang up, and call right back. That way she would know it was Wallace and would run to the phone before her mother or sisters. But one time her mother answered the phone and caught them. The next day at school Uncle Wallace was called to the Dean of Brothers' office and confronted by Janice's father.

"I hope you have intentions to marry my daughter," Brother Robert 16X snapped. "Yeah, you must be planning to marry her if you're calling my house for her."

Uncle Wallace was stunned. "I'm too young to think about getting married," he said. He was thirteen.

Brother Robert shouted back, "Then I guess you won't be calling on my daughter for a while then, huh?" He leaned toward Uncle Wallace. "Future son-in-law," he added.

Adults and young adults could make formal intentions on a potential spouse, but their courting would have to be chaperoned at all times. There had been rumors of Elijah

Muhammad's extramarital affairs and resulting offspring before I was born, but nobody talked about it now. When I was much older, GrandWillie would explain that no one really talked about it then either. She said it was all kept hush-hush because the few people who believed the rumors to be true also believed the actions to be justified.

"The people just believed he was a prophet and he had to do what he had to do and sometimes we wouldn't understand it, but it wasn't for us to understand because he was the one who was the Messenger of Allah," GrandWillie explained.

"Huh?" I asked, my face twisted, puzzled. I was about twelve when I began asking these more serious questions. "How come everybody else had to follow rules except the officials?"

I remembered how strict the rules were for us common rank-and-file folks. And somehow we usually got caught if we tried to do wrong.

This particular Sunday I was worried that Donna and Nunita might get caught talking about trying to get next to a brother. They seemed to have forgotten what happened to our schoolmate, Gloria, when she was eleven and Sister Memphis caught her staring at one of the young brothers while the Messenger's voice was on. Sister Memphis had called her to the stage during one Monday morning assembly and proceeded to "verbally whip" her. (Elijah Muhammad said verbal whippings could be more devastating than physical ones, and I believed him.) Sister Memphis had humiliated Gloria so bad, calling her a disgrace to her family and to the Nation, that tears streamed down Gloria's face. By the time Sister Memphis finished with her, Gloria was crying so hard she was shaking, her head tucked and shoulders hunched in utter shame. I felt so sorry for her.

I remembered the scene vividly for years to come—my first indication that liking boys could mean trouble. Some others, like Donna and Nunita, seemed to get over it real quick. Already they were cooking up an encounter with Markus.

"Hey, Sonsyrea, Salaam-Alaikum," Nunita said as we both stood at the sinks washing our hands. Nunita had about five sisters and three brothers, all enrolled in our school. She never had to worry about getting teased by the neighborhood kids around her way because she had so many sisters and brothers to stick up for her. Plus, their father had an ice cream truck, and sometimes they gave out treats for free.

"Wa-Laikum-Salaam," I returned, not letting on that I had been listening to their conversation.

When I glanced up in the mirror in front of me, I saw two women standing behind us trying to fix their hair in the mirror. They were visitors who had to wear a scarf while they were inside the Temple. They could be their beautiful selves again now that they were going back out in the world. They wouldn't have to hide their beautiful hair—preserving it for their husbands' eyes only—out there. The Messenger wasn't even finished speaking, but these two women were free to leave.

The Messenger talked bad about women like these, women who wore makeup, straightened hair, and short dresses. He said they were trying to imitate white women and that it was degrading for a woman to go out in public revealing her beauty. But these two women didn't seem to care what anybody in the Temple thought about them. In fact, they acted proud and vain, fixing themselves up in the mirror.

"Paulette, you want to check out an early movie?" one asked the other.

"Sure, why not?" her friend responded as they walked out the door.

Something about them was like cool, refreshing autumn air. I didn't know if it was the fact that they were prettier than the women in the Temple or the fact that they talked louder and swung their hips as they left that struck me the most. I knew women, good Muslim women, weren't supposed to be like that, but I liked them. They looked like sunshine. A lot of the Muslim sisters around me looked like rain, some part of them watered down, muffled. They were too refined.

I looked around at the Muslim women tending to their babies and noticed for the first time that the mother of my schoolmate Tiwana looked really sad. She was a squat woman with thick glasses and the look of country poverty embroidered into all her outfits. I knew they were even poorer than us because Tiwana wore taped-up glasses to school. She had a whole bunch of little sisters and brothers, and she had to help look after them at the Temple on Sundays. She was barely seven or eight years old herself, walking around there with a baby on her hip. My Spanish teacher, Sister Brenda, looked miserable, too.

The only sister who beamed was Sister Faulkner, whose husband, Brother Jeyonne, was one of the F.O.I. leaders. Sister Faulkner was tall and beautiful without makeup, and somehow she shined through her layers of clothes. She had five little boys, but they didn't seem to slow her down a bit. She was always busy doing something around the Temple. If I had to be like anybody when I grew up, it was going to be Sister Faulkner because she managed to seem happy all the time.

When I finished in the bathroom, I still wasn't quite ready to return to my seat upstairs, so I waltzed over to the water fountain, hoping to see Donna and Nunita work their little plan on Markus. Next to the water fountain several teenage brothers were helping the men unload doughnuts and pastries off the bakery truck. They had an assembly line going from the truck to the tables set up in front of the kitchen. Inside the kitchen, sisters who were GrandWillie's age were fixing dinners for sale. GrandWillie cooked sometimes, too, but today wasn't her turn. I looked around but didn't see Markus anywhere. So I figured nothing was going to happen and went on back upstairs. One of the sister hostesses led me back to my seat, and I sat and sat and sat for the duration while the smell of bean soup, baked fish, and whole wheat rolls floated upstairs. I couldn't wait to eat. GrandWillie would buy a dinner for herself and the rest of us in her care after the meeting.

When the Messenger's lecture was over we all stood up to sing the Muslim "fight" song:

> We are fighting for Islam
> And we will surely win . . .

We all stood straight—no slouching allowed—and sang out proud. The song was an ode, an ode to us.

This was a Nation I should go to bat for if necessary, I was learning. Islam, the one true religion, would forever have enemies, I was taught. Islam represents truth in its purest, and truth would always be challenged, as it had been since the beginning of time. So Muslims, true Muslims, real believers, had better be ready to stand and fight. But after one of these long meetings I couldn't stand to fight for anything. I was sleepy and tired. Some of the grown-up men, on the other hand, were recharged.

"You know, I really do thank Allah for sending us the Honorable Elijah Muhammad. He truly is a savior," Brother

Robert 4X would say as he wheeled his big blue Cadillac toward our home. He was GrandWillie's friend's husband, and he always took us home if it was dark outside. The brothers in the Temple were supposed to make sure all the women with no husbands got home safe and sound.

"He's a brilliant man. Absolutely brilliant," he continued, grinning from ear to ear like somebody had just reached up in the air and pulled him down a million dollars. GrandWillie nodded in agreement.

* * *

I simply was awed by the Honorable Elijah Muhammad. Not by his smarts so much, but by the power he had over all these people. I believed he was our savior; we all believed he was our savior. Instead of a picture of a blond-haired, blue-eyed man named Jesus, who I was taught people in the black church wrongfully prayed to, we had a photo of Elijah Muhammad—actually light enough to pass for white—posted in the Temple. It was posted above the entrance to the main hall on the second floor, and we saluted it, clicking our heels once or twice, before passing under it. Sometimes our eyelids instinctively snapped shut when we were doing this.

The heel-clicking part reminded me of Dorothy in the *Wizard of Oz*, which was my favorite movie. In the movie Dorothy stood before the Grand Wizard, clicking her heels, repeating, "There's no place like home, there's no place like home," believing she needed the Wizard's magic to deliver her home. But he explained to her that she had had the power all along. I thought Elijah Muhammad was a wizard and that black people needed his power and wisdom to deliver them from all the stuff the bad white people did.

The narrow road to heaven that Elijah Muhammad talked about sounded like it was probably similar to the yellow brick road in the movie, though I had no idea where this narrow road was in real life. I figured that whenever we found it and started walking on it, I would be shocked and frightened by dangerous surprises all along the way. Just like Dorothy and her friends had to prove themselves worthy of the Wizard's help, I thought it was only right that we had to prove ourselves worthy of being in the Nation. All I had to do was memorize all my lessons so I could represent the Nation well to the outside world.

The older people had to do more. There was always something to do at the Temple or for the Nation. We went to the Temple almost every day of the week for something—school through the week, Fruit of Islam (F.O.I.) meetings on Tuesdays for the boys and men, Muslim Girls' Training and General Civilization Class (M.G.T. and G.C.C.) on Saturday mornings for us girls and our mothers, and the general meetings, which were sort of like church services, on Sundays.

Some of the men and women at the Temple were as stiff and uptight as any Tin Man. Some of the officials seemed like the Lion—ready to take charge as soon as some great Wizard gave them permission. But some of the grown-ups at the Temple seemed as brainless as the Scarecrow, acting like they didn't have minds of their own. Elijah Muhammad told us to dress a certain way and we did. Told us to chew our food a hundred times before swallowing, brush our hair a hundred strokes, and think five times about what we're going to say before we spoke. He gave us a long list of forbidden foods and required all of us, kids and grown-ups alike, to digest the historical and religious lessons.

Elijah Muhammad had our minds completely.

One Nation Under a Rule

CHAPTER 4

In the Nation we had our own religious holiday, our own code of ethics, our own constitution. We also had our own traditions—seasonal bazaars and banquets held at public halls.

Sometimes we held events at Crampton Auditorium on the campus of Howard University. When we were on the campus, usually on a Sunday afternoon, all of us dressed in Nation of Islam–styled uniforms. The non-Nation people seemed to revolve around us like we really were gods and goddesses of the universe.

Passersby stepped out of the way for Muslim women in long, solid-colored, straight skirts and headpieces. They seemed to practically bow to the F.O.I. brothers who patrolled the area.

Our banquets and bazaars were held at the Northwest Gardens building, a public hall uptown. Our events usually were fund-raisers for our schools and for a hospital our leader wanted to build for us. Sometimes the banquets would be held in honor of graduating seniors or honor roll students, in which cases awards were presented.

I looked forward to these events because they were so much fun. I dressed up like GrandWillie, wearing the same color outfit as her, and she let me wear a pair of her small earrings and one of her beaded necklaces to match.

Sometimes GrandWillie selected my outfit to match hers the night before and ironed them both in advance. The events always were held on a Saturday evening, and GrandWillie usually took a nap, since she would be staying up past her regular nine o'clock bedtime.

❋ ❋ ❋

"Sonsy-Ray-Ray, won't you lay down for a few minutes so you don't get tired tonight?" GrandWillie suggested as she unfolded our roll-away bed. When she called me that, I could tell she was in a particularly good mood.

"I'm not tired. I was just sitting out here reading," I said. I was sitting on the balcony outside me and GrandWillie's bedroom, reading my favorite "Aesop's Fables" again, so she could see that I was sort of resting. "Can't I just stay out here and read some more?"

I was as interested in saving my energy for the evening as she was. I would get to see my friends from school at the banquet and be surrounded by hundreds of Nation brothers and sisters. This was as close as we got to family reunions. My Christian relatives didn't really come around us and we didn't really go around them, except in cases of family emergencies like a death or major sickness. The other members of the Nation had become our extended family. Some of the teenage girls at the Temple were like young aunts whom I watched and wanted to grow up to be like, and some of the girls, schoolmates whom I didn't get to socialize with at school because of the strict routine, were like cousins.

Ma was busy cleaning and tending to my baby sister, Sakinah, who was a year old, and my toddler brother, Furard, who was three.

"Ma, are you ready to do my hair?" I asked, approaching her with my comb and brush in hand several times during the afternoon. Even though I'd have to cover my hair, it was important for my braids to be fresh and my barrettes to be the right color to match the outfit I was going to wear.

As usual, Darren was out playing with his neighborhood friends or selling *Muhammad Speaks* newspapers with Uncle Hussein and Uncle Wallace. Dad was in the basement rehearsing one of his groups, and I could hear him throughout the house.

"All right, take it from the top." We heard Dad directing the male singing group that sang Dad's original R & B. Mr. Butch was the lead singer. He had shiny, wavy hair and skinny legs like the black Motown singers I had seen on TV.

"Hush, chile, go to sleep. I know you're hungry, and you gotta eat. But tomorrow I might find a job or somebody might show me the waaaaaay."

This was Dad's group called "The Blendells." They sounded smooth. I bopped my head to the beat as I moved from one "resting" spot to another in the house, on the balcony, and on the porch. Dad's music sounded good enough to me to get on the radio. In fact, that's exactly what he was working on.

"So very, very, very very, very black. Just because my skin is a shade of BLACK," Mr. Butch crooned.

It was warm and sunny, a typical spring day. I held my weaving loom on my lap as I sat on the cement floor of the front porch and wove colorful cotton loops into another potholder for the kitchen. The afternoon before a banquet could not pass quickly enough.

Darren came running up to the house in time to get dressed without Ma having to call him.

"What you doing, Ray-Ray? It's time to get ready," he said, beaming. At about three o'clock it was time for our afternoon prayer, which we made individually in our bedrooms, and time to get dressed.

Ma combed my hair and braided it into three thick braids in her bedroom while everyone else took turns in the bathroom. Dad's rehearsal was still going strong. Uncle Hussein and Uncle Wallace were getting dressed, too. They and Darren wore suits. Ma wore one of her colorful pink, yellow, and orange long dresses and matching headscarf. She dressed Furard in brown slacks and a white turtleneck and my baby sister in a short dress and ruffled socks.

"Darren, go downstairs and tell your father what time it is," Ma told Darren. He was clipping his black bow tie on his white shirt, standing in front of the long mirror in the hallway.

When Ma finished my hair, I went back to my room and asked GrandWillie to reach my outfit she had ironed.

"Here, Sonsyrea, make sure you lotion your legs," she said, handing me her rose-scented lotion, which I could use since this was a special occasion.

"Keep a move on," GrandWillie said when she noticed me slowing down. "You know I can't stand to be late."

Even though Dad wasn't an active member of the Nation, he played jazz on his saxophone with some of the other brothers for some of the banquets and bazaars. But today I heard Darren telling Ma he wasn't coming. "He told me to tell you to call a cab," Darren said. Ma hated that. She always wound up taking us someplace with GrandWillie like we didn't have a father.

"I guess y'all would grow up like weeds if it was up to your father," she often said. "He acts like there's nothing to raising y'all except putting food in your mouth and putting clothes on your behinds."

Dad spent most of his evenings and weekends working with his bands, and Ma wished he spent more time with us.

He took Darren and me to a neighborhood ice cream parlor sometimes and took the family out to dinner occasionally, but that wasn't enough for Ma.

GrandWillie, Ma—carrying Sakinah—Uncle Hussein, Uncle Wallace, I, Darren, and Furard rushed downstairs when we heard the cab horn beeping out front.

When we arrived at the Northwest Gardens, Uncles Wallace and Hussein held open the doors while the rest of us climbed out. Other families dressed in Muslim attire just like ours were approaching the building, some in their own cars, some getting off the bus.

At the banquets, which cost ten dollars for children and fifteen for adults, we sat at round tables adorned with red and white linen tablecloths. My family took up a whole table by ourselves, and many other families were the same size or larger. I made my rounds to visit my friends at their family tables before the meal was served. Darren timed his visits in a way that allowed him to get served a meal at a friend's table across the room and then again at our table.

Ma held Sakinah on her lap and fed her pinches of food while we ate baked chicken, carrots, string beans, and rolls. We were served bean pie, which tasted sort of like sweet potato pie, and ice cream for dessert. Of course, Darren visited another friend's table so he could get two desserts.

Uncle Sharrief worked with the other brothers from our own Shabazz Restaurant serving us dinner. The Shabazz Bakery provided the desserts.

After a banquet I could fall asleep instantly. Sometimes I fell asleep in the cab on the way home. And when I climbed into bed that night, I was out before the lights. Completely exhausted, thoroughly delighted. And the next day, I was likely to inquire about the scheduled date of the next event.

❋ ❋ ❋

Some weekends I spent Friday and Saturday nights at one of my Muslim girlfriends' homes and went to the Temple with her and her family on Sunday. But if I knew, if I even thought, Dad was planning to take Ma and us kids out to dinner on Saturday night, I'd stay home and wait.

Some nights when Dad decided to take us out, Ma decided on Chinatown. Ma liked to sample the multicultural experience our city had to offer, and Chinatown was part of it. Chinatown looked like a regular city neighborhood with storefront buildings lined up in a row, except in Chinatown the signs on most of the buildings were written in Chinese.

The same way you saw nothing but black people in our neighborhood, and in the white neighborhoods you saw white people, in Chinatown, where families lived in rooms above their restaurants and storefronts, the streets were filled with Asian families.

In the Chinese restaurants, Darren and I found amusement watching the mostly Asian customers eat with chopsticks and speak in a strange language. We pulled back the corners of our eyes to make them slanted like the children at tables around us.

"Ching. Chang. Chong," we'd say, laughing and making fun of the odd people. We must have looked odd to the people around us—Ma and I in long dresses, and Darren and Furard with near-bald heads—but it didn't bother me. Chinese people were okay. It was just the Caucasian people we couldn't deal with. In the Muslim school, I had learned that all of us people of color were better than the white devil, and we who were darkest were the absolute best.

Most of the times when we went out to eat, we went to the Shabazz Restaurant, owned and operated by our Nation of Islam. Uncle Sharrief, who was nineteen but claiming to be twenty-one, was the manager of Washington's Shabazz Restaurant, and Uncles Hussein and Wallace worked there on weekends.

The restaurant was located in one of the dingy sections of town, along the 14th Street corridor, which was lined with other small black-owned businesses. At night the pimps, prostitutes, and dope dealers came out. But they never bothered us. There was always a long line, Muslim and non-Muslim, waiting to get inside the restaurant.

The brothers in the Nation who had turned the building into a restaurant with a health food store up front and a fish market on the side had done a great job of carving out a nice, spanking clean place for us to dine. But all around it the streets were ugly. Uncles Hussein and Wallace joked about the rats as big as cats that they had to fend off behind the restaurants when they dumped the trash at night. Sometimes they chased the rats, and sometimes the rats chased them.

When we went to the restaurant, Muslim brothers in white chef jackets and hats served our plates from behind a cafeteria counter. Since we had so many restrictions on what we could eat, they served fish loaf instead of meat loaf, brown rice instead of white rice, and brown rolls made from 100 percent whole wheat flour instead of white rolls made from bleached flour, which we were taught had been stripped of all its nutrients. They served carrot fluff, a sweet blend of soft carrots, brown sugar, nutmeg, cinnamon, and enough eggs to make it fluffy like mashed sweet potatoes. We couldn't eat sweet potatoes because Elijah Muhammad said they had too much starch and gas for our bodies.

"Ma, may I have the chicken dinner?" I asked one evening, moving in line behind my mother, pushing my tray along the serving rail.

Carrying my baby sister, Sakinah, in one arm, pushing a tray with the other, Dad set a pretty slow pace moving through the food line at the restaurant.

"Sonsyrea, don't ask me questions right now," my mother said. "I'll do the ordering."

"Ma, I want the fish loaf and the—" Darren said before Ma cut him off.

"I *said*, I'll do the ordering," she told him. Then Dad butted in.

"Moe, let the kids get what they want," he said. My mother was the strict one. Dad just wanted us to be happy. I never really understood who wore the pants, so to speak, between Ma and Dad. As far as I could tell, Ma put Dad in control, like she was saying, "Okay, you be the man, and this is what the man's supposed to do, okay, honey? Kiss, kiss." All the domestic decisions and decisions about raising us seemed to be hers, and she hated when he interfered with that.

"I-want-the-chicken-dinner-with-the-carrot-fluff-and-string-beans-and-I-want-a-roll-with-two-butters-please-oh-yeah-and-a rootbeer-with-a-straw," I told one brother behind the counter, taking advantage of Dad's interference.

Darren jumped in to tell the other brother, "Give-me-the-chicken-breast-that-big-one-right-there-and-the-corn-I-only-want-one-vegetable-and-you-can-make-it-up-by-putting-two-pieces-of-bean-pie-with-it-Brother-George I-mean-SIR!" He caught the mean look on my mother's face. "Please," he said. She was still looking at him angrily. "Thank you," he added.

Ma rolled her eyes at Dad, sighed, then ordered for herself. Uncle Sharrief came from the kitchen to greet us.

"As-Salaam-Alaikum," he said. "Everything okay?"

Everything was okay with me. People who used to laugh at us were eating at *our* restaurant, sucking in the aroma of our special recipes for bean soup and Whiting fish, browsing through our newspapers they bought on their way in. I thought people were beginning to realize that the Muslim way was the right way and that life could be this good for all black people if they only listened to the Messenger.

CHAPTER 5

Brothers Got My Back

Just as Darren learned early on that our mother and all the rest of us women were put on this Earth to serve him, cook for him, and clean up behind him, I learned that men were here to protect and provide for me.

Sometimes I missed the girls' bus going home and had to wait in the girls' bathroom until school let out for the boys, then ride home with my brother and uncles on the boys' bus. I usually sat by myself in the seat behind the bus driver and looked out the window the whole time. The rules said that we couldn't talk on the bus. So the boys buckled into their seats and remained silent as Uncle Hussein, junior F.O.I. captain, paced up and down the aisle making sure nobody talked or ate on the bus. Some of the boys had lunch bags full of doughnuts from our bakery bought after school, and they pinched off bites because they couldn't wait until they got home. If Uncle Hussein caught anybody, he made him hit the floor right there on the bus and do push-ups.

Sometimes as we rode I'd stare at little Chris, whose father managed the Muslim restaurant, and think maybe I could marry him when I grew up. I knew I'd have to marry somebody since that was the only reason I was on this Earth—to become a good wife and mother. I also considered Debra-Mitchel's little brother, Ibn, because he was cute and cool. All of us girls had our favorites, but most of the other girls never got the chance to ride the boys' bus and check out all the brothers like I did.

The boys' bus was more fun than the girls' because sometimes the boys got into fights with the heathen. In one particular neighborhood we passed through, the neighborhood boys, who were heathen because they had not been saved or made civilized by the teachings of the Honorable Elijah Muhammad, would wait for our yellow school bus and throw rocks, dirt, and snowballs. It was as if the boys in the neighborhood had heard about these strange Muslim boys and their reputation for fighting and wanted to see for themselves. One time the neighborhood boys threw buckets of water through the windows of the bus and Darren got all wet.

Generally, Brother Jack didn't let the young brothers off the bus to fight because he told them to learn to use patience when dealing with their uncivilized brethren. Brother Jack said it wasn't right for blacks to fight blacks. But after so many days of taunting, he finally let the young brothers work out a plan. For the next few days no one would even turn their heads to acknowledge the neighborhood boys. Then, on a day they set, Brother Jack stopped the bus, opened the back door, and let the brothers loose. I stayed on the bus and watched as the Muslim boys, who all looked alike with bald heads, white shirts, and dark slacks, chased the savages into the woods.

A few moments later, I asked Brother Jack, "What's taking them so long?"

"Oh, they'll be right back," he said. "They just got a little business to take care of."

"Well, I hope my brother don't tear his coat," I said, knowing that my mother wasn't a live-for-the-Nation-die-for-the-Nation-sacrifice-your-coat-if-necessary kind of member. "He's gonna get in trouble if he tears his coat."

Brother Jack tried to distract me with conversation, asking me about what I had learned in school that day. He had asked several questions before the young brothers came running back.

As we pulled away, they were laughing and slapping high fives. Darren sat on my seat and was trying to catch his breath. Uncle Wallace came back to the front to check on us.

"Did you get some licks in?" I asked my brother. He was a little shaken but tried not to show it.

"Girl, move over," he said.

"Let me see," I said. "Did you tear your coat? I can fix it so Ma won't see." In the Muslim Girls' Training and General Civilization classes for sisters, I had learned enough basic stitches to be able to mend my brother's coat if necessary.

My brother was one of the real soldiers who defended our Nation, and I was proud. Around the neighborhood and on the public buses, I had heard people talk about how sharp, how fierce, how strong "them Moozlem men" were. There were always rumors about F.O.I. brothers here in Washington or in other cities killing people or planning to. I never knew how much of it was true.

One night when I was trying to fall asleep I couldn't help but overhear my uncles and brother in the next room talk about a particular brother—I'll just call him "Todd" here—who was rumored to have committed a murder years ago.

"Uncle Hussein, Ibn said Brother Todd killed a lady before. Did you know anything about it?" Darren had apparently been waiting for them to get home, because he hit them with the question as soon as they walked into the room. "Ibn said Brother Todd thought the lady was a spy and killed her, then found out he got the wrong lady. Is that true?"

"Boy, go to sleep, y'all little kids don't be knowing what you talking 'bout, just trying to repeat what you hear the grown-ups say. Don't be going around talking about that, you hear?"

I wanted to go in there and say "Salaam-Alaikum" to them because I hadn't seen them all day, but I couldn't get out of bed once Ma put me in it. My uncles, who were more like big brothers to me because they were so young, never fussed at me like they fussed at Darren. And they wouldn't let anybody else—except Ma—fuss at me, either. They told me all the time, "Girl, I'll kill a rock for you, make water cry," which meant they would attempt the impossible to ensure my safety.

I knew my older uncles could fight because they laughed with each other about how teens in the neighborhood backed down from them. Not just because they were in the Nation, but also because they were Tates. And just like with the F.O.I., if you messed with one, you had to deal with them all. A girl couldn't have felt safer around them.

❋ ❋ ❋

My uncles were the best. All men in the world should be like them, I thought. They often told me how pretty I was.

"Jane Kennedy! She's downstairs for real," Uncle Avon would tease. "Aw, man, that's Ray-Ray," Uncle Wallace would respond. I didn't think I looked anything like the super black model I saw on TV because when I looked in the mirror, all I saw was this real plain little girl not even allowed to show pretty barrettes on my hair to the world outside. But maybe I was pretty anyway. If my uncles said so, then maybe it was a little bit true, I reasoned.

Everything my uncles told me about myself stuck in my head, and I wanted it to stay there forever. Even when they called me a tattletale and a Rhona Barrett of the projects, after some TV gossip reporter, I figured I must be what they said I was. They called me the ghetto news reporter because I was always telling on them.

Like the time I just happened to go down to the basement to talk to them and caught them playing with a BB gun. They didn't know that I knew they weren't supposed to be playing with it, so they didn't pay me any attention. When I saw them I just turned around and went back upstairs and poured myself a cup of water in the kitchen and calmly told Grand-Willie, "They down there shooting a gun."

"You say what!" she shouted.

"They got a gun, pointing it at some marks on the wall," I said.

She went down there and fussed at them, then came back upstairs and told me I was good to tell any time I saw somebody doing something wrong. She knew they would be mad at me. So she wanted me to know she was glad. Later that evening Uncle Sharrief managed to get close enough to me to whisper in my ear, "Snitch!" and I cried, but I didn't go tell GrandWillie on him because he would just get even madder.

My uncles were growing up, moving out, and making their own living. Uncle Edward and Uncle Avon still hung around with the wrong crowd, but Uncle Sharrief, Uncle Hussein, and Uncle Wallace were becoming clean-cut, responsible men. Uncle Sharrief got married when he was eighteen and moved into an apartment up on 16th Street where I saw a lot of foreigners, but he still came by the family house a lot. Uncle Hussein was fourteen years old and about to graduate and go on to college. Nation officials were trying to open a college for all the high school graduates who were too young to enter colleges and universities out in society. (Some of the kids were smart enough to get into any college anyway, but some of them would fail standardized tests because our history and social science information was so different from what was taught out in the world.) Uncle Wallace had already begun sitting in on Saturday morning math classes at Howard University, since the man who taught it was in the Nation and allowed a few Nation boys to attend.

❋ ❋ ❋

Uncle Sharrief let Darren work with them at the restaurant on the weekends sweeping the floors and wiping the tables clean. But sometimes he had to send him home early in a cab because Darren was around there eating too much and Uncle Sharrief was afraid he might eat himself sick. Darren would be so mad when he got sent home because he was afraid he would miss something if he was at home with the women—and one time he did.

Uncle Hussein, Uncle Wallace, and Uncle Sharrief were working at the restaurant one evening when a group of government inspectors in business suits entered the restaurant saying they wanted to inspect the place. Uncle Sharrief told them they had to wait until the next day because the manager needed to be present. The government men insisted that they be allowed to inspect the building, but Uncle Sharrief knew that he had a right to refuse.

The inspectors went to a pay phone outside and called for backup, and Uncle Sharrief called the Temple for some F.O.I. backup, then locked the doors until they arrived.

It was all a matter of principle, Uncle Sharrief figured. He knew that government officials harassed and tried to intimidate Nation members in little ways, and he just wasn't going to let them this time. Just a year or so ago, in Baton Rouge,

Louisiana, some government men had arrested a few Nation of Islam brothers and charged them with soliciting without identification while they were selling *Muhammad Speaks*. Dozens of brothers went back and held a protest, a fight broke out, gunshots were fired—though F.O.I. brothers never carried weapons—and four men wound up dead. Two of the men were cops, and the other two F.O.I. brothers.

At the restaurant here in Washington, the F.O.I. brothers arrived before the police and formed a barricade outside. Two dozen F.O.I. brothers dressed in their immaculate uniforms or in dark suits with white shirts and bow ties. The only weapon Uncle Sharrief and the others had was their faith. They said a prayer before they went out, and each of them knew that Allah would make them the winners in this battle against the devil. Some of the police who arrived were black, but they were still working for the devil, so that made them devils, too. Uncle Sharrief, the other brothers who worked at the restaurant, and about two dozen F.O.I. brothers stood there stone-faced and ready for battle.

They could kill with their bare hands if a fight broke out. Some were mean dudes who had grown up fighting in the streets. Now that Elijah Muhammad had convinced them that they weren't hoodlums but children of God, they were absolutely fearless. Because Uncle Hussein and Uncle Wallace were just teens, they stood between some of the larger brothers, but they felt as strong and as brave as the bigger men. They lived for the Nation and would die for it.

They told us all about it when they got home that evening. GrandWillie and Ma were just as entertained as I was as Uncles Hussein and Wallace recalled all the details. Darren sat there pouting.

Police troops, armed with tear gas, night sticks, and guns, lined up and faced off with the F.O.I. a few feet away from them. The police blocked the streets so traffic couldn't get through, and hundreds of spectators crowded around at both ends of the street to watch. Uncle Wallace kept his fists balled up and his eyes straight ahead while he listened to Brother Captain Harrell, who went from one end of the line to the other. Uncle Hussein kept his head straight like he was supposed to, but his eyes shifted from side to side sizing up the different policemen. It was very tense.

The standoff lasted about three hours while our local minister negotiated with the police sergeant. They agreed that the manager would be on the premises of the restaurant the next day and the inspectors would be allowed access to inspect. Brother Captain marched to the center of the ranks and told them they were dismissed.

"I'm so glad y'all stood your ground," GrandWillie told my young uncles. "That's one thing about living in this white man's world. You gotta know your rights or they'll push you around and even get other blacks to push you around, too."

I was just happy to know that my uncles were as brave with big ole policemen as they were with the little boys I watched them chase into the woods. My uncles were bad—in the goodest way.

❋ ❋ ❋

I missed my brother now that he was spending more time learning to be a man. Sometimes I sat on the steps near the doorway in the hall waiting for him to come in with our uncles. But when he came in, he'd push me aside and run up to the boys' room with them.

Darren was so happy he was allowed to work with the big boys selling *Muhammad Speaks* and other Nation of Islam products like bean pies and gingerbread and fish. When the bundles of newspapers were passed down an assembly line leading from a truck out front of the Temple to a storage room inside the Temple, Darren was one of the little ones who practically had the wind knocked out of them as the newspapers caught them in their chests.

The men had to take home at least two hundred *Muhammad Speaks* a week. But often brothers took home five hundred, trying to be the top seller. The brother with the most sales would win a free dinner for his family at the Muslim restaurant, but he was more motivated by the feeling of accomplishment.

Brothers who made top sales were called to the platform and praised by our local minister, Dr. Lonnie Shabazz, during Sunday service.

"Brothers and sisters, let's give a round of applause to brother George 12X for selling over five hundred *Muhammad Speaks* this week," Minister Lonnie Shabazz would say. "Just think if everybody went out and did that each week. All praises due to Allah for Brother George. Give him a round of applause."

Our local minister, Dr. Lonnie Shabazz, was a stern yet compassionate figure with high expectations of the brothers. He held a Ph.D. in Education from Cornell University and had moved up through the ranks in the Nation quickly.

Uncle Hussein, Uncle Wallace, and the other teenage brothers looked up to the men in the Nation and worked hard to be like them. The teenage boys didn't have to sell a certain number of papers until they turned seventeen, but they would go out there anyway. By the time Uncles Hussein and Wallace were thirteen and fourteen, they'd stopped taking the school bus straight home after school every day. Some days they went downtown to hustle papers on the street.

The boys traveled in packs with other boys their age, eight to ten heads strong. They'd have *Muhammad Speaks* in one hand, bean pies and gingerbread in the other.

"*Muhammad Speaks!* News for the black man! Brothers and sisters. Only a quarter."

The older teens and the men also spent many evenings and weekends "fishing for the dead," which is what we called recruiting because we considered blacks outside the Nation mentally dead, unaware of their true self-worth. The brothers recruited in night clubs, they caught people coming out of church meetings, and they stopped to talk on street corners. Once one of the teenage brothers, Brother Harold 6X, rounded up so many recruits that Brother Minister had to send a van to pick them all up. A prize also was given to the brother who reeled in the most "lost-and-found" recruits each week.

Uncle Wallace said when the brothers were out fishing for the dead or selling papers, they didn't think about smoking, drinking, or getting into trouble because they all wanted to honor the Nation's code of conduct. Nobody wanted to disgrace the Nation. Helping to build a Nation, being respected in such a Nation, feeling loved and encouraged by the general populace in the Nation made a lot of the brothers feel proud. The Nation was teaching them that strong men don't need dope. That real men don't cheat or look for the easy way out. Uncle Sharrief, Uncle Wallace, Uncle Hussein, Darren, and the other boys believed they were real men, strong men.

❋ ❋ ❋

In the evenings when Uncle Hussein, Uncle Wallace, and Darren would retreat to their bedroom to count their earnings, I stood by the doorway and listened. They could keep only a nickel out of each quarter and had to turn the rest over to the Nation, but they didn't mind. When they were just about finished sorting and counting, I'd knock on the door just as they were rolling their coins, and they all would shell out some silver coins to me. Due to my perfect timing, my penny bank was half full.

My uncles were learning to be providers for—and protectors of—the women in their family. They were taught that the best way to protect us women was to keep us off the streets. We women were taught to conduct ourselves in a way that commanded respect so we wouldn't put our men in a position to have to defend our honor.

One Friday evening while it was still light outside, Darren and I were playing with a group of children when our next-door neighbor, Donald, picked me up and swung me around in circles. Donald was only an inch or two taller than me and didn't weigh much more. I was laughing right up until the time his little arms got weak and dropped me. Then I was on my butt on the ground, crying over my skinned knees, and the other kids were laughing. Uncles Hussein and Wallace came out of the house on their way to the Temple.

"What's the matter with Ray-Ray?" Uncle Wallace asked Darren. Darren shrugged his shoulders like he didn't know.

"Donald dropped me," I cried out.

"Darren, did Donald make your sister cry?" Uncle Hussein asked him. Uncle Hussein was usually calmer than Uncle Wallace.

"Yeah," Darren said. "But he was just playing with her. It was an accident."

"Don't make no difference, boy!" Uncle Hussein snapped. "If somebody made your sister cry, you gotta beat him up!"

All the kids got quiet, and Darren got scared. He didn't want to fight Donald—not only because they were friends, but because Donald's big brother Chris had taught Darren and Donald how to box, and Darren knew Donald could beat him.

"It was just an accident," Darren mumbled, looking kind of meek.

"Sonsyrea, you go on in the house," Uncle Hussein ordered. Then he turned back to Darren. "Darren, get him."

Darren took off his jacket so his arms could move freely. I moved slowly up the stairs, turning back to catch the action. The other kids formed a circle around Darren and Donald the way kids always did when there was going to be a fight. Darren and Donald put up their dukes like they were pro boxers.

I just wanted to see the first jab, then I could go on in the house. The kids crowded in around Darren and Donald, blocking my view. Climbing the last step up to the front door, I noticed the blood coming through the knees of my pant legs. Just dots of blood. But I began limping. I heard the kids cheering the fight, but the noise faded behind me as I went in the house. All my senses were focused on my knees. I was hurt. My dignity and my knees.

Everything was all messed up now. I had caused my brother to fight his own friend, our own next-door neighbor. This could have been avoided if I had stayed on the porch like I was supposed to.

That's exactly why the Honorable Elijah Muhammad said we women should stay in the house, I reasoned in my head. Ever since Adam and Eve, he taught, we women were always stirring up trouble. That's why our Savior taught the brothers to protect us and, furthermore, to control us and keep us in our place. My place as a Muslim girl was on the porch. That's where I should have stayed.

Mother Earth/ Goddess of the Universe

CHAPTER 6

We all had our place—little girls, mothers, and even grandmothers. The rules said no Muslim woman, regardless of age, could be out in public after dark without a male escort.

One time GrandWillie and four of her friends traveled to Chicago for the annual Savior's Day Convention. GrandWillie's friend, Sister Marie, had made plans with a friend to take them to a nice restaurant and then show them around the city. But as GrandWillie, Sister Marie, and the others were leaving the hotel, two F.O.I. brothers stopped them.

"You sisters know you're not supposed to be out after dark," one of them said. "It's our duty to protect you. The Honorable Elijah Muhammad teaches us that . . . "

GrandWillie and her friends just sucked their teeth and returned to their rooms. GrandWillie didn't even bother to turn on her TV because she figured one of the brothers might run in her room and remind her that the Honorable Elijah Muhammad teaches us not to watch the white man's TV shows.

Instead of bucking the Nation's system and standing up to the F.O.I., GrandWillie just laid out her clothes for the next day and went to sleep. She would spend the whole day at the hotel attending seminars and lectures and roaming around one of the ballrooms where Muslim vendors had set up shop. She and her friends did finally go out to a restaurant before they boarded a train home after the conference, but they didn't have time to go sight-seeing like they wanted to.

GrandWillie brought me home a Muslim dollbaby from the bazaar. I heard her telling Ma about the F.O.I. brothers turning them around. She told her that on the last day of the convention when she and her friends went to a restaurant, they saw some of the F.O.I. and M.G.T. officials there eating foods they were not supposed to be eating.

"Meauvelle, they were in there tearing them potatoes up. Now you know we can't eat no white potatoes," she told Ma. "I told Sister Marie, 'You know, I think they give us a whole bunch of rules to follow, but they do whatever it is they want to do.'"

Ma already knew that, because Dad had told her about how hypocritical some of the brothers in charge were when he was little. Ma had joined the Nation just so she could get me and Darren in the school, and for the first five years she liked it. But now she could see how it wasn't all good. For instance, Ma thought it wasn't right how Sister Captain picked certain sisters out to humiliate in front of other people. That's one of the reasons Ma didn't go to the Temple often anymore. Ma also didn't think it was right for the brothers in Chicago to meddle in the affairs of GrandWillie and her friends.

Ma thought the Nation officials were too intrusive, but GrandWillie tried to grin and bear it. At home she even had a little teddy bear holding a sign that said, "Grin and Bear It."

❋ ❋ ❋

Elijah Muhammad said black men should protect black women from the white man by keeping us out of the white man's reach, out of his offices, and out of his world. He said the fight for women's liberation was a white woman's battle; that the black woman needed to stay home and take care of her husband and children. The black man, he said, had enough to fight out in the world without having to fight with his woman over women's rights.

The year was 1974, and out in the world women were pushing the limits on what a woman could and could not do. With the National Organization of Women marching and lobbying for an Equal Rights Amendment, a lot more women were seeking independence and running for public office. Instead of being confined to traditional women's jobs, like working as teachers, they wanted to become principals. Instead of being telephone operators, they wanted the freedom to climb telephone poles. And instead of being secretaries, they wanted to ascend the corporate ladder.

But Ma and GrandWillie both sided with Elijah Muhammad on this one. Working women were the reason our society was going to hell, they explained to me. GrandWillie's own mother had dutifully stayed home to raise her fourteen kids. And GrandWillie said the society was better when women stayed home.

"After the men came home from World War II and told the women they could go back home, the women got hardheaded," she said. "Once they tasted a little bit of that freedom, having their own paycheck, you couldn't get them to go back in the house."

GrandWillie seemed to enjoy cooking, ironing, sewing, and cleaning up behind her half-grown sons. She was very pleasant about it. But Ma always fussed at Dad about leaving his socks lying around for her to pick up. Ma grew up in the 1950s when women were out in the work force, and her own mother, Grandma Thomas, always worked—sometimes two jobs. Grandma Thomas said Ma needed to get out of the house and work like everybody else. Granddaddy Thomas said Ma was lazy and just using religion as an excuse to stay home. They didn't consider baby-sitting other people's children "real work," but it seemed like real work to me. (I hated when anybody said anything bad about Ma, but I was too little to stand up for her.)

Even though GrandWillie and Ma talked bad about career women, I couldn't help but admire those types of women. They looked good on TV. My favorite commercial was a perfume commercial where a woman sang, "I can bring home the bacon." Wink. Wink. "Fry it up in the pan. And never, ever, ever let you forget you're a man. 'Cause I'm a woooo-man." I'd sing it loud all day long, like some kind of freedom call. Ma hated it.

"I've told you about singing that song," she'd say. "It's nonsense, and I don't want to hear it coming out of your mouth."

Then I'd sing it silently. Before Ma got all snappy about it, I might have thought the commercial was just about perfume. Now I knew it was about freedom. Being able to do it all: "'Cause I'm a woooo-man."

❋ ❋ ❋

At eight years old, I knew there was women's work and men's work, and I knew that Elijah Muhammad said we shouldn't try to mix the two up like they were doing out in the world.

At school we never talked about what we wanted to be when we grew up, except when our teachers encouraged our individual talents, privately. Like when Sister Doris told me that since I liked to write, maybe I could write for the *Muhammad Speaks* one day. As a group, we girls learned that motherhood was the most important job a woman could have.

Sister Helen taught us about our wombs in one memorable lesson. She made us all stand up at our seats and said, "Put your hand on your womb." Most of us looked around the room, giggling, dumbfounded or embarrassed.

I folded my arms across my stomach and sighed. "I guess this is my womb," I said to myself. "This is where babies come from, a woman's stomach." I had seen three of them grow big in my mother's stomach—even though one was born dead. Sister Helen walked up and down the aisles surveying us like a sergeant. Even Zina, who was usually tough, looked sheepish now. Vernada folded her hands across her pelvic area. Susan copied her. And Saundra made a pyramid with her fingers and lay the pyramid on her pelvis.

"Sister Saundra, come up here and show your classmates our WOMB," our teacher said. She drew the letters large on the board, and our silly looks turned serious again. "This is the most precious organ in the world," she told us. "Life is created in the woman's womb. Allah didn't give men a womb. That's the special gift he gave the woman. The womb is connected to the . . . " and she proceeded to explain the baby-making process as my mind stayed stuck on the significance of the womb. Some of my classmates were ten and eleven and starting their periods, so they needed to know this stuff more than me, I figured. I copied our vocabulary list off the board—*womb*, *uterus*, and *conception*—to look up in the dictionary for homework, and was glad that lesson was over. The only thing interesting about it was the fact that we could have babies and men couldn't. Nothing else about growing up to be a woman in the Nation of Islam seemed interesting.

❋ ❋ ❋

Some of the women in the Nation worked because they had to help support their families since their husbands couldn't or wouldn't. Some of my classmates' mothers worked. A couple of GrandWillie's friends worked cleaning rich white people's homes—and their husbands fussed at them for all the years they did. Some of them worked as nurses, which their husbands liked just a little bit better. Dad didn't want Ma to work at all. He said no wife of his needed a job. I could have told him Ma needed a job because we didn't have enough money to get a house of our own. But Ma would never let me tell Dad something like that. If she had known I was even thinking that Dad wasn't providing sufficiently for us, she would have gone inside my head and stopped the thoughts.

Ma kept telling me that rich white women didn't work, that they stayed home and took care of their kids like she was doing. I thought it was kind of odd that she was trying to be like rich white people, since we believed they were the devils. But I didn't quite know how to ask her about that.

GrandWillie and Ma made homemaking their full-time job and baby-sitting their business. They kept about a dozen kids during the day. GrandWillie and Ma had a rigorous schedule that included cleaning the house, preparing meals, feeding kids, sending some off to school, and teaching toddlers. When I got home from school, I changed out of my school clothes and helped Ma and GrandWillie with their baby-sitting. I enjoyed bossing the little ones around.

❋ ❋ ❋

Sisters weren't required to go out selling newspapers or fishing for the dead, although many of the sisters tried to recruit old friends and neighbors. The elder sisters, including GrandWillie, cooked dinners to sell at the Temple on weekends. GrandWillie also served on several committees, such as the one that visited sick people and another that organized activities for us children.

Most Saturday mornings, GrandWillie and I went to M.G.T. and G.C.C. (Muslim Girls' Training and General Civilization Class) at the Temple at nine A.M. Ma didn't go to M.G.T. class anymore because she had to stay home with the little kids. Plus, she was slowly but surely easing her way out of the Nation. She went to the Temple only once in a while now, but I still wound up there seven days a week—for school Mondays through Fridays, M.G.T. class Saturdays, and Sunday meetings.

When GrandWillie and I arrived in front of the Temple one Saturday for M.G.T. class, a brother dressed in his F.O.I. uniform rushed to the taxi and snatched open the door.

"As-Salaam-Alaikum, Sister Willie," he said, helping GrandWillie out the cab.

He reached for my little hand and tilted his head. "Little sister," he said. I felt like a queen, a little Goddess of the Universe.

Sister Barbara taught us little girls basic sewing stitches so we could mend our socks and make clothes for our dolls. When we got older, we could make clothes for ourselves like GrandWillie and most of the other women did. We also did arts and crafts in my class, using kits for basket weaving and to make potholders. While newly "liberated" women bought fire trucks for their daughters, we girls in the Nation learned to remain domestic.

Sister Captain Margaret Ann taught GrandWillie's class, and on the days when not enough sisters showed up for the different level classes, we'd all sit in the class for elders that Sister Captain taught. Sister Captain, who was in her late forties like GrandWillie, always showed up no matter what the weather. Distinguished by the gold trim around the high collar and around the edges of the sleeves on her uniform, she drew large letters on the chalkboard: *The Navy Bean*.

"What are the qualities of the navy bean?" she asked the class.

Sister Mariam 3X, one of GrandWillie's friends, raised her hand.

"The Honorable Elijah Muhammad teaches us that the navy bean is very rich in protein," she said. "It is very high in fiber, and it will prolong our life."

We would discuss the nutrients of the navy bean for almost an hour. The teenage girls in the class knew a lot of the answers, too. I admired the teenagers because they were always looking for little ways they could have fun and go around our many rules. They'd go to the bathroom and shorten their long skirts at the waist and comb their hair so that as soon as they were far enough away from the Temple they could snatch off their headpieces.

At the Temple, Sister Captain came down hard on whomever she caught acting out of order. In fact, she could be downright mean. I felt bad for any woman she sent home because her uniform wasn't clean enough. She'd talk about the woman in front of everybody. And sometimes, instead of sending the woman home, she'd take her in the bathroom and talk to her until she cried, then make her go back to the group with a tear-stained face. I knew how mean she could be. That's why I made gifts that I presented to her and Sister Memphis.

I wished I had been there to protect GrandWillie when Sister Captain came down hard on her. It happened when I was a baby, when GrandWillie and Granddaddy Tate returned to the Temple after they had been away for a few years because of Granddaddy's fight with Brother Captain over how many newspapers he had to sell. GrandWillie and Granddaddy returned to the Nation in order to enroll my young uncles in the Muslim school.

GrandWillie and Granddaddy had to reactivate their membership by going to the meetings and other functions again. The first Sunday they went back to the Temple, Sister Captain put a chair outside the Temple's main office downstairs in the lobby area and made GrandWillie sit in it during the whole service, like my grandmother was a kid in the dunce corner in school. She was making an example out of GrandWillie because she had strayed. People walked back and forth past GrandWillie, looking down at her shaking their heads or refusing to look at her at all. GrandWillie just kept her head up and her eyes straight ahead looking at the empty air, saying to herself, "This is not no one person's religion, so I'm not going to let her get to me."

After the meeting, Sister Captain took GrandWillie in the office and challenged her on the twenty-five "Actual Facts." If GrandWillie had missed any one of them or had said it in the wrong way—intonation was important—Sister Captain would have told her not to come back to the Temple and not to send her kids to the school.

GrandWillie recited them all correctly. She wanted her kids to benefit from the Honorable Elijah Muhammad's great wisdom, so she would do what she had to do. Plus, the Nation members had become the only extended family her kids could associate with since GrandWillie's own family had cut her off.

Sister Captain didn't miss a beat. If someone pranced into the Temple with her headpiece pulled back halfway off her head, she'd pull her aside and tell her to stop being vain. If she caught someone coming through the door of the Temple without a headpiece on, she'd stop her and scold her.

"Sister, you know this is not something you carry in your purse and throw on your head once you get in the Temple," she'd say.

A sister could get called down front for being seen in public with her hair uncovered. She could get suspended from the Nation or expelled. Sister Captain—and the other officials, in fact—could make it hard on the no-ranking sisters they didn't like.

I had a feeling that's why Ma stopped coming to the Temple as much as she once did—because she didn't like to witness the other sisters humiliated and because she knew one day they might put her on the spot, too.

❋ ❋ ❋

I wasn't afraid of getting called out by Sister Captain because she liked me—thanks to my gifts, I guess. To me, M.G.T. class was sort of like get-togethers, our own kind of special sister socials, even though it was a class and we had lessons to learn.

Several of the teenage girls were studying extra hard and cozying up to Sister Captain, hoping to move into a junior leadership position, like captain of the junior drill team. But Tynetta seemed to be Sister Captain's choice. She probably would have been chosen for drill team leader if the minister's daughter hadn't been assigned. Some of the young women felt slighted because Sister Captain—and Sister Memphis and the other sister officials—played favorites in who they promoted in the drill team.

I didn't care because I was too little to be picked for anything anyway. I just enjoyed being a part of the sisterhood. To me M.G.T. class was like a tea party with real people and real talking instead of stuffed animals and toy dishes. But for some of the other women it was more like a meeting, an opportunity for them to talk about things that bothered them.

The sisters might discuss a concern about the background investigations that were done before a couple got married. Brother Captain would check the brother's past to see if he had been married before or had kids and to see what he had to offer the sister, and Sister Captain would talk to family members and sisters about the sister's emotional well-being and housekeeping habits. The couple would also have to be counseled before they could marry. All this was supposed to help ensure a successful marriage. But some members found it too imposing.

Ma's sister-in-law, Aunt Leona, who was married to Ma's foster brother, Uncle Lloyd, used one particular M.G.T. class to complain about the demands of the Nation on her husband and herself. She talked about the eviction notice that arrived at her apartment that week. Aunt Leona, who at one time was a Black Panther, joined the Nation with Uncle Lloyd right after they got married. Now she was concerned about Uncle Lloyd's priorities. When she was seven months pregnant with their first child, Uncle Lloyd used the rent money to pay for the *Muhammad Speaks* newspapers he couldn't sell.

Aunt Leona said she could go along with budgeting their money to allow only five dollars a week for groceries like Elijah Muhammad suggested, but enough was enough.

"I don't mind eating bean soup every day," she said that day in class. "But I can't stand by and let us get evicted. We have a baby on the way."

Her teacher assured her that Almighty Allah, who came in the person of Master Fard Muhammad, would make a way. Our job was to stand by our man through the worst of times.

There was going to be a great war of Armageddon, the prophesied battle between right and wrong, "black and white," and the world would be restored to its natural order, we were taught. The black man would win the war, of course, and resume his rightful place of leadership. And we, his black woman, would be his right hand at home.

One subject that no one dared discuss in M.G.T. class was the rumors they'd all heard about the Honorable Elijah Muhammad getting a few of his secretaries pregnant and not taking care of those children. He was above all our laws and the policies he said he set for our own benefit.

Once in a while, Sister Captain had all the sisters stand up in a single line so she could do a random inspection, checking under their headpieces to make sure that they had indeed combed their hair.

"Cleanliness is next to godliness," she reminded us. The requirement that we cover our hair was no license to neglect grooming it, she said. GrandWillie would never get caught with her hair undone. She went to the beauty parlor first thing on Saturday mornings. Every Saturday morning. Before the rest of us even got out of bed.

At M.G.T. class we learned about acting ladylike. We learned not to use profanity and not to raise our voices, and we practiced walking with a book balanced like a crown on our head. If the book fell, it meant that a sister was still walking with her head down. This was as close to charm school as some of us low-income folks would get. Some Saturdays we practiced karatelike self-defense exercises, and Sister Captain reminded us, "The Honorable Elijah Muhammad teaches us that we are never to be the aggressors. But if someone attacks us for our beliefs, then we are to do what?"

"Fight like hell to the bitter end!" I shouted with the other sisters, who had formed a single line to practice lifting their long skirts to kick.

❋ ❋ ❋

After class was dismissed, I sometimes stayed behind for drill team rehearsal. In the kitchen GrandWillie and other sisters prepared fish dinners, beef burgers, and bean soup for sale. Out in the open room the sisters' drill team formed a block five sisters wide and six sisters deep.

"Atten-hut!" Sister Suede commanded, prompting the block of sisters to snap to a stiffened position.

"Present arms!" she continued, prompting them to a righteous salute.

"At ease."

"Atten-hut!" Again they snapped into focusing their complete and undivided attention on her commands.

"Left face!" she commanded. "Right face. Left face, left face, right face, left face, to the reeeeaaaar MARCH!"

The block of sisters snapped and turned and turned and turned to each of the commands, their skirts and headpieces swaying. It was important to be able to follow commands and move swiftly together as one unit. I watched from my position on the sideline, eagerly anticipating the day I'd be old enough to join.

"I think we've got the best team in this region. Am I right or wrong?" Sister Suede hollered, as the sister soldiers marched in place.

"You're right!" they shouted back.

"Two, four, six, eight, who do we appreciate?"

"Elijah," they responded.

"Once more."

"Muhammad."

"Break it on down."

"Elijah." Step. Step. "Muhammad." Step. "M-U-H-A-M-M-A-D!"

They were preparing for a drill competition with teams from public high schools in the area. By winning, they could boost our Nation's image. No doubt the F.O.I. would escort them to their competition, and that would just make these sisters look extra special. Well protected.

❋ ❋ ❋

My other aunts, who grew up in the Nation, had never joined the M.G.T. drill squad because they never liked being in the Nation—and they didn't pretend that they did. Aunt Carolyn made it clear by the time she was fourteen that as soon as she turned eighteen she was leaving home and never looking back. I didn't know why she didn't like the Nation of Islam or our family anymore, but I figured something must be wrong with her if she didn't like my GrandWillie.

Aunt Gay never said anything bad out her mouth about the Nation, but as soon as she was old enough, she blatantly did all the things she couldn't in the Nation. Wearing the shortest and tightest clothes possible was her scream: "See my womanly body." She had gotten pregnant when she was seventeen, but she still had an awesome figure. Aunt Gay, an artist, painted in the brightest colors she could find.

Aunt Carolyn didn't come around to visit GrandWillie except for once in a blue moon. I knew that she worked in the government, paid for her own apartment, and bought herself nice clothes and furniture.

I wanted to be a little bit like Aunt Carolyn and a little like Aunt Gay when I grew up. I also wanted to be a little like GrandWillie, able to make the best of whatever situation I found myself in. And a little like Ma, able to rationalize my way in and out of everything. For now I was just a sponge. A sponge with the last name X—whatever that meant.

Dis-Integrate

CHAPTER 7

Sometimes being special didn't seem so wonderful anymore. It seemed like I was in a glass case, a pretty bird—or a beautiful girl—bred properly like an expensive parrot trained to memorize and repeat.

I wished all I had to memorize was the words to the Jackson Five songs Aunt Gay played. Jermaine Jackson was her favorite, and I liked Michael. I marveled at their album cover and thought they looked cool in their flashy, skin-tight, bell-bottom, fly-away-collar outfits. They could never wear that stuff to the Temple because our minister would have told them they looked like the white man's clowns. Other little girls in my neighborhood got their mothers to buy them Jackson Five records and had fun listening to them together for hours, but I had to spend most of my time studying my lessons for school.

At first when I started learning all that stuff, my teachers said we had to learn it because we black people were the rulers of the world and needed to know about all the planets and everything on Earth so we could control it. But I suspected by now that that wasn't true. We couldn't control the sun. It came out when it wanted to, and sometimes it hid behind the clouds all day. Nope, the only things that seemed controllable were us robots in our little Nation.

Sometimes I thought about all that stuff when I was sitting on the porch by myself. Often my next-door neighbor, Debbie, who was a teenager, invited me to sit on her porch with her.

One particular afternoon we sat on her porch singing a camp song: "Boom, boom, ain't it great to be crazy . . . silly and foolish all day long."

I had a good time, but that night while Ma was combing my hair she told me to watch what came out of my mouth.

"Do you really think it would be good to be silly and foolish all day long?" she asked, tugging at the tangles in my hair as I sat on the floor between her legs.

I shook my head no because I couldn't speak. I had a knot in my throat and tears in my eyes.

The next day, when Debbie asked me if I wanted to come over with her, I shook my head no and held up my potholder kit to show her I'd rather just sit there and make colorful potholders. Ma hadn't said I couldn't go again, but I didn't want to give her a chance to, so I restricted myself for a while. Water gathered in my eyes as I sat on the cool pavement weaving a red loop through a yellow one. Over, under, over, under was all I had to think about while weaving: over one loop, under the next, over, under, over, under. I tried not to think about anything else, but the thoughts sneaked up on me, and before I knew it, tears were rolling down my face. I curled up in a corner with my knees folded up to my chest, balancing my potholder loom in between, wiping quickly at the tears, trying to keep my face dry.

I thought everybody in my home was doing everything the Honorable Elijah Muhammad said we had to do in order to have heaven here on Earth, so I wondered why I didn't feel like I was in heaven. We had learned that heaven and hell are right here on Earth. Heaven—a nice home, a steady job, and a happy, healthy family. Hell—pain, poverty, suffering, sickness, and isolation.

I knew that when we did little bad things, little bad things would happen to us, so I tried to stay good. When Uncles Wallace and Hussein, Darren, and I all caught the chicken pox a few months earlier, I knew it was because we had sneaked to eat potato chips and chewing gum, which were prohibited from our diet. I made up my mind that if Allah forgave me and let me get over those awful, itchy, ugly bumps that popped up all over my body, I wouldn't sneak and eat potato chips anymore.

Some of my other friends had a hard time figuring out why bad things kept happening in their families, too, even though they tried to be good. Some of our families were falling apart, and some of our carefully orchestrated happiness had us feeling discontented, but the grown-ups wouldn't dare admit it. No one would admit that our Nation was anything less than one big happy family, full of delightful children growing up in heavenly homes. A Nation of respectful, righteous men and women who all looked out for one another. The grown-ups wouldn't talk about it, but the younger folks, the teens, did.

* * *

Carolyn, one of the teenagers from school, just all of a sudden stopped coming to school. She never talked about transferring or anything, but after about a week of being gone, the rumors started.

"Her father's trying to hide their whole family somewhere," Debra-Mitchel told Tynetta. "He's in big trouble with Brother Minister."

"Well, I heard Carolyn's father been going behind Brother Minister's back trying to report stuff straight to Chicago," Tynetta answered.

We were having a bazaar at the Northwest Gardens ballroom, and I overheard them talking. There were big balloons, cookies, doughnuts, and little jewelry boxes made out of painted popsicle sticks on sale. I bought two balloons with money I had collected from GrandWillie, Uncle Hussein, and Uncle Wallace. I wore an outfit Ma made for me, psychedelic-colored pantaloons and a uniform top with swirls of orange and pink and yellow in it. I had rubbed so much Vaseline on my patent leather shoes they shined like glass.

A girl named Jenny chased Darren into the girls' bathroom and made all of us laugh. Some of the others started teasing Kim because she had Shirley Temple curls hanging down like bangs from under her headpiece.

"Kim's trying to be white!" Zina teased. "Who put them stupid curls in your hair?"

Kim's aunt, who wasn't a Muslim, thought it would make Kim look especially cute to have hard-pressed curls. She didn't realize that in the Nation we viewed straight hair the same as whites viewed nappy hair. Ugly. Ma never pressed my hair real straight. Just straight enough to be able to comb it. Kim also wore a frilly dress cut just above her ankles instead of all the way to the floor like we were supposed to wear them. So she got teased for that, too.

"You all are just jealous," she said haughtily. She flung her head back, giving emphasis to her headpiece like it was long, beautiful hair, then announced, "I'm going to go browse."

As we looked over the jewelry at one table, we heard Debra-Mitchel and Tynetta talking about Carolyn.

"Well, supposedly," Tynetta said, making a doubtful face, "he's been sending letters to the Messenger saying some of the brothers here were stealing money and changing the reports and stuff. He was trying to say that some of the brothers in the Temple are FBI plants trying to stir up confusion. That's what I heard."

"They don't need nobody to do that," said Debra-Mitchel, who was the sassiest teenager in the Temple. "These people got enough confusion all their own."

The grown-ups didn't like Debra-Mitchel because they said she was just a smart-aleck teenager who didn't know how to respect authority, but Debra-Mitchel could see straight through the grown-ups.

"Carolyn's father probably ain't telling nothing but the truth," she said.

Kim and I pretended we were really interested in the rings and necklaces that had crescent moons and stars on them, but really we were just trying to hear all that we could.

"He said Carolyn's father been writing letters for months, and they just now caught him. They gave him two choices. Take thirty-day suspension and keep quiet about everything, or else."

"Or else what?"

"Or else he would get chastised some other way, I guess."

We all heard of brothers getting "chastised" and winding up mysteriously dead. But none of us made the connection that the deaths and chastisements might have been related. There were different degrees of chastisements, from a verbal whipping to expulsion and being called down front at the Temple. But now, it seemed, chastisement could even mean death.

The Nation had changed so much since my grandparents had joined back in the 1950s. At first the changes were good—more people in the Nation, more money, businesses, schools, and more respect out in the world. But now the changes were bad—people talking about one another behind their backs, accusing one another of stealing money, and all kinds of carrying on. That wasn't the way it was supposed to be. That's the way GrandWillie said people at her old church used to be. People at the Temple were supposed to be better than that.

On our way home from the bazaar, I thought about what Tynetta and Debra-Mitchel had been saying.

"GrandWillie, did the government give some of the brothers at the Temple some kind of plants to kill us?" I asked as our taxi rode through the streets. It was raining, and the dark streets glistened under the crystal raindrops falling everywhere.

"Girl, what nonsense are you talking about?" she answered, looking at me, perplexed. I repeated what Tynetta had said, but GrandWillie just said, "Girl, stop trying to understand everything."

The grown-ups didn't want to hear anything bad about the Nation. GrandWillie and the other grown-ups acted like they couldn't question the officials because they might get in trouble.

I thought we were always supposed to want to know the truth. Sometimes when I listened to teenagers like Tynetta, I thought there was more truth in their words than in what I heard at the Temple on Sundays.

I was thinking about all of this as the cab pulled up to our house. The rain came down harder and harder.

❋ ❋ ❋

At the Temple, I watched as people tattled on one another and sometimes confessed their own sins. Darren thought it was funny when the brothers confessed to the officials.

"Brother Larry was in there crying, talking about, 'Brother Captain, I'm sorry,'" Darren told me one time. He said that during their F.O.I. meeting, Brother Larry broke down. "He said, 'I know I was wrong. God forgive me. I can't keep it a secret anymore. I was with Brother Greg's wife the other night,'" Darren said, laughing so hard he could barely talk. "He was crying like a little sissy in the office, and me and Chris were cracking up."

"That's not funny!" I said. (I'm just using the names "Brother Larry" and "Brother Greg" here. I wouldn't dare use the men's real names. Their sins have long since been forgotten, although the moral of their dilemma lives on.) "Brother Larry's going to have to go to hell now. That ain't funny!" I told Darren.

I knew that being left outside the Nation was hell because that meant being cut off from the only family support some people had. We didn't have jails in our Nation. But isolation from the rest of the group was supposed to work the same way. Members could get suspended from the Nation for thirty to ninety days, which meant they couldn't come to the Temple or communicate with any Nation members during that time.

I didn't know what my family would do without the Nation, because we didn't socialize much with our relatives who didn't believe in the same God we believed in. Elijah Muhammad said it was best since our own family members and friends would try to confuse us and make us doubt our beliefs. Our Nation was our tight-knit security blanket. It was designed to make us feel warm and cozy, but those who wiggled too much, asking too many questions, would find themselves left out in the cold American society where the wicked white man ruled.

❋ ❋ ❋

Now, five years after Ma became involved in the Nation, she was questioning its most essential aspects. For the past couple of years, she'd been questioning the practices of some of the officials. But now Ma was beginning to think that there was something wrong about the belief that one man has the absolute power of God. Could God really be a black man walking the streets right here in America? That seemed as unlikely to her as the idea that God was a white man who died hundreds of years ago. Ma didn't agree with everything Elijah Muhammad said, and for that reason, she often found herself at odds with the sister officials.

"You never questioned your white god," Elijah Muhammad would say during his monthly closed-circuit addresses into all the Temples. "But you would question your own kind."

Ma had thought she had joined a religious organization, but now she realized that she had signed herself and her children into a militant, cultlike institution.

Ma had become skeptical after learning of some of the incidents GrandWillie and others experienced. And she took it personally when the officials approached her. Ma got really upset one time when a sister lieutenant told us we had to sit in the back because Ma wasn't wearing an official uniform from Chicago.

Ma stood up, clutched her purse, yanked my hand, and pulled me out of the row we had been seated in. She sighed and rolled her eyes, trying to look impatient and angry. Really, she was hurt. I wished I could have kicked the sister for embarrassing us like that. It wasn't right to make us feel bad just because of the color of our clothes. Ma was really upset because she thought that by joining the Nation of Islam she had escaped pettiness and divisiveness. When I was older, Ma told me that this incident was a turning point for her.

Ma couldn't afford the official uniforms, which cost forty dollars. So she bought cheap fabric from the five-and-dime store and made us imitation ones. GrandWillie made some for me, too. It was okay for little girls to wear homemade uniforms to the Temple, but it was not okay for women. They were supposed to look official or at the very least wear the right colors—white on Sundays, beige for the Saturday morning M.G.T. classes, and solid colors throughout the rest of the week. But Ma didn't like drab and solid colors, so she made her outfits from bright plaid material.

Bright, psychedelic colors were in style during the seventies, but Elijah Muhammad spoke against his followers wearing them. He also forbade his followers to adopt the traditional African tribal styles; brothers could wear only dark, conservative suits. He said people wearing the wrong colors would be dismissed from the circle of Islam.

Ma thought the Nation was supposed to be different from mainstream society where white people were separated from black people and people who had money to afford certain things were separated from those who didn't. The "Royal Family," the Honorable Elijah Muhammad's wife, children, and grandkids, was treated with special favor, and the rest of us were just the poor masses. Ma was poor and without rank, so she had about as much a chance in this Nation as she did out in the world.

Ma began to question other things, too.

She talked to her big sister, Judy, about these questions on the telephone sometimes. Aunt Judy had sent her children to our Muslim school a few years ago, then took them out when she turned into something called an Orthodox Muslim. Since Ma had so many questions, she started reading lots of different books looking for answers, and her sister kept bringing her more questions.

When Ma began discussing Elijah Muhammad's ideas with her sister who didn't believe in them, she began to notice certain ironies. Our men, for instance, wore European suits instead of African-inspired attire. Even our economic system was capitalistic in concept, and our leader was able to capitalize off the labor of the masses. Uncle Sharrief and the others who worked long hours in the restaurants and bakeries didn't get paid for all the time they worked. But they believed they were working for the good of our Nation.

Another thing happened to open Ma's eyes during this time. The car Dad brought her got a flat when Ma was driving alone on the highway, and it was white folks who stopped to help her change the tire. Now it seemed that not all white people were devils and not all black people were angels.

Ma wasn't the only one who realized that people were being taken advantage of, and her brother, Uncle Lloyd, wasn't the only brother who gave his family's bill money to the Nation some months. Sometimes the women fought with their husbands about this.

The more Ma learned about GrandWillie and Granddaddy's experiences, the more skeptical she became. GrandWillie and Granddaddy would not have dared say anything bad against the Nation even though they had misgivings about some of the practices. They feared the wrath of God coming down on them if they did. My grandparents had learned in the black church not to question God, and even though they had switched gods, they believed that principle still applied.

When Ma began questioning her religion, it meant she was in that seeking mode again. Ma had grown up in a Baptist church but had begun asking her minister questions when she was a teenager. She said that since he couldn't explain how the Father, the Son, and Holy Ghost could all be one and the same, she figured she'd search elsewhere for answers. I didn't know it then, but this would become a pattern for Ma.

A House Divided/ A Change Gon' Come

CHAPTER 8

Ma was pregnant with her fifth child and her stomach was swollen like a big watermelon, and since it was hard for her to move around she had to call me from downstairs to reach her things sometimes. She lay in the bed most evenings, surrounded by books on the floor beside her bed and on the dresser. One particular Friday night, she called me to hand her a thick book called the Holy Quran, which she liked reading.

The Honorable Elijah Muhammad had often talked about the Quran and the Holy Bible, too, but until now we hadn't had a copy of either one in our home because he said that most of his followers wouldn't be able to understand either book without his interpretation. He said everybody should just let him read it and tell us what God wanted us to know. But Ma was reading for herself now. She had a book called *Myth of the Cross* and a copy of the Holy Bible, and she kept her Quran wrapped in a small white towel on top of her TV—out of reach of us kids.

As I was pulling the book down to give it to Ma, I dropped it.

"Watch yourself!" Ma yelled, as if the book was a baby or something.

I jumped. The book fell out the towel, and I marveled at its beauty. The hard cover was dark green like the needles of a pine tree, with gold writing on the front. The pages were some fancy kind of thin paper, and each page was designed with English writing in small blocks on one side, Arabic writing on the other, and a big block of small writing at the bottom of the page.

"*Stafula!*" Ma yelled. I knew this was an Arabic word, but I didn't know what it meant. She rose up and reached for the book on the foot of her bed where I had dropped it. Gently she wrapped it back in its covering. "Girl, you have to be careful," she said.

I knew the Holy Quran was a special book, the book that Muslims worldwide believe is Allah's last and final statement to humankind. It was more special to us than the Holy Bible because we believed that the people in charge of preserving and propagating the Bible had changed it so much that God had to reveal his Scripture all over again. I was taught that after the religious people had been fighting and worshiping idols for years, Allah sent a special angel named Gabriel down to Earth to correct his religion. Gabriel had spoken in Arabic because the man he was talking to, a man named Prophet Muhammad, was an Arab. And the man wrote down what the angel told him in that language.

A few people in the Nation knew that our leader was preparing the younger people for a new kind of Islam, the universal Islam that's practiced by black and white and yellow and red people all over the world. The new teachings would be based on the Holy Quran instead of Elijah Muhammad's *Message to the Black Man* book. But the vast majority of the members in the Nation had no idea of the changes to come.

Ma taught me and Darren a new prayer, the Fatiha, the prayer Orthodox Muslims around the world recite five times a day. We were excited about reciting the Arabic prayer because it made us feel like we were speaking another language. None of our friends at the Temple could speak Arabic beyond reciting the alphabet, so we would be able to impress them. That was the only thing about Orthodox Islam we liked. We hated everything else.

Darren and I both preferred being Nation of Islam Muslims because we still had a sense of connection to other black people and because that's what we had gotten used to. We hated the way Ma made us sit around a tablecloth on the floor like Arab Muslims instead of up at the table, and we hated when Ma took our spoons and forks and made us eat with our fingers like Orthodox Muslims used to do during the lifetime of the religion's founder, Prophet Muhammad.

"She's trying to turn us into savages," Darren joked, looking around, hoping GrandWillie would talk some sense into our mother.

In the Nation we had learned the importance of proper etiquette. All civilized people used proper etiquette, and we black gods and goddesses were the most civilized people on the planet. What was Ma trying to do to us?

I felt embarrassed sitting on the floor eating, especially when one of our uncles walked past and shook his head or laughed at us. My uncles thought my mother was losing her mind.

The main thing I hated about Ma's new religion was the fact that she now wanted to teach me to dress and behave like women I thought were white. I had seen Arab Muslims before. One time Ma took us way uptown for a prayer service to a huge, immaculately decorated building called the Islamic Center, and all the people there looked more white than black. Most of them were Arabs, but some of them were actually white. Why in the world did Ma think she was going to make me dress and act like white people? I was a black princess. That's what I had been taught the whole eight years of my life.

Plus, I thought the Arab Muslim women at the center were stupid because they let the brothers make them sit in a room in the basement of the building where the lighting was dim and the walls leaked. I had been used to the men and women being separated and even to women not being as free as men in the Nation. But there was no way I was going to let Ma turn me into an Orthodox Muslim girl. I might do everything she told me to do, I figured, but deep down inside she would never change me.

Ma changed her name to an Arabic one, and her siblings who were Orthodox did the same. The whole point was to get a new name that had a meaning they could aspire to. Ma's new name meant "to see clearly." My name, Sonsyrea, had a meaning, so I was safe. But Ma tried to change Darren's name to Dawud. He refused to answer to it. She would call outside for Dawud to come in, but he didn't respond, even when he was within earshot. *Dawud* was the Arabic name for David, who according to the Quran was a prophet of Allah.

Sometimes when Ma's Orthodox siblings called our house asking for Ma by her Arabic name, Darren and I would say, "Sorry, you have the wrong number," and hang up. They'd call right back and we'd get fussed at.

Ma began using some other Arabic words. For instance, instead of saying "thank you" now, she'd say "*shukran*." Aunt Gay would flinch and ask, "Who does she think she is? Does she think she's a better Muslim or something because she can speak a few Arabic words?"

I usually stood up for Ma, but this time I, too, was mad at her. All these changes were causing too much trouble in our household. It was like a war had been declared. On one side was Ma, on the other side everybody else.

Ma was looking for some new kind of explanation for the problems in her life since racism didn't seem to be the root of all her problems after all. She had found that even living in the all-black Nation of Islam, she had felt alienated and manipulated.

All her life she had felt like a loner. She was adopted when she was two years old and raised with one foster brother and two church-going foster parents, but she never felt like part of the family. She enjoyed her in-laws for the first few years after she got married, but then that changed. Dad was away most of the time working on his music. Since she didn't belong to the Nation anymore, the only bonds she might have now would be to her ten long-lost brothers and sisters, whom she was just getting to know. Many of them had become Orthodox. The more time Ma spent with these siblings, the deeper she, too, got into Orthodox Islam.

❃ ❃ ❃

Orthodox Islam was beginning to catch on in the black community in Washington and other cities as former Nation of Islam officials became aware of the fraudulence in Elijah Muhammad's Nation of Islam.

Orthodox Muslims, especially the ones from the Middle East, didn't consider what Elijah Muhammad taught true Islam because Elijah Muhammad based his teachings on a mix of the Bible, the Quran, and the nationalist philosophy preached by the late Marcus Garvey. In the Temple we were taught to disregard Orthodox Muslims because they refused to accept the fact that we were the real chosen people referred to in the Bible and the Quran.

Now here I was, caught in the middle. When I was around Ma and her sisters and brothers, I heard comments about how misguided the people in the Nation were. Aunt

Kimba and Uncle Sabu talked about how "blessed" they were that Allah, the real Allah, the real God—not Master Fard Muhammad, who they once believed was God in person—had delivered them from deception and shown them the real Islam.

At home my father's brothers, Uncles Wallace, Hussein, and Sharrief, who were little men now, talked about how foolish Ma, her siblings, and all the other black people were who were trying to imitate Arabs. I didn't care so much who was right or who was wrong, I just didn't like the fact that I felt like I had to choose sides. This was my family and I loved them all.

At home we didn't all pray together anymore because our prayers were different. We had always prayed together in the evenings, and a lot of times—especially during the Holy Month of Ramadan when we fasted—we had all gotten up together for the predawn prayer. But now we couldn't even do that. Since I couldn't tell whose prayers were right, sometimes I prayed one way, cupping my hands in front of me while I bowed my head, and sometimes I prayed the other way, folding my hands across my stomach while I bowed through a series of motions, reciting Arabic.

When going to the Temple or Nation events with GrandWillie, I would wear my Nation of Islam outfits, and when visiting my Orthodox relatives with Ma, I dressed like them. When I was in the house and what I wore didn't matter, I didn't want to look like either. Covering my head with a plain white handkerchief at home was a good way to be in between, because it was neither the signature headpiece for the Nation nor the symbolic veil of Orthodox Muslim women.

I never heard Ma and GrandWillie debating with each other about who was right or wrong, but I would hear comments from other relatives.

Uncle Hussein walked past Aunt Kimba and shook his head when she visited our home wearing what looked like a bed sheet draped over her head, pinned under her chin, and flowing to her feet. If Ma tried to dress me like that, I was going to run straight to Dad for help because I knew he wasn't into being an Orthodox. He wasn't into religion at all anymore, because he had gotten enough religion going to the Temple seven days a week while growing up. He didn't believe in the Nation of Islam anymore because he said too many of the officials in the Nation turned out to be as corrupt as the white American leaders they condemned.

❊ ❊ ❊

I was used to us Muslims being separated from our Christian family members, but now my Muslim relatives had drawn a line in the sand, too.

The friction between my Orthodox family and my relatives in the Nation was just like the friction between Nation of Islam members and Orthodox Muslims across the country.

The tensions actually had been simmering since the Nation was first founded in 1930, and they intensified when Malcolm X, former spokesman for the Nation, returned from a trip to the Middle East and proclaimed Elijah Muhammad's Islam false.

When Malcolm was killed, the Nation was blamed for the assassination, and the feud between Nation Muslims and Orthodox ones was subsequently cited again as the cause of several deaths of black men in major cities across the country.

In Washington on January 18, 1973, a family of Orthodox Muslims, including two toddlers and a nine-day-old infant, were killed by men believed to belong to the Nation. Now, a year later—1974—the trial was under way and came on the news every evening.

I was practicing my penmanship when I heard a loud man's voice coming through the TV saying, "These men shot my babies because I teach Islam is for everyone, not just for blacks." It scared me because even though I had heard about the F.O.I. brothers threatening men like Carolyn's father, and even though I had seen the young boys run off our school bus, chasing boys their age into the woods to fight, I never imagined that men in the Nation would kill babies.

Years later, I would read that one of the men arrested struck a deal with the government, agreeing to tell on everybody else to save himself. But he changed his mind after a visit from a black Muslim minister. Meanwhile, then-spokesman Louis Farrakhan delivered an alarming message on his radio show.

"Let this be a warning to those of you who would be used as an instrument of a wicked government against our rise," Farrakhan said. "Be careful. . . . In the ranks of black people today there are young men and women rising up who have no forgiveness in them for traitors and stool pigeons."

I never found out exactly what happened, or who got ahold of the man who was going to cooperate with the government. But he was found hanged in a jail cell before his trial date arrived. Newspapers reported that his body also bore signs of a severe beating. He had been in a cell block with a large population of black Muslims, but the warden of the jail told reporters he had no idea the young man's life had been in danger.

I can remember hearing Uncles Hussein and Wallace talk about it.

While they were talking, I remembered them a few years earlier, studying their lessons about killing four devils each for the Honorable Elijah Muhammad, and I wondered if they believed that it was divine justice that the man wound up dead.

Out in the World

CHAPTER 9

It was bitterly cold but sunny on February 26, 1975. It was Savior's Day, the day we normally celebrated the birth of W. Fard Muhammad, who founded our Nation. Sunny except for the cloud of uncertainty hanging overhead as we all wondered whether our leader and lifesaver, the Most Honorable Elijah Muhammad, was really dead like the news reported.

Many believed that he wasn't really dead but that, like Moses, he was leaving us behind to test our faith, planning then to return. They thought he was up in the Mother Ship Plane, which he said would come back for all righteous people in his Nation. Others, who believed that he had died, suspected that the hospital had killed him.

GrandWillie and I stood in a long line waiting to get in the Washington Coliseum, where the day's events would be broadcast live from Chicago. Two lines of people circled all the way around the block. Sisters dressed in white skirts that hung beneath their coats huddled with their children in one line. Solemn brothers in dark suits formed the other. A lot of people sporting big bushes, obviously not members of the Nation, had come, out of respect for the Honorable Elijah Muhammad, to stand in line with us.

In the street, brothers in F.O.I. uniforms directed traffic, stopping cars, questioning drivers who moved too slowly, while sister and brother lieutenants patrolled the sidewalks. Across the country, lines were formed around other public halls as well. The lines moved slowly because everybody had to undergo the body, purse, and pocket search before entering the building.

"GrandWillie, my feet hurt," I said. The frozen pavement was cutting through my shoes.

In previous years GrandWillie had journeyed to Chicago for the annual Savior's Day, but this time she stayed home and I was glad. Even though she said hardly more than two words to me the whole time we waited, she held onto my hand tightly. Everyone was silent and serious looking. Some folks attempted conversation, but their anxiety was clear. I balled my gloved hands tight and stuffed them into my pockets to keep warm and leaned on the wall to rest.

"Chile, stand up straight!" GrandWillie snapped. "You know better than to be slouching."

"My feet are tired," I mumbled.

"I don't want to hear no back talk out of you today," she said. I pulled my coat up to my nose to keep my warm breath close to me and started wondering about things.

What was the big deal anyway? I wondered. So we were going to find out for sure whether Elijah Muhammad really did die like they said on the news. Big deal. Ma already had me doubting that he was a real prophet. GrandWillie was acting like I'd better not move or say anything. Like I'd better save all my energy and all my breath for whatever was about to happen. We finally reached the entrance.

"As-Salaam-Alaikum," I said happily to Sister Helen at the door.

She nodded without parting her lips. My uncles Sharrief, Hussein, and Wallace were directing brothers to their seats and across the lobby. Darren and some older brothers were selling books written by our savior and *Muhammad Speaks* newspapers. GrandWillie grabbed my shoulder and pulled me with her to our seats down front. Behind the reserved space where we uniformed Muslims sat, uniformed officials guided others to their seats.

Heavyweight boxing champion Muhammad Ali, who had joined our Nation, was on the stage in Chicago, and we could see him on the closed-circuit TV screens at the Coliseum. A famous Baptist preacher named Jesse Jackson was also on stage, along with some of our Messenger's sons and other officials from the Nation. They showed a long documentary on the history of our Nation, starting with a picture of W. Fard Muhammad, the man who we believed was God in person. The documentary ended with pictures of our businesses, restaurants, bakeries, schools, temples, and farms all over the country.

I was bored with the video but thrilled to see that so many people came out to join us on this particular Savior's Day. On the news that morning, I had heard city government people saying good things about our leader, and now to see that so many regular people loved and respected him, too, made me feel good that I had been under his guidance all these years. I couldn't sit still like a little princess with my hands in my lap and my eyes straight ahead this day because there was too much going on around me.

We had to evacuate the building because of a bomb threat, and the mood remained tense after that. Also, GrandWillie and the sisters around me looked nervous and anxious because they weren't sure what was going on. We didn't know if he had died of congestive heart failure like the hospital said, and we didn't know who was going to be the new leader. Five brothers, including his son named

Wallace D. Muhammad and the New York minister Brother Minister Louis Farrakhan, were being considered.

A voice on the loudspeaker announced that our Savior had died of natural causes two days earlier. There was a collective gasp. Tears flowed down many cheeks, but no one cried out loud in pain because we had been trained to be unemotional.

GrandWillie didn't cry at all because she sort of expected her dear Savior to be passing on soon. She and a lot of other members knew the Messenger had been sick, though no one was supposed to talk about it.

On the big screen a brother led us through our opening prayer, then speaker after speaker went to the microphone and talked about how great the Honorable Elijah Muhammad was and how he lived on in spirit.

"No one can tell you he is deceased," said one of his sons, named Nathan Muhammad. "No one can tell me he is deceased because you have him in your heart, I have him in my heart. . . . He lives today."

The crowd on the big screen began chanting, "Long live Muhammad! Long live Muhammad!"

The people around me in the coliseum joined in chanting, clapping our hands, and stomping our feet in cadence.

"Long live Muhammad!"

Some of the sisters who still wouldn't break their composure stood stoically at their seats to show their utmost respect without breaking our code of behavior. I stomped my foot and clapped loud like the brothers and refused to stop when GrandWillie gave me the eye and when she discreetly yanked my arm. I was feeling delighted inside and free just to be able to open my mouth so wide and shout like this in public.

Our leader's son named Wallace D., the one who had rebelled against his father about ten years earlier, came to the podium on the big screen and raised both his hands high in the air to hush the crowd. He was to be our new leader, he explained.

Looking serious and unmoved by the praise for his father, our new leader began:

"In the name of Allah the beneficent, the most merciful, to whom we forever give praise and thanks. . . . We were a people who just a few years ago were unable to think without having a portion of the white man's mind to think with. . . . We were unable to agree on an issue unless approval had previously been given by the white man. . . ."

I figured he must have been talking to the people who were not in our Nation or to the people my GrandWillie's age who used to be out in the white man's world before Elijah Muhammad created our own. I couldn't remember a time in my little life when I thought I needed the white man for anything.

I looked up at the huge portrait of the Messenger that hung from the ceiling and knew that even though Ma had recently told me he wasn't a god or even a real prophet of God, he was very powerful, as powerful as any white man I'd ever seen on TV. His son read from the Holy Quran and talked some more, and when he finished, some of the F.O.I. brothers lifted him up on their shoulders and the crowd shouted again, "Long live Muhammad! Long live Muhammad! Long live Muhammad!"

At home that evening our house was quiet, the same as it had been when Granddaddy died. GrandWillie and my uncles were somber, but again Ma went about her business as usual. School was closed for the rest of the week, but we had Muslim Girls Training class the following Saturday morning. I could tell a lot of the sisters, especially the older ones, were sad and confused. The god who had told them how to live, what to wear, what to eat, how to eat it, and when to eat it and had directed every aspect of their lives for many, many years was now gone.

❋ ❋ ❋

Two months after Elijah Muhammad's death, I celebrated my ninth birthday with ice cream and cake. By the time I turned ten our Muslim school closed down. Our new leader, his son, no longer made people pay dues and sell a certain number of newspapers, so our Nation no longer had enough money coming in to keep our schools open.

I had liked the University of Islam, but part of me longed to go to public school with the other children in my neighborhood and play the same games they played. It was nice to feel special belonging to the Nation of Islam, but part of me wanted just to feel normal and fit in with everyone else.

It was April 1976 when our Muslim school closed down and I had to transfer to a public school, two months before their school year ended. It was chilly outside the morning Ma walked us to Kingsman Elementary to enroll us. Inside, the walls along the empty corridors were painted a sickly greenish blue color, and the odor wafting from the cafeteria smelled nothing like the wholesome beef burgers and wheat doughnuts I used to buy after school at the Temple.

I missed Sister Memphis who used to greet us at the door with a welcoming "As-Salaam-Alaikum" every morning. And I missed Vernarda, Kim, Saundra, Nynita, Aisha, and the other young Muslim sisters with whom I had shared friendships and a very comfortable sense of sameness. They had transferred to the schools in their own neighborhoods. At my new school, my languid, long clothes distinguished me from my classmates, who were wearing fashionably tight designer jeans. I was moving into new territory and wasn't sure what to expect.

Growing up in the Nation of Islam and then having to go out into the real world was like moving to another country, adjusting to a culture and philosophy we had been trained to despise. As enthusiastic as I was about seeing how the other people lived, I also was nervous about how I would fit in. I wondered if they would like me and welcome me like a sister since they were black like me or if I would find out that they really were mean and uncivilized, as I had been taught. Maybe they would teach me their games, which I hadn't had a chance to learn in the Nation, and maybe I could teach them some facts about how great we black people really are, which they didn't learn out in the world.

I was wearing a long orange and brown patchwork dress with a white headpiece for my first day of school. Darren looked like a normal kid in regular pants and a pullover shirt.

Darren, for the most part, was simply overjoyed because he knew that the teachers in public schools couldn't put their hands on him or even make him stand in a corner with his hands folded across the top of his head like they used to do at the Muslim school. Darren's close-cut haircut was the only thing that distinguished him from the other boys, who wore short Afros.

As a Muslim boy Darren enjoyed a certain level of respect in our neighborhood. As a Muslim girl, I was respected, too, but it was a different kind of respect. It would keep boys from catcalling out to me, but it would not thwart the taunts of girls who thought Muslim women were crazy or weak for allowing men to dictate what we wore and how we behaved.

We had a lot to learn about people out in the world, and they had a lot to learn about us, too.

On the first day of school, Ma marched us up to the principal's office. Dressed in pants, a long top down to her knees, and a matching scarf on her head, Ma looked like the myth of the meek Muslim woman. The secretaries turned to watch as we blew into the office. Within moments the myth would be destroyed.

The school principal, Mr. Moore, greeted Ma from behind the linoleum-topped counter and shoved several papers across the divide for Ma to sign. Ma snatched them up and held them close. She knew to read things thoroughly and ask a few questions before signing. Seemed like she was always at odds with official types. Now she was arguing with Mr. Moore because he wanted to put me in the fourth grade with other kids my age while Ma insisted I finish out the sixth grade, since that's what grade I was in at the Muslim school.

Ma wasn't mean or nasty, just serious and unyielding. She didn't smile a lot or turn on any feminine charm to get Mr. Moore to see her point. I was so glad my mother wasn't a weak pushover or a tight-clothes-wearing floozy like some of the other mothers I noticed around our neighborhood.

"No," Ma told Mr. Moore frankly, she would not take us back to the neighborhood clinic for polio, measles, and chicken pox shots.

"I have decided against immunizing my children," she told him.

"I'm sorry, Mrs. Tate. It is the policy of our school system to require complete immunization of all our students," Mr. Moore intoned.

"I understand your policy, sir. But as a parent, I have the right to decide whether or not to immunize my children," she said. "My children have had the chicken pox already, and if and when God sees fit for them to come down with something else, I'll keep them home and take care of them."

Finally, Mr. Moore pointed to the space where she could offer her explanation. "I conscientiously object" was all she wrote. But I knew the real reason was because she didn't trust any agency of the U.S. government to inject anything into the arms of her children. She had explained to us earlier that experimental medicines are tested at the free clinics in black neighborhoods. She had learned this, she said, when she used to work as a nurse at D.C. General Hospital.

Shortly before the lunch bell rang, Mr. Moore guided us up two flights of stairs, where we dropped Darren off at his classroom. Ma told Darren's teacher that she and Dad would support his disciplinary actions against Darren with a strong arm at home. Darren sucked his teeth and sighed. How could she set him up like that?

When we walked through the door of my new classroom, all the kids stopped what they were doing to stare at the small girl in the long orange and brown patchwork dress and white turban on her head. I looked past them and noticed the bulletin board with the "A" papers from last week's vocabulary test. Immediately, I determined I was smarter. *Atmosphere*, I thought to myself, we learned that word in the fourth grade. Above the blackboards, which were actually green, there were small placards with science and history information. This science and history would also be a breeze compared to what we had studied at the University of Islam.

My new teacher, Mrs. Hardin, was a round and robust woman, her skin the color of oak wood. She rose from her desk where she had been picking out the bones from her fish sandwich when we walked in.

"Good morning," she said, smiling as she walked over to us. "You must be Mrs. Tate."

"Yes." Ma smiled back, extending her hand for a shake. "And this is Sons-Sere-Ray," pronouncing it phonetically.

"Class, say good morning to Sons-Sere-Ray," Mrs. Hardin commanded.

"What kind of name is that?" one of my classmates demanded from the front row.

"It's Indian. It means 'Morning Star,'" I said with pride.

"Is that some kind of Moozlem name?" he persisted.

"It's Indian," I repeated more forcefully.

This was a few years before African American parents began naming their children foreign names and names the parents themselves created. Before inner-city mothers across the country would look at their daughters and name them Imani because they wanted them to know they represented "Faith." Before a father named Shawn and a mother named Nina would put their heads together and come up with the name "Shawnina."

At school the next morning, when I declined to rise with the rest of the class for the Pledge of Allegiance, followed by a run-through of "America the Beautiful," Terry Gomillion, a dark-skinned, bubbly girl who sat to the right of me, wanted to know why.

"Because the United States doesn't care about black people," I told her.

"What do you mean? It's just a little thing we say and a little song," she said.

"It's not just a little song," I said with the earnestness of someone trying to enlighten a poor fool.

Elijah Muhammad had trained us well. At the University of Islam, the only flag to which we pledged our allegiance was the flag representing the Nation of Islam, and the song we sang at the beginning of our Monday morning assemblies was the Muslim fight song.

In fact, we had learned to despise the American flag. The red in the American flag, we were taught, represented the blood of the slaves, our forefathers. The white represented the skin color of our oppressors. And the blue represented the illusion that white people continually created for blacks. "When you look at the sky, it appears blue," the minister used to teach on Sunday. "But it is not really blue. Blue is the color of illusion. When you look at the water, it appears blue. But it is not." And the fifty stars in the American flag represented how divided was the country. The Muslim flag had one star, representing one Nation, unified.

Now how would I explain all of this to my eleven-year-old classmate, who clearly was not as enlightened as I?

"It's not just a little song," I said. "Every time you sing it, you're supporting the government. The government brought black people over here as slaves and still, even today, refuses to treat black people fairly," I said.

Mrs. Hardin interrupted our chatter and told us to do our work. We completed a few verb-subject agreement assignments, then were told to read a section in our history book. By the time the bell rang for recess, the girls' curiosity had temporarily vanished. It was play time. Out on the blacktop playground, Terry invited me to jump double dutch, a game I had not yet learned.

"Sonsyrea, all you gotta do is this," Terry said, half bouncing on the balls of her feet, about to jump into the twirling ropes. "All, all, all, all . . . " the girls sang a tune for her to jump to. After several minutes of fancy spins and high jumps in the ropes, Terry exited the ropes to give me a chance. She saw that I didn't know how to jump. "Come on. Hold your dress like this," she said, drawing my long dress up to my knees. "Okay, okay," I said, while the other girls started the tune over for me. "Jump in!" one of the girls shouted as they started the tune over again. I finally jumped in, and instead of finding harmony in the ropes, I found myself tangled among them. The girls all laughed, all except Terry. She could see that I was embarrassed.

"Okay. Just try it again," she said. She was such an upbeat kind of girl. I liked her a lot. I tried it a few more times before the girls' laughter became too much.

"That's why Elijah Muhammad forbade sport and play anyway," I thought to myself. "I never had to worry about jumping double dutch to win approval at the Muslim school. Our grades were the only thing that mattered. Whoever got the most As got the most attention." I wished I was back at the Muslim school, back among friends, among girls who looked and behaved like me. As I stood alone with my thoughts on a playground full of children, Darren ran past me and I called out to him, but he kept running like he didn't hear me. "DARREN!" I called again, but he was out of earshot now. I hated when he tried to pretend like he didn't see me, like by ignoring me somebody might not realize that the girl in the long clothes and turban was his sister. But anybody could tell we were related, we looked just alike.

As the days passed, I began to feel shy and alienated. During the next few weeks, during recess out on the playground, I got tired of my classmates' stupid questions: "Do y'all have hair? I heard Muslim girls were bald headed."

"How come y'all can't eat pork?" someone would ask.

"Because it gives you worms," I'd answer.

"Don't you miss eating ham and pork chops and stuff?" someone else might inquire.

"Nope. Never tasted it."

"Never?"

"Who said it gives you worms? It don't give you no worms. I eat it and I didn't get worms. People don't get worms. . . ."

"People do get worms, they just can't see them. They get little tiny worms inside their stomachs and get sick with all kinds of diseases," I explained.

"Y'all missing some good stuff. You can't eat pickled pigs' feet, either?"

"The pig is the nastiest animal on the face of the Earth. The pig is grafted from the rat, cat, and dog," I said, sounding kind of robotic by now.

When Darren and I would go home for lunch, I was thankful for the respite. There were two more months of this playground dialogue before finally it was graduation day.

On June 12, all the wooden seats in the hot auditorium were filled with the joyful faces of mothers in Sunday dresses and fathers in slacks and button-down shirts. I looked around to find my relatives. Only they would understand why I was the only child there in this stupid long light blue dress and matching headpiece while the other girls wore white dresses.

At first Ma wasn't going to let me participate in the ceremony because she said that the society shouldn't be making us think that we've accomplished something by completing sixth grade. "You'll graduate when you finish high school," she said. But GrandWillie finally persuaded Ma—the day before the ceremony—to let me participate.

GrandWillie and I shopped around and could not find a long white dress anywhere. So here I was in a long polyester light blue dress with a panel of spring flowers down the front. I was very angry at Ma for making me such an oddball. I was out in the world now and thought she should let me dress like everybody else. Walking down the aisle with the other little girls in short white dresses and shiny curls in their hair, I felt like an ugly duck. At home, my uncles had always told me how pretty I was, and among others in the

Nation the little girls in short dresses would have felt ugly, but I was out in the world now.

I was glad when I spotted GrandWillie's turban in the back of the auditorium. Dad couldn't be there because he had to work, but I didn't mind because he was doing what daddies were supposed to do. Ma was home, too swollen with her latest pregnancy to leave the house. But Grand-Willie was there, and so were Grandma and Granddaddy Thomas. I raised my dress a bit when it came time for me to walk onstage to do my poem, so I wouldn't trip. I stood behind the podium, and the audience laughed when they saw that I couldn't reach the microphone even standing on my tiptoes. The audience thought this was cute, but I wasn't there to be cute. I was there to deliver a poem. Someone brought me a step stool and I began:

> I have to live with myself and so,
> I want to be fit for myself to know.
> I want to be able as days go by,
> Always to look myself straight in the eye.

I recited it slowly and with as much drama as I could muster. I stood poised and spoke with conviction, just like I had rehearsed it.

> I don't want to stand with the setting sun,
> And hate myself for the things I've done.
> I want to go out with my head erect.
> I want to deserve all men's respect.
> But here in the struggle for fame and wealth,
> I want to be able to like myself.

It was a good thing I had learned to like myself in the Nation of Islam, a good thing I had learned I was smart and decent and good all the way through. Out in the real world,

I was beginning to realize that I often would have to stand alone.

After I finished my poem, our school choir stood to sing a song I'd heard them rehearse for weeks:

> Oh, freedom, oh, freedom, oh, freedom over me
> And before I be a slave, I be buried in my grave
> And go home to my lord and be free.

The ceremony was full of poems, songs, and speeches. Our principal congratulated us on having completed the first phase of our education and told us that at the next level, junior high school, we would have more freedoms and therefore would have to be more responsible for ourselves.

My classmates were lucky, I thought. All they had to think about were the changes in school. I had to worry about going to a new school, fitting in out in the world, *and* changes in the religion that had been my way of life.

Wake Up, Everybody

CHAPTER 10

Our new leader changed the name of the Nation to World Community of Islam in the West, saying there were lots of Muslims of all colors out in the world. He even opened the group to white people, but I was glad I didn't see any in our Temple. I didn't know what I would do if I had to sit next to one of them.

I'd learned they were wicked, that they smelled like wet dogs when it rained, and that, in general, they had unsanitary habits such as picking up food and eating it after they dropped it on the floor—and not wearing underclothes. I thought I might start itching if one of them sat next to me. Moving out into the real world in my neighborhood where everyone was black was hard enough, I couldn't imagine trying to adjust to white people, too. There would be so many other adjustments to make.

The brothers in charge at the Temple removed the Honorable Elijah Muhammad's photo that we used to salute because our new leader said his father had not been a prophet or messenger of Allah, just a man with good intentions, trying to save black people. So Ma had been right all along. When she began adopting these Orthodox customs, my

Nation of Islam–born uncles said she was foolish, but now the people at the Temple were doing the same things. The Temple wasn't even called a Temple anymore. Now it was called a Masjiid.

The brothers got rid of our flag and the blackboard with all our symbols, then they tore down the stage so our minister could stand on even ground with the rest of us when we prayed. All those changes were easy enough to get used to. But when GrandWillie and I walked into the main hall of the Temple one Sunday morning and I saw that all the chairs had been taken out, replaced by carpet for us to sit on, my mouth dropped to the floor.

Still standing in the doorway, I looked down on the floor in the main hall and spotted a light tan woman whom I had never seen before. She appeared to be Arab, wrapped in sheer fabrics and seated in a lotus position, her feet as bare as everyone's around her.

"Hand me your shoes here, Sonsyrea," GrandWillie said, shoving my shoes in her large handbag.

We had just gotten used to not having to be searched coming into the Temple, and now we were expected to leave our shoes out in the open where any of these strangers could take them. GrandWillie didn't think that was a good idea. I don't think she was comfortable with sitting on the floor, either, because she and her friends made cushions out of blankets they carried and sat up against the wall. I joined my friends Saundra and Susan on the green carpet with other sisters we had never seen before.

The Masjiid was full with lots of people who joined us now that we didn't have so many rules and restrictions. People who had left the Nation were coming back since they wouldn't be forced to sell papers and buy special uniforms. And Orthodox Muslims of all colors came, too.

We sisters and brothers still sat separately, but now the brothers sat in the front half of the Temple and we sat behind them instead of beside.

"I think my grandmother don't like all these new things," I told my friends. "She said she's just gon' go along for a little bit to see what happens."

"Well, my mother said it's good that we don't have to be *dictated* to anymore," Saundra said.

She was always trying to use big words and sometimes I didn't understand. She was three years older than me.

"Dictated?" I asked, squinting my face. "What you mean?"

"Oh, Sonsyrea, you know what I mean. You know *dictate*, when you have a ruler telling you everything. Well, my mother said it's good that the Honorable Wallace D. Muhammad is telling people to wake up."

Our new leader explained that what we had learned and practiced all those years before his father's death was called a First Resurrection. Black people had to be awakened from a mental state of death, from not knowing ourselves and loving ourselves, and move toward doing positive things for ourselves. Now we were moving into the Second Resurrection, and we were supposed to come alive even more and think for ourselves—individually—and read the Holy Quran and Bible for ourselves and discipline ourselves. GrandWillie and her friends—and maybe even some of the teenagers—understood what was happening. But it was all I could do to keep up with the program.

Years later I would appreciate the spiritual sojourn that I unwittingly had traveled with my grandmother and mother. They both had evolved from disenchanted Christians, which they each had been as young adults, to mindless servants of a religious demagogue to women becoming more aware of their own self-worth. Now GrandWillie felt less responsible for duties at the Temple. She could go and help when she felt like it and not feel guilty—or fearful of Sister Margaret Ann, who used to be captain.

Ma was feeling more independent from Dad, and she began searching for a house without him. In my own little ways, I was growing, too.

❋ ❋ ❋

Our house was getting crowded now that Ma and Dad had five kids: me, Darren, Furard, Sakinah, Atif, and Takiya. Aunt Gay was still living there with her son, and Uncles Hussein and Wallace were getting bigger and needing more space. There were twelve of us living in this three-bedroom house, which my grandparents had bought to raise their family in. Through the week, Uncle Avon's daughter, Robbin, stayed with us, too.

Ma and my aunt and uncles were starting to fuss at one another about little things like cleaning the bathroom and leaving dishes in the sink, but mostly I tuned them out. Then Ma started fussing at us kids, and that was harder to ignore, but I tried my best.

The living room was reserved for adults and company, but I would get permission to go in there to listen to the radio and the albums that my uncles were buying now that they were allowed to spend their money on entertainment. This first summer out of the Nation, they joined other teens in the neighborhood on trips to Hershey Park and even went to parties. Darren was allowed to play football in the neighborhood league, and I felt more freedom, too.

I put on earphones in the living room and played my uncles' Stevie Wonder albums over and over and over again. Lying flat on the floor, I played "Songs in the Key of Life" and read the words from the booklet that came in the album jacket. When I listened to the Spinners I danced, and when I listened to Aunt Gay's old Aretha Franklin albums I pretended I had a microphone and performed.

I looked forward to playing all day like the other neighborhood children—for a change—since I had the whole summer off from school to vacation with the other kids.

On the first clear and sunny day, the girls on the block gathered in the middle of the road on our one-way street to bounce and shake and yell, doing the popular street cheerleading of the day. Unsure whether I'd get in trouble for joining them, I watched from the porch as they formed a line. They looked down the line to make sure it was straight, then put their fists on their barely round hips and bounced on their toes, yelling out the name of the first cheer, "Partay!" as in *party*, in their collective voice.

With that, the hand-clapping, feet-stomping, call-and-response routine was in full swing.

"My name is She!"

"Her name is She!"

"I par-tay."

"She par-tay."

"I party with . . ."

"She party with . . ."

"My niggah."

"Her niggah."

"We party for . . ."

"They party for . . ."

"The tutty-fruity-bump-my-booty-watch-now-watch-me-shake-my-booty. Oooow-good-god, oow-oow-good-god."

She-She, the hot-to-trot from up the street, was out in front of the crowd gyrating her adolescent hips, arms open, shoulders moving back and forth trying to shake the tiny buds on her chest. At one point she lifted her leg, like a puppy on a tree, and socked it to the boys seated front row on the curb. She-She, whose real name was Sheila, was a slender beige girl with dark hair parted down the middle and braided in cornrows on all sides. Pink sponge hair rollers had curled the braid ends the night before so that today could find her showcasing her vanity in the middle of the street. She didn't seem the least bit worried that her orange tube top, a sleeveless, strapless elastic band around her torso, might slip down with all that shaking. But the thought crossed my mind. Her matching striped shorts weren't tight, but they were shorter than anything I could have dreamed of wearing outside the house. She obviously thought she was cute. I thought she was ignorant, but I envied her freedom.

She was free to yell and scream in the middle of the street, free to raise her leg and sock it to the boys who watched in awe. To top her, Marlene, the loudmouth next door, lay on the ground face down, humping it.

Marlene and She-She were the same age, but Marlene was darker, with shorter hair and more roundness about her butt and breasts. Her white jeans shorts were just as high, and her matching polkadot halter top equally flimsy and revealing. She yelled just as loud and bounced and shook her body just as freely.

A couple of younger boys, my brother included, ran past the girls, slapping them on the butt and grabbing at their barely budding breasts. "That must be what Ma means by women inviting men to disrespect them," I figured. Ma said that a woman's actions and the clothes she wears invite a man to disrespect her or guard her from disrespect. Those girls had no right to be throwing their stuff around like that in the first place, I thought. Of course the boys would be tempted to grab them. What did they expect? It was the girls' own fault. Besides, they seemed to enjoy the attention, cursing the boys and chasing them down the street.

I leaned against a pillar on the porch and watched without much expression. My Muslim friend Lamia, a fat girl who came to our house every day with her younger brother, Latif, and sister, Layla, while their parents worked, sat on the top step, resting her chin in the palms of her hands. And another girl named YoShawn, who had very long braids, sat next to her. She was twelve, another one of the kids Ma and GrandWillie baby-sat.

Behind us, GrandWillie approached the screen door with a bottle of vinegar in one hand and a crumpled sheet of newspaper in the other, cleaning the window at the top of the door. The younger children that she and Ma watched during the day were taking naps now that it was just past noon.

Ma and GrandWillie structured our whole day with "constructive" activities, so the same high-noon sun that shone on the girls in the street usually found Lamia, YoShawn, and me reading or playing an educational game in the shade on the porch. But many times we got distracted anyway, watching the girls play in the street.

Most days we got a chance to burn off some of our energy when Ma walked us two miles north to the swimming pool for swimming lessons, then about two more miles east to the library.

I loved going to the swimming pool, but I hadn't been there since before Ma first became a Muslim when I was three years old. As Muslims in the Nation of Islam, we had been forbidden to go to public pools because we would have been required to wear the proper attire, a bathing suit that would have left most of our body exposed. But now that we were Orthodox Muslim, only females past the age of puberty—considered women—were forbidden to be half-naked in a public place. At ten years old, I was still a girl—thank God.

We were lined up along the edge of the pool, waiting for our swimming teacher to blow his whistle for us to jump in, I looked up and down the line of boys and girls and was happy to be rid of my special coat of armor, my long clothes, even if only temporarily. I was for once free to look like everybody else, free to be like them.

I found that I loved the swimming pool, the strong smell of chlorine opening my nostrils, the pretty blue cushion ready to catch me when I jumped from the edge, the sense of oneness with the other kids. My world was opening up.

❋ ❋ ❋

As an Orthodox Muslim mother, Ma was more serious about making sure we made all five of our prayers every day. When we were in the Nation, she was more concerned with us memorizing Elijah Muhammad's prayers and recitation so we could excel in school. As an Orthodox Muslim, I began learning that no man or worldly pursuit such as school, and certainly not frivolous play, should come before Allah. I was learning this, but I didn't like it. The midday prayers were quite a nuisance to a kid trying to function out in the real world. None of the other kids had to quit playing to pray.

"I get tired of praying all the time," I snapped at Ma as she held the front door open for me and Lamia.

"You don't want Allah to get *tired* of looking out after you, do you?" she responded.

I stomped up the stairs to the bathroom and rolled up my sleeves to prepare for prayer. Sulking and sighing, I washed my hands up to my elbows three times, since three was a magical number for us Orthodox Muslims. (We didn't have a magic number in the Nation.) As I rinsed my mouth three times, poked my wet index fingers up my nostrils three times, and washed my face three times, I could hear the kids running across the street. I looked out the window and saw Freddie and Bernard running to find hiding places. Darren, no doubt, was trying to find a hiding place around the corner so Ma couldn't see him and call him in for prayer. With the water still running, I wiped my dripping hands three times over the white handkerchief on my head, then cleaned inside my ears. I also had to take off my tennis shoes and socks and wash my feet three times.

This ritual was *wudu*, Arabic for ablution or cleansing. We couldn't pray if we were dirty, I was taught, because Allah didn't accept prayers from dirty people. Even in the Nation of Islam we had to wash for prayer, and we often were reminded that "cleanliness is next to godliness."

* * *

Within weeks I got tired of explaining to the kids over and over again why I had to stay on the porch, why I had to wear long, hot clothes, and why I always had to go in the house to pray. So I just stayed in the house and talked to GrandWillie most of the time. Sometimes we played board games like checkers, Chinese checkers, and Monopoly.

"GrandWillie, want to play a quick game of Chinese checkers?" I'd ask.

The smell of bean soup might be wafting from the kitchen and the sun just beginning to turn evening orange when GrandWillie and I sat down to play. If all the day-care kids got picked up on time, we would have a half hour or so before it was time for our evening prayer and dinner. "GrandWillie, y'all didn't have Chinese checkers when you were little, did you?" I asked as we set up the game. GrandWillie liked the green marbles. I liked the blue.

We talked through the game, but our conversations usually came down to questions and answers, I guess because a ten-year-old and a fifty-four-year-old didn't have much to talk about except the whys, what-fors, and hows of things. Plus, I liked to hear her talk about the way things were when she was little.

Over one game, I found out my great-grandmother was only fourteen years old when she got married and migrated north to Washington, D.C., from North Carolina.

Moving one of my marbles across the board, I asked GrandWillie my great-grandparents' first names.

"Fennessie Loudella?" I laughed, repeating what GrandWillie said. "That was her name, for real?"

GrandWillie nodded and laughed as she moved her green marble. "And your great-granddaddy's name was Tennessee," she added.

I remembered GrandWillie had taken Darren and me to visit them a few times in my life. We picked strawberries from Great-Grandma's garden. Over the years, I'd learn that my great-grandparents had grown fruits and vegetables and canned them themselves so they didn't need to depend on the white man's grocery stores. They knew to be self-sufficient long before the Honorable Elijah Muhammad came along.

"GrandWillie, do you still like your sisters?" I asked while moving another marble across the board.

"Of course," she snapped.

"Just curious again," I said.

"Girl, you're always curious. You know what curiosity did to the cat."

I didn't think curiosity could kill me. I was curious about a lot of things. Like why we didn't spend any time with our family the way I saw families on TV do. On TV, families always got together for the holidays.

GrandWillie's sisters and brothers had cut her off when she joined the Nation of Islam. For nineteen years they didn't speak to her. Her father had forbidden them to. Her mother had to sneak to visit, and so did two of her younger sisters, Aunt Shirley and Aunt Naomi.

The only relative who ever came to our house now was GrandWillie's baby sister, Aunt Shirley, whom GrandWillie baby-sat for. Now that I was finding out about all these aunts and uncles whom I had never spent time with, I wanted to know more about them. I wondered why none of the others ever came by.

GrandWillie usually won the games by landing her last marble in home base before I did. We scooped up the marbles, lay the board back in its box, and generally headed for the kitchen to check on dinner. I stayed right at her heels.

❋ ❋ ❋

When I spent the weekends over at Aunt Shirley's house, I went to the family church with them on Sunday, and there I heard relatives talking about my GrandWillie, saying she was pitiful for having joined that "Moozlem" group, making her kids and grandkids suffer through it.

Two women I called Sister Know-It-All and Snooty-Toot always had something to say about somebody, and when I passed them, wearing my long dress, I heard them talk about GrandWillie.

"Whose child is that?"

"Oh, that's Willie's grandbaby," the answer would come.

"I don't know why they got to have the children all mixed up in that foolishness."

"Don't make no sense they got to make the children suffer."

They might have looked at my second-hand dress and thought "suffering," but I felt fine.

I liked the sound of the gospel music at Aunt Shirley's church. And the sights, whew! Somebody was always getting "happy" and "filled" at the Bethlehem Church of God and Holiness. Once, a lady got the Holy Ghost and jumped around so much she fell to the floor and hit her head on one of the benches. The men ushers and women nurses had to run to her rescue.

"What's the matter with her?" I asked Sirene, my cousin.

"She got the Holy Spirit," Sirene said. "Stop staring like that."

I had never seen anything like it. I thought the lady was jumping and shouting because the music was getting good to her. It was getting to me, too, but I knew better than to jump all around like some fool in public.

As much as I enjoyed the gospel music and got filled with the good spirit, I still couldn't sing the praises of Jesus. I didn't want to go to hell with the rest of these people for praying to the wrong God. I wondered why my Christian relatives didn't know better.

Elijah Muhammad said that what he taught came, in part, from the Bible. Didn't they read their own Bible? We had been taught at the Muslim school that Jesus never claimed to be God. That it was the blond-haired, blue-eyed devil who twisted the Bible and made Jesus God.

I turned side to side while I was singing, so the blue-eyed man hanging from the cross at the front of the church wouldn't get the wrong idea and think I was singing to him. No one noticed that I was changing all the words. They were full of their own song and praise. The preacher would be preaching or the choir singing, service in full swing, and still certain relatives' pointing and staring managed to make me feel uncomfortable. The junior choir, full of my cousins, even brought the congregation to its feet, singing:

Sign me up for the Christian Jubilee
Write my name on the road
I've been changed since the Lord has lifted me
I wanna be ready when Jesus comes. . . .

The sound and energy hit the walls with such force that the old stained-glass windows seemed to rattle. The cracks and pores of the old building seemed to open up.

Ma didn't mind me going to church with Aunt Shirley sometimes because she knew that wherever I went, I knew who my God was and would pray to him regardless of what anyone else was doing. The picture of a Caucasian Jesus in front of GrandWillie's old church didn't bother me, either, because I knew that picture was a figment of the white man's imagination because the Bible really said Jesus had bronze skin and hair like wool.

I was happy to be in GrandWillie's old place of worship. I was glad our new Muslim leader no longer condemned religions that were different from ours. He told GrandWillie —and I think Ma even heard him—that all religions were good and it was okay to mingle with our relatives who weren't Muslims. Within a few years, he would begin holding interfaith events to bring Muslims and Christians and Jews all together. For now, I was just happy to be able to experience life.

I enjoyed all these new sights and sounds.

Fight the Power

CHAPTER 11

As the summer of 1976 drew to an end, commercials for back-to-school clothes caught my attention when I watched my favorite sitcoms, *Good Times* and *The Jeffersons*. One evening, when commercials came on with little kids in back-to-school jeans, shoes, and shirts, my siblings, my cousins, and I tried to outshout each other saying what our mothers were going to buy us.

"My mother gon' get me two pairs of designer jeans and some Dirty Bucks," my six-year-old cousin, Robbin, said. She wanted a pair of jeans with *Sasson* on the back pockets and a pair with *Jordache*.

You had to have at least one pair of designer jeans or you were nothing among your peers. Dirty Bucks were tan suede tie-up shoes, which all the kids in the neighborhood wanted. Robbin was sure she could get a pair because her mother, who saw her only on weekends, often took her shopping and bought her whatever she wanted. Since my wardrobe consisted of only old Muslim school uniforms and other Muslim girl outfits—balloon pants, long tops, and long dresses—I was sure my mother would buy me whatever I wanted, too.

"I'm gon' get two pairs of jeans *and* a pair of slacks and some Dirty Bucks," I said.

I realized school would be starting in about two weeks, so I decided to make sure Ma was aware that we had only a short time left to get ready. During the next commercial, I bounced upstairs to Ma's room and asked her if we were going back-to-school shopping this weekend or next weekend.

"You have clothes in your closet," she said, looking up from changing my baby brother's diaper.

It was a good thing I came to her now instead of waiting for her to realize on her own that I needed new clothes. Sometimes Ma just didn't seem to understand things. Everybody knew that wearing the right clothes to school was even more important in junior high school than in elementary school. I was already going to be smaller than everybody else in my new school because everybody else was at least two years older than me. While most kids were twelve years old when they started junior high, I was ten. My long clothes had kept me from making any new friends in the elementary school I went to, and I didn't want the same thing to happen in this new school. I was going to be attending Elliot Junior High School, about a mile from our home, and I didn't want to be the only one from our neighborhood walking over there dressed in funny clothes.

"Ma, I need new pants and shirts and shoes," I said, trying to sound calm even though my heart started beating faster.

"You can start out the school year in the clothes you have," she said, no longer even looking at me.

She couldn't be serious, I thought. She must be crazy if she thinks I'm wearing my Muslim clothes to my new school.

"Ma, I *need* new clothes for school," I pleaded, as Robbin, who had come up to see what was taking me so long, watched from behind me. "Everybody wears new back-to-school clothes on the first day," I continued.

"Since when do we do what everybody else is doing just because everybody else is doing it?" Ma responded. "You do not *need* new clothes. You *want* new clothes. I'm not about to go out here and get caught up in this so-called back-to-school madness. We'll get the school supplies that you do *need*. You *need* a notebook and a book bag. That's all you *need* for so-called back to school. That other stuff is just a rip-off. They jack the prices up in stores, then put out a whole bunch of commercials to make you kids think you *need* new jeans for school. What does a pair of new jeans have to do with you learning anything? That's what you go to school for—to learn, not all that other stuff."

She was making this into a bigger deal than it was, like she always did. I almost didn't graduate from elementary school because of her. Now she was going to mess up the beginning of junior high school, too. Dad and GrandWillie never made such a big issue out of little things. That's why I wished she could get run over by the ice cream truck and I could just live with my GrandWillie and Dad—even though I hardly got to see him.

All I wanted was back-to-school clothes, and here was Ma giving me a lecture about life. Why couldn't she just say the truth: that she didn't have any money to buy new clothes because she refused to go out and get a real job like her parents, Grandma and Granddaddy Thomas, said she should do? The few times they did come over to visit to bring me or my brother something for our birthdays or to see their newborn grandchild, I heard them tell her that she could make more money if she became a nurse like they planned for her, instead of laying home having a whole bunch of babies. I'd heard her telling her parents that she kept getting pregnant because "Allah manifested" she get pregnant even when she was trying birth control. They didn't believe her, so I became skeptical about her excuses, too. She blamed Allah for everything.

"Allah tells us not to get ripped off by the material pursuits of this world, wanting everything we see," she told me.

I didn't know what no "pursuit" was, and it wasn't just that I *wanted* school clothes. I did *need* them. GrandWillie understood, and the next morning she came up to our bedroom as I was getting dressed—she always woke up hours before the rest of us—and handed me an envelope with some money in it. She said she was paying me for having helped her and Ma baby-sit through the summer. I had helped by entertaining the little kids while she and Ma fixed lunch, and I had helped march them upstairs to the bathroom in an orderly fashion so they could wash their hands. I opened the envelope and saw clean, crisp bills, unfolded.

"One twenty-dollars, two twenty-dollars, three twenty-dollars," I counted out loud. "GrandWillie, this is *five* twenty-dollars!" I shouted. "I can have all of these twenty-dollars?"

"You earned it, Sonsy-Ray-Ray," she said, folding up the cots we slept on, rolling them off to the side so the room could become a play area for my younger siblings.

"You put one of those bills in your piggy bank and save it, and we're going downtown so you can get yourself some school clothes—if you want—with the rest of it," she said, leaning over, whispering to me. "Your mother don't have to know nothing until we get back," she added.

My mother would've been too proud to take the money from GrandWillie because she already felt bad that GrandWillie had to give us a place to live since my father kept spending his money on music equipment and going in the studio trying to make records. My mother was twenty-eight years old with five busybody kids, a hard-headed husband,

and nothing else to show for her life. So she was getting meaner and meaner and taking it out on us little kids. I looked up, happy that GrandWillie was helping me get around my mother again.

"I'll deal with her when we get back. You were good all summer, and you deserve a little something," she said.

I hadn't considered my helping out "work," but since GrandWillie said it was, I decided I was going to help out more in the future, so maybe I could earn more money and buy myself whatever I wanted whenever I wanted. Darren had been allowed to earn his own money selling newspapers and working in the Muslim restaurant with our uncles since he was eight, and this year he had money for his own school clothes because they still worked at the restaurant, which wasn't closed down yet. He had teased me, showing me his jar full of money, bragging about buying back-to-school clothes, and I couldn't wait to show him all my money now.

I couldn't remember the last time I'd been shopping downtown, so I was excited. Ma was in her room still asleep when GrandWillie and I left. We rode the bus downtown and went in Hecht's department store and Woodies, and I marveled at the tall mannequins wearing striped pullover shirts with their hair flipped up like a lady named Farrah Fawcett I saw on a TV show once a week. Even the black mannequins wore their hair like hers. We went to the section filled with little girls' clothes, and I saw red and yellow back-to-school signs everywhere. So I knew we were in the right stores. I couldn't get to the racks of jeans and slacks and shirts fast enough. Green pants, red pants, plaid pants, flower pants, and matching shirts.

"You like this little set, Ray-Ray?" GrandWillie asked, holding up a dark green flowered double-knit pants set. I shook my head no, delighted that she even asked, allowing me to make my own decision.

"I like this one," I said, having spotted a plain dark blue shirt with matching slacks. She checked inside the clothes and put them back because they weren't my right size.

"You'll need to try them on," she said.

Ma and GrandWillie had made all my school clothes and ordered my school uniforms from the Nation up until now, so all I'd had to do was stand still to have my hips and legs and arms measured for specially made clothes. I was happier now to be buying regular clothes from the stores like everybody else. Years later I would realize how privileged I had been to have clothes specially made, even by my mother's and grandmother's own hands. But for now I just wanted to be like everybody else.

Thanks to my GrandWillie, it looked like I was going to do just fine. We returned home carrying shopping bags in both our hands, and Ma was standing in the kitchen when we walked through the door. GrandWillie said she would deal with her, so I ran upstairs with my bags before Ma could say anything to me.

❋ ❋ ❋

Ma still made me wear a scarf on my head, I guess just so everybody would know I was a Muslim girl. But at least I didn't have to wear long dresses anymore.

Ma came to the school the first week to meet all my teachers, then came back to explain to my gym teacher why I couldn't wear the shorts uniform for our forty-five minutes of physical fitness like everybody else. They reached an agreement that when class was indoors with just us girls, I could wear the short outfit and participate. But when class was outside on the baseball field, I'd have to remain fully dressed and sit on the sidelines because Ma didn't want the vulgar little boys from our neighborhood looking at my legs and trying to touch my butt. At the swimming pool, all of us half-naked kids were supervised, so no one could get out of line. But Ma thought public schools gave kids too much freedom and that in junior high school, my long clothes would be my only protection. She didn't realize that my clothes were the cause of most of my problems because they alienated me.

The girls wanted to know why I didn't just sneak and wear the shorts for gym and why I didn't snatch my head-piece off my head in the mornings when I got far enough away from home.

"Just because," I told them. The reason was because I knew Allah was watching my every move even when my mother couldn't see.

At the Muslim school some of the teenage girls took off their headpieces and hiked up their skirts when they got far enough away from the Temple. But to me, it wasn't worth it to risk the wrath of Allah. I might be able to go around Ma's back and get GrandWillie to buy me the right clothes, but I knew there was no getting around Allah.

Once during gym class a girl named Sylvia asked, "Sonsyrea, why Moozlems can't wear shorts?"

"We cover our bodies so men will respect us," I told her.

She burst out laughing. "Y'all think men suppose to respect y'all just 'cause you don't wear shorts." She was loud and obnoxious, creating a little sideshow.

"Hey, Paulette, come here. Come here. Sonsyrea, tell me again why Moozlems can't wear shorts."

"It's just our religion!" I snapped, turning to walk away. If I had been bigger or tougher, I would have punched her for making me feel so small.

"That's not what you said at first," she yelled. "My father said y'all Moozlems are crazy!"

I rolled my eyes and walked away because I didn't think I could beat her if we got in a fight. Even though I'd learned self-defense at Muslim Girls Training classes, I never thought I'd really have to use it. Now, here I was out in the world and this Sylvia was confronting me about my religion. I remembered Sister Captain telling us that if ever challenged on our religion, we were to "fight like hell to the bitter end." But I had doubts about my religion now since so much of it was changing so quickly.

"Mess with somebody your own size," one of our classmates named Antoinette (not her real name) said, pushing Sylvia, who stood taller than me but a few inches shorter than Antoinette. I was feeling all shaken up inside. All the girls in class formed a circle around Sylvia and Antoinette, cheering them on to fight. But our teacher came out of her office in time to stop it before it began. At my Muslim school, we hadn't had any fights. I'd seen the boys run off the bus to fight heathen children, but they always fought as a team. I didn't know what I was going to do out here alone, but I figured out quickly.

"I'm gon' get you at three o'clock," Sylvia told me as the crowd dispersed. Little did she know, I was going to be walking home with Antoinette—today and every day for the rest of the year.

I became friends with Antoinette and a girl named Mechelle, who was about five-feet-five and two hundred pounds, pecan brown with acne and long hair that she always wore in two cornrows, and Belinda, who was about the same size, had smooth skin the color of almonds, and wore her hair pressed and curled. Antoinette, who came to school wearing dirty or wrinkled clothes a lot because she was living between two unstable homes, got in a lot of fights. The other kids at our school teased her and called her "dirty girl" or "alley cat," but she usually wound up beating their butts. She was the only tough one in our little group. Mechelle and Belinda were kind of shy like me, but nobody messed with them because they were so big.

The four of us walked to and from school together and talked between classes. I didn't eat lunch with them because they had either lunch money or a government-subsidized lunch card to buy lunch in the cafeteria. Since my parents were too poor to provide lunch money every day and too proud—for now—to accept a handout from the government, Ma packed me a brown-bag lunch every day. But I dropped it in the sewer on my way to school because it was uncool to show up at junior high school carrying a lunch bag like a little kid. At lunch time, I stayed in the school library studying instead.

Then I signed up to write for the school newspaper so maybe I could spend my lunch hour talking with my English teacher about journalism or working on an article for the paper. My fourth grade teacher at the Muslim school had read parts of my plays and short stories aloud in class, telling me to keep up the good work. So I figured working with the school paper would be fun.

I got mostly As that year because the year had been a breeze after a few initial adjustments. There was only one other Muslim in the school, a boy named Talib-Diin who sometimes wore a *kufi* to school. Talib-Diin was more shy and withdrawn than I was becoming. Darren made friends with the baddest boys in the school and got in so much trouble with his teachers that he would eventually be kept back. At the end of our seventh grade year, I got promoted to eighth but he had to repeat seventh grade. He said I was just a little bookworm but he had "street smarts," so he didn't care that I passed him.

By the time Christmas came during my eighth grade year, I still found myself having to explain things to my classmates. After our Christmas break when my classmates bragged about all the new clothes and other gifts they got, I had to explain that I didn't get anything except a couple of gifts from my Christian grandparents. I had to explain that we didn't celebrate what we Muslims considered a pagan holiday.

I became friends with a girl named Yvonne who wore a dress to school every day and came from a strict religious family, too. Her family were Jehovah's Witnesses, and she said she didn't mind that she had to wear a dress every single day. She was dark brown with glasses and a long ponytail, and she looked more like a bookworm than me. Sometimes I even had to explain things to her. When she tried to tell me what the Bible said about not having boyfriends and running around being loud and savagelike, I told her her Bible was fake, not really God's words. As an Orthodox Muslim, I was learning not to trust the Bible.

Once when Yvonne and I got in an argument about the Bible during class, our teacher, Mrs. Hickman, made us stay after school so she could have a talk with us.

"I'm going to share a little story with you," Mrs. Hickman told us as we stood at her desk waiting to be scolded. Mrs. Hickman was tall and very light skinned and looked like Sister Memphis from the Muslim school.

"Once upon a time, there were five students who lived in a city called Washington, D.C." She paused, puckered her lips, and folded her hands under her chin for dramatic effect. "All the students were assigned to Elliot Junior High School, and they all had to decide on how to get there.

One of them decided to walk, one of them rode the bus, another one got a ride from her parents, one rode his bike, and the other one decided to just stay home and not try to get there at all."

Yvonne and I looked at each other, puzzled. I had no idea where this story was going, but I was hoping Mrs. Hickman was almost at the end.

"Every one of them who set out to get to school got there," she said, looking serious. "Regardless of whether they came from near or far and regardless of what means of transportation they used." She stood up and came from behind her desk. "You see, it doesn't matter what religion you're in or what holy books you read, there's only one God, one heaven, and he doesn't care how you get there."

I would remember and reflect on her little story for years to come, but right then I was just hoping Sylvia wasn't waiting outside the school to beat me up since I didn't have Antoinette there to protect me.

❋ ❋ ❋

My biggest problem in school was that some of my classmates thought Muslims were crazy or violent or both. They thought we were crazy because their parents told them we were, and they thought we were violent because the only time they saw us on TV was on the news when Muslims were fighting or dropping bombs over in the Middle East.

One incident in particular reinforced such stereotypes. On March 9, 1977, groups of heavily armed Hanafi Muslim men stormed three public buildings in the city and held 134 people hostage.

At school the next day, that same loud-mouthed girl named Sylvia tried to tease me.

"Hey, y'all, did y'all see Sonsyrea's father on the news last night? He took the District Building hostage," she said, laughing.

I'd seen the news, too, and knew that none of those men looked like my father. Three groups of Hanafi Muslim men had stormed the District Building, our city hall, where the mayor of the city worked, and taken hostages, killing a radio news reporter and wounding a popular D.C. city councilman. They had also taken over the Islamic Center uptown and seized the B'nai B'rith building, headquarters for the world's largest and oldest Jewish organization. They threatened to chop off the heads of their hostages and throw the heads out the windows if they didn't get what they wanted.

The city was frozen in terror, everyone glued to television or radio. The Muslim men demanded to see whomever was in charge of releasing a movie called *Prophet Muhammad: Messenger of Allah* because they considered the movie blasphemous. They wanted police authorities to deliver to them the seven Nation of Islam Muslims convicted of murdering the family of a leader of the Hanafi Muslims in Washington a few years before.

This hostage ordeal lasted three days but would stay in my classmates' minds for the rest of the year. I was so sure that this had reinforced the ideas they had about Muslims, I distanced myself from them even more.

I looked forward to getting away from them on the weekends. GrandWillie took me, my siblings, and my cousins to the movies sometimes. We saw *Let's Do It Again*, with Bill Cosby and Sidney Poitier, and a movie about boxing champion Muhammad Ali when it came out later that year.

GrandWillie loved watching Muhammad Ali fights because he was a Muslim and he showed the world that Muslims could fight and win.

In preparation for one of Ali's big matches, GrandWillie tore open a large bag of potato chips and a bag of cheese puffs and mixed soda and juice together like we were having a party, just her and us kids. The men always went over to Uncle Avon's house to watch so they could be as loud as they wanted to. At home my cousins Robbin and Beyete, my brothers Furard and Atif, who were too little to go with the men, and my sister Sakinah and I all sat around the coffee table in the living room, munching as GrandWillie leaned in toward the TV.

"Some people say you have a big mouth," a short white man with a cartoonlike appearance on TV said, holding his microphone up to Muhammad Ali's face. Before the heavyweight champion of the world responded, GrandWillie was cheering him on.

"That's all right!" she yelled at the TV screen. "Tell him you can back it up. You keep on talkin'!"

"I'M THE GREATEST!" Mr. Ali boasted, his bearlike body half naked in only a pair of boxer shorts and his boxing gloves. The crowd around him was busy and noisy with anticipation. "I'm gonna float like a butterfly and sting like a bee," he said into one of the cameras. "Leon Spinks is going down in round three."

I thought he was awesome. GrandWillie was on the edge of the couch midway through round two. "Get 'im!" she coached, her lips twisted and fists balled up in front of her like she was about to box herself. "That's right!" she shouted, breaking her normal composure for this special occasion. "Get him! Get him!" Her fists punched the air as she shouted.

I stopped munching and shouted, too. "Don't let him off the ropes!" I yelled. "Do the rope-a-dope. Do the rope-a-dope!" I'd heard my uncles say that before, and Darren had taught me about uppercuts and left and right jabs. I enjoyed boxing and was counting on Muhammad Ali to win so I could feel proud about being a Muslim when I returned to school after the weekend.

❋ ❋ ❋

By the time I turned twelve, in April 1978, I had met new Muslim friends because my mother and aunts and uncles who practiced Orthodox Islam met other Orthodox Muslim families. They had enough people to form our own Muslim community, and they organized Sunday school classes for us kids. Sunday school rotated among the families' homes, mostly apartments in the Mayfair and Paradise Mansion projects.

Most of the Muslim homes in the projects were clean, but some of them still had roaches because of the dirty people who lived around them. We had to step out of our shoes before entering any of the Muslim homes, but most of them had nice carpet on the floor.

None of the homes had pictures on the walls because we believed it was sinful to take family portraits or hang pictures of people or animals on the wall. That was considered idol worship. Everyone burned incense—strawberry scented, musk, coconut, sandalwood—I think to purify the air. And everyone had beautiful Persian-style prayer rugs in the easternmost corner of the living room for prayer time.

Several of the families threw out their furniture and had only large pillows to sit on because we believed Allah didn't want us to have any kind of luxury—like furniture. Most families did not have a dining room table because we believed Allah wanted us to sit on the floor around a clean cloth we called a spread. We used three fingers on our right hand to pick up our food instead of using utensils because we were trying to do everything the way the prophet Muhammad had done 1,400 years ago.

"Ma, they probably ate with their fingers because they didn't have spoons back then," I challenged.

I had been doubtful about Ma's wisdom for years, and now that I was a preteen, I thought I could challenge her directly. I didn't need GrandWillie to plead my case anymore.

"You're getting to be a mouthy little brat," Ma said. "Don't let your lips get you in trouble."

Ma had whipped me only one time in my life, and that had been five years ago, so I wasn't worried about any kind of "trouble" she was threatening. She whipped Darren often because he always got in trouble at school. But I had been a good child. I had gone over her head to GrandWillie to get my way through the years, but that wasn't really outright being bad, I thought. I stayed on the porch when I was supposed to most of the time, I came in the house when I was supposed to. I made my prayers when I was supposed to. I kept my headpiece on at school and didn't sneak to wear shorts. But now she was demanding even more, and I had to draw the line.

"When in America do like the Americans," I said once when Ma had me helping prepare Middle Eastern–style rice dishes for dinner at Aunt Kimba's home. I frowned and mumbled the whole time, and when Ma came back in the kitchen to help, I wanted her to know I was not happy. So I repeated myself in case she didn't hear me the first time.

"When in Arabia do like the Arabians. When in America, do like the Americans," I said louder but to no one in particular. Aunt Kimba just rolled her eyes, expecting that Ma would straighten me out. But this time Ma simply ignored me.

I carried a large plate of rice into the living room where everyone was ready for dinner and placed it in the center of the spread so everyone could eat from it. At the end of the meal we passed a jar of herbal tea around, and everyone sipped from it. I thought this was disgusting.

❃ ❃ ❃

Darren and I both began losing faith in our religion. Only a couple of years had passed since we had been told that the history and other information we had learned at the Muslim school were false. Elijah Muhammad's son said those lessons we had been taught were not based on actual facts. Now Ma was expecting us to obediently go along with a set of new principles and practices, but we couldn't. We coped the best we could, though, making jokes about certain practices and outright rebelling against others.

Darren managed to spend many weekends at Uncle Sharrief's house so he wouldn't have to be with Ma and her new Orthodox Muslim friends. I could have spent more weekends over at Aunt Shirley's and gone to church with her, but I liked a particular boy in our new Orthodox community. I looked forward to going to our Muslim Sunday school just so I could see him.

A stick of jasmine incense was burning when I stepped inside Sister Ayana's apartment for Sunday school one morning. I stole a quick glimpse of Billy as he neatly lined his tennis shoes along the hallway wall with the other shoes. Surveying the two rows of shoes, I could see who was there. Uncle Sabu, our Arabic teacher, was already present. I could tell by his green and white leather Nikes. They looked like two weather-beaten ships in a sea of tiny vessels on the shoe line near the doorway.

Billy paused to bless me with a moment of attention before moving into the living room where Sunday school was being held.

"Is your brother coming?" he asked.

I blushed, leaning against the wall, balancing myself on my right foot as I untied the shoe on the left. With my chin almost buried in my chest, I answered, "No. He spent the night over Sharrief's this weekend."

I could tell that Billy knew I liked him. It was something about the way he looked at me this time. My shoes removed, I found my way into the living room and sat on the girls' side of the circle, folding myself into a skinny pretzel like the rest of them. In the middle of the circle, Uncle Sabu was using his long, skinny wooden rod with a rubber tip to point to each of the letters of the Arabic alphabet. I had learned the Arabic alphabet at the Muslim school but was not the least bit eager to show it. I didn't want to be here except to see Billy, whom I was hoping to marry someday. But I think Uncle Sabu was thrilled to have this opportunity to use some of the skills he had acquired at the University of Islam.

"Alif," he said, pointing to the first letter in the set he had drawn on the small blackboard.

"Alif," we complied.

"Ba," he went.

"Ba," we echoed.

And so it went until we had recited all twenty-eight letters in unison. Then, with a point of his rod, he began directing each of us to stand and recite as much as we could without looking at the board. Billy could recite more than most of the others. It was too bad that English and other subjects in regular school didn't come as easily to him. Nashad and Nzinga, my two best friends, teased me for liking Billy.

"Girl, you gon' be out of high school and Billy's still going to be trying to get out of junior high," they joked. I was in ninth grade, about to advance to tenth grade in high school, and Billy was in seventh grade, where it seemed like he would stay for a third year.

"Yeah, y'all gon' be married and your children gon' have to teach him how to read!" they teased.

"He ain't dumb," I insisted. "He's street smart."

I never did figure out how Billy could memorize so much Arabic, the alphabet and Quranic verse, but couldn't keep up in school. I was the opposite. I was an honor roll student at school and had learned to recite the American Pledge of Allegiance in Spanish. I realized I had to learn Spanish to get through school and get my diploma; I didn't see how learning Arabic could help me in my life.

❋ ❋ ❋

During some Sunday school sessions, we also read stories about Allah and his wrath and why we should fear him.

Stories of Allah punishing idol worshipers by bringing their large statues, small figurines, and photos to life titillated us by day but frightened me at night. Even though I was about to go to high school, I was just a twelve-year-old girl, and the fear of Allah had been instilled in me since I was three.

I had learned that putting a statue of a person or animal in one's house was viewed by Allah as idol worship, a heathen practice condemned by God even before Prophet Muhammad came along. And on Judgment Day these idols of worship would come to life to haunt their owners. So, sometimes at night, I worried that our neighbors' sins might reach into our house, too.

What if Allah decided to end the world this very night? I worried while trying to fall asleep. Mrs. Downie's unicorn plant stands would come to life! She lives right next door, so if the unicorns get her, they might come over to our house and get us, too. And what if Allah brought to life the huge, larger-than-life statues of white American heroes downtown? Would they come charging into our neighborhood, too?

When I spent the night at Grandma and Granddaddy Thomas's house, I worried about the painted picture of a chubby white boy in shorts and his little fat sister in frills on the bedroom wall. I didn't want Allah to think I was worshiping these images. Eventually, I began to hang scarves or towels over the pictures at night. Now I only had to worry about Allah punishing my grandparents' household for their sin of having a dog. According to the Muslim books we studied, the prophet Muhammad hated dogs and said that the angels would not enter a home where there was a dog. We believed that the dog was the devil's beast. Uncle Sabu told us to notice the way a dog's eyes glow at night. That was proof they were evil. Meanwhile, my grandparents' dog, named Ren, watched TV with them in their bedroom at night, eating ice cream from his bowl when they ate ice cream in bed.

Grandma said she prayed for us all the time. Prayed that God would forgive my parents and show her grandbabies the light.

"God said there would be impostors to come," Grandma said, her tall and sturdy stance adding conviction to everything she said. "And he said the impostors would lead a lot of people away. I just pray that he lets some of y'all get saved before it's too late."

I certainly couldn't argue with my grandmother about her religion because I had to respect the wisdom of her age. But all this religious stuff was confusing me. Who was right?

❋ ❋ ❋

The adults in our Orthodox community talked often about preparing for Judgment Day.

We could be having a picnic on a bright summer day with families all around us barbecuing pork ribs, drinking beer, and playing cards, enjoying life without worrying about God. But we couldn't forget about Allah for even a few hours. When our scheduled prayer times arrived, we had to stop, wash, and pray. Sometimes we couldn't find a working water fountain or restrooms in the park to complete the preprayer wash, but this wouldn't stop us.

"Come over here! I found it!" Uncle Sabu yelled from a distance one particular afternoon. Patting his hands in a patch of dust or sand, then wiping his hands on his face, he proceeded to wash with "Allah's clean dirt."

The first time he suggested this, I rebelled strongly.

"We're supposed to clean ourselves with dirt?" I said sarcastically, talking to my mother like she was the child.

"Yes, Allah says that when you don't have clean water, you can use clean dirt," Ma said. I could see that she was a bit embarrassed that I was challenging her in front of everybody.

"But that's stupid!" I said. Ma cut her eyes at me, and I knew I had gone far enough for now. I'd have to put dirt on my face, arms, and legs, too. Not only did I not like washing with dirt, I also didn't like having to pray in public. But Ma didn't understand that, either.

"You shouldn't be ashamed to worship Allah," Ma said.

"I'm not ashamed," I argued. "I would just rather say my prayers in the privacy of the car instead. Allah knows what's in my heart." But Ma didn't buy it. Surroundings and circumstance should never prevent us from stopping to pray, she said.

Nzinga claimed that her period came on so she could be excused from prayer. Females were not supposed to pray during the menses cycle because that was a period of being unclean. Nashad said that she was still clean from the morning because she hadn't used the bathroom or eaten or drunk anything that would have made her too unclean to go before Allah. "I'm still in *wudu*," she explained.

I remembered Ma saying that Allah kept a running log of every deed and misdeed, every sin and every lie. On the Day of Judgment, Allah would open his book of deeds and ask me, "Why didn't you make *Asr Salat* on August 12, 1978?" I could almost hear Allah's big bass voice in my ears. I knew I couldn't look up at him and tell him, "Because I didn't feel like it." He might reach down out the sky and punch me in the head for an answer like that.

I was beginning not to like him because he had too many religions and his religions caused confusion in my head, in my family, at my school, and in my city. But I couldn't do anything about it.

Making Modest Maidens

CHAPTER 12

By the spring of 1978 I had successfully argued and convinced Ma that sending me to school in headpieces was anything but "modest." Ma argued that one reason we Muslim girls had to dress modestly was so we wouldn't draw undue attention to ourselves. But I insisted that in the Middle East where everyone wore veils, wearing one would be the modest thing to do.

"Ma, these clothes draw *everybody's* attention to me. People can't help but stop and stare. It's like I'm begging for attention. Like everybody's gotta know I'm a Muslim. That ain't modest."

Once I was no longer wearing my headpieces, I asked for permission to become a cheerleader for my junior high school basketball team. But I couldn't convince Ma to allow me to wear a miniskirt.

"It's only for a couple of hours, a couple of days," I pleaded one morning as I headed out the door to school.

"No!" she yelled. "And you better not call yourself going behind my back asking your grandmother."

I was twelve and learning just how far Ma could be pushed these days. She was becoming more lenient in some ways, but in other ways she would become even more strict. Last year, when I was in seventh grade, she had allowed me to stay up past my bedtime to watch a TV miniseries called *Roots* about a black family surviving slavery. But this year, she wouldn't allow me to watch *Rich Man, Poor Man*, a show about a rich white family, even though I told her all my classmates were watching it.

Ma allowed me to join the Booster Club, which sat in the bleachers with pom-poms during the games and cheered the team in singsong shouts. Dressed in jeans and sweatshirts, we yelled, "Jump baaaaaaalll. Shoop, shoop, take that ball through the hoop, hoop!"

When I was a little girl in the Nation of Islam, shouting in public wasn't even allowed. So I should have been satisfied just to join the loud girls now. But there was so much more I wanted to do now that I was free.

I joined the school choir, with Ma's only condition being that I keep my mouth shut when the choir sang about Jesus. As long as the songs praised "God," I could sing, she said. That seemed fair enough, although I would have to excuse myself from performing in the Easter program. I was allowed to audition for the annual spring musical and landed a role in our drama club's version of the Broadway musical *Bye Bye Birdie*.

❋ ❋ ❋

Nzinga, Nashad, and I spent many afternoons on the telephone taking turns calling one another. The telephone for us was our lifeline. On the phone we consoled and counseled one another through our common problems.

"Girl, I think my mother is pregnant again," I said into the phone one afternoon. My mother was acting mean all the time and hibernating up in her bedroom. So I figured that's what it was.

"For real, girl? When did you find out?" Nzinga queried.

"Well, she hasn't said anything yet. But I got a feeling she is. She's going around here snapping at everybody again. Whooping and hollering all the time. GrandWillie even had to have a little talk with her to tell her she can't be disturbing everybody's peace like that."

"Girl, whatcha gon' do if she is pregnant?"

"I don't know," I said.

"I guess my mother'll be next."

All our mothers got pregnant every year or every other year, it seemed. They said the more babies they had, the better their chances of getting into Paradise. Nzinga, Nashad, and I thought some of this stuff was downright silly. For instance, my mother's real mother, whom I didn't call Grandma because I'd disowned her, had eleven babies, but I couldn't imagine Allah letting her into Paradise with all her evil ways. She had given most of her children away, in fact.

I was already sick and tired of hearing my aunts and uncles complaining about us taking up all the space in the house. Ma said she tried natural birth control methods—and some store-bought kinds—but they didn't work. Then, after the babies kept coming, she started holding out that paragraph in one of her Orthodox Muslim books called Hadith, which said that ten babies guaranteed a Muslim woman entry into Paradise. My Muslim girlfriends and I didn't believe it because what we were experiencing, having to change diapers and clean up vomit and baby-sit all the time, seemed more like hell.

"Girl, I get tired of them having all these babies. We're the ones who get stuck with all the work," I said. I had been excited when my first siblings were born, but now that I was older with more responsibilities, the novelty had worn off.

"I know. I told my mother I'm running away the next time she gets pregnant," Nzinga said. "That's why we don't have nothing as it is. Umar don't have a job. Ain't trying to work." She hated her stepfather. He actually did work, selling incense and oils. But as far as our little Americanized minds could tell, a job wasn't a job unless it came with a regular paycheck, signed by a big man in a big company or government office. Umar considered himself employed, working long hours, hustling products on foot. We thought he needed a job, though. "All he do is walk around here bossing everybody around. He need to be out trying to find a job somewhere. And my mother, she's so stupid, she just does whatever he says. One baby after another. She should've learned her lesson last time."

"Girl, my mother ain't no different. Wallace and them already complaining about us crowding their space, and she's going to bring another baby in here. I don't know where she think the baby's going to sleep."

I was stretched out on the convertible couch in the basement talking on the phone while my uncles' twelve-inch orange-cased TV played *The Flintstones*. Overhead, big feet thumped from one room to the other and smaller feet shuffled around, too.

"Soonsyreaaaaaaaaa," my mother called.

"I'm doing my homework," I shouted back.

"Come up here. I need you to sit with your brother while I put dinner on."

"I gotta go. I'll call you back later," I whispered into the phone, since Ma was standing at the top of the stairs now.

I pulled my little brother Atif out of his playpen in the dining room, balanced him on my hip, and headed for the front porch. My little sister, Sakinah, and my brother Furard were on the back porch with GrandWillie and the other children in the day care. Darren, who never had to baby-sit, was out playing ball in a churchyard with his neighborhood friends.

After dinner I told Ma I had a report to do, so I'd be in the basement using the encyclopedias for a while. As soon as I got back downstairs the phone rang once, and I snatched it up. It was my cousin Nzinga again.

"Girl, I'm glad you answered the phone," she said. "I only got a few minutes to talk, but I just had to call you back. Girl, guess what."

"What?"

"Sister Razia is expecting again."

"No!"

"Yep. I called Shawn as soon as I got off the phone with you. She said her mother is going to leave her job after the baby is born so she can be home with it."

"Girl, ain't they some trips? What did Shawn say she's going to do?"

"She might try to go live with her father."

"Umph."

"I don't blame her. I might go live with my father, too."

"Well, I don't got nobody I can go live with. My Aunt Gay would let me move in with her. But I know my mother wouldn't let me."

I had considered my options a few weeks ago when I got angry at my mother over the way she beat my older brother. I was used to hearing him yell when she lashed his legs with a piece of the plastic tracks from his racing car set. But what I saw the last time really made me angry.

Ma was angry because our junior high principal had called her and reported catching Darren in the stairway urinating against a wall. Ma was very embarrassed.

At home, she whipped him with a belt, and he grabbed it and refused to let go. She was standing there huffing and puffing, "Let go of this belt! I said let go!" Then she picked a yardstick off the dresser to finish whipping him.

He didn't cry. When she left the room, he reached in the closet and began stuffing his clothes in a duffel bag. I waited until Ma was in the bathroom, then I went in his room to console him.

"Come on, Ray-Ray. We're leaving this place," he said.

Ma heard him and came in the room. "Sonsyrea is not going anywhere!" she said. "You go!"

He did.

"Girl, Darren ran away again," I told Nzinga. "I hope he can stay this time. You should have seen what my mother did to him."

Ma and the other grown-ups said the discipline had to be strict. "Spare the rod and spoil the child," they'd say, quoting a Bible phrase they remembered from their own youth. For a time, she had tried a new kind of child psychology from somebody called Dr. Spock, who wrote books about being kinder to kids. Then, using his advice, when Ma wanted to discipline us for hollering at each other, she simply made us stand in a corner facing each other until our anger turned to humor, staring in each other's silly faces. She also tried to talk to us to try to help us understand why we shouldn't fight. But now that she considered us unruly preteens, she was going back to basics—her belts and eventually the back of her hand across my lips.

"This is nothing compared to the wrath of Allah," Ma would say. I don't remember the first time she said it or the last, but it became a familiar refrain: "You don't get away with *any* sins. If I don't get you, eventually the police will, and if the police don't, then Allah will."

What did Ma know? She acted like she knew everything just because she read a bunch of books in her bedroom. I was going to go to college and become much smarter than her, and then she wouldn't be able to tell me anything. Already,

I was beginning to think I was as wise as her because I had been studying philosophy since elementary school. I was only twelve, but I considered my reasoning skills as sharp as hers. After all, I had been a little X. She had sent me to Elijah Muhammad's University of Islam so I could get a better education than she had gotten in her primary schools, and now it should come as no surprise to her that I would be smarter. We argued often, but for now she still had the final word.

❋ ❋ ❋

Ma organized me and my Muslim girlfriends into a group she named the "Modest Maidens," which was her Islamic version of a Girl Scout troop. Having attended classes for women in the Nation, she understood the need for structured rites-of-passage groups for teenagers. We didn't have uniforms like Girl Scouts, but as Muslim girls we had an identifiable dress code. Shaheeda, Fatimah, and Aisha wore shoulder-length veils pinned under their chins. Nzinga, Nashad, and I had talked our way out of veils by now, but we still had to wear a long blouse over our pants to cover our hardly noticeable hips and behinds. I had regular clothes now. But I had to wear them in a Muslim-like way.

Ma was serious about the Modest Maidens. She planned tea parties for us and trips to the downtown ice skating rink. She also gave us cooking and sewing lessons. But our interest in the domestic activities lasted only a few months. After that, the mothers took turns taking us places and hosting activities for us. Sister Razia, for instance, would drive us to a movie theater to see a movie that the mothers had deemed appropriate.

But a trip to the movies was never as carefree and frivolous as we girls thought it should be. For instance, when we went to see a teenage love story called *Endless Love* starring teen sex goddess Brooke Shields, Aunt Nagiyah went with us and afterward analyzed each scene, making sure we could separate decent loving feelings from naked passion. When we went to see *Grease* starring Olivia Newton-John, Sister Razia quizzed us on the way home.

"So, how did y'all like the movie?" she asked, her eyes straight ahead on the road.

"It was good," Nzinga said.

"They had this one girl who was like the oddball," Fatimah added.

"She was a trip," Aisha chimed in. We were all trying to tell the story.

"She liked this boy who was supposed to be cool," Nashad said. "But he didn't like her, and all the other girls teased her because she was so homely. And one of the girls got pregnant because she was so fast, then the boy didn't want her after that. Then the homely girl changed her hair and bought this tight outfit so she could get the boy she liked."

"Well, when she saw the boy didn't like her, she should have just said, 'Forget him,'" Nzinga added.

"She wasn't changing just for him, though," Shaheeda added. "All of them treated her like a nerd."

"She was a nerd," I said.

In some ways, I think each of us could relate to the lead character. Our religion with its daily dictates, mind-boggling principles, and foreign dress code had at some point left us all feeling ostracized at school and in our neighborhoods.

"Well, she shouldn't have tried to change just to please everybody else," Nzinga said.

That's what Sister Razia had been waiting to hear.

"That's right, Nzinga," Sister Razia beamed. "In the end, everybody else came around. Didn't they?" We all paused to ponder this for a moment. Come to think of it, that's exactly how the movie ended. All the characters evolved a little, not just the oddball one. But how could Sister Razia have known this? She hadn't seen the movie.

"You see, as it turned out, she didn't have to change so much to try to be like them. They did come around to accept her the way she was, didn't they?" She didn't pause for an answer. "And don't you think they learned to respect her more?"

Ma and all her sister-friends didn't miss a chance to teach us something. Something about life, something about ourselves, something to help us become good Muslim women.

❋ ❋ ❋

Being a good Muslim woman meant pleasing your husband, according to what we were learning from our books, the Quran and the Hadith. Aunt Kimba told me more than once that the Prophet Muhammad said the best woman is the one who doesn't ask for anything. She had never gotten so much as a wedding ring from her husband, and welfare helped pay for their housing, food, and medical expenses.

"Allah says a woman can get into Paradise only if her husband is pleased with her," Aunt Kimba explained once while we were cleaning and cutting fresh chickens to fry for dinner. Across the room, Nzinga peeled onions for a rice dish.

"So we're just supposed to do whatever they want, whenever they want?" I asked.

"That's all a woman has to do," Aunt Kimba said plainly, her facial expression calm and pleasant. "That's why Allah says marriage is half your faith," she continued.

She went into the whole spiel about Allah saying Muslim parents should arrange to marry off their children as soon as the children reach the age of puberty so they can go forth and bear fruit, which is the only reason Allah put us here in the first place. Aunt Kimba and Sister Razia were already matching up their children for marriage. It started off as a joke. Maybe Aunt Kimba's Nzinga could marry Sister Razia's Bilal since they were about the same age, and Sister Razia's Nashad could marry Aunt Kimba's Ali, since they had already shown a liking for each other, and Aunt Kimba's Buhira, who was about seven years old now, could grow up to marry Sister Razia's Biyeenah, who was a year younger. That's how the Muslims in the East did things, they mused, and that's how rich white royalty in England did it, too.

For my part, I was planning to marry Billy when we got out of high school. His mother knew I liked him because I sneaked to call him on the phone, only to hang up when she answered instead. She said that we could sit down with both sets of parents and "get intended" if we really wanted to get to know each other and intended to marry soon. But I wasn't thinking about getting married anytime soon because I was planning to go to college and become a career woman.

I was only in ninth grade, and for now I just wanted to talk and date and kiss the way most American girls my age did. Billy and I sneaked kisses in the upstairs bedrooms at Aunt Kimba's house, and he gave one of the little kids a quarter to stand lookout for us.

We Muslim girls had pajama parties, most of them at Aunt Kimba's home, a peaceful place where the walls were painted a light lavender. Aunt Kimba let us pop popcorn with as much butter as we wanted and stay up all night talking and giggling as long as we made our *salats* and did "something for the pleasure of Allah first." We should put Allah first in everything we do, she said. So we'd sit in a circle and take turns reading from our religious books early in the evening to get that out of the way.

One night I read from *The Teachings of Islam:* "We ladies stay for the most part within the four walls of our houses. We remain pinned to our jobs of fulfilling the sexual desires of men, bearing their children for them, and looking after their homes . . . and yet, they seem to benefit more than we."

I passed the book on to Nashad and she read: "The authority responded 'when a woman seeks the pleasure of her husband and carries out her domestic functions to his satisfaction; she gets the same reward as men get for all their services to Allah. . . .'"

Then Nzinga read: "A woman whose husband is pleased with her at the time of her death goes straight into Paradise . . . . A woman is cursed by the angels if her husband is displeased with her and she stays away from him for the night."

Nzinga was more bothered by these stories than were Nashad and I. She slammed the book closed. "I'm finished," she said.

"Our thirty minutes is not up yet," I said. I found the stories interesting.

"Well, I think we read enough," Nzinga said, cutting her eyes at me. She thought I was such a bookworm, a brainiac, a nerd because I enjoyed learning about new stuff, even if it seemed ridiculous. The other girls considered our duty done as well and began breaking up the circle. Aunt Kimba, who had been putting her small children to bed, came back downstairs.

"You girls all finished?" she asked, moving toward the kitchen.

"Um hmmm, but I have a question. Aunt Kimba, this book said that a woman is supposed to do it with her husband every night or she can go to hell," I said, genuinely intrigued. "What if the woman doesn't want to?"

"It's her duty," she said.

"Just because the husband wants to?" I continued.

Nzinga piped in, "Hmph. I'm not going to be having sex just to please no man. I ain't doing nothing I don't wanna do." She hated the way her mother seemed to jump or bend at her stepfather's beck and call.

"*Inshallah*, you'll learn," Aunt Kimba said. "It's all about pleasing Allah. Allah says this is how we can please him."

While the women catered to their men in varying degrees, there were a few things they collectively would not tolerate. When the men used the Quran and Hadith to justify abuse and infidelity, the women banned together to stand their ground. While the brothers noted passages in the Quran where it said men could beat their wives if their wives became disrespectful or disobedient, the sisters found the passages in the Quran instructing husbands to use, as a first method of punishment, abandoning their wives' beds. And when the brothers pointed to the passages condoning up to four wives as proof that "Allah knows a man needs more than one woman," the sisters came back with the passages that said, "It is better to have only one."

"Umm hmm. Allah says right here," Aunt Kai said, pointing to a passage in the Quran during one of the sisterhood slumber parties, which included us girls and our mothers. "A Muslim man can have more than one wife only if you can provide for them all equally and treat them equally."

"Well, I'm about all Abdul Raheem can handle at one time," Sister Kadijah said as she walked across the living room to the coffee table full of munchables. "He has to do all he can just to keep up with me."

Sometimes, after the little kids were put to bed, our parties got wild. Ma would break out the nonalcoholic beer for the women, though Pepsi was the strongest drink we teens could have. Everyone came out of their veils and extra layers of clothing, stripping down to their real selves. We danced to songs by the Emotions and Sisters Sledge, and we played old Motown hits. We formed a Soul Train line sometimes, and we girls went through the line doing the bump and the robot.

"Let us show y'all what a *real* dance is," Ma would say, breaking into dances from her youth, the Slop, the Twist, and the Funky Chicken. Ma and her sister-friends grabbed partners and showed us how to do the Bop, and we laughed at one another's stumbles.

"Look, Uncle Saeed taught me how to do the Bop," I said, grabbing Nashad's hands, pulling her into my dance. She was as clumsy and uncoordinated as I. The sisters cracked up laughing.

"That ain't how your Uncle Saeed danced with me when we first met!" Aunt Kai shouted. "He didn't want to do nothing but slowdrag!"

Aunt Kai was the youngest of the women, and she still was madly in love with her husband of five years. When they were together, they looked like high school teens, bumping up against each other, patting, and pinching. He bragged that his wife was the best cook in the world. She bragged that her husband was the best everything. I thought that if Billy and I ever got married, he better love me like that.

There were some things that some of the Muslim sisters allowed that I simply wasn't going to tolerate from my husband. I decided that if Billy ever spent our rent money on drugs, I would divorce him. I wouldn't let him tell me whether I could get a job or not. And I wouldn't let him bring his friends over to our house all hours of the night. When I voiced my position at our sisterhood parties, the grown-up women told me I was too bossy and too independent and no man would want to marry me unless I changed. My teenage sisters laughed that Billy was just going to have to pop me in the mouth often for talking too much.

"I wish he *would* try to put his hands on me," I snapped. "I'll have Darren over to our house so fast, he'll wish he hadn't."

"How you gon' call your brother on your husband?" Nzinga asked.

"Easy. Just like I always called him if a boy did something to me," I said.

"Y'all say all this stuff now," Aunt Kai said. "But things will be different after you fall in love. Trust me. You won't even see things the same way."

"If my husband ever puts his hands on me, he's gon' be the one feeling different," Nzinga snapped.

My girlfriends and I were already developing deep-seated rebellion that no man would be able to understand, much less control. We were going to do what we wanted to do when we wanted to and how we wanted. Our walls would be difficult to penetrate, especially mine. I had a double dose of domestic training—first in the Nation, now with this Orthodox community. I would become doubly resistant as I got older.

For now, our sisterhood parties were fun. Sometimes Ma came up with a theme for the party to make it more fun. One time she made it a "Come as You Were" party and told everyone to come as they were before they became Muslim.

Aunt Kimba and Ma both wore pleated skirts, bulky sweaters, ankle socks. Aunt Kai picked her hair out into a wild bush. Aunt Nagiya came looking like the prudish secretary she had been. Another sister had tied a red bandanna around her Afro. It seemed to me like nothing much had changed about the sisters except their clothes. The sisters who had been feisty before Islam still were feisty, and the ones who had been mild mannered before still were meek.

I admired the strong sisters but didn't pity the weak. From the time I was in the Nation, I was taught that women had a clearly defined role and domestic responsibility. But I wasn't taught that we should be physically abused. In fact, I was taught that we shouldn't be. I remembered our self-defense lessons in Muslim Girls Training class. It was all right for a sister to stand up for herself, I had learned. If somebody, anybody, even your husband, kicks you, you'd better kick back and kick harder. If you gotta go down, you'd better go down swinging. We were taught that it's better to report a husband and let the brothers in the family or in the Temple deal with him. But in cases of emergency, no Muslim sister better stand still crying if she's under attack.

At home I had never heard Granddaddy Tate raise his voice, certainly not his hands, at GrandWillie. Dad slapped Ma once because she stayed out partying too late with Aunt Kimba. But Ma said she made sure it was the last time he would try that. She didn't tell me what she did, but she said she made it clear she wouldn't be slapped around.

Years later, when I found myself fighting with my fiancé for about the fifth time, I wondered how I let it get so far. I wondered why he was still trying to subdue me. He should have learned his lesson during our last bout when I staved him off with a steaming iron. My fiancé couldn't figure out why I kept fighting back. Through the grace of God, our relationship ended before either of us was severely wounded. He wasn't a Muslim man, but he thought he was lucky to have gotten a Muslim girl because he thought I had been trained in subservience. He had no idea how complex my training had actually been.

Among my Orthodox sisters, I had learned to admire Nashad's mother, Sister Razia, because she seemed the strongest. She was like a queen warrior, graceful and all woman one moment, quick to curse out her husband—or any brother—in the next.

"I told Muhmoud he can have another wife," Sister Razia said, feigning seriousness as she sipped punch at one of our parties. "He can have another wife." Then there was a brief moment of silence. "But she might not want him by the time I finish with him." Everyone burst out laughing.

Sister Razia was the main sister all the brothers despised. Some of the brothers, especially Nzinga's stepfather, Uncle Umar, said she was haughty and arrogant and there was no way Allah could be pleased with her. Sister Razia would challenge her husband in front of them.

Sister Razia and her husband had been partners, working together, neither of them making all the decisions all the time. But the brothers now said Muhmoud was too soft because he wouldn't subdue his wife. Sister Razia quit her job as a secretary for a public legal defense organization so she could fulfill what she thought was her Muslim duty, but after about three years at home she went back to work.

I wanted to grow up strong-willed and independent-minded like her.

❋ ❋ ❋

"That stuff they teach y'all in those schoolhouses ain't real education," Aunt Kimba told me one day as we pinned wet laundry on the clothesline in back of her house.

At first I felt painfully disillusioned because she was telling me that the math, science, history, and language lessons I grew up believing were important weren't important after all. In the Muslim school, grades had been important; now she was trying to tell me otherwise.

"This is education," she said, giving importance to the chore of hanging laundry. "This is what you need to be learning."

Teaching me how to hang clothes on the line was teaching me practical art and domestic duty, things she thought I needed to know as a Muslim woman. The grades on my report card would mean nothing in the sight of Allah on Judgment Day, she said. Allah would look into his record of deeds and see if I had fulfilled my duties as a Muslim woman. So what I needed to be learning at this stage in my development was that the sheets should be pinned up first, then the towels, then the diapers, then the washcloths. Hanging them in this order created art on the line, she said.

We both could look around the desolate complex of gray cinder blocks and concrete and ascertain a need for art. The dry dust in the flower beds where no flowers grew was a dead giveaway. Aunt Kimba's Christian next-door neighbor, Ms. Wilson, a single mother who took her five children to church every Sunday, had planted tulips in her garden, and they added specks of color to the otherwise drab surroundings. Indeed, the environment was crying out for art. Perhaps Aunt Kimba was crying out, too. Crying out for her life, for a better way to live. Later in life she would look back on these years and describe them as her "coffin years." She had not been in a stupor on drugs or alcohol these years, but her consumption of a foreign religion had left her no less at odds with her own reality.

It seemed that my mother was out of sorts, too. When I was younger, my grades had been very important, but now she was taking me out of school on Fridays for *Juma* prayers and during our Orthodox Muslim holidays. She said it was more important for me to observe these religious rites than pursue a worldly education. I didn't like being taken out of school for religious activities because I was already set on an earthly endeavor: education and career.

Somehow, the intense training I'd gotten in the Nation during the foremost formative years of my life stayed with me. I had been trained like a robot to believe I had a responsibility to correct some wrongs in this world, and now not even my mother or aunt could shake that belief. In the Muslim school I had been taught that motherhood was the most important job a woman could have, but I also had been taught that I had a talent for writing, which perhaps could do some good. I felt it was my responsibility to pursue this talent.

I later learned that Aunt Kimba was adamantly opposed to working outside the home even before she met her chauvinist husband who wanted to keep her in the house. She had made homemaking her job before she became a Muslim, but when she found Islam, she found ample scriptural evidence to support her views. She scoffed at the current women's liberation movement, saying it was a Western idea intended to lead women away from God's natural order.

"What about the women who can't have babies?" I asked Aunt Kimba another time while we were hanging laundry.

"Well, those women can find other ways to please Allah," she answered.

"What if a woman just decides she wants to please Allah in a different way other than having babies?" I continued.

"That's not something a woman can decide," she said. "If Allah sends you babies, then that's the task that he put you on Earth to do. Allah tells us to marry, and he tells us to be fruitful. It's not for us to try to decide how much fruit to bear."

I doubted her. At school my social science teacher had talked to us about birth control, and I had learned that in some parts of Asia the government restricted the number of children each family could have. My Christian grandparents considered it irresponsible to have babies you couldn't afford.

"Allah gives us common sense and self-control," I said, trying not to sound disrespectful.

Aunt Kimba, who was veiled from head to toe, sighed and pinned up another diaper.

"You're going to be one of these defiant American women," she said, keeping a calm tone. "Arab women aren't exhausting themselves trying to be men. They're spoiled. They like staying home, being taken care of."

I didn't know where she was getting this information from, but it didn't sound correct to me. I had watched a television special about Arab women on the educational channel and it said that the women felt oppressed and were trying to progress beyond their dark roles as subservient, second-class citizens. Ma, who still carefully monitored what we watched on TV, explained that the information on that show was "Western propaganda," another ploy by Americans seeking to condemn and discredit a Muslim society. Ma said the American media would never show strong Muslim women who actually honored their domestic role.

Although Aunt Kimba and Ma insisted—at that time—that they were happy homemakers, I knew this wasn't the kind of happiness I wanted when I grew up. I knew I didn't want to dedicate my whole life to having babies and raising them. There had to be more to life than serving my husband, getting pregnant, changing diapers, and teaching the hard heads right from wrong.

When I was very young GrandWillie had told me that society was all messed up because mothers took jobs outside their homes instead of raising up respectful children. But I noticed that one of my aunts and a couple of my uncles had gone wayward despite GrandWillie's best efforts. No sense in me sacrificing my goals and ambitions, I figured. I liked writing, I liked making money, and that's what I was going to do with my life. My elementary teachers had identified my writing talent, and GrandWillie had shown me I could make my own money when I helped her with the day-care kids.

I turned thirteen that April in 1979. In June I finished ninth grade and was set to begin high school in September. In many ways, I was already the woman I would become, smart, determined, and independent, though *arrogant*, *manipulative*, and *defiant* were the words Ma used to describe me.

Higher Learning

CHAPTER 13

Ma's baby sister, Aunt Nell, took me shopping for more sophisticated school clothes—trendy Chinese-collar blouses and tweed slacks. She drove out to a shopping mall in the suburbs, and we spent the whole afternoon there. Aunt Nell, who was twenty and single with one baby girl, wanted to make sure both Nzinga and I had a nice enough wardrobe to survive high school. She understood the social pressure to dress right.

Aunt Nell had plenty advice for us, too. She jokingly told us to be leery of the cool guys at school. She'd hear the music from the soundtrack of *Cooley High* blasting from the basement, and she'd come down to join us. As Darren and Ali mockingly poured wine "for the brothers who ain't here," acting out the roles they'd seen in the movies, Aunt Nell laughed because she remembered guys like that from her school.

"Them the kind of niggahs y'all better watch out for," she said. "Them real smooth, real cool niggahs, the ones'll have you knocked up."

As my mother grew closer to her natural family, we spent more time with this side of the family. Her mother, Grandma Fuller, was different from any woman I had ever met. As a young child I simply thought she was a witch, but now I wanted to understand how she got so evil. I was at the age where I was defining myself and what kind of life I wanted to live. These new relatives would give me a lot more to think about.

Grandma Fuller, who was short and wide, with mean all over her face, hated our religion and said so often.

"Y'all doing all that silly-ass shit. God ain't worried 'bout what you got on your damned head," Grandma Fuller would say as she stood in her narrow kitchen fixing dinner.

Grandma Fuller was the nastiest, most foul-mouthed woman I'd ever met, and she scared me. Granddaddy Fuller died of throat cancer in 1975 before I got to know him well. A picture of him in an army uniform still decorated the living room wall, right next to a black-and-white photo of Grandma Fuller in her younger days when she was pretty, with long black hair. Her hair was gray now and her face wrinkled with bitterness. When I asked Ma why she was so nasty, Ma said it was because she had violated God's commandments by having an affair with a married man and conceiving eleven babies out of wedlock.

Most of the time when we visited Grandma Fuller's house, we kids ran straight to the basement to enjoy our aunts' albums. Upstairs, the grown-ups spent much of their time trying to convert their mother. They were afraid she would die before she accepted God in her heart and would wind up in hell.

"How you know there's a heaven, goddammit?" I'd hear Grandma Fuller say. "You ever seen a god? Silly-ass nonsense. Look around here. You think a damned god been up in here? I been on this Earth fifty-some-odd years, and I ain't never seen no god."

Grandma Fuller cursed my mother for no good reason, and once, when we were little, she tried to trick me, Darren,

Nzinga, and Ali into eating ham by telling us it was really turkey. We'd learned about swine in the Muslim school, and even though we were kids, we knew better than to eat any pink meat. Still, after all these years, she hadn't grown to like me any more than she liked my mother, who she said never should have been born.

"I tried to abort all y'all's asses," I'd heard her tell Ma and her other kids, who were trying to save her soul. "Y'all lucky they didn't have legal abortions back in my day or none of y'all would be here."

Aunt Nell found humor in Grandma Fuller's comments, while Ma and the others took offense. Aunt Nell knew her mother frightened me, so when she took me back to the house after our shopping trip, she tried to prepare me for whatever might come out of Grandma's mouth.

"Just take whatever she says like a grain of salt," Aunt Nell told me as she pulled her green Pinto into a parking space in front of the house.

Aunt Vicky, Aunt Nell, and their brother, Uncle Kenny, were the only ones who had grown up in this house. Their eight other siblings, Ma included, had been given away as babies and didn't meet again until they were all teens or young adults, when one of Grandma Fuller's sisters found them all and began bringing them together. Darren and I had been visiting with this side of the family only for a few years—since Ma started pulling out of the Nation—but Darren immediately decided that these relatives couldn't replace our grandparents, aunts, and uncles we had loved all our lives. I embraced them all, the more the merrier—except for Grandma Fuller.

When Aunt Nell and I got in the house, we headed for the kitchen because she promised to press my hair real straight and curl it for school. Grandma Fuller heard us bumping around in the kitchen and came down from her bedroom. She pushed past me as I sat next to the stove and didn't even say excuse me as she squeezed her behind past my face. She poured herself a glass of water, but I didn't think that was her real reason for coming downstairs.

"No sense in pressing that girl's hair," she snapped. "Soon as she gets home, she's gon' have to wrap it up in that Moozlem rag again."

I knew she just came downstairs to be mean, but I thought about what Aunt Nell told me in the car and didn't let my feelings get hurt.

"Ma, go on back upstairs somewhere," Aunt Nell told her, pulling the hot comb through my hair. "You always got something nasty to say out your mouth. You act like it's gon' kill you to be nice sometimes."

I knew Allah said you shouldn't talk to your parents like that, but sometimes you had to because sometimes parents were wrong. Grandma's meanness was broken by Aunt Nell's comments, and Grandma smiled.

"It just might kill me, you never know," she said as she placed her cup in the sink and turned to leave. "I'll never find out." Then she disappeared back upstairs.

Aunt Nell went in the living room and popped an Isley Brothers cartridge in the eight-track player so we could groove while she curled my hair under in a trendy mushroom style.

❋ ❋ ❋

Two of my bookworm buddies from junior high school were enrolled in McKinley High, a school for college-bound kids. My junior high school teachers wanted me to go to that school, but Ma wanted to keep me closer to home. So she enrolled me in Eastern High School in our neighborhood.

My high school was just across the street from my junior high. My high school principal there looked at my school records and determined I was college material. So he assigned me to a program of advanced courses. For my three years of high school, I would be grouped with the other academically "gifted" kids, singled out for special treatment.

On the first day of school, I ran into a girl from my junior high school who had been in the same classes as me. I was glad to see Pam (not her real name) because I needed a friend in this big new school. Pam wasn't assigned to the advanced group like me, but we agreed to meet at my locker at lunchtime and go to a greasy grill down the street for lunch. Most of the corner stores and neighborhood grills in the 1970s still were black-owned, which made us feel like we were being served by family. I had lunch money saved from monthly allowances Ma began giving me and Darren.

Pam looked like my bodyguard because she was so much taller and tougher than me. We joked about our teachers and classmates and discussed who we thought were the cutest boys in school. Hardly any boys tried to get my phone number, and it would be years before I learned that the word had gotten out that I was Darren Tate's little sister, a Muslim girl, and I was not to be approached. Some of the cool boys tried to talk to Pam, but she told them she didn't have a phone because she didn't want to be bothered. She didn't care if they teased her and said her family was too poor for a phone, because she knew the truth in her head.

It was a good thing I no longer had to wear Muslim clothes, making me an easy target, because my religion came under fire again a few months after school began. Iranian militants took sixty Americans hostage in Tehran, demanding that the United States release Iranian Shah Mohammad Reza Pahlavi so he could be prosecuted for murder and corruption. But now I didn't have to worry about my classmates asking me dozens of questions about Islam and Muslims as if I knew all the answers. Now I was just a normal high school kid, having fun with my good friend at lunchtime.

One day when we stopped at the store on our way home, she noticed me taking rolled-up dollar bills out of a small brown envelope.

"Girl, where'd you get that envelope!" she yelled, as if something was wrong.

My mother had put my allowance money in a small brown envelope, the kind of envelope given out at the bank. But what I didn't realize was that it was also the kind of envelope used to package small, nickel-bag quantities of marijuana. Years later Ma would explain that she didn't know about this alternative use for the envelopes either.

"My mother gave me this," I said. "What's your problem?"

"Girl, those the envelopes they sell reefers in. I know, 'cause my uncle sells it," she said.

I was confused, but I couldn't ask my mother about it because we didn't have the kind of relationship where I could just go up to her and ask her any kind of question or talk about anything. Our relationship was developing into a very formal one. We talked when she asked me a question that required a response.

I decided not to ask anyone at home about the envelopes. Instead I would snoop around and find out for myself. I searched everyone's closet and peered under my uncles' beds and under my parents'. Jackpot! I found, inside a beige tin file box, a plastic bag, the size of a two-quart freezer bag, full of weed under Ma and Dad's bed. Under the weed were a bunch of brown envelopes. Without understanding what the dried, crushed leaves were or what they could do for me, I stuffed one of the envelopes full and hid it in my coat pocket. When I showed it to Pam the next day, her whole face lit up like a light bulb.

"Girl, I told you!" she said. She smelled the weed and added, "Girl, this is some good stuff!"

I didn't know what she was talking about or what the smell of the stuff in the envelope had to do with anything.

"Gimme some papers," she said as we stood in front of my locker.

She was still sniffing the stuff as I pulled out a sheet of notebook paper. I thought she wanted to take some of the weed for herself, since I'd brought enough to share. I thought she needed the paper to fold it into an envelope for her stash.

"Not that kind of paper," she said. "Some Tops." All of a sudden I was supposed to be cool, I guess, and know what "Tops" was.

"Some what?"

"Top papers to roll some joints," she said.

I had never actually seen any rolled reefers, so I couldn't imagine what she was talking about. I later learned that my father, Uncle Avon, and Uncle Edward had been smoking and selling the stuff for years. But somehow, my mother had managed to keep me sheltered from that part of our family business until now.

When I first found the stash of marijuana, I didn't think about all that it meant. In a few days I would begin to see that the grown-ups around me must have been hypocrites because they were making me follow a whole bunch of religious rules while they were disobeying the laws of this land. At first I didn't think about anything except moving quickly enough to fill my envelope and push the tin box back in its place without getting caught. There was always a time right before dinner, before our evening prayer, when both Ma and GrandWillie would be downstairs and Uncles Hussein and Wallace would not be home yet. That's when I made my move.

I didn't think to pray for forgiveness for stealing the weed or smoking it because I didn't really understand what was so wrong about it. How wrong could it be if the adults had it in our home? I figured I had to sneak to get it because it wasn't for children, and that's probably why my parents had hid it. But I didn't feel much like a child anymore. I had a lot of responsibility helping with the smaller kids and keeping the house clean, responsibilities my older brother could shirk. And the mental and moral demands pressed upon me were far more rigorous, it seemed to me, than for other girls my age.

Some of my childhood joys had been stripped away the summer before because I had gotten my period and, according to Islamic law, become a woman. All of a sudden, I couldn't go swimming anymore because our religion dictated that after a girl reaches the age of puberty, she can't expose any part of her body in public. I had loved going swimming. But this past summer, I'd had to wear a long-sleeved leotard and shorts cut off just below my knees, an outfit that made me the target of many stares, taunts, and teasing.

In some ways, I felt stressed and worried beyond my years. I had to argue with Ma about the importance of my staying in school Friday afternoons because I understood the importance of getting grades good enough for college even if she didn't. I was thirteen now, and thirteen only in age. Most of the other girls my age had to worry only about how to style their hair and keep the style from dropping before the end of the day. I was two years ahead of most girls my age in school, thanks to the head start I had gotten at the Muslim school, and in many other ways I was growing up faster, too.

Pam was transferred out of the school, and I felt alone with no other friends. I couldn't relate to the other kids. My weed became my best friend, and I got high three times a day. I smoked half a joint walking down an isolated street on my way to school, puffed on the same joint in the bleachers on the football field outside at lunchtime, and got high again on my way home. This was routine practically every day for the rest of the year. But none of the adults around me suspected anything. To them, I was a well-mannered, studious child.

When I fell asleep in my morning homeroom class and in my first class after lunch, I told my teachers I was just tired because I had so many responsibilities at home. My eyes were bloodshot from the weed, but they believed I truly was weary. My grades slipped through these years to Bs and Cs—and even Ds in math, because I couldn't concentrate while I was high. But life seemed nicer; everything seemed funny.

* * *

Darren and I both were losing respect for our religion and the adults who preached it to us. It seemed like my mother and her friends were making up new stuff as we went along.

"This ain't Islam," Darren declared. "It's *His*lam. This is Uncle Uball's religion," he said, poking fun at Uncle Umar.

It seemed that every time Uncle Umar learned something new and told Aunt Kimba to do something, she did it, and when she told our mother about it, our mother would do the same. Aunt Kimba acted passive and mousy around her husband, so my mother tried to do the same. All of a sudden, she started *asking* my father if she could go a certain place or do a certain thing, and he looked at her like, "Why are you asking me?" Darren and I looked at her the same way.

Because of our religion, or despite it, Darren, who came home after a few months living with Uncle Sharrief, and I both became quite rebellious. I was stealing marijuana and getting high three times a day. Darren was stealing it, getting high on it, and selling some of it, plus stealing cars with his buddies, breaking into people's homes when he was supposed to be at school, and gambling in the alley down the street in the evening. Tensions in our household had gotten bad, and we weren't praying together every day anymore. As far as I could tell, everyone just preferred to pray his or her own prayers in privacy now. Uncles Hussein and Wallace would walk past Ma and refuse to speak. GrandWillie constantly yelled at Ma, telling her to stop yelling at us kids, and Dad stayed out all night sometimes, performing with his bands.

Dad was home enough to correct Darren sometimes, though. Once, Dad found out that Darren had burglarized the home of one of our neighbors, Mr. Stevenson, and Dad made Darren return the jewelry he'd stolen, apologize, and do chores for Mr. Stevenson free for a whole month. Mr. Stevenson, one of very few whites in our neighborhood, had been generous about hiring Darren and other neighborhood boys to cut grass and run errands. And he had done the same for my father and uncles when they were boys. Darren was quite embarrassed when word of his theft spread through our household. Our uncles teased him unmercifully.

Darren and I were no longer as close as we had been. While I envied his freedom, he resented my having passed him in school. He was trying even harder to prove that he was "street smart" as opposed to book wise, like me. I wasn't bound to the front of the house, but whenever I wanted to visit my friend YoShawn, down the street, I had to get permission. I often caught Darren kneeling in a circle with his buddies in the alley rolling dice and scooping up dollars. I'd run home to tattle. If one of our uncles was home, since Dad hardly was, he'd rush to the alley, embarrass Darren in front of the guys, and pull him home by his neck. I'd wait on the porch to see him scolded.

"Tattletale!" he'd yell while being dragged or pushed past me. Sometimes he would ball up his fist and place it over his eye or nose, signaling to me that that's where he planned to hit me for tattling. Then he'd get slapped in the head and scolded some more.

"Boy, what I tell you about messing with your sister!"

Even though Darren and I were growing apart, he could still count on me for favors. For instance, when he got in trouble at school, he could pay me a few dollars to help him write a hundred copies of the school rules, which was required. He was in the ninth grade in junior high school, but he was well known in my high school, which he visited often while cutting his own classes.

Most of the rough guys, the hard heads, spoke in passing, addressing me as "Little Tate" and asking the whereabouts of my brother, who was getting a reputation for being "thorough," which we called cool, rough boys. I was always hearing about my brother's antics in the halls at my high school. I heard things like "That little niggah can scrump!" which meant he could fight. Boys still fought with their hands back then, in the late seventies, and the biggest fear was a boy getting pounced on or "jumped" by a group of boys or beaten with a baseball bat. Guns were only beginning to emerge as a weapon for daily use. The few boys who had guns were the roughest and toughest, and usually the ones who had been kicked out of school already.

The first time I saw a gun was when a grown man leveled one at my brother in a fight after school. As I was leaving the building to go home, a couple of people ran up to me and yelled in a panic, "Your brother's in trouble, girl! You better go get your peoples!"

I ran around the corner and spotted a big crowd across the street. The crowd was cheering and laughing. I pushed my way through to the center and saw a grown man beating up my brother. Darren threw a few more wild punches while the man hit him steadily in his head and body. I clutched my books and turned in circles in a panic, looking around for his friends to make them help. Darren stopped swinging and ran through the crowd to a path up a hill across the street. The crowd stood watching and waiting, and the man lingered in the middle of the circle catching his breath. I started to run after Darren when I saw him running back toward the crowd with a big stick. The crowd opened and let him in, and he slammed the stick across the man's back before the man realized he was back. Darren kept swinging the stick, getting some good hits in, then the man broke through the crowd, opened the trunk of his car, and leveled a gun at my brother. I screamed and ran and heard screams and scampering all around me. I ran all the way home to GrandWillie's house, dodging cars in the street because I wasn't stopping for any stoplights.

"GrandWillie! GrandWillie! Darren got beat up and this man, this big man, GrandWillie . . ." I was frantic and out of breath. "GrandWillie, this tall man was punching him in the face and—" Before I could finish, she cut me off.

"Your father will take care of it when he gets in," she said with no emotion. She was busy with the day-care children. "Where's Darren?" she asked.

I panicked all over again. "GrandWillie, the man had a gun! He had this big gun and—"

GrandWillie rushed to the basement steps, calmly calling down to Uncle Wallace to go out and get Darren.

I sat on the porch waiting as Uncle Wallace and Darren marched down the street in a huff. Darren looked particularly short and skinny now. His right eye was swollen, his lip busted, his face bruised, and his clothes torn and dirty. Uncle Wallace was talking to him. They seemed to be planning something.

"You okay?" I asked, approaching them as they came up to the porch. They brushed me off like they didn't even notice me. This was serious, I could tell. Since their days as bald-headed, clean-cut "Black Moozlems," the Tate boys had a reputation for defeating their opponents and standing up for one another.

My cousin Sirene came running up the steps. Sirene had seen the fight, too, and we talked about what kind of retaliation there might be. We still were doing our homework on the front porch when Uncle Sharrief and Uncle Hussein returned from work about six P.M. As quickly as they went into the house, they came right back out, in a pack with Wallace and Darren, all of them dressed in their fighting clothes, old cotton sweatsuits and sneakers. As soon as they reached the corner, Sirene and I ran behind them. They couldn't know we were following or they would make us go back. They marched around the corner, across the street, down two more streets, and around another corner. Sirene and I stood on the corner, hiding behind a brick wall. Three women were sitting on the porch.

"'Scuse me, is your brother home?" Uncle Sharrief asked the women, assuming they were the man's sisters.

"Which one?" one of the women snapped. She sensed trouble.

"The one who went after my nephew," Uncle Sharrief said calmly. "Just tell him to come outside. I want to talk to him."

She turned around and yelled through the open door. "Craaaaaig! Somebody wanna see you!"

The man, who looked slimmer and less imposing now, bounced down the steps on his toes and came to the gate. His little brother stood at his side. Darren and Uncles Hussein and Wallace were right behind Uncle Sharrief. Sirene and I couldn't hear the exchange, but within moments it looked like they had reached a resolve. The man and his brother had turned to go back in his house when I heard a dissatisfied Wallace yell, "The next time I see your little punk-ass brother on the street, I'm gonna kick his ass like you did my nephew."

The man turned around and boasted, with his head coolly cocked to one side and his arms gesturing, "We can straighten this right here."

Uncle Sharrief, still calm, told him, "Well, if you come out of your yard, it's out of my hands."

The man opened the gate and proceeded down the first step to street level where my brother and uncles were. As soon as he stepped, Uncle Sharrief punched him square in the face, and all hell broke loose. All the guys were in a rumble, and the women on the porch were screaming. Sirene and I picked up rocks and moved in closer, throwing them at the women, mostly missing. I heard one of the women yell something about "gun!" and I started screaming, "Sharrief! Sharrief! They're gonna get the gun! Sharrief!" Sirene and I ran, and my uncles and brother must have heard me because they ran, too.

Back at the house, they quickly changed clothes, and Sirene and I realized we might get in trouble for having left the porch without permission. GrandWillie and my mother weren't there. Before my uncles could come to the porch to scold us, a police car pulled up. We saw the man sitting inside holding a rag to his mouth as the uniformed police officer walked up to the house.

"Is this the Tates' residence?" the officer asked.

"Yes. Who would you like to see?" I asked politely, as if I didn't know.

"Mr. Tate."

"Which one?"

"Darren Tate's father."

"He's not home," I said. I had learned not to like, trust, or respect police officers back in the early seventies when I heard the people in my home and neighborhood referring to them as "pigs," as in "fascist pigs."

"My dad won't be home until late," I said sharply.

We were talking when Uncle Sharrief came out the door. He was polite to the officer, inviting him inside. Before GrandWillie and my mother and siblings returned from the garden, the officer was gone and the whole mess had been cleared. There weren't going to be any charges against my uncles. If anything, the man could have been charged for threatening a minor, my brother, with a gun. We knew our rights.

In order to keep Darren out of trouble, Uncle Sharrief hired him at the exclusive senior citizens' home where he worked as the executive chef. Over the years, Uncle Sharrief would hire Darren, a few of his friends, and other family members who needed jobs. Uncle Sharrief had learned in the Nation that black men should create jobs for one another.

Sirene's mother, Aunt Shirley, picked me and Darren up some weekends and took us skating with our cousins to keep all us teens occupied, but through the week, Sirene and I sneaked to visit our new boyfriends while their mothers were away at work.

My new boyfriend was Vincent, a short guy, shy like me. Vincent wasn't cute like Billy or as rambunctious and exciting as Billy, but he was fun to be with. I would've stayed with Billy, but I kept hearing stories about him trying to get other girls' phone numbers at my brother's school. Billy's junior high school was across town, but he had stayed back again in eighth grade, so he cut school more and more to hang with my brother.

Vincent knew Darren and Billy, but he wasn't afraid of either because his big brother was a part of Darren's crew. Vincent, who was in ninth grade at my old junior high school, was an honor roll student and respectful of adults. He carried my books home, turning around at the corner so my mother wouldn't see him. I called him on the phone when I thought my mother had gone to bed. Sirene always went with me when I went to Vincent's house, and we worked out a plan so I wouldn't find myself alone with him long enough to get into trouble. Sirene watched the time and would start pounding on the door saying it was time to leave right about the time Vincent's hands tried to roam up my blouse.

Vincent eventually called his friend Tony to kiss and entertain Sirene, but we knew what they were up to and wouldn't let each other go too far. Ma and her sister-friends had me convinced I'd burn forever in hell if I fornicated. Fear kept us in check.

❋ ❋ ❋

At school my classmates and I talked about politics in social studies class, and we debated who would make a better president, our current one, Jimmy Carter, or his Republican opponent, Ronald Reagan. Some of us agreed with our parents, who said it didn't matter who was running for office because all the politicians lied. But a few kids had more insight for our debate.

"Republicans have never been good for black people," one of my classmates insisted during one of our class discussions.

"The Democrats neither," another student shot back. "What have they done? At least the Republicans let you know right up front they don't like you and don't plan to do anything for you. If the Republicans get in there and start cutting programs, at least black people will know we have to come together to help each other more."

Up until now I hadn't considered politics important because in the Nation of Islam, we had been told to stay out of the white man's politics and concentrate on building our own nation. Now that I was out in the world, I began to consider I might become a politician myself after I became a news reporter. Or maybe I would become a news reporter and write about the politicians. Ma and I got into heated debates about my career plans because she insisted I should only be planning to become a wife and mother. GrandWillie believed motherhood was an important job, but she told me I could be anything I wanted to be. She said I could do anything I set my mind to do. But soon I wouldn't have her daily moral support, because we were moving out of her house.

❋ ❋ ❋

We moved out of GrandWillie's house in the summer of 1980. We moved into a three-story brick townhouse that also had two bathrooms, a basement, and a fenced-in backyard. The walls were a bright shiny white. A big bay window in front of the house and glass double doors in the living room at the back of the house let in plenty of sunlight. I finally got my own room.

We were among the first families moving into the townhouses in Wylie Courts. The wooden playground equipment out front was new. Flowers in the tree boxes out front were about to blossom. The townhouses were located on the back side of H Street, a busy corridor that had been burned down during the riots following Martin Luther King, Jr.'s, assassination. Everything in this newly built complex seemed perfect, except the huge red and white billboard out front announcing that this was a "Project of the District of Columbia."

Wylie Courts was a new experiment in housing projects. Residents were allowed to buy their homes from the government. They were required to attend workshops on budgeting, and we all had to participate in Saturday morning cleanups.

The first summer we were in these new houses, we kids around the neighborhood had fun getting to know one another. We girls would spend the summer evenings sitting around on the play equipment in the courtyard laughing and joking, having returned home from summer jobs as clerks in government agencies, tutors at summer schools, counselors at recreation centers, and street sweepers.

As long as I made my prayers, I could sit out front with the girls until dark. When the street lights came on, I, Zola, Chee-Chee, and Tina knew it was time to go in the house. I was glad that some of the other girls had rules, too, so I wouldn't feel like the odd one out.

Darren hung out at the arcade around the corner from our home, feeding quarters to a new video game called Pac Man. He didn't come in from playing to pray during the day, but he prayed with the family in the mornings and at night when Dad led us. Now that it was just Ma, Dad, and us together in our new house, we all prayed together again because we all believed the same Orthodox Islam.

Dad talked Darren into taking music lessons at school so he could learn to play the trumpet. At home, Dad taught him the keyboard on our old piano in the living room and helped Darren organize his own band with other boys from school and our neighborhood. Billy and his big brother, who was the same age as Darren, joined the band, playing congos and a cowbell. The band also had a boy on saxophone, one on drums, two singers, a bass guitarist, and a lead guitarist. They called themselves Key Stone Funk, named after I don't know what, and they played a heavy rhythmic go-go music that at the time was unique to the kids in Washington.

I envied all the attention Darren got from Dad and decided I wanted to learn to play the clarinet so Dad could give me lessons, too. Instead, he gave me a beginner's book and told me I could teach myself. Dad thought I had plenty of household duties to keep me busy and that it was more important for me to train domestically under Ma. Plus, Dad had no reason to suspect I might get into trouble if he didn't occupy my time. I was the saint, so they thought.

❋ ❋ ❋

I enrolled in a music class in school. I had to catch up with the other students who had been playing their instruments since junior high school. So I spent my lunch break in the band room practicing. I used the discipline I had learned in the Nation and at home. I could master anything I put my mind to, I was taught.

My band teacher at school, Mr. Sands, who had known my father from when they used to perform at the same nightclubs, was impressed with my talent but not surprised.

"You're pretty good, Sonsyrea," he said one afternoon, patting my shoulder as I ran through my scales. "Your father must be working with you."

"Nope," I told him. "I'm teaching myself."

In the band room I got plenty of attention, not only from Mr. Sands but also from the boys in the band, since I usually was the only girl spending lunch break there. Most of the girls in the band were majorettes or flag twirlers, and the girls who played instruments played either flute or clarinet but rarely sacrificed their lunch break to practice.

After school we started rehearsal by going through our classical sonatas. Mr. Sands said learning to play this kind of music was more important than learning the music we heard on black radio stations. We couldn't get into any college band playing pop music.

Our chairs and stands were lined in a semicircle with Mr. Sands standing in the center, directing us with the movements of his baton. His sloop feet and slightly hunched back made him look like Dr. Suess.

We had to sell candy, organize bake sales, shovel snow through the winter, and wash cars to raise money to buy band uniforms. Mr. Sands showed us a catalogue picture of the slick, navy blue and white uniforms we could get, and we worked diligently for them.

When May arrived and the parade season in our town began, we hit the streets proudly. We were the Blue and White Marching Machine—a big family, proud of the music we made together. At home, most of us had problems. At school in the band room, we found peace and joy in our music.

"HEEEEEY, BAND!" our drum major called to us as we stood in neat block formation at stiff attention, preparing for our first big parade.

"WHAAT!" we responded, leaning back on our heels all at once.

"ARE YOU READ-AY?"

"YEAH!"

"I SAID, ARE YOU READ-AY?"

"YEAH!"

"HIT IT!"

And we did a series of swift moves, dips, and a spin, landing in attention again, facing forward. The drummers hit the drums once, and we all snapped our heads to the left, shaking our fluffy plumes in the process. They hit the drums again, and we snapped our heads to the right. My heart beat fast with anticipation, and I felt aglow inside. I'd wanted to march like this ever since I was a little kid watching the Muslim teens in the Nation of Islam. I had learned about the power of unity watching those drill teams. Now I felt it.

As the band blew and stormed down the street, the crowd cheered wildly. Out the corner of my eye I saw Ma, my brothers, sisters, and cousins cheering us on, waving and yelling my name. I finally knew what it felt like to march down the middle of the street and be the center of attention. And to think, I didn't even have to shake my booty and get raunchy and nasty like the girls in my neighborhood, whom I had once envied. Most of my life people had stared at me because I was the odd one. But now, here I was the center of attention, being stared at and cheered as a member of a talented group.

❋ ❋ ❋

Next stop: Florida. Mr. Sands said we were invited to participate in an annual national competition for high school bands the following school year. We would have to raise money again and practice even more. The principal and teachers and our family members all pitched in with donations. A local black-owned weekly newspaper ran an article soliciting support.

We would probably be the only black band down there. But we could beat the white concert bands, Mr. Sands told us, as long as we mastered classical music more difficult than theirs.

I understood what Mr. Sands was saying, because in the Nation of Islam we had been taught more advanced studies than our white counterparts in public schools.

I was beginning to see how my Muslim school training was paying off. Uncle Wallace graduated two years ahead of his peers, and Uncle Hussein, who graduated from the Muslim school when he was fourteen, would become the class salutatorian at the prestigious George Washington University, a white school. Now, at fourteen, I was finishing my junior year in high school.

Believe I'll Pray On . . . See What the End's Gonna Be

CHAPTER 14

Although I was fifteen years old and a senior, Uncle Hussein still escorted me to school dances. At nineteen, he looked more like a high school boy than a college man about to get his bachelor's degree in chemistry.

He took me to high school dances where live go-go bands pumped funky jams—heavy on the percussion. I hopped around the dance floor doing the Happy Feet while some people still did the Freak, a dance in which boys moved their hands all over your body to "freak" you. Uncle Hussein, who kept an eye on me as he leaned against the wall with his arms crossed, would have yanked me off the floor if he saw me "freaking."

Uncle Hussein was studying for exams to get into medical school, and I was glad he still found time to take me to dances. We both missed Uncle Wallace, who at sixteen was at Hampton Institute in Hampton, Virginia.

Dad organized a band with a couple of his friends and a few of Ma's brothers, who were Orthodox Muslims and different from my Nation of Islam–bred uncles. Some of the Orthodox brothers refused to get regular jobs because they said no employer would allow them to take off time to perform their midday prayers and take off Friday afternoons to attend prayer service at the mosque. But my Nation-bred uncles believed in hard work.

Although Elijah Muhammad's son, Wallace D. Muhammad, who changed his name to Warith Deen Muhammad, was bringing the old Nation members in line with Orthodox Muslims, there was still a little tension between the two sects. That friction had been reflected in my own family for years.

I didn't have a lot of respect for the Orthodox men who didn't work because I had learned while in the Nation that a man is nothing if he's not providing for his family. Anything my Nation-bred uncles told me, I believed without questioning.

Ma tried to set up our new home like a humble Muslim abode, making everybody take off shoes at the door and keeping the house plain and undecorated. Like most of the other Orthodox Muslims in our circle, we didn't even have furniture. No living room set, no dining room table. Ma's parents offered to give us furniture, but Ma declined. In the living room, we had only two large pillows to sit on, an old wooden coffee table, and Dad's big piano. There were no pictures on our walls, in keeping with Orthodox tradition still, and no cute little statues or figurines because of the Muslim rule banning idols. I wanted to hang posters of my favorite teen singers, New Edition and Michael Jackson, but Ma forbade it. Thank God, Ma allowed us to have beds in our bedrooms. Some families we knew slept on mattresses of blankets on the floor, trying to sleep the way we believed Prophet Muhammad slept.

My Orthodox uncles even tried to dress like the Prophet on Fridays. Usually, when Uncle Saeed arrived at our home for band rehearsal, he still was wearing a white turban and an ankle-length white shirt over his jeans and designer tennis shoes. He carried on his shoulder a duffel bag full of incense and perfume oils that he sold. He looked every bit a cross between an Arab and an urban African American. I thought he looked funny and couldn't keep a straight face when I saw him dressed this way.

When the brothers were at our home, they made prayer with us on the prayer rugs Ma kept rolled up in one corner of the living room. Sometimes Dad led, sometimes one of my uncles led. Then we kids disappeared into our rooms and the brothers into the basement, where they plugged in the speakers and the amplifiers, which carried their music throughout the house.

I enjoyed their music—conscientious lyrics about living righteously, set to beats similar to what I heard on the radio.

Lying flat on my back in my bedroom, staring up at my blank walls, I grooved to their beats. An aroma that I was familiar with came up to my room through the heating vents. I went to the basement to investigate. I banged on the door until Dad came and opened it.

"Yes?" he said, his eyes bloodshot and a cloud of white smoke pushing through the doorway past him.

I knew it! It was weed. I still remembered the smell from two years earlier when I was stealing it from Dad's stash. I was wrapped in my bathrobe and tried to see all I could in the few seconds he held the door open.

"Nothing," I said. "I was going to ask you something, but never mind."

He closed the door, and I stomped up the stairs to my mother. It wasn't fair. As a Muslim child, I had lots of rules I had to obey. I thought it was unfair that these Muslim men didn't have to obey laws themselves. They were disrespecting our home. A bunch of hypocrites. I didn't get a good look inside the basement to see exactly who was down there this time. But I had a good idea. I knew that Sister Bushora's husband, Brother Abdullah, probably wasn't down there because he was one of the brothers who actually practiced what he preached. He'd join the brothers for salats and family dinners, then leave before they descended into the basement for rehearsal. I wished they were all like him. I wished my Dad, at least, was more like him. I was so angry at Dad and whomever he had with him in our basement. They should have had some respect for us kids living there, I figured. They were supposed to set some kind of example. My little sisters and brothers would be going to junior high school soon, and when they smelled the stuff in the bathrooms or stairwells at school, it would be so familiar to them, they wouldn't know how to turn it down.

"Ma, they're downstairs getting high," I said to my mother, who was sitting up in bed reading a geography book.

"Sonsyrea, mind your business and go to your room," was her response. She didn't even look up at me.

"It is my business," I continued. "They're disrespecting our house!"

"Go to your room!" she snapped.

I slammed the door behind me.

❋ ❋ ❋

Saturday mornings Dad got together with some of the other Muslim brothers who also had large families and went to a wholesale market to buy our fresh produce and meats at a discount. Sometimes they also bought enough eggs and fruit to sell to our neighbors at prices cheaper than those at the nearby grocery stores.

The rest of us spent the morning sweeping, mopping, and cleaning the walls throughout the house, with Ma on our heels making sure we didn't miss the corners and crevices. Then we had to go outdoors and join our neighbors cleaning up.

When Uncle Avon, his wife, and two children moved in our basement, my workload doubled. I had more dishes to wash and had to clean the bathrooms twice as often. When I complained to Ma, she said Aunt Camille hadn't had the privilege of attending Muslim Girls' Training classes in the Nation. So, she simply was not properly trained in handling domestic details. I thought that was a bunch of bull.

"She knows how to clean up behind herself!" I said. "She's just trifling!"

"You'll get all the blessings," Ma said.

"I don't mind sharing these blessings," I said.

"Don't get cute!"

She must think I'm a damn maid! I thought to myself as I pushed the mop back and forth across the floor. And that trifling-ass Camille, I should tell her about herself—ole pseudo, fake-ass Muslim. Aunt Camille began wearing Muslim woman's garb after she married Uncle Avon, but that didn't make her no doggone Muslim, as far as I was concerned. Tying a damn rag around her head didn't make her no damn saint. If she was really so righteous, she wouldn't leave her chores for me to do. She knew that when she didn't pick up behind her kids, I'd have to. I was glad they stayed with us only about six months. I was so happy when they moved, I offered to help pack.

So long, fake-ass, I said to myself as I waved them good-bye.

I was beginning to think all these Muslims, my parents included, only used the religion for convenience. They used it as a reason not to work and a reason not to get involved in society. I understood that when GrandWillie and Granddaddy Tate joined the Nation of Islam, it was because blacks *couldn't* really be a part of mainstream society. There was segregation and there were Jim Crow laws, and there weren't powerful black Congress members who could rectify these situations. But life had improved for blacks even though the NAACP and black politicians were decrying Reaganomics, President Reagan's cuts in social programs benefiting blacks.

I thought my parents had no excuse for remaining on the sidelines. They should be out forging ahead, making more progress. But it seemed like they were just resting back now, like blacks had arrived and there was no more fighting to be done. It seemed as if my parents and their Muslim friends with their anti-American sentiment declared themselves morally above this society.

My Orthodox uncles told me they didn't obey the American government's laws about smoking pot because American politicians had no moral authority to tell anyone what to do. They reminded me of the racist police officers who viciously beat blacks and set upon them with dogs and fire hoses during peaceful civil rights demonstrations, and they reminded me of the Vietnam War, which they said America had no business fighting.

I wasn't sure what to think anymore. In the Nation we hated the white man, but we were taught to obey the laws of this land while we worked toward getting our own piece of land, where we could have a separate nation. Before we could achieve that goal, however, Elijah Muhammad died and his son, our new leader, changed a lot about our religion, like what we had learned and practiced had been wrong.

Our new leader, who changed his name from Wallace D. Muhammad to Warith Deen Muhammad, opened our temples to the white man, changed our collective name from the "Nation of Islam" to "World Community of Al-

Islam in the West," then again to "American Muslim Mission," and drastically changed the structure of the organization so that we had no more captains and lieutenants. Although I had been glad about some of the changes, like not having bossy officials anymore, I was really angry that I had been made to abide by a bunch of strict rules that now were considered invalid. I was realizing that you just can't trust grown-ups. The more I thought about the incidents and events of my lifetime, the less I trusted adults.

I thought about the fact that when I was two years old, the Reverend Martin Luther King, Jr., a peaceful minister who had championed civil rights for blacks, was gunned down in cold blood. I was six when America pulled out of the Vietnam War. But by that time, too many black men had already died. When I was seven, President Richard Nixon was under indictment for stealing documents from the Watergate building.

In my own household, hypocrisy reigned as we followed a strict Muslim diet and observed all our prayers through the day, then indulged in dope at night. The Quran forbade intoxicants. But Dad and the other brothers considered marijuana a natural, mild antidepressant medicine, not dope. I knew they were simply justifying their actions.

Ma didn't understand why Darren and I had become so defiant. She thought it was just normal teenage rebellion. I felt like I had a lot to rebel against. I believed Dad was spending some of our family money buying the weed that he and his band members got high on. Darren believed Ma was using Islam as an excuse to stay home and have babies. We expressed our anger in various ways.

It was all Ma could do to try to survive and feed us on what little money Dad gave her. She bought lots of rice because she could use it to stretch a meal.

"That's all we eat," Darren complained once while we were seated on the floor around the tablecloth for dinner. "Rice and eggs, rice and peas, rice and chicken, rice and beef, rice and butter, rice and rice."

Ma got angry. "Some children around the world don't get that! You better thank Allah that he blessed you with another meal."

"Ma, this rice is burned!" I said after I tasted it.

"It's not burned, it's smoked!" she snapped. "Sonsyrea, eat your food," she said. "Y'all some ungrateful little children. I ought to let your asses go to bed hungry one night and see how you feel after that."

Darren and I looked at each other, shocked, and the younger children were caught off guard, too.

"You didn't used to curse at us," I said. "When we were living at GrandWillie's house, you didn't talk like that." I was offended.

"That was your grandmother's house," she said.

"Oh. So you had respect for GrandWillie's house, but you don't respect ours?"

"I've had about enough of your mouth for one day," she said, snatching my plate up. "You go on upstairs somewhere out of my face."

"Why should I have to go upstairs?" I insisted. "I'm not the one around here cursing and carrying on." With that, she reached across the spread and slapped me in the lips.

"Did I ask you something?" she said through clenched teeth. "You're going to learn when to open your mouth and when to keep it shut!"

"Why you gotta be slapping her?" Darren shouted.

"You want some, too?" Ma said.

"I'm going to call the police and report child abuse," I said, rising to my feet. I had rights, I knew my rights. I reached for the phone on the kitchen wall, and she grabbed the receiver from my hand.

"You better go somewhere before I abuse you for real," she said. So I marched upstairs, defeated.

Later that evening, while Ma was reading Islamic stories to my younger siblings seated in a circle on the grass in the backyard, I watched out my window as the girls out front laughed and played. I practiced my instruments (I had learned flute, too) for a while, then got bored with my music.

I went into my brother's old coat pocket in his closet to find some excitement. I figured, what the heck, why fight it? Ma was starting to curse, and Dad and his friends were getting high in our home. If the grown-ups didn't care about being righteous for real, why should I bother? I used to smoke joints three times a day, then stopped when we moved and I didn't feel so stressed out anymore. Now I wanted to get high because I didn't care about being righteous anymore.

Of course, Darren wasn't home now. He was out having fun somewhere, free as a bird. I took out enough weed and papers to roll myself two skinny joints, then went down to the kitchen to get incense out of the drawer and to make sure Ma was still sufficiently distracted with the younger kids in the backyard. Sitting on the edge of my bed, looking at the girls outside, I fired up one of the joints. The stick of incense I put near my door would camouflage any odors coming out of my room. I smoked the first joint and felt mellow. My hands were moving slower, like they were floating all by themselves as I moved the joint to and away from my lips. This is nice, I thought. I smiled and almost giggled. So what if I get stuck in the house all the time. . . . My thoughts trailed off before I could finish thinking them.

For these few moments my brain could rest and I could actually exist without thinking at all. I was tired of thinking all the time, trying to figure through things and weigh the many odds and consequences. I lit the second joint. The images of the girls out front faded. The cars racing by became a blur. The red fire engines tucked inside the open doors of the fire station across the street looked comfortable. I smiled, lay back on my bed, and looked up at my ceiling, which like the rest of the room was painted white.

The room began to spin. I wanted to close my eyes but couldn't move my eyelids fast enough. The room spun faster and faster. My arms pushed my body back into an upright position on the edge of the bed, and the room stopped spinning. I sucked on the half of a joint left in my hand a few times before I realized the flame had gone out. In movements that seemed to take forever, I patiently watched my hands trying to relight the joint.

Once the joint was finally lit, my hand dropped the flaming match in my paper trash bag. The bag poofed up in flames, but I couldn't respond quickly. I waltzed to the bathroom a few feet away from my room and filled a small bathroom cup with water. Suddenly, fear hit me. I ran back and forth between my room and the bathroom, trying to put out the fire with the small cup. The fire alarm buzzed as my room filled with smoke. Ma ran up the stairs with a bucket. She put the fire out quickly and ran back downstairs to answer the firemen pounding on the door.

I thought quickly about what I would tell my mother when she returned to my room. The matches and joint had burned with the bag. I got the mop and ammonia to clean up my mess.

"What were you doing to start a fire?" Ma asked.

I looked at her with feigned sincerity and lied.

"I was trying to light another stick of incense and accidentally dropped the match in the trash bag."

She seemed to believe me, or she just didn't know what else to say.

"I was just about to make Mahgrib," I said, referring to our evening prayer.

"Well, I suggest you make it right now, and I suggest you ask for Allah's forgiveness," she said. "You don't want to mess around and bring Allah's wrath on yourself."

I realized that I had almost burned down my home. So I decided to stop getting high—at least for a while. But I didn't think Allah was trying to tell me something. If Allah was going to come to our house to speak in the form of a burning trash bag, he would have done it a long time ago, I figured. He would have spoken when Dad and his band members were in our basement getting high.

* * *

By the time Ma was three months pregnant with twins, her doctor put her on bed rest. I then became the mother of the household, with five younger siblings to cook for and to clean up after. Since Darren was a boy, his only domestic duties were taking out the trash and mopping the floors once a week. My chores seemed to last from sunup to sundown. This was February of 1982, a few months before my graduation. Most high school seniors were thinking about the prom and the senior class trip, but my life was different.

Everyone in the household woke up moments before dawn for prayer. Then Dad went to his job as a security officer. Everyone else went back to bed for an hour or so before it was time to get ready for school. But I had to stay up and stick to a strict schedule I had designed to make sure everything ran smoothly.

A typical day found me in the kitchen cooking breakfast by seven o'clock. At seven-thirty I woke up all the kids and ran back and forth between the kitchen and their bedrooms, scolding them for taking too long or for arguing with each other loudly enough to wake our sleeping mother. Between seven-thirty and eight I might clean and season a chicken for dinner, wash greens, or grate carrots according to the weekly menu Ma had written down for me. I stashed dinner in the refrigerator so all I had to do later was cook it. By the time the kids came downstairs, I had a cloth spread out on the floor for them and their plates already fixed. They knew better than to complain about their cold eggs with no salt or their lumpy grits because I had disciplined them by sending them to school hungry a few times. I told them I didn't have time for no foolishness.

Once I served them, I ran back to my room and jumped into a set of clothes I had ironed at the beginning of the week. Ma made me iron all my clothes at one time to save electricity. I rushed back to the kitchen to hurry the kids out the door and clean the kitchen behind them, then I vacuumed the living room floor. By the time eight-thirty rolled around, my girlfriend Chee-Chee was ringing the doorbell so we could walk to school. She could look at my frantic face and see I wasn't ready.

"Dag, girl. You always making us late," she said.

"Just wait a minute. I got two more things to do."

I had to take my mother her plate of cold food to her room and clean the bathtub behind my father.

Sometimes I complained.

"I don't see why Dad can't clean the tub behind himself in the mornings so I don't have to be late for school all the time," I mumbled loud enough for my mother to hear.

"Your father's a man, and he goes out there and works

every day! He shouldn't *have* to do any cleaning around the house. He pays the bills!"

"Well, I shouldn't have to do all the work either," I snapped. "Sakinah and them can do something, even if it's just sweeping the steps down!"

I had drawn a chart with chores for everybody, but Ma rejected it, saying the little kids were too young and my older brother was too irresponsible. This would only be temporary, she said. This was a test from Allah, and the test wasn't just for her, it was for *all* of us. She said these weren't *her* babies, they belonged to *all* of us.

Chee-Chee knew I was mad at my mother, but she had the nerve to be friendly with her anyway.

"Good morning, Mrs. Tate," she yelled. "Ray-Ray's going to make us late again, huh?"

"You need to talk to her, Chee-Chee. She knows what she has to do in the mornings. I don't know why she doesn't just get up earlier. She would rather stay up late, sneaking on the phone to chase these little boys around."

The *witch!* I thought to myself. I knew for a fact that she used to sneak on the phone and call my father when they were in high school. And at least I wasn't having sex like she did with my father when they were teens.

I grabbed my books and my flute and clarinet cases and headed out the door without saying "Salaams."

"Your mother *is* right, Ray-Ray," Chee-Chee said. "You know what you have to do in the mornings."

"You got a nerve," I said as we walked toward the bus stop. "Your ass get up in the morning and don't have to do shit but eat and get dressed. I got all this shit to do."

"Aw, bitch, quit whining."

"Wait a minute, hold up, hold up," I said. "You know I don't play that bitch shit. Don't call me no bitch." A lot of girls around our school played calling each other bad names, but bad names was where I drew the line.

"Oh, what you gon' do?" she asked, still playing. "You can't fight."

"That's all right," I said. "You know I'll get you back. When you least expect it. Expect it."

She pushed me, I pushed back, and before long we were both laughing. By the time we got to school I had forgotten about how mad I was at my mother. I could be myself again, the ambitious student who seemed naturally smarter and more disciplined than many of her seventeen- and eighteen-year-old fellow seniors. I was still shorter and smaller than my classmates, and I wore my hair braided in two thick braids along the sides of my head, while most of the girls wore curls and fancier cornrow hairstyles.

But at school I was happy. In my advanced literature classes, we studied authors like Henry Thoreau and Edgar Allen Poe. When we reached the midway point in our senior year and realized that our teacher, who was one of three white teachers in the school, did not include any African American authors, we refused to go in his class. Finally, he agreed to add Ralph Ellison's *The Invisible Man* to our list of books to discuss in class.

At school I felt like part of the real world, whereas my home life felt like some kind of cartoon gone wrong. We were trying to live like foreigners, trying to practice the religion of foreigners. Also, I felt like an old woman when it came time for chores but a little girl again when it came to things I wanted to do—like date and go to parties.

I liked school so much, I wanted to stay there as much as I could. School was my escape. I joined the drama club, the newspaper staff, the "It's Academic" team, and the marching and concert bands. One activity or another had kept me at school two or three more hours in the evenings during my tenth grade and eleventh grade years. But now that Ma was pregnant during my senior year, I hardly got to stay after school for two hours of band rehearsal because I had to go home and feed my younger siblings dinner. I prepped the dinner in the mornings just so I could be allowed to attend band rehearsal after school. My music classes and band rehearsal meant everything to me.

The clarinet section was still lagging behind as we prepared for the big competition in Florida, so I suggested Mr. Sands make me the assistant section leader. I could get us in shape. First I had to prove I could play better than the leader, who had been playing since she was in seventh grade. So I spent long hours practicing difficult moves.

I didn't have a music stand, so I set my music books on the windowsill in my bedroom. I could see the other girls out front laughing and joking. Sometimes they looked up at me and waved. Now it didn't matter that they had more free time than I did, because my discipline was self-imposed. I was on a mission. Dad said that if I rehearsed hard every night, I could guarantee myself a music scholarship to college. Music was going to be my ticket out of my house.

❉ ❉ ❉

In March of my senior year, the band went to Florida to compete in the national competition we had been preparing for during the past year. I had become section leader and had replaced the girls in the section who refused to practice through lunch break with a few guys who were more dedicated. We were the only black band in the competition, but we felt confident. We won three trophies, including first place for the concert band category.

I turned sixteen—with no sweet fanfare except for Uncle Wallace taking me to lunch and other relatives giving me cards with money inside. It didn't bother me. I didn't expect a party because Ma was still on bed rest with her pregnancy. In fact, I had to get home in time to cook for the family on my birthday.

My graduation also came with no big celebration. Grand-Willie came to the ceremony, along with Aunt Nell and my grandparents Thomas. Ma couldn't come because of her pregnancy, but Dad was there, Uncle Wallace was away at school, and Uncle Hussein was at a hospital taking tests to find out why his legs were weakening.

I performed a solo on my flute, and was glad my relatives were there to see me. I paid little attention to the speakers, but I took note when our principal read the names of students who had earned scholarships. I should have been among them, but I'd had to turn down two music scholarships because Ma refused to give her consent. I needed her consent because at sixteen I was considered a minor. She said I wasn't mature enough socially to handle college and that, as a Muslim girl, I should be more concerned about getting married.

I had gotten so depressed the few months before graduation and contemplated suicide. Some nights I curled up in the windowsill in Darren's room while he was out late and wondered if I jumped whether I would die before my body hit the ground below. That way I could die without feeling the pain. I was tired of living, tired of thinking, and tired of feeling. Tired of feeling the anger, confusion, depression. And the thought of having to spend the rest of my life tied to the role of a housewife and mother seemed like a lifelong sentence.

On the other hand, I wanted to do the right thing and please Allah, mostly to avoid his wrath. But I wasn't clear about what the right thing was anymore. For the next couple of months I was so depressed I couldn't eat, and my clothes began to sag.

As the summer ended and Ramadan, our sacred month for fasting, approached, I decided to take my fasting and prayer more seriously. In addition to refraining from all food and drink during daylight hours, I also would pray more and read the Quran from cover to cover during these thirty days. I was desperate for clarification and understanding. I had heard so much philosophy and witnessed so many contradictions, I decided to resort to the Quran and study Allah's laws for myself.

Since my mother would not support my going off to college, I decided to pray about that dilemma, too. When I learned to pray in first grade, I was only repeating after my teacher without even understanding what I was saying. I moved through my Orthodox prayers, simply reciting Arabic in my head, feeling nothing in my heart.

This time I prayed in my own words. When I opened my eyes again and raised up off my knees, I knew beyond a shadow of a doubt that I was going to college and I was going to get a job in the media. I wasn't sure about any of the particulars, like when and how I would get there, but I knew at that moment that I was going to be fine.

Back in elementary school at the University of Islam, my teachers had told me that God gives everybody a purpose in life and to fail to follow through would be disobedient. They had told me God gave me a talent for writing and I should use it to serve him. I wished Ma could understand, but she seemed confused about a lot of things right now.

I knew that just like she grew up believing in Christianity, then changed to the Nation of Islam, then changed to Orthodox Islam, she might change again. I couldn't keep going through her changes. I had to go with what I believed now.

Epilogue

Sure enough, Ma changed religions again—sort of. Her understanding of Islam changed again. In the very beginning, she'd understood Islam to be based on a black supremacy philosophy, as Elijah Muhammad had taught. Later she was sure practicing Islam meant eating, sleeping, dressing, and praying the way Prophet Muhammad had done some 1,400 years ago in the Middle East. Now she—and most of her sister-friends—were beginning to believe their salvation had little to do with tying veils around their heads. So they came out of them. They still dressed modestly in loose-fitting clothes. But they took off their veils.

They still prayed five times a day for guidance and forgiveness, but they no longer saw the need to submit themselves to poverty, shunning material gain based on the belief that Prophet Muhammad would prefer all his followers to live that way.

I enrolled in the University of the District of Columbia to study journalism so I could write newspaper and magazine articles to help people make more informed decisions. I was happy I'd decided to proceed with my life, living it my way. Otherwise I would have been caught up in the storms of change that swept through our small Muslim community of family and friends.

Some of the Muslim brothers came to their senses about the same time their wives came to theirs. Ma was left alone to face her worst fears and oldest unattended pains after Dad was sentenced to jail on drug charges. She would later become a minister in the Church of Scientology, explaining that its philosophies in no way contradict those of Islam. She preaches universal love and universal understanding and forgiveness now.

Aunt Kimba left her husband, taking their ten children with her. She later got a job in real estate and landed herself a beautiful, spacious home, where she spent much time nurturing her younger daughters to become strong, independent, faithful young women. Aunt Kai left her husband long enough for him to correct some of his personal problems—and she hers. When they reconciled, with a better understanding of Islam, she took a job as a nurse, they moved out of public housing into a suburban house with a pool in the backyard, and they helped their sons and daughter find scholarship money for college. Sister Razia returned to work as an executive secretary, helped her oldest daughter, my best friend, Shawn, through two years of college, then encouraged her—strongly encouraged her—to marry the navy soldier she became pregnant by. My cousin Nzinga married the Muslim boy the community pressured her to marry and later fell in love with him. They have three beautiful children whom they are raising with a healthier understanding of Islam.

I married my career goals. Actually, I married my next-door neighbor who had become Muslim while in jail. But that union lasted less than two years. I fell in love with the idea of working in the media. So I pursued that goal relentlessly and landed jobs at my hometown newspaper, the *Washington Post,* before moving to Virginia and Chicago to work at large daily papers there.

Most of my Muslim relatives and friends have graduated to a better understanding of Islam and now practice their beliefs in a way that doesn't choke the life out of their younger children and doesn't isolate them from the larger community around them. I probably will not return to the Muslim mosque for daily worship because the experience was too intense. I found that I enjoy gospel music on Sunday mornings in my home. Occasionally I attend a church service because I enjoy the fellowship.

When my Christian relatives suggest I need to commit myself to a particular church or at least a particular religion —choosing one over another—I explain to them the main lesson I learned growing up: they're all good.

I'm happy to see Elijah Muhammad's son, Warith Deen Muhammad, promote interfaith conferences in cities across America now. He encourages congregations to celebrate their own understanding of God and to celebrate their neighbor's understanding, too.

I've looked back over my life with some anger and resentment and bitterness. I blamed my parents, their parents, racist American leaders, and even God for making conditions in this country so wretched, so oppressive, so confusing that my grandparents—and hundreds of thousands through the years—felt the need to go to such extreme measures seeking salvation. Now I consider all those feelings to be simply a growing process and the restrictions and ridicule I suffered merely growing pains.

Everyone involved in my experience has grown in some way. Some have moved further from their original ideas and understandings than others. Even the Nation of Islam seems to have grown. I see Nation members involved in the communities where they live now, some as community leaders, some running for office. Thirty years ago no minister in the

Nation of Islam would have conceived such an idea as a Million Man March on Washington, much less have the grass-roots community support to pull it off. I do hope that the Nation has evolved in its philosophies of life and understanding of Islam as well.

I can look back and laugh at many of those experiences now. Someday I'll be able to count it all joy.